# THE PERFECT SINNER

Also by Will Davenport

*The Painter*

# WILL DAVENPORT

# *The Perfect Sinner*

HarperCollins*Publishers*

HarperCollins*Publishers*
77–85 Fulham Palace Road
Hammersmith, London W6 8JB

www.harpercollins.co.uk

Published by HarperCollins*Publishers* 2004

1

A catalogue record for this book
is available from the British Library

ISBN 0 00 718453 0

Typeset in Meridien by
Palimpsest Book Production Limited, Polmont, Stirlingshire

Printed in Great Britain by
Clays Ltd, St Ives plc

*In memory of Tony Dixon who knew this story.*
*The estuary wil always be his merchant.*

## Acknowledgement

I owe a debt of gratitude to that fine story-teller Clive Fairweather for first lifting the veil on Sir Guy de Bryan.

In all his life to any, come what might
He was a true, a perfect gentle-knight.
Speaking of his equipment, he possessed
Fine horses but he was not gaily dressed.
He wore a fustian tunic stained and dark
With smudges where his armour had left mark.

Geoffrey Chaucer.
Prologue to *The Canterbury Tales*.

# CHAPTER ONE

All my life I have been burdened with a good reputation. I do not deserve it. I will be ripped on the racks of Purgatory until the Day of Judgement for what I have done.

Do you know what that would be like? I'm not afraid of wounds and I have had plenty of them. In battle the pain arrives later and always passes in time. A man can stand that. To be burnt and torn and stabbed for a thousand ages is another thing entirely. The fear of it stalks in the animal form of my sin. It scratches at my door and leaps on me when I wake and I cannot keep it away. My three sins came one after the other, a year between the first two and then two years to the third. I have confessed the first of them and been given inadequate penance. I have tried to confess the second, but the priests will not see it my way. I have kept the third and greatest entirely to myself, saving it for my deathbed.

The worst of it is that my wife Elizabeth shared that first sin and in the long and lonely years since she died, I have feared for her even more than for myself. Time crawls by in Purgatory and the punishment there is dreadful.

Now, in this year of 1372, on the day of the consecration of my Chantry, I was given hope because I saw Elizabeth again. I looked up from where I was doing my stiff best to kneel in prayer and I saw her standing up there in the new stained glass blazing with sunlight. She was young again and she spoke with that angelic voice which always plucked directly at my heart and she used it to bring me a gift.

I have been trying to make up for my second sin, you see. It took place in war and was a sin of omission. There was an act I failed to prevent. War has battered into me the slow realisation that it is man's most natural state, a base business painted with glory only for disguise, but this act was the basest of its parts. I will speak out now as I should have spoken then. Our war with France has lasted all my adult life and now at last I know the shape of what I want to say. For an entire year I have been struggling for the right words. Now she came to me and flamed up there in the December sun. Elizabeth, a creature of pure light, gave me my opening line.

'Old men who stay behind,' she said, 'old men who stay behind, do not inflame the young with words of war.'

Perhaps it came from inside me and not from her at all, but I don't think so.

There are days which lie in ambush for you from the moment you are born. I had thought it was a day of endings, the dedication of my chapel, the setting in stone of the knowledge that came too late, my plea for forgiveness. Instead it was the very opposite, and before this winter day was finished I was to meet a man who would make me look at it all afresh.

As I stared up above the altar, Elizabeth slipped away from where she had stood smiling in the window and there was the Madonna Maria Virgine in her place, no less fine than she ought to be, but a picture on flat glass and no more than that. I fought down my keen regret because one should never feel regret at the sight of the Madonna, and there was some comfort to be taken. Elizabeth had seemed serene and the

Madonna had let her share her space. She could be saved.

When Elizabeth died thirteen years ago, I had Hugh's tomb in the Abbey opened and laid her next to him and there they lie, the two Despensers, just as if she had never been Elizabeth de Bryan, just as if two of my sins had never taken place. As if I had never been. It was not because I thought she loved him more than me. Indeed, I knew that could not possibly be the case. We had our years together, Elizabeth and I, and though they started later than they should have done, they were as sweet a time as I could ever have hoped for. Together, we had a natural harmony in everything we did, and our marriage felt to me like a long-delayed arrival home. It was just that in the Abbey, in the immediate sight of God, there was sin to consider and it seemed more proper that she should lie there with Hugh. When death comes for me they will put me close by, just across the aisle, in a tomb to match hers so that I will be but a hand-clasp away.

Hugh Despenser, you see, was the bravest and most admirable of men and he had to steel himself, against his natural inclination, to act that way, which makes my sins all the greater because two of them were against him. We first fought side by side a quarter of a century ago at the crossing of the Somme. He won the day for us at Blanchetaque, struggling through the water to beat the enemy off the far bank. He saved an entire English army that day with heroism that took your breath away and should have taken his.

Bad memories are the hardest rock and stand out more and more as the softer stuff gets washed away. What happened two days later in that August of 1346 ranks among the worst. We were across that bloody valley and they were coming up at us in numbers you could not believe. It was a typical late summer evening and, with the low sun behind us, they stood out so clearly, every detail of their equipment and their weapons, the straps and the steel, as fine and precise as a painting. In the glare they could not see how thin we were

3

in our tired lines. We were dark reapers against the sun and we scythed them down until we were astonished by the slaughter and unsure if they would ever stop.

My post was by the King up on the hill, behind in his final reserve, and my duty was to watch, which is the hardest thing. They came in ranks a hundred soldiers wide, pushed forward by the weight of thousands more behind. Those behind had no clear view until those before them fell. Only then could they see that they were already as good as dead, invincible certainty draining into despair in the very last yards of their advance.

My second sin is coming with the smell of sulphur on its breath.

This tale will not allow the absence of its villain for a line longer, and there's a pity. He has to come into it now. Sir John Molyns. Molyns the robber, Molyns the murderer. The King had hunted Molyns for his destructive violence. Now he was valued for that same quality. Now he was restored and there he was just ahead of me, down there in our line, about to commit a terrible act, and I should have prevented him from doing it. The King gave me the power to stop him and I chose not to use it. That was my second great sin.

My hands and my arms were shaking with exhaustion, holding the butt of the pole, and the wind got up again, whipping the King's long standard, the Dragon banner of Wessex, as it billowed over my head. I was groaning from the concentrated effort it took to hold that standard upright and immobile and I knew how much it mattered. The flag, tugging at me in the gusts, was the weathercock of the battle, the final symbol. You could see the men snatch glances behind for the evidence that the Royal Will did not waver, that the Royal Person was resolute, sharing their own danger. The upright immobility of that standard was the proof. All very fine, but chivalry died that day.

There, in the torn and bloody earth of Crécy, chivalry died and perhaps I could have saved it.

A drizzle of holy water across my cheek pulled me back from that past, back to my new Chantry. In this other folded valley, a mile inland from the marching waves of Start Bay, I was pretending to kneel down. I was the sole member of the congregation in my own brand-new chapel, and there was nobody else here bar the priest to spot that my backside was still supported by the edge of the pew and my knees were a hand-span short of resting on the hassock. If the priest had noticed, he would have said nothing. William Batokewaye knew what a beating those knees had taken in the service of the King, after all, he'd been there for much of it.

A fine mist of sawdust still filtered down from the roof's new-cut beams, filling the air with a spray of stained-glass sunlight. The pews smelt of sap and the stone itself showed the fresh face of sliced cheese. It was the forty-fifth year of the reign of his Royal Majesty, King Edward the Third and it should have been a red-letter day.

I watched William stumping up the aisle towards the altar as if he were attacking in the front rank of God's army. He had always been a good man in a tight corner. Within a year of losing his sword-arm to a Frenchman's axe, the stump barely healed, he had learnt a left-handed flick of the wrist which reaped soldiers like barley. These days, his only weapon was the holy water, but that same left wrist flicked back and forth to spread eternal life just as he had once spread death.

I was still in my reverie, half nightmare, half myth, embellished over years of remembering until it shone with the untrustworthy precision of a jewel from the devil's diadem. I was remembering that moment in August of 1346 when three horses, lashed together, thundered at us through the piles of the dead. Then that rain of water arced across my face and shocked me out of my trance.

5

'Wake up,' rasped the priest, glancing back at me. 'This is all for you, so you might at least pay attention.'

For a moment, I wasn't quite sure which was then and which was now because that voice belonged to both times, but in those days the priest had all his limbs and I had a clear conscience.

He stopped his chanting and his spraying, stared around him at all the gilt and the fresh paint and the no-expense-spared glory of the place. He pulled an oddly irreligious face.

'It's done,' he said, swivelling to stare at me. 'Blessed and dedicated. Are you happy now? You should be.'

I could only look at him, and perhaps he saw something in my eyes because he put his thurible down, reached out to take me by the arm and helped me clamber to my feet.

'Come on. Outside,' he said.

There was complete and unexpected peace in the court-yard. It was warm for December. I had expected the usual scraping and hammering of the masons working on the rest of my buildings, forgetting I had sent them all off to work in the quarry to guarantee silence for the consecration. There was no sign of human life or so I thought for a moment. Then a tiny movement up above caught my eye. They are as keen as they ever were, my eyes, and I depend on them all the more now that my body is no longer quite so agile. It has always been second nature to watch for that betraying move-ment in the undergrowth that might save you from an ambush.

There was a man up there on the high ground, the hill which overlooks my village and my Chantry, and I saw him stand up. He didn't look familiar.

'Tell me what's going on,' William demanded and distracted me. We sat down side by side on a bench, the priest folding his robe under him. He looked at the mud drying on the back of it.

'I wish you'd put drains down the street,' he said. 'I went right over on my arse.'

'They like it the way it is, the villagers.' I replied. 'It's always been like that. You know that better than me. This was your place before you ever brought me here. I didn't even know about it until you told me.'

'Slapton, eh?' said the priest, looking around him, 'It's thirty years since I lived here last. There's no kin of mine left here now and I feel almost a stranger. I went away to see the wider world and I've learnt to like a drier path to walk on. My grandfather used to call it Slipton because of that slippery old street. If I'm really going to live here again, I might have to do something about that.' He looked around him and sniffed the air. 'Now, shall we take stock? What have we got here exactly? One brand-new chapel, for the ease of souls and your soul in particular. One chapel, not staffed by one priest, oh no. Not even staffed by two priests. Your chapel will be staffed by one chaplain, which is to be me, plus five priests and four clerks, am I right? At a cost, I am told, of forty pounds a year. Forty pounds a year *for ever*. Not to mention a stone-built college for us all to live out the fullness of our lives in prayer, study and, if I know anything about my fellow priests, in dice and wine and maybe even the odd woman.'

I frowned.

'Oh yes,' he went on. 'It won't all be holy and they may be *very* odd women.'

That wasn't why I frowned. I knew William Batokewaye well enough to overlook the licence he had just allowed himself. I'd often heard he had a wife tucked out of sight though if so, that was one of the few things he had ever tried to keep from me. My reputation again, you see. That sort of thing was allowed for lower orders but not for a mendicant friar as he was, or at least had been. Would he presume to bring her here to Slapton? That might test our friendship. I frowned because since that moment in the chapel the echoes of sweet Elizabeth's forgotten voice, waking

7

all my love, had been gradually fading in my head and now, knowing I had lost the sound of her, I was bereft.

'My question is this,' he said. 'Forgive me, I'm not complaining. I look forward to a comfortable retirement from the rigours of the last thirty years. It is generous of you in the extreme to provide it, but, quite apart from the fact that I would have been prepared to mumble masses for you all day and most of the night for half that sum all by myself, what's it all *for*?' The priest was a year older than me and had been asking me that sort of question for as long as I could remember. Having no arm for defence, he only ever knew how to attack.

'It's a Chantry. You know what it's for.' I opened my arms to indicate the courtyard in which we sat, the church we had just left and its new stone tower which soared into the air, dominating the little village, overpowering the spire of the village church below.

'I know what a Chantry's for. What I'm asking is why do *you* need one?'

I looked at him, suspecting a trap. He had always been a plain speaker and not one to follow slavishly along dogmatic lines, but this was going too far.

'You can't disapprove, William. You and I usually agree on what's right and what's wrong. I've built it so you and your priests will sing masses for my soul and for Elizabeth's.'

'And if we didn't? If your soul had to stand up for itself without a lot of people, most of whom don't know it very well, all singing flat on its behalf?'

I stared at him. I was deeply disturbed by his tone. This was dangerous ground. 'You know the story? The story of de Mowbray?' I sometimes felt it was all I had thought about for years now.

'I might. Tell me anyway.'

'He begged his chaplain to sing a mass for his soul the moment he died. Do you know what happened?'

Batokewaye sometimes looked as if he had been hewn from the huge trunk of an old elm tree and that look came upon him now, dense, unchangeable, so I went on. 'The chaplain ran straight from the deathbed. He was racing to the chapel but something stopped him. De Mowbray's spectre, twisted and tortured. "You've broken your promise," said the spectre. "No, I came straight here," said the chaplain, "you died only a moment ago." "In that time, twenty years have passed in Purgatory," the ghost replied, "I have suffered twenty years of torment for your neglect. It is worse than Hell."'

He just went on looking at me. I thought perhaps he hadn't been listening.

'Worse than Hell, William' I said again. 'If a few moments here is twenty years there, imagine how it will be. Your soul stays there, paying the price of your sins, until Judgement Day itself.' It turned my guts around to think of it, to think I had that coming, hurtling at me.

He sighed. 'Wherever I've been in the country, I've heard that story,' he said. 'I've heard it said about Montague, Mauny, Beauchamp, Scrope, every single knight who has given up the ghost.'

'Are you saying you don't believe it?'

'I'm saying that Purgatory is a very good idea from the clergy's point of view. I'm delighted at the chance to live in luxury off a terrified Lord.'

'Should we not be terrified of Purgatory? If we die in mortal sin aren't we bound to suffer there? Isn't that what the Bible says?'

The priest stared back at me, unblinking. 'I know you, Guy. I've known you since long before you were a knight. I've heard everything you have to confess and I must say it's been mild stuff. If you came to me to confess a real mortal sin, I'd know you were lying. All right, lying might be a sin but you'd have to try a lot harder to get committed to the eternal flames than by a grammatical paradox.'

He thought he knew me. He didn't. I had told him nothing of the last and greatest of my three sins.

'There's Heaven and there's Hell,' he went on, 'and each of us is bound for one or the other. You have to earn your way into both of them and all we can do is pray to Saint Peter that he'll be kind if we're somewhere in between, which is where most of us are. And by the way, no it's not what the Bible says at all. The Bible is fairly silent on the precise question of Purgatory. It's a modern invention.' The priest stood up, turned to face me, looming over me.

'Look at you. Sir Guy de Bryan, noble Knight of the very choice Order of the Garter,' he growled, 'King's companion, steward, holder of the Great Seal, ambassador, royal envoy. Thought of throughout the length and breadth of the land for years past as the finest knight there ever was, so clearly honest that you cast no shadow in the sunlight. It passes straight through you. So fair, you've been called in twenty times a year since you were old enough to wear a sword to sort out every brawling squabble the greedy nobility gets itself into. Trusted equally by the King and the Commons and that's rare enough. Not a spot on your soul and yet you're so afraid you've hired a phalanx of priests. You're getting much too pious. You need to ease up on the piety. Do you understand *anything* about our Lord?' He wheeled round and thrust his hand, finger outstretched to the top of the tower.

'What's that up there?' he demanded.

I looked up, squinting against the sun. 'The crucifix?'

'That's it. Don't we take it for granted? Wasn't it lucky Christ died on a cross?'

Unsure where this could be leading, I frowned at him. 'It was surely more than lucky, it was blessed,'

'That wasn't what I meant. Supposing Pilate had given him the option,' rasped the priest, bending down to put his enormous face right in front of mine. 'Supposing he'd said, all right Jesus, it's up to you. Your choice. You can either be crucified or you can be stung to death by bees.'

More heresy was in the wind. I stared at him.

'Well, imagine,' said the priest impatiently. 'If he'd chosen the bees, what an inconvenient sign we'd have to make then.' The priest waggled his hand around his face, fingers jabbing back and forth and let out a hoot of laughter.

I crossed myself quickly as the rooks took off from the trees around the tower adding their shrieks to the echoes of the laugh. Remembering the figure up on the hill, I looked up there to see if there had been a witness to this blasphemy. There was nobody there now.

'Oh come on, man,' said the priest. 'I suppose you think that's another hundred years of Purgatory added to your sentence. If God hasn't got a sense of humour, what hope is there for the world? Indeed, what hope is there for any of us if someone like you has to spend half your fortune on a place like this?'

'Have you lost your faith?' I asked. 'It's a few years since I've seen you, old friend. You don't sound like a believer any more.'

'Oh, don't you dare doubt my belief,' retorted the priest. 'I may be old-fashioned, but I believe all right.'

'Do you believe in good and evil?'

'In their place,' said the priest, 'I am not sure I have ever met a truly evil man. Have you?'

'Oh yes. One. Just one.'

The priest looked at me. 'Molyns?' he asked.

I nodded.

'All right, I'll grant you that,' the priest went on. 'One. But good and evil notwithstanding, what I don't believe in is all this modern blackmail.'

'You know what I did.'

'I know what you *think* you did. Seems to me other people had a big hand in it.'

He didn't know about my third sin. That was the problem and somehow I wasn't yet ready to tell him. I had tucked it so far out of sight that I no longer quite knew its shape.

The wicket gate creaked open and a face looked round. It was the man from up on the hill. I didn't want to be interrupted and certainly not by a stranger.

'Not now,' I called, perhaps a little impatiently, and the face disappeared abruptly.

'Ah,' said the priest, 'sorry, he's with me. I was just about to mention him.'

'Who is he?'

'He's a squire in the King's household. Well connected. Trusted. In with the people who matter. They send him to sort out things, very like you were at that age, I'd say. Oh and he's married to the beautiful Philippa Roet, so that puts him in with Lancaster.'

'Really? Why's he here?'

'You're off travelling again. He's going with you.'

'Who says he is? Come to that, who says *I'm* going anywhere?'

William looked at me with a smug expression. 'I am trusted with certain information, you know. He came down with me. I was asked to bring him to you. Up at court they thought he'd never find Slapton by himself. I know where you're going.'

He'd tried that sort of trick a few times before. 'I don't think you do,' I said.

'You're journeying overland, avoiding France and all its friends. Your final destination is Genoa by way of the Rhine valley and the Alpine passes. Your purpose there is to negotiate an agreement whereby the Genoese will trade freely with us, using one port specially nominated for that purpose and hopefully granting free use of Genoa by English ships in return. Am I right?'

That removed any chance that he was guessing. 'It's supposed to be a secret. Who told you?'

'Calm down. It *is* a secret. Lancaster told me. Is that high enough authority for you? This young man has been sent to give you a hand on the grounds that, many qualities though you undoubtedly have, fluency in Italian is not known to be one of them.'

'I speak some Italian,' I said, a little stung.

'Enough to order food. Not enough to conduct high level negotiations.'

'But why is he here now? We're not leaving until the beginning of April.'

'You mean nobody told you?'

'Told me what?'

'The King sent word last week. There's a rush on. It's all been brought forward. You really didn't know?'

I shook my head.

'You're leaving in three days time from Dartmouth on the afternoon tide, on board your ship, *Le Michel*, captained by John Hawley, although why you should trust yourself to that rogue is a mystery to me. You are sailing up channel to Dordrecht in Flanders where you will join Sir James di Provan and John di Mari, two of the most irritating and self-regarding clots it has ever been my misfortune to meet, and with them you head south as soon as you possibly can.'

'William, you know as well as I do nobody travels across the Alps in winter. Even the Brenner Pass is tough going now.'

He looked uncomfortable. 'It seems the King believes in your ability to do it. Someone apparently has to and he thought sending you would give the best chance.'

I knew him well enough to make an accurate guess. 'Come on, you know more about this than you're saying. What's it really all about?'

He squirmed. At least he gave a tiny involuntary wriggle which is as close to a squirm as a man of William's size and experience is ever likely to get.

13

'I've heard a few things,' he said eventually and I just waited.

'It's his bankers,' he said in the end. 'You know he still owes those Florentines a huge fortune?'

'The Bardi family? Yes, I have heard.'

'They're pressing him hard. The Genoa deal is something to do with it. He has promised them agreement by the end of February, otherwise he is in default.'

I knew all too well what default would mean. Humiliation for the English crown. We all remembered the last time he'd had to pawn the crown and the shame that brought, and I wouldn't have been surprised to learn he'd done the same again. I loved my king, but sometimes he behaved like a complete idiot.

I rubbed my brow, suddenly aware of the enormous practical difficulties of this whole enterprise.

'Three days to get all this ready? I don't even know if Hawley's in Dartmouth and the *Michel* hasn't left his mooring since October.'

'Hawley's ready. I saw him on the way. The King's messenger got that far, at least.'

'Well, he didn't get here. Oh, wait a minute. They found a man on the rocks below Strete. He'd been thrown off the cliffs, stripped of everything but his jerkin.'

'That was him. Someone's killed a King's messenger in your lands. There'll be a big fuss about that.'

'There's no time to lose. Is Hawley provisioning the ship?'

'Yes. I told him to do it well. I can't eat that vile stuff you usually serve on board.'

I stared at him in astonishment. 'You're coming to Dordrecht?'

'No, no. What would be the point of that? I'm coming all the way to Genoa.'

'Why?' The thought of getting William's great bulk over the Alps in the snow was appalling.

'It sounded like fun,' was all he would say, then before I had a chance to argue, the priest played his trump card.

'I also hear, if the masons are to be believed, you're going to leave your message on the walls here for all to see, and as far as the future of your soul and come to that, your neck, is concerned that seems to me to be the more pressing concern right now.'

That made me blink. 'You know about *that*?' I had thought the Declaration was a secret. There was nothing of it yet to be seen. It was all still forming in my head and the words had to be right before I would let the carver pick up his chisel. Second thoughts are best avoided when you set your words in stone.

'I get to hear most things. Is that something to do with the clerks? I keep wondering why a Chantry needs all those clerks.'

He was a perceptive man and he knew me better than any now alive, perhaps better than anyone bar Elizabeth ever had done.

'To a point. I have a great work in mind. The message, as you call it, is a small part of it. The clerks will work to draw together the thoughts that lie behind it.'

'Has it struck you that the only ones likely to have learning enough to read your message are also the ones most likely to disapprove?'

'I don't care.'

'And if the King reads it?'

'Does the King know about it?'

'Not yet, but when he does . . .'

'All the better.'

'Where's it going to go?' he asked. 'If it's going to be displayed on *my* church for all the world to see and disapprove, then I'd better know.'

'I'll show you.'

The plaque lay ready on the stonecutter's bench. Its surface was smooth to the touch and the border had been chased out in folds to frame it.

'Either you've got a lot to say or it's going to be carved in big letters,' said the priest. 'What exactly *is* it going to say?'

'You can read it when it's finished. It's too close to me, too raw. I can't tell you yet.'

'You don't trust me?'

How could I not trust him, the man who came closest to understanding, the man who had risked the King's fury to back me up in the days when we were all young, when he was a mere deacon, without the age and reputation to keep the royal wrath at bay?

'I'll tell you the first line,' I said.

'I'm listening.'

Elizabeth's words came to me fresh. '*Senes qui domi manent, nolite juvenes verbis belli accendere.*'

'Oh dear,' said the priest. 'I was afraid it would be something like that. Where exactly is it going?'

I turned around and gasped as the old wound in my knee caught at me. I pointed at the chapel porch. 'Right above the door,' I told him, 'for all to see.'

The priest looked where I pointed and then cocked his head up to follow the height of the tower as it soared high into the air.

'I predict trouble,' he said. 'If you want to enjoy a quiet old age, you should put it higher up.'

'How much higher?'

The priest looked at the rooks wheeling around the summit of the tower, a dizzy height above us.

'What about up there,' he suggested, 'right at the top. That might just save your neck.'

# CHAPTER TWO

This is not a complaint, but I have spent more than half my life away from my own bed and probably a quarter of it away from any bed at all. This past year I have served Edward mostly at sea in the Channel against the Castilian galleys and I have now been granted the extra responsibility of Admiral of the Western seas. Oh, and I also had to address Parliament on his behalf, asking them for still more money. The King is no longer quite the active man he was, but a year or two ago he told me that if I had wanted a quiet life, I should have taken care to seem more of an idiot and more of a coward. I think it was a compliment.

When I began to notice the discomfort, I realised the King's business took me along some well-worn routes and there was no good reason why I should put up with strange beds. I have therefore bought myself houses on some of those frequented paths, personal hostels for a personal pilgrim carefully spaced at a day's travelling distance and now, most of the time, I can sleep in one of my very own beds. That's England I'm talking about. Now we were going abroad and it was back to the bad old ways.

I was brooding on that when the *Michel* took a wave right over the bow and staggered almost to a halt. He is a good ship and he'd been built just the way I wanted him. He can go further to windward than any other ship I know, but it was asking a lot to expect him to fight his way up-Channel in a down-Channel gale. I called him after my dear old horse, the first of my chargers, killed under me by a Frenchman's sword in his throat, and in truth they behaved the same way, the ship and the horse. The first Michel was there with me through thick and thin just as long as I kept him properly fed and properly shod and didn't ask him to charge straight into a low sun. He didn't like it when blades came at him out of the glare. He carried me for six years in the King's service, which is quite a record when you think how much of that time was spent at the exact places where two armies were colliding. We talked to each other a lot, Michel and I. The second Michel, the wooden one, felt the same way about the wind as the first one felt about the low sun. The weight of the water forced his head further and further off course and the big sail slatted and cracked. I had seen this one coming and braced myself on the backstay, but the King's squire, face down on the deck, short and fat with his head in a bucket, hardly seemed to care about the distinction between air and water any more. He was already soaked through before the wave hit him, so that the flood only lifted and swelled his sodden woollen jerkin as it passed. The priest was braced against the weather rail as ever, glaring at the vague horizon as if he were hoping for a fight. It was the fourth day of our three-day passage up-Channel, and I only minded the delay because William wouldn't perform the office of Mass in any kind of storm. It was one of his few orthodoxies. He said he had seen too many people vomit up the Host and that was definitely disrespectful and possibly blasphemous. I was standing behind the steersman, staring forwards beyond the port bow, to where the sea blurred into the low, cantering clouds. White-caps were whipping from the wave tops in the wind that came driving from behind him again as the bow swung back on course. We had seen no sign of the sun for many hours and, though there should be nothing ahead of us, who could tell for sure whether it was wind, rock or sandbank that broke and frothed the sea?

My sailing master caught my eye and jerked his head down towards the well-deck. Hawley was not known for his soft heart or his thoughtfulness for those who didn't share his complete indifference to the discomforts of the sea, but he seemed to like the squire. They had made friends in Dartmouth before we sailed. Not many people ever managed to make friends with Hawley. He didn't like to cheat his friends, which may have been why he chose to have so few. The young man was showing signs of movement, doing his best to get to his knees. I dropped down the ladder and stood beside him. 'How are you?' I asked, and he swung his head to one side and then the other as if he could not quite locate me.

'I'm still breathing,' he gasped, 'at least when there's air to be had. The rest of the time I'm drinking. Are we nearly there?'

'Visibility's bad. I can't see land at the moment,' I said, knowing a fuller answer might nip this brave attempt at recovery in the bud.

The squire made a huge effort and reared his head higher than it had been since dawn. 'The Channel never seemed this wide before,' he said uncertainly. 'How far is it?'

I could not evade a direct question. 'We're a little west of where we started, doing what we can against a north-east wind.'

The squire reached out for the rail and hauled himself unsteadily to his feet. I put out a hand to make sure of him as the next wave heaved the bow higher. He had been a plump man when he came aboard, but I realised that the past four days had already served to trim him down a bit. He was looking around him aghast.

'West? That's the wrong way. Will the storm sink us?'

'Storm? No, it's not really a storm.' I had another look at

the sky. The clouds ended in a dark line which was drawing nearer all the time. 'It will blow itself out in a short while, then we'll make our way back up-Channel. At least it keeps the galleys away.'

'What galleys?'

'The French galleys, the Castilians. Take your pick. No galleys are good news. We are at war, you know.'

He was doing well for a man who'd been so sick minutes before. Standing up does that for some people. His habitual interest was showing itself again. He had an eye for everything, did this young man. He looked up at the rigging and seemed to be trying to frame a question. 'I think you had better dry yourself,' I said. 'Come into my quarters.'

It was relatively peaceful in the cabin and I was able to study the squire as he rubbed himself as dry as he could, the first chance I'd had since he had come on board at Dartmouth.

'I know your face,' I remarked. 'I've seen you before, haven't I?'

The squire nodded and managed to look both pleased and a little wary through his pallor. 'First time was thirteen years ago,' he said, 'in France. That is, I was a nobody in the retinue of Prince Lionel and you were the great Lord Bryan with retained men of your own.'

I was even more impressed by his powers of recovery. The younger man showed resilience and that quality had always prompted my approval. 'Thirteen years ago?' I did the sums. 1359, the year my dearest Elizabeth died. 'Rheims? You were at the siege?'

'I didn't get as far as Rheims. I was captured.'

'How on earth did you manage that? There wasn't a lot of fighting that year. Rethel, was that it? That little skirmish at the bridge? Were you captured there?'

'No, no. Nothing so noble. You'll remember how hungry we all were, surely?'

'How could I not?' Foul weather for week after week and

20

the French had finally learnt their lesson. With his father, the King, a prisoner in England, Dauphin Charles changed the rules, decided taking the English on in battle was a mug's game with only one outcome. Instead his French armies burnt the crops, laying the country bare so that we'd starve. It wasn't glorious and it wasn't at all chivalrous but it worked all too well. Starve was exactly what we did. Still, I suppose that after Crécy we could hardly claim the high ground on chivalry.

'We were sent off to search for food,' the squire explained. 'Three of us, me and two Welsh archers. We walked into a farmyard and the barn was full of French. They thought I might be worth something. The other two got the knife.'

'Who sent you off like that?'

The squire looked a little embarrassed and I wondered why, then I guessed.

'It was me, was it? Did I send you?'

'It's all a long time ago,' he said as if that made it less important. 'And you also fixed my ransom.'

'Did I now?' I had fixed many, many ransoms. 'How much were you worth?'

'Sixteen pounds' said the squire proudly, 'and the King paid it.'

'Sixteen pounds, eh? And how old were you then?'

'Sixteen years.'

'A pound a year.' The man was twenty-nine now. I wasn't sure he looked worth twenty-nine pounds, but someone thought he was if they had entrusted him with this mission. He wasn't just a travelling companion. My instructions laid down that I must consult him over every aspect of the diplomatic negotiations once I got him to Genoa, though I was, in every other way, the leader.

'That wasn't it,' I said with certainty. 'That wasn't what I remembered.' I didn't explain, didn't say that grief had driven all other details out of that year, leaving only the black hole

21

of tears which stood where Elizabeth had once been. 'It was more recent than that.'

'The year after? I was there at Calais when the Treaty was signed. You came straight from Paris. You swore observance for England in the King's name. It was a fine moment.'

I shook my head. There had been huge crowds at Calais. It had been hard lawyer's business for me, trying to see the holes in the Treaty through the blinding smoke of ceremony.

'Where else?' I asked.

'The other time?' he looked reluctant and his head drooped so that he looked down at the deck. 'I suppose that must have been when we were with Lancaster,' and I knew why he looked like that.

'That bloody business at Limoges.' Slaughter for its own sake. Licentious revenge on a town that had done no more than stand up for itself. It was the moment when I knew Lancaster for what he was, a bad commander and an unprincipled man, not a man to follow in war or in peace. The ending of the siege of Limoges had been another stepping stone on the way to my declaration. I'm not talking about old Lancaster of course, not Henry of Lancaster. He had been the noblest of men. This was new Lancaster, John the King's son, made Duke by marriage and by convenient death.

'There were things there I would rather forget,' said the squire. 'I decided at Limoges that war could do without me. I have not been in the wars since.'

'If you have the chance of that choice, then make it so.' I sat down to ease my leg and rubbed my knee. 'I am sixty-five years old, young man. I should have made that same choice long ago. I wish you could know what I know. But you puzzle me. There were many thousands of us at all the events you mention and yet you seem to have singled me out.'

'There were many knights, I grant you that, but I would not agree that there were many like you.'

My door flew open with no trace of a knock and the priest, spraying water like a dog leaving a pond, ducked his head to come inside and slammed it shut behind him.

'Hawley says the wind's backing,' he announced. 'It's northerly.'

'Thank you William,' I said mildly, looking at the puddle forming under him. No crewman would have had the nerve to soak my cabin floor like that. 'Will you join us in a glass? We'll be heading back for Flanders in an hour or two, I should say.'

'I will. Has he started interrogating you yet?'

'Who?'

The priest jerked his head at the squire. 'This one. It's what he does best. Ask, ask, ask. He's known for it. Unless he's scared of you.'

The squire went a little pink or perhaps it was just that his colour was improving anyway. The motion of the boat had eased as the wind backed further. I could tell the wind and the tide were both moving to the east together.

'No he hasn't. What would he ask me? I've got nothing much to say.'

'There was something,' said the squire meekly. 'That's if you don't mind?'

I wouldn't have minded at all if the priest hadn't said that thing about being scared of me. 'What?' I asked.

'Sluys,' he said. 'You were there for the battle of the ships. Would you tell me what it was like?'

Sluys? I hadn't thought of Sluys for a long time. He was a clever man, I realise now, opening my door like that, starting me off with a question he knew I would want to answer. I know now that he had no particular interest in the ancient history of Sluys, just as well as I know that William Batokewaye colluded with him, nudging him in the right direction in everything he did. It was only later on, when I saw that squire at work on other people that I recognised the technique of a master. Get them talking about anything at all, then when they're moving, give them a nudge. It's easier to steer a wagon when it's already rolling. Oh, he was clever all right and, though I didn't know it yet, they had a plan, those two.

Sluys, my first sea-fight, though you couldn't really call it a sea-fight, with the French boats crammed together in the narrowing estuary of the Zwin and the wind, blowing straight in, keeping them there and carrying us to them. It was not so different to storming a town, a town with masts and wooden walls. So he got me talking, remembering the archers up our masts, shooting down, remembering the hand to hand on decks that might as well have been streets except for the splashes as the bodies went into the water, and even that splashing only lasted a short time. In no time at all, the sea was so thick with the corpses of dead French that the next ones in made little more than a soggy thump.

We were away. He knew more about it than I did in some ways because I had been in the middle of a struggling mob on the *Saint-James*, the big Dieppe ship. It was a grunting, heaving fight, too close to stretch out a sword arm and too crowded to see six feet away. That was all I knew about it until we had them subdued, four hundred bodies lying on the decks of that ruined ship alone, and by the time our friendly Flemings, seeing it going our way, had finally come out from Oostburg and Termuiden and Sluys itself and hacked into the rear rank of the smaller French boats, it was all but over. He knew the figures, this damp, little man, 'Sixteen thousand French dead,' he told me. 'One hundred and ninety ships taken or sunk.' He had it by heart, and from the look in his eyes, he was trying to live inside the flimsy house he was building out of my slow words.

'It was the worst sight I had seen up to then,' I told him. 'Butcher work. Hacking and cutting and piercing with no time to know your enemy, but for all that there was still chivalry.'

He asked me this and that for a quarter of a candle's length, then, having loosened my lips with old war stories, he made his one mistake. He turned much too sharply to the subject he really wanted to talk about. 'Molyns,' he said. 'Tell me about Sir John Molyns,' and I looked sharply at William Batokewaye, wondering for the first time if the priest had put him up to it. Old William looked back at me, eyes wide and innocent, waiting for me to speak.

'Molyns has been dead ten years and more,' I said. 'He's a man best forgotten. Nothing he did is worth the effort of our memory.'

The squire closed his mouth and kept it closed.

'He helped put the King on the throne,' said the priest mildly.

'He did that,' I agreed, because what else could one say?

That thought was still in my mind a few days later, once we had swapped the *Michel* for horseback and were plodding south. Thinking of the far past, at my age, makes the present much more painful. I could ride for hours back then because I was so much lighter in my saddle and my joints had youth's oil in them, but there was much I didn't know in those days. I didn't know how to scan the landscape ahead, to measure the dangers of the blind places which might hide who knows what. I didn't have the voice of command which could still make even the toughest trooper do what I said without a moment's question.

There was quite a crew of us by this time. The two Italians, di Mari and di Provan, would have little to do with me and I didn't mind one bit. They weren't my kind of men. They talked to each other in their own babble. Di Provan had a high-pitched mocking laugh which made me wince, with a carry to it shrill enough to tell any brigands we were coming

25

a mile away. Occasionally, if they wanted something, they would refer to the squire, but they seemed to find me barbarous, unfashionable, useful as some sort of bodyguard, but no more. The squire asked me, rather anxiously, if he should explain that I was not only the leader of the party but also its designated chief spokesman. I got a certain amount of wry pleasure from letting them dig the hole of misunderstanding ever deeper. They were Genoese, these men, and a bit full of themselves, and they had two of their own crossbowmen with them. Now, I've seen a lot of men killed by crossbows and mostly they were the men who were holding them, not their targets.

I watched it close up sixteen years ago at Poitiers when we were creeping up on them through the woods. It was dreadful standing still while we waited because I had splits in my feet at that time, the awful itch that is best dealt with by keeping moving. Either that or taking off your boots to have a good rub though that never lasts long. Elizabeth cured it for me after years of torment with an oil of hers, and I remember her sitting on the floor of our bedroom in my house of Pool as she worked it in to my toes, looking up at me all the while, making the shape of little kisses with her lips, and when she had done, she spread the rest of the oil over both of us and we rubbed it in with the skin of our bodies. Anyway, back at Poitiers, trying to take my mind off my feet, I watched one of their crossbowmen at work and understood what a dreadful business it was, winding that string back up after each shot. He didn't see us until we were well clear of the wood, and before he got off one shot, Gwynn put two arrows into him. It was always like that with crossbows. They pack a punch but they don't always get to punch twice.

In an ambush you get one chance and that's it. If you haven't dealt with it by the time you count to five, the chances are you're dead. On this journey the safety of these

Genoese, of William and of the squire, depended entirely on my Welsh archers who now went ahead and behind, ready to chase away any band of hopeful brigands who might not be familiar with my standard and might imagine we were some sort of easy pickings. Of course we took the Dutch way, as they call it, down towards the Rhine as we'd been ordered. The French lay to the south west and France was barred to us by the war. We'd need more than a half-dozen archers to see the French army off. A few more anyway.

We had left the comfort of Bruges well behind, leaving the town after a Mass for travellers to which I had obliged William to add a personal mass for my own list of souls. The Italians had chafed at that but I ignored them and now we were all ambling through dull, open country. It was nothing like campaigning. The December rain was surprisingly warm and I knew we would sleep the night in one of Ghent's fine inns.

In a dream prompted by the talk of the old days which seemed to please the squire so much, I was back in my youth, twenty years old and on my first long cross-country journey. The royal summons had come in the summer of the year 1327 and it was the single most exciting moment of my life until then. I was entirely delighted, not so much at the prospect of fighting Robert Bruce's Scots, though ignorance invested even that with glamour, but more with the relief of getting away from the draughts of Walwayns Castle. My father's ancient fortress stood by the corner of Wales where one coast faces the Atlantic and the other turns eastward to confront England. Even in summer, a cold wind straight off the endless sea blew through the stone walls as if they were chain mail and my father's increasingly mad rages threatened all our lives.

'You're going to the bloody *King*?' he screamed when the summons came. 'I'm the King round here. Have I said you could go? Have I? You'd leave me with the goblins, would you? The goblins speak to me, you know. I could tell you what they think of *you*. You're no better than I am. You just think you are.'

The Scots gathering to invade our northern borders could not be more dangerous than him. He was a normal man one moment and murderous the next. You needed eyes in the back of your head when he was like that. From the earliest moment I could remember, I had vowed to stick to reason and predictability in my own life and watched anxiously for signs in me that his blood might show.

Outside events got me out of there. Even in far Walwayns, miles from everywhere, out there on the very edge of the kingdom, we knew it was a year of divided loyalties, and the Scots had chosen a good moment to threaten invasion when attention was elsewhere.

Called to arms. A blast of trumpets rang through those words. However mad he was, my father couldn't safely keep me there against the royal summons, so off I went, equipped as best I could manage, with the captain of the castle guard and his three best men, all of us pleased to be away from the mad rage of Walwayns. I pretended to command them and they indulged me by pretending to listen. We made our way across the country, accumulating others as we went, all experienced men-at-arms except me, and I was agog to hear their tales. The journey up to Durham took ten days, enough time to get used to my horse, my borrowed saddle and the heft of my grandfather's old sword, but not nearly time enough to sort through the complex loyalties and mixed feelings of that band of fighters. By the time we reached the army's gathering place in the north, a land I knew nothing of, I at least understood where the majority opinion lay.

The throne was effectively empty. The country lay somewhere between two kings. No one regretted the end of the second Edward, a vicious, corrupted waste of time who had entirely deserved his comeuppance. His wife Isabella was right to come back from France and kick him and his favourites out, that was the majority opinion. She was not so right, most men thought, to flaunt her lover in the way she did, and that lover, Roger Mortimer, they all agreed, was a most dangerous man. The pity of the country was that the second Edward had proved such a poor shadow of the first Edward, his brave father. All hope now lay in the new young king, the third to bear that name and the whispered slogan of the times was 'third time lucky'. The signs were good. Physically he took after his grandfather, not his father, and people said he had the kingly manner.

The question everyone asked was, would Mortimer ever let him rule?

Our journey reached its destination one evening on a hilltop where a large patrol challenged us and then ushered us down into a valley so full of armed men that I could not understand what my eyes were telling me. They looked like a swarm of bees, jostling for position for their tents and their cooking fires. I had rarely seen more than fifty men in one place, and here were fifty fifties and ten times that again. All we lacked was an enemy. We moved down into that valley and found a place and slipped into the ranks. It was decided that we belonged in Montague's troop, though as we were not part of his official retinue we had to fend for ourselves as far as food went, which was a hungry business. For days that stretched out into weeks, we patrolled those hills with absolutely no idea where the Scots were. I had time to set my old chain mail to rights and get something like an edge put on my sword, though it wavered in and out as you looked along it and would just as easily have sawn wood as sliced flesh. The Earl of Lancaster, the old Earl that is, was in command, and he was a fine man, but on my fourth day there, I saw young Edward, the new king, for the first time, and there was an even finer man. He was five years younger than me, but he was already bigger.

Those Scots had us looking like fools from the very first.

They were light on their feet. They brought no baggage trains like we did. Each man carried a little bag of oatmeal, I heard, which they would mix into a paste and cook on a stone. We drank wine which the carts brought and they drank water which the rivers brought. How could we catch them? Rivers go faster than carts. We followed them, slogging through the thick country while they danced ahead in their own natural element, taunting us with smoke from the villages they burnt. I craned for another glimpse of the King and, as our numbers thinned, the footmen left trailing and lost as we who had horses did our best to keep going, I saw more and more of him. It got worse and then it got still worse again. Our rations grew shorter and shorter, our horses were going lame, and then the biting flies of summer were driven away by even worse downpours of driving rain. Rain gets into armour and rusts it and rubs your skin raw if you're stuck in that armour all day and all night. Mine had been made for someone else long ago and it fitted only where it touched.

So far, it was a contest only with hunger and the weather, and I could stand up to that, but I needed more. I was desperate to test myself against an enemy, to know what it really was to stand up to another man in a real fight. It wasn't that I wanted to spill another man's blood, more that I needed to know how I would be. The strain of fearing that I might turn out a coward in the company of all these tough, quiet men was getting too much for me. I knew the rules of chivalry. I knew what was considered a fine way to fight and what was not. The Scottish knights had a brave reputation.

We found them in the end, mostly by luck. We crossed a river in a barren land and saw them on top of a hill ahead of us, in a well-prepared position with no way to attack except slowly and uphill into waiting steel, and we weren't in a hurry to do that. Instead, we faced them for three days from our own side of the valley. They looked as though they grew from the landscape and belonged in it, in their rough cloth, while we, though the shine had long gone from our metal, seemed entirely out of place. I could not imagine what it would be like to attack them, to climb that hill and face those deadly men, but the moment of finding out was postponed. After the third night we woke to see the far hill was bare. They had slipped away.

I felt frustration but I also felt relief, a little song in my soul that my death had stepped a few paces back. Then our scouts returned and the word spread that the enemy had not gone far. They had found an even better protected hill and the stalemate set in all over again.

It was three days later that I met the King face to face and in the oddest manner. My wish had come partly true. I had experienced battle, but not in any ordered way, not in a way covered by the rules. My first taste of combat consisted of waking abruptly, confused as men rushed over my legs in the night, shouting 'Raiders! To arms!' Searching desperately in the dark for my sword, I found it with the scabbard all caught up in the tent ropes and got it out, cutting my other hand in the process, just in time to take a wild slash at a man who appeared out of the darkness in front of me with an axe. I missed him completely and that was just as well as he turned out to be one of ours. We beat them off, or they chose to leave – a bold party barely three hundred strong, who left mounds of our men behind them. The next night had us all wide awake and jumpy, peering into the mist fearing a repeat, but when day dawned, we found we were looking up at what seemed once again to be an empty hillside. Had they gone? As I looked, a band of our men rode up from behind me on horses.

'Are you armed and ready?' said the nearest. 'If you are, come with us and let's see what's up there.'

I was about to question the man's right to command me in that way when he half turned and I saw that he had every right. I had taken him for a full-grown man, because he was big but the face I now saw was younger than the body. My king, Edward, aged just fifteen, was a fine man and his face had a smile on it which would have inspired loyalty in a piece of solid rock. I climbed into my saddle to follow him, thrilled, repeating his words to myself so that I had them by heart, the first words my king spoke directly to me. Ten of us went carefully up that hill, all in plain armour with no surcoats, no crests. There were three riding ahead in case all was not what it seemed. I had spurred forward to join them, but was waved back to my proper place. They were hard men, those others, men you wouldn't want to tangle with, and as I looked around, I saw that only Edward and myself did not yet fully fit that description, though it was plain from the look on his face and the way he held himself in the saddle that for him, it was only a matter of time.

What a strange sight we found at the top. We rode through a band of mist which had us staring hard again and drawing swords, then it dispersed as we reached the summit so that we seemed to climb up into a place all of itself, remote from anything else I knew, floating in its own world. For a moment I thought we were the only living beings present, but then I heard a groan and saw ahead of me a slumped body, lashed to the trunk of a tree.

'See to him,' said the man next to me.

'Who is he?'

'He's one of ours, snatched on a raid. Look to him.'

At that stage of my life, I was no good at tending the wounded, scared to face the pain of others without the knowledge to ease it. This man hung from the ropes, naked, and his face was somewhere behind the blood which ran in crusted streaks down his body. Both his legs were splayed out at an angle which showed the bones were smashed, and he whimpered when I tried to support him while I cut him down.

I gave him water and did what I could to wash the blood from his eyes.

'I'm Guy,' I said. 'Help is coming.'

He croaked something in reply but it sounded more like a curse than a name. Laying him on the ground, with no idea what else to do I saw that beyond him there were four more, each lashed to another of the twisted mountain oaks. Three of them looked dead, but the fourth was tugging hard at his bonds as he saw us coming. Then he heard our voices and knew we were English and calmed down.

I did all I could for my man, and as I cleaned him I realised the extent of his wounds was worse than I could ever have imagined. He stared at me with gratitude as I mopped away the blood, but my kerchief was soon so drenched that it could take no more. I was kneeling over him, calming him with a hand on his forehead, talking to him in his pain so that he would know he was not alone, when a hand came from behind me and roughly thrust me to one side. I overbalanced backwards and saw the man who had led the way up the hill. He was perhaps approaching thirty with sandy hair and small, reddened eyes, close together. For just a moment, I felt sharp relief that he had come to help me, then I saw the knife in his hand. He held the knife out so that the poor soul on the ground would see it and the injured man began to shake his head from side to side, trying to raise his arms to protect himself.

'Don't do . . .' that, I was about to say, but before the word was out, the knife had slit his throat and the rest of his life was bubbling and spurting out into the grass.

'Why did you do that?' I said to the sandy-haired man, and he turned his head to look at me with a grin on his face.

'To spare his pain.' His voice was shriller than you would expect from a soldier.

'If that was the reason, why did you show him the knife?'

'Every man should have the chance to prepare himself for death.'

'That wasn't it. You enjoyed . . .'

33

The next thing I knew, his left hand was clutching my throat and the knife in his right hand was pricking the skin just above my eyelid.

He shot a quick look around, but there was nobody near us to see.

'I am not bound by your rules,' he said in a whispered hiss. 'You will be dead in a second if I choose. I kill who I like, when I like. You have qualms. You're a baby. You're worthless. Learn to respect me, young man. I am a true soldier and I am worth a hundred of you.' The knife dropped away out of my sight and I tensed my belly for its thrust, but a voice was calling. His other hand let go of my throat and he turned away.

'You're wanted,' he said.

I was sickened by the sight and the sound and the smell of him, but I couldn't help staring at his face in fascination. I had no idea that I had just met the man who was to be the bane of so many years of my life.

'Go on,' he said. 'The chief wants you.'

I thought he meant the King, but the man who was waving his arm for me was much older. I had seen him in the camp with everyone paying him their respects, but I did not know who he was. Clearly of high rank, he wore a blue cape over gilded chain mail. Everyone except the King deferred to him and I should have asked his name of someone the first time I saw him. Now, I had left it too late and it would have seemed absurd.

I ran to him and made an awkward bow.

'The King wishes to stay behind here with his thoughts. You stay with him,' he said in a deep and slightly slurred voice. 'Escort him back down as soon as he is done,' he added. 'There is no danger. They are gone.'

They all went off down the hill taking the surviving soldier with them and there we were, just me and the young King in unimaginable proximity. He looked at me, shrugged and turned his attention to the rest of that trampled hilltop, wandering through what had been left behind, with me close behind him. The horror of the last few minutes was still in me, but there was now more pressing business. I felt extremely important and kept my hand on my sword hilt, enjoying fantasies of an unexpected ambush and me gloriously saving my sovereign from a murderous Scot or two. No more than two I hoped.

They had departed in a hurry. Dead cattle, partly butchered, lay in a row in the heather. Stewpots full of cooling water stood by them and further off were heaps of something I could not at first identify. The King knelt by one of these mounds and I stood back, studying him, expecting him to show signs of kingship, perhaps even of immortality. He got up, turned to me and held something out.

'Shoes,' he said in a baffled tone. 'Shoes beyond number. Why have they left us their shoes?'

He was right. There were shoes enough for the whole army, heaped up. I picked some up and looked at them. They were at the end of their lives, worn nearly through.

'What is your name, silent one?' the King asked me.

'I am Guy, sire. Guy de Bryan of Walwayns Castle.'

He smiled at me. 'Well Guy, tell me what you think of these shoes.'

I did not know enough to be talking to a king so I said the first thing that came into my head.

'I think, sire, that by refusing battle, they have had to leave their soles behind them.'

As soon as the words were out of my mouth, I knew both that it was a miserable attempt and also that someone like me should never have dared to try to joke with the King. I watched him anxiously and I saw his expression set, his mouth clamping shut and his eyes narrowing, then his mouth twitched and his shoulders shook and, to my vast relief, I saw he was choking back laughter which now burst and

35

rolled out of him until tears streamed down his face. He laughed and laughed as if he had not been allowed to laugh for a great length of time. All I could think of was that Edward the Third, King of England, was laughing at *my* joke.

'I thought you were the right one,' he said. 'I saw you down there at the camp and I liked the look of you. Might you be my friend, Guy de Bryan?'

'Of course I might, I mean of course I will, sire.'

'When we are alone, you don't need to call me sire.'

I felt my ears heat with delight.

'What did Mortimer tell you to do?' he asked, grinning at my reaction.

'Mortimer?' I bit off the 'sire'.

'You don't know Mortimer?' He sounded incredulous. 'The man who spoke to you last.'

'The man in the fancy chain mail?' I asked and wondered if I had gone too far again, but that only started the King laughing once more. *That* man was Roger Mortimer, the man who had set himself where this young king should be?

'He said to bring you down as soon as you were ready.'

'It is good that you don't know him. I never know who he has in his pay, but none could doubt you're telling the truth.'

'I don't know anyone really. This is the first time I have been called to arms.'

'Not Molyns either?'

I shook my head. 'Which one is he?'

'The one who seemed to have a knife pressed to your face.'

'Oh.'

'John Molyns. Remember him. What did you think of him?'

I could only say what was in my mind. 'He's a dreadful man.'

'He's certainly worth dreading.'

'Why . . .' I stopped. My question was too direct.

'Why do I have him in my army? Was that what you were about to ask?'

I nodded.

The King sat down on the grass and patted the ground next to him. 'It's not my army,' he said. 'It's my mother's army possibly and it's Mortimer's army possibly, but it's definitely not mine.'

'It *is*, sire,' I insisted. 'Everyone I've talked to thinks so.'

'You may be older than me but you're not necessarily wiser,' he replied. 'I don't suppose the latest news from the court often gets as far as . . . What's your castle called?'

'Walwayns.'

'Just before I have to be a king again, I want to tell you this. My earls and barons killed my father. My mother rules with Mortimer who acts as king instead of me. I'm not in a strong position. Mortimer has the taste for power and once you start murdering kings it can be hard to stop.'

'My sword is at your service.'

He smiled. 'I'd rather have your smile at my service, if it's all the same to you. No, don't look hurt. I don't mean to be unkind. It's just that I need a few more Molyns around me at the moment. If I'm ever to sit properly on the throne that is.'

'Molyns?'

'Guy, if you're to live at court, you'll have to get better control of your face. Sometimes you need a John Molyns around. The rest of the time, it's better to be nowhere near him.'

'What do you mean, live at court?'

'If you'd like to, you may join my household, Guy. I need a page, but above all I need a loyal friend. Now, it's time to get back.'

'Are we going after the Scots again?'

'It's a nice idea,' he said, 'but the truth is they have left us these piles of old shoes as a sign that they are now well-shod in new ones and there is no point in us attempting to overtake them.'

# CHAPTER THREE

It was early evening in New York and Beth Battock was already running ten minutes late when she got into the elevator heading down to the hotel lobby. She had wasted five minutes of that in front of her mirror trying to look American and thirty years old instead of English and twenty-seven. The other five had been spent watching the end of her recorded interview on NBC. Now she regretted all that lost time and she began to fret when the elevator stopped again on the next floor down. The middle-aged couple who got in were talking animatedly and barely gave her a glance and she began to fret even more when it dawned on her that what they were talking animatedly about was *her*.

'She comes over here and starts telling us what we should be thinking. I'm sorry. I find that quite unacceptable,' said the woman, frowning.

Her husband nodded. 'She doesn't understand our culture. She comes to this country for the first time and starts shouting her mouth off. She's doing all this for her own self-importance and they're all being fooled by it.'

His wife was so worked up she could hardly wait for him to finish his sentence. 'You got it. That's exactly what it's all about. It's all about her ego, that's what it is. The bottom line is she's too goddamned young to have opinions like that.'

It was quite clear to Beth that they had just been watching her on television. Cold anger rose in her and as the elevator ticked down the floors to the lobby, she couldn't help herself.

'Excuse me,' she said. 'You might not have noticed but it's me you're talking about, isn't it? Well, I think that's quite rude and I also think you're letting yourselves down as Americans by . . .' but something was wrong. Instead of looking embarrassed or angry, they were staring at her with pure puzzlement written across their faces.

'I'm sorry, miss,' said the man. 'I don't have any idea who you are. We were just discussing my niece from Brisbane, Australia. Have we offended you in some way?'

The elevator door opened onto the lobby and Beth bolted out to the waiting limo.

'You're looking fine tonight, Ma'am,' said the chauffeur as she ducked into the back seat, and she had no idea whether that was the sort of thing New York chauffeurs always said or whether he was stepping out of line, so for once she said nothing, breathing deeply and trying to refocus on the evening ahead.

'Park Avenue?' the man asked, and she nodded as he closed the door. The traffic was slow moving and she looked at her watch anxiously. Tonight mattered. She slowed down her breathing, deeply and deliberately, and by the time the car drew in to the kerb she felt she was back in control. The chauffeur opened the door for her and she thanked him as she got out, still unsure of the etiquette. It wouldn't do to hurry, however late she was. Beth looked up for a moment, abruptly dwarfed and dizzied by the soaring perspective of the building above her. There was a banner above the doorway ahead and the words on it said, 'To reach the future's heights, freedom is the only ladder.'

Checking her appearance in the reflection of the glass door, she frowned at what she saw. However much time she spent scrubbing away with the hotel toothpaste, she still had English teeth. However much she had spent on new American clothes, she still wore them as an Englishwoman would, folding and crumpling and migrating to parts of her body where they weren't meant to be. The women of this city seemed to have glued their clothes straight to their skin. However carefully she applied make-up, she could not achieve that perfect, sprayed-on look that she now saw on every side. The people entering the building around her wore that look effortlessly and Beth desired above all to merge with them, to show she was with them in body as well as in spirit. At that moment Beth thought that to be English seemed so dull. Her compatriots were so literal, so lacking in vision and suspicious of power. Above all else, she wanted to be taken seriously by the woman she had come to hear because, finally, she was somewhere where her ideas fitted in.

The revolving door took her into a crowded lobby and heads turned towards her. A photographer took her picture and suddenly there were people approaching her, breaking off their conversations and pushing through the crowd to greet her from all sides.

Beth had learnt to hate that certain sort of male smile that was aimed entirely at her face and not at the mind behind it. In most fields of human endeavour it helped to be a good-looking young woman but in the cynical world of the British political system, dominated by battered bruisers, it could count against you. Four years ago, they'd thought Beth too pretty to take seriously but then her tough message had started to chime with the shocking events of the times. She needed to be sure it was those ideas, not the way she looked, that had helped her up the political ladder. This crowded tour of the power-souks of America was her reward and it had already showed her just how good life could get. Her aide, her very own aide, had met her at the airport. Her schedule had been presented to her in the latest and tiniest of electronic note-books along with the gift of the notebook itself. When she realised just how inappropriate her wardrobe seemed, so carefully chosen in London and so deeply provincial here, Marianne, her aide, had sensed her doubts and conjured a selection of New York's best, brought by smiling women to her hotel room for her to try. They assumed payment would be no problem and so Beth had handed over her credit card and crossed her fingers.

The whole swirling mêlée of a Manhattan evening in spring was intoxicating. For a year, she had been the silent voice of her master, doing just what the chief adviser to a government minister should, breathing cues into his ear, drafting his speeches, stiffening his resolve. In these last few days, she had come out from her master's shadow. People all along the East Coast had come to hear *her*, Beth Battock. Those people had risen to their feet and applauded her. Journalists had inter-viewed her, quoted her because what she had to say was just what they wanted to hear. She was no longer invisible. Her star was on the rise, the people now converging on her the proof of that, and tonight was the high point of her journey.

This time Beth had come to listen, not to speak. Tonight she would finally be in the physical presence of the woman who had been her inspiration and whose every word she had studied, borrowed and adjusted to fit the contours of British politics.

She checked the lobby quickly with her eyes but could see no sign of the woman she sought and then there was a man in front of her shaking her by the hand.

'So glad you made it, Beth,' he said. 'It's our great pleasure to have you here with us tonight. Athan Tallis, Vice President of External Affairs for the Institute.' He let go of her hand and swept an arm towards the back of the room. 'There are some members of our committee over here who are just dying to meet with you.'

41

She followed him through the crowd to a small, expectant semi-circle of older men and women and tried her best to catch all their names as a cold glass of white wine was pressed into her hand.

'Miss Battock,' said a gaunt woman in a long silver gown. 'We've been reading your views with great interest and, if I might say so, with enormous approval. It's been reassuring to see that some people in your country appreciate what our President is doing for the security of all of us.'

Beth nodded and was about to answer when another man joined the circle. Athan Tallis broke in. 'Beth, this is Senator Packhurst. We've asked him to be your host for the evening.'

She turned to shake hands and the group broke up, leaving the two of them together. He was fifty-ish, tanned, attractively grizzled and decidedly predatory. 'Forget the Senator crap,' he said. 'Call me Don.'

'Beth Battock.'

'Oh, I know that. I've been reading all about you, young Beth, and it makes a very interesting story. Hey, maybe we should go through and get our seats and then you can tell me how we get back all those British hearts and minds.'

She took a sip of the wine and looked around for somewhere to leave the glass.

'Bring it in with you,' he suggested. 'We might need some refreshment.'

'I don't think I will,' Beth replied a little sharply, and he raised an eyebrow.

'I see you're true believer,' he said.

They went into the auditorium and sat down in the seats reserved for them right at the front. Don Packhurst started on a long anecdote about the last visit of the British Prime Minister as the other seats filled up but Beth was only half listening, her gaze fixed on the empty dais, eager for the event to start. She was more excited than she had ever been waiting for a play to start.

The speaker was announced by a former Vice-President. 'Ladies and gentlemen,' he said after an introduction hinting that he was responsible for many of the ideas they were about to hear, 'I give you our inspiration, *Christie Kilfillan,*' and Beth was on her feet, clapping with all the rest.

'And so in conclusion,' said Christie Kilfillan ninety minutes later, 'I would ask you all to keep this idea firmly in your minds through the difficult months ahead. This country, this administration, this President, our brave men and women of the armed forces, they have all acted as they have done for the very best of motives and they deserve our continuing support. It has become fashionable to insist that democracy calls for a slower and more muddled approach to international affairs but I have this to say to you.' She hunched nearer the microphone and narrowed her eyes. 'You don't mess around with a cobra.' Waiting until the eruption of applause faded away, she wagged a declamatory finger in time with her words. 'You don't call in the United Nations. You don't put down a motion. You don't set up an inquiry. You don't consult the people. You take out your sword *and you cut off its head.*'

This time, the applause went on and on and on.

As the crowd filed out again, buzzing with the reaffirmation of their beliefs, Don Packhurst took Beth firmly by the arm and led her to the side of the stage where the star of the evening was holding court. She went up to Christie Kilfillan with all the thrilling trepidation of a pilgrim approaching a saint. Kilfillan stood there as the crowd swirled around her, fifty looking like forty, her face in profile as fine and fierce as a goshawk, tolerating the adulation as people manoeuvred to shake her hand, congratulating her on her speech and seeking to engage her in unsuitably long exchanges. Beth waited until Senator Packhurst, standing just behind her, urged her forward.

'Just get in there,' he said. 'We don't stand in queues like you Brits.'

Still Beth held back, watching for the right moment. She had waited seven years for this, more than two and a half thousand days since she had first read Kilfillan's books and fallen under the spell of her argument. The strength of Kilfillan's principles, the realisation of the complete and utter rightness of her stance on the world, had been as over-whelming as falling in love. Taking those principles, bending them to fit the softer politics of old England, arguing for a new form of the special relationship between America and Britain at the head of a new world order, had put Beth where she was now.

There was a second when a gap appeared and Kilfillan's eyes focused on her through it, narrowing, considering. She knows who I am, Beth thought with delight. She's read about me, been told about me. Maybe she's even been to hear *me* speak. In the smaller Washington meetings at the State Department, at the Pentagon and the like, she had scanned the private audiences, hoping for a glimpse of Kilfillan, and she had been disappointed. The New York and Boston meet-ings which followed had been much larger, public events and anyone could have been there, lost in the haze of faces. Someone else wanting Kilfillan's papal blessing filled the gap before she had taken more than a step, then Don Packhurst seized her by the arm and pushed her in front of her idol, so that there they were together, shockingly together.

'Christie,' he said. 'This is our new British friend, Beth Battock. You've been hearing about her, I'm sure.'

Beth waited for her response, for the slightest sign of approval.

'I can't say I have,' said Kilfillan with her characteristic rasp, failing to take Beth's outstretched hand, giving her no more than a quick and supercilious glance.

'You haven't read the *Post*? "Message of support from

Britain's bright hope"? This kid's the future of the old alliance and by the way, she's also your greatest fan.'

Beth studied Kilfillan's face while Kilfillan looked at the Senator with no hint of interest. Beth waited, mute, still certain that at any moment the woman in front of her would begin to engage, would smile, would reach out.

Kilfillan did look at her then, just for a moment, just long enough to say, 'Right. That one. Yes, I caught it.' Then she narrowed her eyes again. 'You've got a way to go, little girl. A cute face won't do it. You got backbone? I don't think so,' and turned away into the crowd.

Packhurst grimaced. 'That's our Christie,' he said. 'Come on, I booked us a table at a place I know you're going to love.'

Over the meal he did his best to persuade her it meant nothing.

'She's a tricky bitch, always has been,' he said. 'You're the future. She sees that, you bet she sees that. The green-eyed monster was riding her back.'

'Maybe she was right,' Beth had said, not believing that for a moment as she chased seared scallops round her plate. She wished she'd picked something else which didn't drip butter on the way to the mouth.

'She was not. Listen, so far as we're concerned, you're Miss Great Britain. It's all been music to our ears. Remember what they called you on CBS? Winston Churchill's brain in Jennifer Lopez's body? We thought our old allies were going cold on us until we heard you. Back to back, the Yanks and the Brits. Together we fear no one. That's the stuff to give the troops.'

In another ten minutes they'd covered the full range of agreement on that one then he asked her, inevitably, to tell him all about herself.

'Start at the beginning,' he said. 'I want to know how you got so smart. Your parents must have been something special.'

45

'My mother died when I was born,' Beth answered, slowly. 'My father was a historian.'

'Oh really? What's his first name?'

'Guy, Guy Battock.'

'What's he written?'

'Nothing you would have come across. English medieval social history.'

'I'll look out for it.'

'Oh, it was mostly academic monographs. Regional stuff. You won't find it in the bookshops.'

'Is he still writing?'

'No, he's dead too. Died a few years ago.'

'OK. That's tough. So you're a poor little orphan.' He reached across and squeezed her hand. 'Are you a Londoner?'

'Yes, born and bred there.'

'And where did you study?'

'The London School of Economics. I did my doctorate there.'

'And then?'

'I did the usual thing, I suppose. I got a job in television. I was a researcher on one of the political shows. And then I met Alan Livesay.'

'A good man to meet.'

'It was just after they made him a minister. I went to see him about a programme we were planning. You can guess the sort of thing, "the new hawk in the dovecote". We got talking over lunch and I suppose he must have liked my ideas. He offered me a job.'

'Every politician needs someone behind him with good ideas,' said Packhurst. 'You have to shake so many hands there's never enough time for thinking. You've sure got the ideas. Your Mr. Livesay can count himself a very lucky man.'

'It was lucky for me,' Beth said. 'No one took his ideas seriously enough until the war on terror started. He's the right man at the right time.'

'Well, I guess we're all very happy that he sent you to us. Remind me, why exactly was it that he couldn't come?'

'The international situation. You know, after the Embassy bombs. He just couldn't leave the Foreign Office at a time like that.'

Packhurst gave her a slow smile. 'Oh sure. Even a junior minister has to feel indispensable. We're all glad you came in his place. I guess you're a star now.'

It was only then, trying to guess what lay behind that smile, that Beth first wondered if this trip had been wise. Advisers were meant to be invisible. They weren't meant to step into the limelight and articulate the truths their masters didn't dare utter.

When the check had been paid and the limo door was held open for her, Packhurst took her hand.

'You've had a pretty full evening. If you want a little company and a chance to relax, I have a nice, quiet apartment nearby.'

It had a horrible inevitability about it and a few weeks earlier Beth might have said yes to a night with a US senator who combined power and good looks, but now her life was too complicated.

'Sweet of you,' she said, 'but I have some work to do.'

Flying back to London the following day didn't help her mood. First Class was full. There were no upgrades and the man next to her in Business Class wanted to tell her in detail all about the range of flashing jewellery he had just sold to a US mail-order giant. She closed her eyes and thought about the future.

At twenty-seven, Beth was on the young side for a British government minister's political adviser. All advisers live in the grey area between politics and public service and are mistrusted by all sides. There was a food-chain at work and many other hungry mouths were clamouring for a bite of her master's favour. Alan Livesay, junior minister in the Foreign Office, was busy climbing his own ladder while all those around him clung to his coat-tails, trying to hitch a free ride. Beth was good at getting noticed, and that was the key. She needed to catch the attention of Livesay's boss, the Foreign Secretary. She had to get to the point where they needed her views to shape their speeches, their policies. It had been dog eat dog and she had lost a lot of flesh before she learnt to bite first.

Then, six months ago, she had played an accidental trump card and got ahead of the game. Six months ago she had widened her sphere of influence from Livesay's private office to Livesay's private bed. It hadn't been a calculated decision. Beth had found out for herself how well power and desire cohabit and, being a new experience, it had not seemed at all like a cliché. Recently, lying together in the soft afternoon sheets, she had nearly let out the love word. He had forestalled her, for which she was grateful afterwards, fearing it would have proved a fatally mistaken kind of intimacy. Just as it was forming on her lips he had turned his head.

'What planet do you really come from, Wonderwoman?' he had asked. 'I don't know anything about you.'

'You've read my CV.'

He traced the shape of her mouth with one finger. 'That was for your job. This is for me. You don't need a Cambridge degree for what we've just done.'

'Oh, I don't know. Fluid Mechanics might help.'

'Don't be flippant. I want to know.'

'There's nothing to tell. My parents are dead. No brothers or sisters. No family at all,' she said and thought, but did not add, *unlike you*.

'But you must come from somewhere?'

'Not really, just London.' Then she had blocked his mouth with her own to shut him up, because it was all lies. When they'd done it all again, in a hurry this time because both were aware of their alibis trickling to a halt, he had forgotten about it. As they were finding their scattered clothes, he had told her she was going to take his place for his American speaking trip. Even then, she had wondered if it represented a reward or simply funk on his part, putting her in the line of fire, a stand-in to replace a master who found it politically expedient to have his views expressed in a way he could disown if he had to. Perhaps he even *wanted* her to go too far, so he could get her out of his life. The career risk was enormous.

That thought had made no difference at all to the line she knew she must take. In her student days and in the doctoral dissertation that followed and which got her to the Foreign Office, Beth had developed the academic ideas that backed up her conviction, held since childhood, that to beat an attacker, you should always strike first. At school it had often got her into trouble. In the early twenty-first century, it got her into power, and Beth was starting to adore power. She decided she would take the chance with both hands and it had worked.

She woke from a short sleep to find the brief, uncomfortable night had passed and a stewardess was heralding their unpalatable return to English airspace with a tray of breakfast. All the glamour had evaporated somewhere over the Atlantic. London looked low, grey and drab as the plane sank slowly towards Heathrow. Beth switched her mobile on in the baggage claim then switched it quickly off again when the voice told her she had twenty new messages. She walked out through Customs, then stood in the arrivals hall wondering why there wasn't a driver holding a sign saying 'Ms Battock'. There was one likely-looking potential chauffeur but he was immersed in the *Mail on Sunday*. She walked closer and as the headline caught her eye, she suddenly understood why there were so many messages and no car waiting for her. 'Love-Rat Minister Quits', it said and the photograph was of Alan Livesay.

She walked quickly to the book shop, grabbed a *Sunday Times* and there it all was in banner headlines.

A cold wash of dread ran out to her fingers and all the way down to her toes. Her first thought wasn't that her prized job had just gone down the pan. It was even less creditable than that. Her first thought was that Helen Livesay, patient, supportive Helen Livesay, who invited her down to Sunday lunch when she thought Beth needed feeding up, who sent her Vitamin C tablets and bottles of herbal cures when she heard her sneeze, had just found out that she, Beth Battock, had been sharing her husband's bed in his afternoons and on his nights away from home. Then she looked further down the page to the blonde caught on a hotel step, kissing Livesay goodbye, and it all got even worse because the woman Livesay had resigned over was someone she had never seen before and not her at all. 'His long-term mistress', the story said.

The taxi took her to Clapham and she told the driver to drop her at the far end of her street just in case, but there was no one waiting for her outside. *They* arrived the following morning, when she went downstairs and found two men in her kitchen.

# CHAPTER FOUR

The larger of the two men said, 'Hello Miss Battock,' as if this were a normal social occasion. His nose and mouth were submerged in pale cheeks as if his head had been over-inflated. 'Sorry to walk in but the door was open. Thought we ought to check you were all right.'

'The door? Which door?' she said stupidly.

'This one,' he said.

The door to Beth's flat was on the second floor. 'What about downstairs?'

'Someone was coming out. We walked straight up.'

She was absolutely sure her door had been firmly closed. 'That doesn't give you the right to walk in.' Who were they? Not police.

'Derek Milverton,' said the first man, putting out his hand, 'from the CPA. This is Phil.' Phil was hiding behind him, taking in the room in jerky gulps of his eyes.

CPA? 'Do you mean the Child Protection Agency?' They must be in the wrong place.

'No, Cunningham Press Associates.'

'Which is?'

'A news agency.'

51

She'd heard of. Specialists in sleaze. Always somebody else's problem, until now.

'We just wanted to know if you might like to say anything about your boss and his . . .'

'Reporters? You're reporters and you come busting in to my flat?'

'No, no. Like I said, the door was open.'

'Bullshit. You can open it again and go straight back out.'

'Look it's in your interests. You'll be under siege here in half an hour. Talk to us and we'll help keep the reptiles off your back, see?'

'What do you mean? You *are* the reptiles. Why am I going to be under siege?'

The phone rang and all their eyes switched to the machine on the side table. She didn't want to answer, not while they were still here. It rang three times, then the answering machine cut in and she realised, as she heard the caller's voice, that it was switched on to 'monitor'.

'Hello, Beth my darling,' said Alan Livesay's unmistakable voice, 'I'm so, so very sorry about . . .' She hit the button and killed the call but it was far, far too late and the balance of power in the room had changed irrevocably.

'Well, how about that, *darling*,' said the larger man. 'Isn't that just our lucky day?'

'He calls everyone that,' she said, but she could feel the heat in her cheeks and she knew they could see it. The smaller man produced the camera he had been holding behind his back and something in her snapped. She reached for the closest object she could find, her kitchen fire extinguisher, pressed down the lever and sprayed foam all over both of them.

She propelled them out of her flat, downstairs and through the front door on a wave of sheer fury, then went back up and looked out of her window to see them stopping on the pavement for the larger one to use his mobile phone and the smaller one to take pictures of the front of her house. It was still only half past seven in the morning.

After a long time the phone rang again. In the intervening hour, she hadn't moved from the kitchen chair where she sat staring at the table and her unopened pile of mail. The room already seemed to belong to a time line which had come to an end.

'Beth, pick up the phone,' said a familiar male voice, the voice of authority, of tradition, of the way things are meant to be done in the Civil Service. Sir Robert Greenaway, Permanent Secretary at the Foreign Office, was not somebody you could ever ignore. She picked up the receiver as if it were a landmine.

'Is that you, Beth?'

'Yes, Sir Robert.'

He dispensed with courtesies. 'There's a story starting to run on the wires. It's linking you and Livesay.'

'Two men broke into my flat this morning. They said they were from a news agency.'

'They were. Be quiet and listen please. I'm not going to ask you if it's true. That can come later. We have quite enough on our plate here already thanks to your friend the late minister. Now, understand me clearly. I don't want you anywhere near this place until further notice. I strongly advise that you leave your house in the next ten minutes if not sooner. After that you'll have the whole of Fleet Street camping on your step. Go away somewhere they can't find you. My office will call you on your mobile in a day or two. Don't talk to anybody and get going now. Understood?'

'Understood.'

'Officially you are on sick leave. Pack what you need and get going.'

That was that. He had put the phone down.

The first of them arrived as she was leaving. He was very young and, as she came out of the gate, he was running

53

down the street from a taxi stuck behind a truck a hundred yards down the street.

'Elizabeth Battock?' he called as he ran towards her.

'No mate,' she said in the best Australian accent she could muster. 'She's up on the second floor,' and she left him ringing the bell as she got in her car and drove away.

West seemed the best direction, west out of London by the quickest route. She drove down the M4 for an hour and then the full irony of what she was doing struck her as she realised she had absolutely nowhere to go. Hotels were out of the question. She'd have to pay by credit card and after her New York shopping spree there was a double risk, identification and credit refusal. Friends? She could stay with a friend. No one in London, that wouldn't do, anyway they were all in the politics business, people to share your triumphs with, not your crises. She wouldn't trust any of them at a time like this, not when there were useful points to be banked by helping out a journalist or two. There was Maggie. Where did Maggie live now? She hadn't seen her since graduation. Her address was somewhere, probably on the Christmas card list in her kitchen drawer. Beth could see the list in her mind's eye. It was just the start of a list really.

Something quite like tiredness came over her then and she pulled over at the next service area. Wiltshire felt like a safe distance away and, after she'd unloaded her bitter-smelling coffee and pallid sandwich on to the most remote table, she rummaged in her bag for an address book just in case it showed she had a forgotten best friend somewhere. Instead, she found the stack of post that she had stuffed in there on the way out of the flat and, for want of anything better to do, she started opening the envelopes.

It was mostly dross, bills, junk mail, one wedding invitation from a colleague she didn't much like and an invitation to speak at an Institute of Strategic Studies seminar, but there underneath was the other letter she had accidentally swept up with the rest, the letter she had left unopened before she went away to America, waiting for a right moment to open it, a moment which might never arrive.

The envelope was handwritten and postmarked Devon. It bore her old address in Fulham and someone had crossed that out and forwarded it, which, a whole year since she had moved, was the sort of miracle she would prefer not to happen. She stared at it for a long time before using a table knife to open it as if something inside might lunge at her fingers.

'My dear Beth,' it said, and she really had almost forgotten how to read his handwriting. 'I know you are very busy these days, but I wonder if you might be able to come down to see us soon. It seems such an age since we talked and there is a lot to talk about. It is very beautiful down here at the moment. The flowers are out around the Ley. Eliza misses you. She would be glad to see you. She had a postcard, I know. Ring the Turners if you can come. They'll give me the message. All my love, Dad.'

Tainted sanctuary. An invitation to the one place where nobody would go looking for her, the place nobody knew about. An invitation to the last place she wanted to go. There was no other hiding place in prospect but even then it was the most reluctant of decisions.

The motorway ended at Exeter and the endless stream of traffic heading towards Cornwall and the south-west tip of England clogged both lanes of the A38. Absurdly, she had to stop and check the map to be sure of her way. She had owned her own car for four years now and it was the first time she had driven down this way.

Below the teeming A38, Devon bulges down to the coast and that bulge is known as the South Hams. It is marked at first by miniature rounded hills, wearing clumps of trees as toupees on their very tops to stop the wind blowing the soil away. Further south, towards the coast, a gentle oceanic swell of ridges prepares you for the real waves ahead. Signs of tourism are all too plain on the larger roads that skirt around it, but in the middle of it all, inland from Start Bay, is a less trampled area of fields, lanes and not much else which retains some of the utter remoteness of past centuries.

Beth was not in a mood to be charmed as the hedges crept in on her and slowed her pace. She was a London driver to the depths of her soul, carving others up and expecting to be carved up in her turn, always ready with the quick hand gesture and always reacting in fury if she was given one first. The road from Totnes to Kingsbridge began to test her patience. With blind corner after blind corner, crests and hidden dips, there was nowhere to overtake for miles, The Dartmouth turning took her on to a road which was little better, but when she took the long-forgotten right turn sign-posted to Slapton, even the white line in the middle of the road disappeared.

It was a warm afternoon and she was driving with the window down, but the scent from the high banks bordering the road only made her feel uncomfortable and out of place. She hated the way the banks pressed in on her as if she were going down an ever-narrowing trap which might not allow her the space to turn around and escape again. After a mile or so she came up behind a small, silver Nissan which was being driven with quite unnatural caution. On the infrequent straight sections the driver, a very old man, would speed up to nearly twenty-five miles per hour, but when confronted by anything approaching a bend, he would slow to fifteen, restrained it seemed by his equally old wife who could be seen waving her hands in the air at any sign of a hazard. Once and only once the road straightened and widened enough for Beth to try overtaking, but the old man had no idea that she was behind him and pulled into the middle of the road as she began to pass. Neither occupant showed any response to her horn-blast so she added deafness to the list she was compiling of their characteristics and fell back in behind them again.

After a very long time and a fairly short distance, they came to a road junction where the couple in front, missing their chance to pull out, waited instead for a very slow tractor to pass in front of them. The tractor was followed by a long line of cars. When the road cleared, they still showed no sign of moving. She waited a little longer and gave another peep on her horn. There was no response. She got out, walked up to the other car and looked inside and her heart thumped. The man and the woman inside were indeed extremely old. They also looked quite dead, their heads lolling forward and their eyes closed. A series of irrational possibilities came to her. Had she killed them? Had her hooting given them both heart attacks? Could their exhaust be leaking? Maybe the carbon monoxide had been blown away by the wind until they stopped, then the inside of the car had filled up with a lethal dose. She took her courage in both hands and opened the driver's door, and that was when the driver woke up.

'Hello,' he said with a puzzled smile, 'can I help you?'

'I don't believe it,' she said. 'Were you *asleep*?'

'Asleep? No, no. Oh. Oh dear, yes, perhaps I was.' He looked around and seemed to find nothing particularly unusual in that. 'I think we must have been having a little nap. Been for a walk you see. Did you want something?'

'You're in the middle of the road.'

'Bless my soul, are we? I'm so sorry. Did you hear that Em? We've been asleep. In the road.' Em showed no sign of waking.

'Look I'm in a hurry,' said Beth. 'Can you just pull over and let me by.'

'Let me see, yes, of course, of course,'

Beth got back in her car and the car in front started to move, but instead of pulling over, it meandered off again in the same direction as her and she swore viciously. Then it occurred to her that it really didn't matter. She couldn't have been in less of a hurry. No one knew she was coming and she didn't even want to arrive. It was just that there was nowhere else to go. As the road became still narrower, the car in front suddenly put on an unwise burst of speed and shot off out of sight, suggesting that some physical need more urgent than sleep had overtaken its occupants. Beth didn't speed up. The lane she was now driving down, and it was no more than that, should have been intensely familiar. She had walked it a thousand times in her childhood when it had been the lane home, but that didn't help. She recognised it as if someone had spent many hours describing it to her, not as if she had lived there for two thirds of her life. Adding to that feeling of disjuncture, she caught a momentary glimpse through a gap to her right of something genuinely unfamiliar, a large house down in the valley below the road where she had no memory of such a place. Then it was too late for unfamiliarity because she was coming down the hill. Slapton, steep, cramped Slapton crowded in on her, and there ahead, looming over the cottages with its squadrons of rooks flying around the ivy wrappings of its derelict battlements, was the dark tower which was all that remained of Slapton Chantry.

The main road was a twisting gulley running down between stone walls as the village came rushing in to smother her, and when she finally found a tiny gap to squeeze the car into, she sat in it and waited for the courage to do what came next.

The front door of Carrick Cottage opened straight on to the road and the flaking blue paint on the door was just as it had always been. Beth looked to the side and saw the same frayed blue curtains. She put her finger to the bell, then hesitated and ran her hand up and down the stones beside the door until she found the gap where the key used to be hidden. It was no longer there. No one else needed it these days. For a moment she was the child who had lived there, but only for a moment. She rang the bell just as a stranger would.

The man who came to the door was not at all as he had always been. He had changed so much that for a moment she thought he was someone else. He was two stone lighter than when she had last seen him, but despite that he had put on far more years than the calendar showed. He looked at her as if he were equally bemused.

'Beth?' he said, 'It's Beth!' and she saw a gleam of moisture appear immediately in the corner of each eye.

'Hello Dad,' she said and, being unable to kiss him, she put out both her hands and took his as they stared at each other.

'I didn't think you'd come,' he said, 'being so busy.'

She wondered if he still read a paper, if indeed he had any idea that the hounds were baying at her heels.

'Yes, I've come,' she said. 'Can we go in?'

'Can you stay for tea?' he asked as if he expected her to disappear again at any moment.

'I was hoping to stay a bit longer than that,' Beth replied, 'if that's all right.'

He nodded. 'That would be nice. Your room's all ready, just in case.'

Beth suppressed a feeling of irritation.

He went into the kitchen and she heard him filling the kettle. It still made precisely the same sound it had always made, the tinny drumming of the water into thin metal. He had always filled it through the spout with the tap on full. She heard him light the gas.

Nothing had changed inside the house. The parlour was a dark place with split leather armchairs and the old prints of clipper ships on the walls. She crossed over to the bookshelf to distract herself from her discomfort. There were all the bird books and the botanical guides, but there also, to her astonishment, was a spine she knew well, her own little book from last year, *The Opportunity of Crisis*. It was in her father's political section sandwiched between Will Hutton's *The State We're In* and Christie Kilfillan's *Last Chance*, as if keeping matter and anti-matter apart.

He came back in from the kitchen and caught her looking at them.

'I thought I'd better read what you had to say,' he said quietly and sat down. 'Won't be long. The kettle takes a minute or two.'

She almost said, I know that, kettles are the same everywhere, but she bit it back. 'What did you make of it?' she asked instead, caught between a reluctant pride in his interest and a flash of anticipatory irritation.

He thought. He had never minded waiting to get his words right and that had stretched out the hours of Beth's childhood often to breaking point. 'It's a great achievement to write a book,' he answered in the end. 'You feel passionately about it. I admire passion.'

'But you don't agree with what it says.'

'You wouldn't expect me to, would you?'

'I suppose not, but surely you can see . . .'

He held up a hand. 'There are other things to talk about first,' he said. 'The world can wait until after we've had our tea.'

She stood there and watched him go back into the little kitchen. That had always been their relationship, him doing the job of both parents and her doing the job of one child. Until she'd left.

He came back with two mugs. Hers had a picture of an otter on it, which was no surprise.

'You're still not on the phone then,' she said.

'No need. The Turners take messages. Peggy bangs on the wall if it's urgent.'

'Is it often urgent?'

He looked at her as if trying to detect sarcasm. 'We had an injured egret down in the marsh last week.'

Beth wasn't entirely sure whether an egret was an animal or a bird. For the first time, a part of her found something valuable in the relentless simplicity of his life. Her mobile was switched off and nobody could reach her. Not one single person in the outside world had any idea where she was. No one outside Slapton even knew she had a father. Here she could be safe while she sorted everything out. London political gossip wouldn't reach down here. Her own father didn't even know exactly what she did, who she had been working for.

That was when, looking down into his tea, he said, 'Tell me, love. How bad is it with this man Livesay?'

# CHAPTER FIVE

There is a chapel in the town of Ghent which owns a toe-bone of Saint Paul in a fine gold reliquary chest, and if you go to pray there, you may ask the priest for a twenty day notice. I went there alone as soon as I had seen to my men in their lodgings. The door had sagged so it caught on the sill and shook as I pushed it open, letting out a miasma of rotting cloth. Inside, it was very dark with only two candles burning and I didn't see the priest sitting waiting at the confessional until he challenged me with a quavering voice.

'Who are you?' he demanded in the Flemish which I knew a little, and then in slower and imperfect French. 'Are you a pilgrim? You don't look like one.'

He probably thought I was a robber.

'Tonight I'm a pilgrim,' I answered, also in French. He stood up, held up one of the candles and looked doubtfully at my style of dress.

'You have no scallop shell,' he remarked.

'I am not only on a pilgrimage,' I said, 'I am on the King of England's business, but I intend to stop for prayer at wayside shrines along my way. I have come here to pray to your relic of the blessed Saint and to ask you for a certificate.'

That seemed to reassure him. 'Do you need confession?'

'Thank you, no. I have a priest with me. I make my confession to him.'

'Have you sinned since your last confession to him?'

Had I sinned since the morning? I searched my memory and I couldn't come up with anything immediate, so I said what I have always said when a strange priest asks me that.

'Father, there is a sin I fear I have not yet confessed, the full weight of which is gradually becoming clear to me. Because I do not wish to confess less than the totality of that sin, I must wait before I ask forgiveness for it.'

He peered at me and in the dim light I could see his lips moving. He reached for a paper and held it out. It struck me he hadn't understood a word of what I had just said.

'I asked,' he said doubtfully, 'because tomorrow is our festival and if you come then I will give you forty days not twenty.'

'Can I have twenty days now and another forty tomorrow?' I asked, looking at the paper he had just given me.

He looked doubtful. 'I don't think so,' he said. 'It is one or the other.'

I gave it back to him reluctantly, thinking I would regret my action if I died that night. Forty days would take my sum of indulgences to a total of more than two thousand days. For a moment, my heart lifted at the thought of nearly six years less in Purgatory, then I remembered how much faster time moved there and I thought how many, many more certificates I would need to make much difference. My six years certificates might win me six years in the time of this world, but that would only be a few minutes of relief in the time they follow in Purgatory.

I gave him five coins for five candles and said I would be back in the morning, then I returned to the Boar's Head Inn and joined my men sitting down at the long tables. William Batokewaye was on the far side of the room, with several women at his table. He told me once that he was a priest when he was in England but that it was a precious burden best left safe at home when he was travelling. I have known him for too long to question that, apart from wondering whether, even in England, he could be regarded as entirely priestly, but at the centre of that man is something so solid, so true, that I do not feel qualified to judge him. He believes he will be forgiven and I hope he is right because I would not wish him to pass an age in Purgatory. When he dies, there will be masses said in my Chantry for him, though he does not know it.

The food came in those huge chafing dishes with the boars' heads at each end for which the Inn was named. Lentils in a spiced sauce and three different meats with spitted duck shredded over the top of them all. The fine gentlemen from Genoa didn't like it. I thought it was excellent. When I'm travelling, I'm on campaign and when you're out there scouring the countryside, you're grateful for anything that keeps your belly button away from your backbone. The squire was getting the worst of their complaints and doing his best to explain to the landlord what they wanted to eat. It wasn't going to get him anywhere. I knew the landlord, Garciot, from old times, and no one had ever got the better of him yet. Before he bought the inn with the proceeds of his ransoms, he'd been one of John Hawkwood's men for many a year. Hawkwood always said Garciot scared him stiff and, coming from Hawkwood, that was saying something. They lived for fighting, Hawkwood's bunch, but they always knew what was right and wrong. You might well call them mercenaries, and it was true that they fought for money but they wouldn't take that money from just anyone. They lived by a tough set of rules, but they stuck to them.

The evening ran its predictable course. The Genoese persisted with their complaint. Garciot stared at them without expression, then he took their food away and came back with something that looked almost the same but smelt far, far worse. He winked at me as he put it in front of them and I wondered what he could possibly have added to it out of sight in the kitchen to make it quite so repugnant. He excused himself for a moment to deal with the two Brabanters at the end of the table who had been making a drunken nuisance of themselves. He held the larger of them off the ground with one hand, while he patted his pockets for dinner money with the other, then he put one under each arm and showed them how to fly into the street. After seeing that, the Genoese managed to eat a surprisingly large amount of whatever it was on their plates and left to go to their rooms as soon as they could get away.

My men went about their own business, drifting towards William's table while Garciot came and sat with us, the squire and me.

'What are you doing, travelling with pants-wetters like those?' he asked.

'King's orders. King's affairs,' I replied, not wanting to encourage him. Familiarity is to be expected when you've spilt blood together, but it wasn't for me or for him to question the nature of the business my sovereign had charged me with.

'I hear the King's in his dotage,' he answered, 'watching his debts mount up, piling jewels on to this ugly mistress of his and letting the upstart John lord it over the country.'

The squire stiffened and, unbelievably, I saw his hand go to the grip of his sword.

'Enough, Garciot,' I said, and I thought I had said it quite quietly until I saw how many turned to stare.

He raised a hand quickly. 'My apologies, Sir Guy. While he commands your loyalty, he is still a great king.'

He turned to the squire and whispered something. The squire's indignation drained out of him. My hearing is still sharp, but the room was full of the noise of feasting men and when Garciot had gone off to see to his guests I demanded to know what he had said.

'Nothing bad,' said the squire quickly.

I wasn't sure I believed him. Garciot was certainly capable of a final sarcastic quip. 'Then what?'

'He told me I should study at your feet and mark every word you spoke.'

Oh really. 'Are you sure that's what he said?'

'I don't lie, Sir Guy.' For a short, fat studious man, he suddenly looked quite fierce.

'I'm sure you don't. Please excuse my bad manners. It's just that I will not tolerate people abusing our king.'

He nodded. 'And I won't stand for people abusing my lord Lancaster.'

I didn't show my amusement at the thought of him in hand-to-hand combat with Garciot because he so clearly meant what he said. The fight would have been over before a man could sneeze.

'You have a high regard for Lancaster?' I enquired.

That was who Garciot meant by his 'upstart John'. King Edward's youngest son, born only yards from where we now sat in Ghent and therefore known as John of Gaunt, as his mother, a Hainaulter, called the town. I wouldn't have wanted to upset the squire further, but privately I had some sympathy for Garciot's opinion. John had lately styled himself 'King of Castile', which seemed to me to be coming it a bit rich. He was never a man who had much understanding for those below him and I couldn't fully forgive him for that slaughter at Limoges.

'I had the highest regard for his Duchess.' The squire sounded sad. He crossed himself, giving a deep sigh. 'I wrote a poem to her.'

The beautiful Blanche. I thought of her and joined him in his silence because whenever I had seen Blanche I had thought immediately of Elizabeth, who had the same hair and the same forehead, but who shaded Blanche like a cathedral choir shades a tavern singer. I still long for Elizabeth every

66

single day. We did not have enough time together. I know this life on earth is only our qualification for whichever place comes next, and I would not fear my time to come in Purgatory if it were just for myself. I deserve to suffer. No, what I cannot bear is the thought that I might spend an aeon there, locked away from her. Even worse is the other possibility that, through our sin, I might meet her there.

They sang her mass every day at Tewkesbury just as they would be singing it now at Slapton. I prayed that would work.

In the years we had together, right up until the end, she had a way of looking at me which suspended time and conscious thought so that we would gaze at each other in private delight. From across a room our souls could still embrace.

'Sir Guy,' said the squire, a little hesitantly, jerking me back to this noisy inn.

'Yes?'

'I would not wish to upset you or intrude upon you in any way,' he said, waving a hand for another jug of wine, 'but I have a great desire to hear men's stories, and there is still so much I want to ask you in particular.'

'Why me?'

'Because I know that what the landlord said was right. Whenever I have heard your name spoken, it has always been with respect and trust. I want the chance to hear the story of great events told without having to worry about discerning truth and falsehood in the telling.'

'Oh now be careful, young man. My memory is sixty-five years old. All memories are changed in the use and the retelling. I cannot guarantee you truth.'

'I will take the risk.'

'We have a long way to go,' I said, 'and precious little other company worth the name.' It was clear we both felt the same way about our Genoese companions, and my archers, all fine fellows, were men of few words. 'Ask what you want.'

'When did you first meet this priest?' he asked, staring over at William who was singing vigorously in the crowd of girls.

'On the twenty-seventh day of August in the year thirteen hundred and forty six, just after the middle of the night.'

'And you question the power of your memory?' He raised an eyebrow. 'That is a fuller answer than anyone could expect. Where was it?'

'In the Valley of the Clerks.'

'I don't know of it. Where is it?'

'It is some two hundred yards below the windmill on the down-slope of the plateau beside the village of Crécy-en-Ponthieu.'

'Oh.' He made a face. 'That valley. Stupid of me. The great battle. Do you still remember it well?'

Remember it well? I thought of it almost as often as I thought of Elizabeth.

'It's an old tale and well-known,' I said. 'Were you born then?'

'I was three.'

'I met William in the night when the battle was over. The windmill was burning to light the battlefield and there were fires everywhere to honour the dead.'

'More of theirs than ours.'

'Oh yes. Far, far more. It had been a slaughter.'

'Not just a slaughter,' he objected. 'An honourable and magnificent fight, surely? You had been outnumbered by ten to one.'

'Time and willing lips will always twist a tale. Some say it was four to one, others say five. All the same, you could have searched high and low for honour on that field and not found quite enough of it.'

I hadn't meant to say that out loud. He pounced on it. 'What do you mean?'

'Nothing,' I said, 'another time perhaps.'

'Please go on. What happened that night?'

'Nobody slept. You never do after a battle. You know that yourself, but the French didn't seem to know it was over. More and more of them kept blundering up the valley like moths to a candle. They were wandering in from the far end, for hours afterwards, thinking to join in the spoils. They just didn't seem to realise that all the bodies heaped up were their own countrymen.' I drained my wine and he refilled it.

As ever, what was in my mind was the moment when the troops parted for the doomed charge of a blind king, John of Bohemia, lashed between his friends' horses.

It was blind John's fate that drew me to the heaps of dead. I thought I knew where I had seen him fall. A stupid thought. From up on the ridge by the windmill I had marked his passage fairly well, but then chaos hid his end and now, down below in the dark there were hills of dead piled to head-height, horses and men mixed together in heaps which had formed a rising barricade. The French had gone on leaping and clambering over that barricade, taking arrows for their trouble and piling it ever higher in the process.

I was weary to my bones, barely able to drag myself through the churned earth of the battlefield, stumbling over arrows and helmets and arms and legs, and I turned over a battalion of bodies before I found him. It was only when I saw the lashings around a harness that I finally knew where to look. Pulling the other corpses off the three of them left me sweating and soaked in crusting blood, and I couldn't get them free, you see? There was a black horse lying across them, a real charger, solid, stiff and utterly dead. In the morning, they were using teams of men with ropes and poles to prise those piles apart, but there in the night, there was just me and the flickering light of the nearest fire. The legs I thought belonged to John were sticking out from under the horse, and I was pulling as hard as I could when I found I was no longer alone. A huge man in a woollen tunic had joined me.

'You take one leg,' he said, 'I'll take the other.'

'I'm not looting,' I said sharply, because most of the men out on that field were our camp followers, using their knives to dispatch the nearly dead and cut from them whatever they could find of value. I had taken off my mail and I was in a plain jerkin. I could have been anyone and I didn't need another fight.

'I know that,' he said. 'I've seen you with the King all day, holding up the Standard. You did a good job. I don't expect you need to loot, I guess you've got a castle or two of your own.' There was nothing subservient about him, but right across that battlefield that night, in the aftermath of the desperate fight, men were talking to other men as equals and no one could be so proud as to mind.

'One castle,' I said, 'and it leaks.'

He laughed harshly. 'I know why you're here. You and I saw the same thing,' he said, 'or thought we did, and we both need to know, don't we?'

'I'm Guy de Bryan,' I said holding out a hand.

'Are you indeed?' he said as if he knew me. 'Well now, there's a fine thing. I am William Batokewaye,' he squeezed my hand in his own much larger one. In those days he still had both arms. 'In the service, for the present, of young Lord Montague, which is why I am here rooting around the carrion in the dark.'

Montague again. The Montagues were always embedded somewhere near the heart of my story. Let me get this right because, looking back, the order of all these events does get a little muddled in my head. That's because so many of the things that really mattered in my life happened in such a short space of years, and so many of them involved the Montagues. They had given me no great reason for gratitude. Old Montague had harboured the villain Molyns, then imprisoned me, then done all he could to see his daughter, my dear Elizabeth, marry another man. When it came to the precipice of my sin, it was me who plunged over, but it was Montague's hand that led me to the edge.

Now we had the new Earl of Salisbury, the younger Montague, and he was a fighter too, just like his wily, warrior father. Would he now set a curve of his own into the passage of my life? Molyns was still in his retinue. Molyns had done the deed that brought the two of us to root among these corpses in the dark.

I looked at the outline of William Batokewaye against the flaring firelight of the windmill collapsing behind him. 'You'll have to explain,' I said. 'What business does young Montague have here?'

'His dead father's business. Don't you know the story?' He looked at the leg he was holding, 'This man saved the old Earl. Six years ago, soon after Sluys?'

'Montague was captured.' It was a busy time. I had forgotten the details.

'Montague and the Earl of Suffolk, and something went amiss with the ransom,' said Batokewaye. 'Phillip of France threatened to kill both of them, and the only thing that stopped him was this man here. John of Bohemia taught young King Phillip a thing or two about chivalry that day, and he shamed him into letting them live. My master wishes to make sure blind John gets a Christian burial before the crows get to him. He deserves it after a death like that.' He sighed.

I wasn't sure if he meant the feathered crows or the human variety which were creeping around us on the edge of the darkness. I let go of my leg for a moment.

'It was magnificent,' I said and crossed myself.

'Of course it was magnificent, but what did he think he was doing?'

'He was riding to the aid of his men,' I answered.

71

'Lashed to his knights? As blind as a mole? What difference could he hope to make?'

'You know the answer to that as well as I do. It's a question of the spirit.'

'It's a question of being dead.'

We were both silent again and I knew we were both thinking about the means of his death.

'If you're in Montague's retinue, you will be familiar with Sir John Molyns,' I suggested.

He spat.

I waited, but it seemed that was all the answer I was going to get. It was certainly the sort of answer I most wanted, because I liked this man.

I pressed him. 'Were you with Molyns today?'

'Molyns was on his own business today, or perhaps the King's business but certainly not Montague's.'

I wanted to see where he stood.

'What business do you think that was?'

'The devil's business.'

We agreed on that.

'Come on then, heave,' he said. 'Let's get it over with.'

We heaved and he came out with a wet slither like a very old baby being born. He had new armour plate around his chest, one-up on chain mail, but it hadn't done much for him. Batokewaye strode off and pulled a brand out of the nearest fire. By its light we examined the sad remains of King John of all the Bohemians, and it confirmed my very worst fears.

'I'll find a priest,' I said. 'We should say a prayer to see his soul through to daybreak.'

'No need,' said the big man as he studied the corpse. 'You've found one. I *am* a priest.'

He didn't look like a priest. He looked like a man who'd been on the winning side of many bloody fights, but we said our prayers, the two of us, there in the flickering dark, in a

72

night that was threaded with the moans of the dying, and then we both sat down on the blood-soaked ground to keep the old king company until the sun rose.

'I couldn't do anything,' I said. 'I knew Molyns was planning something, and I couldn't prevent it. No one else seemed to think it was wrong.'

'It's not your fault,' said Batokewaye. 'You're a young man still. You can't stop what can't be stopped.'

'It was a great sin and it should have been prevented. We're not animals. There are rules. Even in battle we must remember . . .'

'No.' His voice was loud, cutting across me. 'We may not be animals, but tell me this. You're alone, walking in the darkest forest and you hear something rustle behind the next tree. What would you most want it *not* to be?'

'A wolf,' I said.

He shook his head.

'A bear?'

'Not a wolf, not a bear, not a snake, not a lion.'

'What then?'

'Another man.'

'Yes.'

'I tell you, we're not animals, we're more dangerous than any animal.' He looked down at poor dead John. 'When did an animal do *that* to one of its own?'

We talked until the sun first showed itself far away across the Somme, and by that time we were, what? Friends? Not exactly, not yet. Two people who sensed they were to know each other for years to come. Two people bound down the same road. I already knew that William Batokewaye would be a good companion on that road.

At dawn, we saw King Edward's great mathematical exercise begin, his clerks edging their cautious way onto the butchers' field to reckon exactly how many flowers of the French nobility we had plucked. Sir Reginald Cobham, that stalwart soldier, called together anyone with knowledge of the French colours, because in so many cases, it was only paint and crests and armour which still distinguished one pulped face from another. I closed my eyes when I had seen enough, but the distinctive noise of the aftermath made just as vivid a picture through my ears. I could hear the horse teams snorting and stamping and the sliding apart of the piles as they pulled. The clank of armour against armour and the wet thud of dead flesh hitting the ground as the bodies of horses and men were tugged apart. Every now and then there would be a sigh or a moan as air squeezed from dead lungs and, in amongst it, all the time, there was the cheerful shouting of men who found what they were doing to be perfectly acceptable.

'I want to find a peaceful place,' I said. 'Somewhere to think and to gather those thoughts and to say prayers. Somewhere away from Molyns and his like. Somewhere away from war.'

'You have your leaky castle,' said Batokewaye.

'Walwayns? Walwayns is a hard place to get to and a harder place to stay in. Walwayns spells struggle not peace. It is all I can do to stop it coming to pieces around my ears. Every day I spend there, I am beset by troubles. The people are full of complaints, the air is full of rain and falling rocks, the fields are full of weeds and the kitchens are full of rats. Walwayns is a penance.'

'I know a better place,' he said quietly.

'Tell me about it.'

'It is in a fold of valleys and gentle hills, a short stroll inland from a friendly sea. A long lake, full of fish, protects it from that sea and there is a drawbridge on the lake to keep off raiders. The village is sheltered from the winds and it soaks up the sun like a sponge. It has a twisting narrow street, houses built of stone and the fields around it are full of fat beasts. It is close to Heaven and there is always beer in the jug and food in the pot.'

'You come from this blessed place?'

'I do.'

'I wish it were mine to live in,' I said.

'It is, Lord,' he replied.

'I'm not a lord,' I said.

'The place I'm talking about is Slapton in Devon,' he said, looking at me expectantly. 'That's why I call you Lord.'

'What?'

'You have not heard of it?'

'No,' and then, slightly irritated, 'why did you laugh? Is it such a famous place?'

'It should be,' he answered, 'to you at least. You are Lord of the manor of Slapton, as well as Nympton St George, Satterleigh, Newton, Rocombe and Northaller.'

'Me?'

'Yes, you. Did your father not tell you?'

For the last ten years of my father's life he had told me that I was the child of Satan, that he could fly like a bat, that we could eat the stones of the castle's tower if we only boiled them long enough, and that he was the rightful king of the lost tribes of Egypt. He had never mentioned Slapton. 'No, he didn't,' I said. 'Does that mean you knew who I was all along?'

'Not until you told me your name,' said Batokewaye. 'I knew Guy de Bryan was serving the King, but I didn't know which one you were. I'm glad it was you.'

'Did you know my father?'

'I was ten years old the last time he came to Devon. It always puzzled us that he didn't come again. It's a fair place and there are rents collected year by year.'

'Who collects them?'

'My father's the steward. He's an old man now, but he's honest.'

'Is there a house?'

'There is Pool.'

'What's Pool?'

'The manor house, a great house indeed. It lies in the bottom of the little valley that runs inland from Slapton. It is a shaded place but well built in stone and it has more chimneys than you ever see in that part of the world, and there is enough wood stored in Pool's barns to make smoke come out of every one of them. You'll like Pool.'

'I'll come to see it, William Batokewaye. I need a quiet place. Shall you and I go there together when this war is through?'

'There's a lot more Frenchmen where these came from,' he said. 'That may be a while yet.'

# CHAPTER SIX

Having erased Slapton so successfully from her own story of herself, it had simply not occurred to Beth that Slapton's inhabitants would not have done the same. If no one in London knew she came from Slapton, it seemed that everyone in Slapton knew she had gone to London and even had quite a good idea of what she was doing there. It didn't occur to Beth that her father might be proud of her, that he might talk about her as if they were often in touch. Carrying in her head the scornful childish caricature of this place as somewhere so cut off from the modern world that it lacked television, radio and newspapers, she had been counting on anonymity. It had come as an absurd shock to find that her father knew exactly what had been happening to her in the past forty-eight hours, that the neighbours had told him, that people here were gossiping about her.

Head down, hurrying, Beth left his house and took refuge in the back lane. It led out of the side of the village towards her grandmother's cottage, and it had served the younger Beth as an escape route many times before. There was nobody around in the lane, but she imagined eyes inside every window, looking at her, matching her to the stories in their morning papers, and it was a relief to leave the houses behind.

But Slapton wouldn't leave her behind. It was coming back at her from the closed cupboards of memory, the stony surface of the path, the gate she used to sit on when she had somehow got annoyed with both parent and grandparent at once, and the fence where the dog had cornered her. In the first field, she saw the bushes where she used to make her camp and where, on her tenth birthday, she had buried a tin filled with the toys she decided she had outgrown, vowing to herself that she would never dig them up again.

The path led downhill between two more fields, then up into trees and by the stile she took the old branch to the right that led to Quarry Cottage. This was the spot, she had always felt, where you started to feel Eliza's presence spreading out through the countryside around her house. She was going to take the familiar short cut straight through the deserted quarry, but something had changed. It was no longer deserted. New gates closed the gap between the trees. The roofs of the old sheds beyond had been repaired, the brambles had gone and a truck was parked on fresh gravel where the big puddle always used to be.

Eliza's path ran around the far side of the quarry between the trees and Beth intended to take it but, out of mild curiosity and more from an unexpressed wish to delay her arrival at the old woman's house, she walked towards the new gate, opened it an inch or two and looked in, straight up into the face of the man who had been walking quietly towards it from the other side. He wore overalls and he was pulling off a pair of heavy leather gloves. His face was painted with matt grey dust which accentuated the sharp planes of his cheeks. He was smiling at some private joke and his eyes shone. What was even more surprising was that he stopped, looked at her calmly and said 'Hello Beth, I heard you were back,' and for a moment, she had no idea who he was.

'Lewis?' she said, after a giveaway pause. 'Is it you?' For just one absurd moment, she had taken him for Lewis's older brother, but Lewis didn't have an older brother. Seven years had filled him out and toughened him. She knew it was seven years because the last time she had seen him, they were each home from university and she had given him the cold shoulder. Then they'd both moved away.

'You went off somewhere,' she said. 'Scotland?'

'Ireland. I came back. What about you?'

'I . . . seem to be back too. Just for a day or two.' She looked in through the gate. 'What's going on here?'

'Hasn't Eliza told you? I reopened the old place.'

'As a quarry? I thought it died on its feet years ago.'

'Come in and see,' he suggested, 'if you're not in too much of a rush.'

'I ought to go on.'

'It'll only take a minute. I can't be too long myself. I've got to be in Dartmouth in half an hour. It would be handy because I've got a bag of Eliza's shopping in the shed. You could save me time by taking it with you. That's if you don't mind?'

Seven years on, and they were talking about Eliza's shopping. She didn't know whether to be annoyed or relieved.

Inside, the tall face of the quarry loomed out of the trees to their left. Rows of rough-cut stone slabs were laid out on the ground. He took her to the larger of the two sheds.

'You remember, this whole place was my granddad's?' he said as he unlocked the door. 'He never worked the stone, not after the war anyway. When he died he left it to me, so I decided I'd have a go.'

'By yourself?'

'Me and Rob. He's here part-time.'

'Who's Rob?'

'You must remember Rob. Robin Watson? He was in primary with us. He went to the comprehensive.'

For a moment Beth rejected the very idea that she might remember someone from junior school, that even more connections might be waiting in this place, ready to trap her and wind her back in, but all the same she had a vague memory of a large, shambling boy. The comprehensive? She and Lewis had both gone on to the grammar school, the only ones from Slapton who did. Seven years of that long bus ride together, twice every day.

'You make a living out of this?' she asked, looking around.

'You mean is it just a hobby? No, it's a job.'

She bit back her words. She wanted to say, you were bright, you could have done anything. Why are you wearing dirty overalls with stone dust in your hair? Why are you wasting time in Slapton? You got away, why did you come back?

His eyes changed as if he remembered her capacity for scorn. 'It's a little gem, this place.' He checked his watch, 'Do you know anything about geology?' he asked.

She shook her head.

'Have you ever been to Purbeck?'

'No.'

'On the Dorset coast? Maybe, oh I don't know, sixty miles east of here. The Isle of Purbeck? It's not really an island. They just call it that. It's this side of Weymouth.'

'I haven't been there, no.' He talked as if he could persuade her she had.

'Well, it was always famous for Purbeck marble. There's not much left to be had now. Come in and have a quick look, I'll show you.'

On a bench inside was a carved and fluted column in a stone so dark green it was almost black. It glistened.

'It's not really marble,' he said, running one hand over it. 'That's just what they call it. It's a sandstone, you see, but it's packed full of tiny, hard shells and when you cut it clean you can get a real shine on it. Beautiful, isn't it? They always used it for the fine work in churches and places like that.' His voice had an unexpected reverence in it.

Despite herself, the stone drew her attention and she traced the path of his fingers with her own. 'So you get it from Purbeck and you carve it here?'

'Oh no, no. This came from here. That's the whole point. This is a geological oddity, you see, our very own little outcrop of the marble on the south-west, north-east line. The only place you find it west of Purbeck itself.'

'So people still want it?'

'Oh yes.'

'What's this bit for?'

'Restoration work for a church in Winchester.'

'And they come all the way here for it?'

'Beth, this is where they came originally when they were building that same church. The marble looks just a little bit different in every seam, you see, the colour, the shade. You want to match it, you got to come back to the same place.' He had always had enthusiasm and she could remember how much that had annoyed her when enthusiasm in any form was the last thing she admired. He bent down and pulled out a section of a column from the floor below the bench. It was dull and half of it had crumbled away. 'This is the bit they want to replace. I've been down into a few of the old holes and I reckon I've found the very same face it came from in the first place. I'm carving the exact same stone.'

'Why's it in such a state?' Beth asked, looking at the crumbling piece on the floor between them.

Lewis frowned. 'It was just poor stuff. There was a pocket of mud in it and they carved it badly anyway. They should never have let it leave the quarry.' He sounded irritated, almost angry, as if the family had let someone down.

'When was that?' Beth asked, thinking perhaps it was back in the fifties or sixties when his grandfather was still working.

'Thirteen twenty-two,' said Lewis. 'They've still got all the old records. Very bad. You shouldn't let anyone down like that. This stone should be good for thousands of years.'

81

She looked hard at him and saw he meant what he said. He was annoyed with stone cutters who had been dead more than seven centuries for letting the business down.

'Any chance you can come back tomorrow?' he said, looking at his watch again, 'I'd like to show you the rest. See what you think.'

'Maybe,' said Beth. 'I'm not sure how long I'm staying.'

'Do you mind giving this to Eliza?' he asked, picking up a shopping bag. 'Her change is in it.'

'If she's there. I was going to take potluck. She doesn't even know I'm here yet.'

'Oh yes she does,' said Lewis. 'That's how *I* knew you were here. She told me.'

Eliza already knew she was here. How could that be? All at once Beth found she needed to be out in the fresh air again, away from people who knew things. There was no escaping her grandmother though. Not if she knew.

'Do you see much of her?'

'She drops in most days for a chat and a cup of tea.'

She was heading for the door when she first noticed the fragments of the old stone slab. They were laid out on a flat table, eroded and camouflaged with lichen. She paused for a moment to look and Lewis stopped too. It had once been a stone rectangle, but at some point, long ago, it had broken apart into a dozen constituent pieces and the jagged edges had been softened and blurred with all the time that had passed since. Someone, Lewis presumably, had laid it out carefully on the wooden table, fitting it together like a jigsaw, but there was a large gap where one piece was missing. Faint lettering was incised into it, but that too had eroded almost away.

'What's this?' she asked.

'I'm doing some restoration,' Lewis said. 'It came from the Chantry tower. They want me to put it back together if I can.'

'Who's they? English Heritage?'

'No. The tower's privately owned. The house and the tower. Don't you remember? I think it's changed hands since your time.'

She did remember, vaguely. The great tower had never been an important part of her life in Slapton, having no function.

'What is this? A memorial of some sort?'

'Maybe.'

'Do you know what it says?'

'Only part of it. You've heard of Guy de Bryan?'

'No.'

He looked surprised for a moment then glanced at his watch yet again. 'I really should get going. Come back when you've got a bit of time. I'll tell you all about it.'

So then he was gone and she was alone again, outside the quarry, watching him drive away and pushing down the memories which seemed too childish to be allowed. She turned back to the path to Eliza's, knowing there was no alternative but to walk on down it and knowing that at the far end was the wonderful, dreadful woman who was her grandmother and who loved her and disapproved of her in equal measure.

She sighed and started walking. It had never before struck her as odd that when the path bent around to the left and delivered her, still unprepared, to the house, it was the rear of the house that she saw and not the front. The house sat in a clearing in the trees facing the wrong way, as if it had one day heaved itself up in a sulk and turned its back on its visitors. The garden was here, on this side. The front faced nothing but the dense and ragged trees which Eliza had left untended for years so that they pressed against the front windows, scraping the glass when the wind blew and shading the sitting room. Eliza never bothered to open the curtains. She lived in the kitchen most of the time, except when she was out in her sheds doing obscure jobs with the wrong tools.

Eliza was standing there outside the back door as if she had been expecting her.

'Have you come by yourself?' was the first thing she said, taking the shopping bag and peering past Beth at the trees as though she might have to repel an invading horde.

'Yes,' said Beth 'Hello Gran.'

'You'd better come in before anyone sees you.'

That made Beth look around too, but all was quiet in the clearing in the trees and there was no one there but the two of them.

Eliza's kitchen was the same as ever. In the middle stood an old oak table and around it were a sofa and three armchairs which, even before they had sagged with half a century of use, had been much too low for the table. Since Beth had first known this room, which was as far back as she could remember, she had always had to lean forward from the swaying nest of springs and horsehair to reach up to the table for her plate or cup. Meals at Quarry Cottage were eaten on your lap, and if Eliza was sitting opposite, you wound up talking to the top of her head because that was all you could see.

'I've got elderflower or mead,' said Eliza. 'The mead's sweeter but the elderflower's older.'

'Could I just have a glass of water?' Beth nearly said mineral water before she remembered where she was.

'From the tap?' Eliza sounded shocked. 'I'd have to boil it.'

'Oh.'

'It's coming out a bit green. The pump's been greased.'

'A cup of tea then?'

Eliza went into the larder and came out with two tumblers of a thick amber liquid. Beth recognised the sweet honey smell of her mead and resigned herself. Her grandmother put one on the table and drained most of the other one at a gulp. She was the same as ever, as thin as a kipper, as she always said, and much the same colour. Eliza's skin was as tough as tanned leather. She looked as if she'd been smoked. Scorning hairdressers after a woman in Dartmouth had once tried to charge her a pound for a cut and wash in the nineteen seventies, she had bought a pair of electric clippers and kept her white hair shorn in a bristly crew cut. She was not much more than five feet two inches tall, but she was not in the slightest bit fragile.

She stood looking down at Beth, who was trying to find a section of the sofa where the ends of the springs weren't so sharp.

'You've got yourself in a pickle, girl,' she observed. 'I never thought going off to London was a good idea. Don't know what's wrong with Slapton.'

Eliza didn't read the papers. She said bad news would come and find you soon enough if it mattered. There wasn't a radio in the house and Beth was pretty sure her grandmother had never watched television in her entire life.

'I asked Lewis,' the old woman said, divining Beth's puzzlement. 'They were talking in the churchyard yesterday. I heard your name before they saw me.'

So Lewis knew all about it too.

'You got thinner,' Eliza observed, inspecting her.

'Thank you.'

'Don't thank me. That's not a compliment. You look like a refugee. Have you been doing what I said? A mug of hot milk every night, with local honey in it? Got to be local. The bees give you what you need, see? The pollen from the flowers around about where you live, that's the best thing for you.'

'There're not many bees in central London, Gran.'

Eliza snorted. 'Course there are. There's bees everywhere. You're just too busy to notice as well as too busy to eat properly. Well, I suppose I thought you'd be more different.'

'I haven't been away that long.'

'Oh yes you have. Two letters and one postcard in getting on for three years? I suppose I should be counting myself lucky. It's more than your dad's had.'

'I'm sorry. I'm always so busy.'

'I don't know what you've done to your hair. Still, it's nothing a good blowy walk won't fix. Needs a bit of sea breeze in it, does that hair. What's the inside like?'

'The inside of my hair?'

'The inside of my little girl. You might not have changed on the outside, but what about the inside? You're not as tough as you think you are. Never have been. Have you taken a bit of damage?'

Beth could only stare at her in silence.

'Lizzie-Beth,' said Eliza, and the old, kind name brought Beth to the edge of tears. 'Listen, Lizzie-Beth. Do you love the man?'

'You mean Alan?' she said when she could control her voice.

'I don't know. The political one.'

Apart from brief, vulnerable moments in bed, Beth hadn't let herself think that way. There was the excitement, the intrigue and the power. There was the passion, but love?

'That's enough of an answer,' said Eliza. 'I don't reckon you do.'

'Well, I . . .'

'Doesn't mean it doesn't hurt. You still want to smell the smell of him, eh?'

They had talked of many, many things in the years before Beth went away, but she had somehow never expected to sit in Eliza's kitchen discussing the earthier side of sex.

'Yes,' said Beth in a voice that came out smaller than she expected.

'I know what that's like,' said Eliza, and that was the first time she had ever said anything which hinted that her son

Guy had been anything other than some kind of immaculate conception, a one-off event in which no man had played a part.

It was only at the grammar school, in Beth's second year, when her English homework had been an essay on 'My family as a historian would tell its story' that she had realised how little she knew about her grandmother. The sentence she had written had been crossed out by the teacher. 'My grandmother, Eliza Battock was born in Slapton like me and so was her mother who was also called Eliza Battock.' The English teacher had written in the margin in red ink, 'If she was your *grandmother*, her maiden name would not have been the same as her mother's as she would have taken your grandfather's surname.' It had taken her days to puzzle out what it meant. She had been so cross with her father all that year about all kinds of things, the old-fashioned house they had to live in, how little there was to do in Slapton, and about his complete inability to understand what she was going through in the frightening discoveries of growing up, that she had never been able to ask him.

'Do you?' she asked, interested.

'Do I what?'

'Know what it's like?'

'Oh yes. You saw what young Lewis has done to the quarry?'

Beth knew that when Eliza decided to evade an issue there was no point in pursuing it directly. 'He showed me a bit.'

'There's a good young man. He's a fine craftsman.'

'Oh Gran. It's a waste. He was a clever boy. He could have done anything he wanted to.'

'Like being a politician, you mean? Like lying for a living and fighting wars when you want to stop the people seeing through you. Fighting wars to make you feel big. That's better, is it? Is that what you mean?'

The other Eliza was back. Her eyes changed when she was

like this. She stooped a little more too, as if waiting to spring at you.

'No, I don't mean that. He was a good writer.' She was remembering the tussle they had each year over who would win the prizes. It was always one or the other of them. Nobody else in her year got much of a look-in. She'd done Latin as an extra GCSE to get one up on him, but he'd joined her a term late and got the same 'A' grade that she did. Straight 'A' grades right through, both of them. 'He was brilliant at languages too.'

'And now he's good at stone carving and that's a proper skill, a skill to treasure so don't you start putting him down. He's done just what he wanted to,' said Eliza. 'You can't tell lies in stone.'

'Not all politicians lie,' said Beth.

'No that's true, the dead ones don't.'

'Anyway, what do you mean, you can't tell lies in stone?'

'Well, you can't – not without being found out. Words last in stone. You get found out.' She walked across to the dresser. 'I kept your postcard,' she said. 'From New York. I thought they'd knocked down all those tall buildings with their aeroplanes.'

'Not all of them, Gran. Speaking of buildings,' she wanted to change the subject, 'I wanted to ask you. When I was driving in, I saw a house I never noticed before.'

'Where?' Eliza had swung around on her.

'On the way in, coming down the hill, just down below the lane. Down in the valley.'

'What sort of house?'

'Quite big. Sort of a manor house. Have they cut the hedges or something? It surprised me.' It shouldn't have been there, not a great big house in the village she grew up in.

'Manor house? Must be Pool. You've seen Pool.'

Beth waited for more, but Eliza went back to rummaging around on the dresser. She wasn't to be easily deflected.

'I got this too,' she was opening out a folded page of a newspaper. 'It was given me in the shop.'

Beth hadn't seen it before. It looked as if it came from the *Telegraph*. She could read the headline. 'Livesay aide talks tough in DC'. A quick thrill went through her before she remembered that nothing with Livesay's name in it could be good publicity now. It must have come out before she came back.

'Says here you're flat out for war, girl. Says you think we're all spineless if we don't fight people we don't like.'

'That's not exactly what I said . . .'

'Where's it now? Where's my glasses? Says here, Beth Battock, speaking in the something club, I don't know, foreign something club, says Beth Battock said the people of Great Britain are behind the President and even when their leader's nerve fails they know that resisting oppression with something or other, what's this, calculated that's it, *calculated force* is always right. Is that right? Is that what you believe?'

'Yes, it is Gran.'

'Well, I'm people of Great Britain and I don't think so.'

To move her off the subject, to get the kind Eliza back, the Eliza who would defend her to the death, Beth tried distraction again.

'Oh Gran, I wanted to know something. Lewis showed me the stone slab from the tower. You know? The one he's repairing? He said it was something to do with Guy somebody.'

'Oh don't you go bringing him into this. He wouldn't be on your side not neither girl, I can promise you that.'

Thinking Eliza was confused, Beth said, 'No Gran, not that Guy, not Dad. This is some old man from centuries back.'

'I know what I'm saying. You know very well who he means.'

'No, I don't.'

'Have you forgotten everything I ever told you about this

place? Lewis means Guy de Bryan. Let me tell you if Guy de Bryan was here, he'd put you straight about your ideas. He wouldn't have had any truck with you, my girl. Why do you think he built the damned Chantry?'

# CHAPTER SEVEN

After Ghent, we began to settle into the journey. William and his horse weren't getting on, but I was expecting that. Both of them wanted to be in command and the horse was not clever enough to give up quickly. I always took two horses everywhere, and if the worst came to the worst he could ride Arcite. Arcite was a gelding and would treat him gently. My other horse, the stallion, Palamon, was as fiery as they come. He was named after Hugh Despenser's horse, because the two of them together, horse and master, put up the bravest fight I ever saw at Blanchetaque in our crossing of the Somme, and if my honouring his master was a little hollow, the very least I could do was to honour the memory of the horse. My own Palamon wouldn't tolerate anyone but me in the saddle, but Arcite wasn't like that. If I handed him to another man he would treat that man as well as me.

The men from Genoa had been angry at the late start that first morning out of Ghent. I told the squire I had been at prayer and I made the mistake of showing William my forty-day certificate as I rode next to him.

He looked around to see if anyone was in hearing range. No one was.

'You don't need that,' he said. 'I keep telling you, it's purest nonsense. God doesn't need bits of paper.'

'It's not the bits of paper,' I said. 'It's the prayers behind them. They're what matters.'

'Stop hissing,' he said.

'I'm not hissing.' I hated these disagreements, fearing the consequences of his pig-headedness because in every other way I regarded him so highly.

'You're starting to sound more and more like a heretic,' I said.

'That was a hiss.'

'Well, what do you want me to do, shout it? Do you want the Italians to hear you're an anti-papist? '

'I'm not,' he said mildly, 'but I don't believe there's any special holiness in your average fragment of the true cross.'

'You're not following Wycliffe are you?' I asked. I was a little shocked. John Wycliffe's preachings were stirring men up at home. 'That's blasphemy, surely.'

He laughed. He actually laughed. 'It would be if I were talking about the real thing. Look, I've already seen enough bits of the cross to make up ten whole crosses and I can't have seen more than one in ten thousand of the total.'

'The Bishops say it's miraculous,' I answered. 'It's like the loaves and the fishes. The Lord in his goodness has allowed the wood of the cross to be multiplied so that all may have the benefit of the relics.'

He just looked at me and then he did that foolish thing with his fingers around his face again, making the loud sound of buzzing bees.

'You don't need your bits of paper,' he said. 'You *are* an indulgence, a walking indulgence.'

I gave up, wheeling Palamon around. What William never understood about me was that whenever in my life I have done something men regard as good, I have known that the possibility, the idea of the exact opposite was wriggling away deep down inside me. You squash that wriggling thing. You crush it down into the darkness inside you and then men praise you for what you do, but perhaps that's why you do it, why you crush the wriggling seed of evil. I know what William would say. He would say that even a saint feels that sinner inside him, but that's the difference. A saint who ever lets the sinner take control is no saint. I was no saint. William was wrong. I needed my pieces of paper.

I looked back at William and he seemed to be laughing as he plodded along. I feared for him. He was too good a man to lose to a heresy and its consequences. The Dutch had a name for Wycliffe's followers. *Lollaerds*, they called them, which meant babblers of nonsense. The priest of Ghent had given me a list of the shrines and their relics on the next two days of our journey, and I would show William a thing or two. I decided I would visit every one.

The weather stayed fine for that part of the way, though there were frosts in the morning and our reins were stiff until the sun rose. Palamon wasn't at his best on mornings like that. He'd plod along with his head down until the day warmed up, still half-asleep and only when the sun brushed the frost powder from the path would he join me in my watchfulness, jerking his head at anything he thought I might have missed, and whinnying his thoughts to Arcite when I wasn't sufficiently appreciative.

We were approaching Maastricht and intending to take a late midday meal there. I had accumulated another ninety days' certificates by that time. This was already becoming a difficult time of the day. The Genoese believed such a meal should consist of a copious variety of dishes in which fruit and fresh Italian vegetables should figure large. My bowmen wanted hearty food, as indeed they did at any time of day or night. I didn't care. What we got was what was available in the cold north at that time of year, scraps of dead cow, dead pig, dead hen or dead horse, surrounded by a mound of beets and as much cabbage as they could eat. There were complaints of course, but the squire bore the brunt of them because I found it was a lot easier to pretend I didn't speak any Italian at all. I knew perfectly well what they were saying because on campaign, you pick up 'soldier's language', which is to say all the phrases you need in regard of military emergencies, food and warm, dry beds. Plus, for younger and unprincipled men, the matter of women.

What happened was not in any way my archers' fault. They led us round a bend and there in front of us, sitting beside the road, was a man drinking from a leather bottle. He didn't even glance at us, but my archers, all six of them, behaved exactly as I had trained them to do and checked for ambush immediately, it being second nature. Gwynn spurred his horse up the bank with one of the Owens backing him up, and circled the only cover nearby, a copse fifty feet from the road. Llewellyn rode ahead and the other three spread out, facing outwards against any threat. Then Gwynn hollered the all clear and they took up their normal formation again but sadly, precautions such as that are for guarding against the very sane, not the very mad. I kept an eye on the man as the Genoese rode past him but at that exact moment, he pulled a knife from his sleeve and sprang at James di Provan. It was an insane act. Perhaps he was goaded beyond endurance by the loud whine of the man's voice and the absurd brightness of his red coat, in which case I had some sympathy for him. It would all have been easily dealt with. Little Dafydd, Gwynn's son, had an arrow notched to his bowstring before the knife was half-way to di Provan. Then the damned Italian crossbowmen committed two unforgivable errors. One of them swung his horse across Dafydd's line of shot without a backward look. The other fired his crossbow before it was firmly at his shoulder and the bolt missed its target, whizzed past my leg and hit something immediately to my right. I just had time to see the squire's

94

horse rear and fall on top of him before I had my sword drawn and was riding down on the attacker, but I needn't have bothered. As soon as there was a finger's width of clear space, Dafydd had an arrow in him, and if that arrow parted the hair of the nearer crossbowman on its way, then I think Dafydd regarded that as part of the point.

Well, there was that usual sick moment when we all went from going full tilt to a standstill again and turned to reckon the cost. The horse had scrambled to its feet, but the squire was groaning on the ground. There was a dark and spreading pool oozing from his jerkin and I took it for a death wound. You don't get a crossbow bolt through the chest and live to tell the tale. In that moment of clarity, I knew I would feel sorry for his death and very angry indeed at the idiotic incompetent who had caused it. You learn to abandon sentimentality when enough men have died around you, and then you save your regrets for those who really deserve it, but there was something most unusual about this man, a way of looking at the world, an unquenchable enthusiasm for discovering other people's point of view, which I would miss. Most people are ten times more keen to tell you their thoughts than to find out yours.

Then the squire sat up, wrinkled his nose, said a very rude word and pulled the remains of a broken flask from his pocket.

'My ink,' he said. 'I've broken my ink.' There were a few more words in there, but that was the essence of it and, having built him up, I will spare you evidence of his earthier side.

I looked at his horse and that was when I saw where the bolt had gone. It was sticking out of his saddlebag and the heavy leather had saved the horse. The squire didn't seem to share my relief.

'Oh no,' he said, clambering to his feet. 'Oh damn, damn, damn.' He wrenched the bolt out and hurled it away, then he opened the straps and brought out a great wad of vellum with an irregular tear straight through the middle of it where the bolt had gone in at an angle. That seemed to make him even angrier.

I had moved on to the next matter once I had satisfied myself he was intact. Di Provan was shouting at my men. I dismounted and put myself between them.

'Speak to me,' I said, 'not them.'

He did, but his Italian came a little too fast for me. I reckon he understood me perfectly well though.

'Your men nearly got you killed,' I said, loudly and slowly. 'Their behaviour was disgraceful. They will give us their weapons until I am sure they have mended their ways.'

He burst out again and I wasn't in the business of negotiating, so I plucked the crossbow from the nearer man's hands and tossed it on the ground by Dafydd who was standing near with another arrow notched. That got them. There was a torrent of outrage and a slightly shaky voice from behind me began to translate it into English. The squire was back in business.

'He says you are no use. He says you should have seen the man's knife. He says you should give his man his weapon back or they will arrest you. He says . . .'

'Tell him to shut up,' I said. 'Use whatever language you like.'

Whatever he said, di Provan's jaw fell open and he looked at me as if he could not believe his ears.

'Now,' I said, 'tell him and his men that no soldier who rides with me has ever missed his shot at twenty feet. Tell him I have never known Dafydd miss at two hundred feet. Tell him when in action no soldier ever moves without knowing just how and where his comrades stand. For all these reasons these two men are not proper soldiers and I will not have them carrying weapons. They are more danger to us than to anyone else.'

Di Provan became even more furious, then the squire,

without bothering to translate, broke in on him and covered his tide of Italian with a counter-tide that stopped him in his tracks. It went on and on and on and as he talked, di Provan's face changed so that he looked at me at first in disbelief, then in surprise and finally in something approaching respect.

When the squire finally fell silent, di Provan made as if to say something but thought better of it. We remounted and I had the dead man slung over a spare horse's back. We disposed of him in Maastricht, which was easier than it might have been because the sheriff there was Wim the Cleaver who had been the Bascot of Mauleon's lieutenant in the early days of the war. The Bascot was a friend of mine. We had a similar approach to life and he had picked sound men under him. Wim was as honest as they come. I had met him many times and he came out in person when the guard at the town gate summoned him.

'Don't know him,' he said, pulling the body off my horse and turning it over with his foot. 'I'll have him buried.'

'Christian rites,' I said, reaching into my pocket for a coin or two, but he wouldn't take them.

'I owe you one, Sir Guy' he said. 'Are you staying at the Feathers?'

'If they've got room.'

'They'll have room. I'll send a man around to arrest a few if they haven't, that'll make space. I'll see you there for a glass later on.'

The Genoese made less of a fuss this time. They all four shared a room and we had two between us. Fine treatment indeed,

William ate with us because there were no girls to be seen at the inn. 'Fish' he said glumly when they told us what they had. 'I didn't know it was a fish day. I hope it's lake fish. We're too far from the sea for my liking.'

I had bought us all a fish indulgence before we left because you need proper food when you're on campaign and it seemed worth making sure we could always eat meat. I hadn't thought to tell the inn on arrival because it wasn't what we would normally regard as a fish day. Turned out it was their local saint's day and we were going to have to eat it because they hadn't got anything else except peas and I firmly believe that when you've eaten one pea, you've eaten them all.

'We can drink while we wait,' said William, 'a day like that deserves more than one jug of wine.'

I fixed the squire with the gaze that only allows the truth. 'Now listen young man, I want to know what you said to di Provan that shut him up so smartly.'

'Oh,' he looked a little flustered. 'Nothing you could possibly mind, Sir Guy. I told him about your reputation as a fighter. I thought it was only fair. He looked half-way to drawing a sword on you.'

'And what did that tale involve?'

'The story of the Garter tournament, well, the short version, anyway.' William lifted his massive head. 'You've done it now, young man,' he said. 'There are some tales whose telling should be left to those who know them.'

'I was told it when I was a boy,' said the squire indignantly. 'My father was there. He told me over and over again.'

'It wasn't his story and it's not yours.'

'William,' I said, 'it is not yours either and it is so long ago it no longer feels like mine. Let us hear what new life a young man's lungs can breathe into it. I might prefer a different version.'

That was a silly thing to say. There are some stories should be allowed to grow cold.

'It is a most noble story,' said the squire. 'The tale of how a knight gave up his love for the sake of a friend. It was in the year 1343, the sixteenth year of the King's reign, and he called a great tournament at . . .'

'Wait a minute,' I said. 'Let's go back a bit. If the tale

must be told, then let it be told properly. Let us begin at the beginning.'

The squire nodded eagerly. 'Of course. That's the moment when the two knights, imprisoned in the same cell, looked out and saw . . .'

'No, boy. It's a long time before that.'

'I don't know it then,' he said sadly, 'but I'd like to.'

Then, perhaps because earlier that day I had thought him dead, or maybe because I needed to be young again for just a while, I told him how it all began.

'You have to go back another five years to 1338. I was thirty years old then, pretty well-trained by that time.'

'You were a knight?'

'No, no. I was just a man-at-arms. I was knighted at Crécy. Anyway, I was serving under Montague and Arundel at the siege of Dunbar, old Montague that is.'

'Was that a great fight?' asked the squire eagerly.

'Far from it. Dunbar was the sort of siege where nothing at all happened, where nobody came out to negotiate or tried to take us by surprise by a night-time sally or even bothered to show their heads over the parapet to hurl the odd arrow at us. It went on right through a freezing Scottish winter and spring. We were rigid with frost and boredom in equal quantities. They sat inside in warmth and comfort, laughing at us.'

'Didn't you attack?'

I phrased it diplomatically. It has never been my way to undermine the reputation of those above me. 'Arundel found the fortifications a little too strong. He thought it best to conserve our energy and outlast them, so we did just as little as they did and that starts to prey on your mind in the end. I mean, at least they had walls around them. Their complacency made me quite convinced they had got word that help was coming, so I spent a lot of time quietly scouting the countryside around without asking permission because it was better than doing nothing. At the end of May, just when it was warming up, with little prospect of anyone having the energy to actually storm the damned castle, I was south of Dunbar and a man came galloping.'

I remembered that so clearly. I heard him first. I was riding around the edge of a wood and I heard the drumming of horse's hooves in front getting louder and louder. I remember looking quickly around me because the trees were thick there and filled between with brushwood and I could not get off the track, which curved out of sight just ahead. You imagine the worst at times like that, knowing that whatever is about to burst into sight might be the death of you. I did not want to die at Dunbar. A moment later, he appeared, a young man on a wiry horse, going full pelt, and when he saw me, he nearly came off it.

'Hold,' I said, turning my horse across the track to give my sword arm free play, and he slewed to a halt, looking all around him for escape. He was about to turn and run when we recognised each other from the previous year's campaign.

'Guy,' he said, 'well met. I have a most urgent summons for all of you. Where's Arundel?'

'John Mowbray,' I said, 'he's back at camp. Follow me,' and we raced back to the siege camp together.

I was silent for a moment trying to remember where it was that John Mowbray died. I cradled him trying to staunch a wound that bled like a river, but I just couldn't remember where.

'Well, King Edward's new war on France was a few months old and the message said he had decided it was time to cross the Channel, to confront the King of France in battle.'

'So you rode away?'

'Let Sir Guy tell the story,' William said, annoyed, but I hushed him. It was good to hear the squire's enthusiasm. It wasn't common to meet anyone who wanted to know about the past.

'It was a rush. It always is. As usual, by the time the news reached us, the date for us to gather at Dover was impossibly close, so we charged south as fast as our horses could take us leaving the wagons to straggle after us as best they could.'

'The whole army?'

I laughed at the idea. 'No, just the fifty of us, the men-at-arms and the knights, riding in a mad dash. That's always costly, but there were still forty-five left when we passed through London. We only stopped for long enough to change horses.' I found myself frowning. 'John Molyns was with us of course. He never moved far from Montague's shoulder in those days. He was a man of property now, much of it gained by foul means. The tales they told of him were terrible.'

'Why talk of Molyns?' William interrupted. 'You'll only upset yourself, and the bugger's dead and buried now.'

'He won't understand this story unless he understands Molyns,' I said, and the squire nodded eagerly.

'Molyns was still on the up,' I said. 'He'd been well rewarded by the King's favour a year or so earlier for doing some dirty work, rounding up all the foreign merchants in London, save only for the King's Italian banking friends. He was good at tasks like that, where a touch of natural violence helped to do the job, but some of his earlier work was starting to catch up with him and he'd been currying Royal favour against the day when that would come home to roost.'

'More dirty work?'

'It was one of the vilest tales I ever heard. He had his heart set on the manor of Stoke Poges, which was owned by his wife's uncle, Peter Poges, a good, plain man.'

'A pompous mass of piety,' said William, 'but he still didn't deserve what happened to him.'

I took no notice of him. 'Molyns didn't want to wait to inherit, so one November night he sent his henchmen to the house and they butchered both Peter and his son.'

'But they were *family*. What did Molyns' wife say about that? It was her *uncle*.'

'Gill Molyns? She was always loyal to her husband. I don't know what she said in the privacy of their bedroom, but she went along with it all. She even managed to bully her grandfather into surrendering the rest of the lands around the manor.'

'And he was never tried for the crime?'

'Oh yes, he was, but he was smart. He fixed it so that friends of his brought a murder case against him.'

'*Friends* of his?'

'That was the smart bit. They scrambled all the evidence on purpose. To make sure of it, he had a bent Justice of the Peace in his pocket and he stacked the jury with his own men. They acquitted him, as they were always going to do, and he couldn't be tried again for the same crime. And we think we live in civilised times.' I shook my head. 'After that, he seemed to accumulate wealth and land in a most extraordinary way,' I didn't want to say it but I never understood how he managed to stay under the protection of the Montagues, whose nobility should have put them above all that.

'Go on with the story.'

'We rode hard from London towards Dover, but nightfall stopped us somewhere west of Canterbury, and Montague sent a rider ahead to a great house there, where he had a connection of family.'

I stopped. Of course I knew the shape of this old story, but it wasn't until I *said* those words that I called that house out of the past and became suddenly aware that this story was taking me to a strange place, long unvisited. My first glimpse of my dearest Elizabeth now lay just ahead.

'What house?' the squire prompted.

'The house was Badlesmere,' I said slowly.

'Montague's family, you said?'

'Yes. We were welcomed at the gates by Giles, Baron Badlesmere. You see, he had been married to Montague's daughter, Elizabeth since she was nine and he was fourteen.' Elizabeth at nine. How funny she must have been.

'Not by choice of his,' put in William in a particularly deep growl, taking another jug from a passing servant. Perhaps he guessed where my thoughts had got to. 'Badlesmere was never one to find much appeal in a woman.'

'That's your opinion,' I said. I approved the intention, but felt I had to stand up for Badlesmere's reputation, especially in the light of what was about to happen to him.

'In ten years, there were no children from that marriage,' he replied defiantly. 'Everyone knew why.'

'I have heard Badlesmere met a strange death,' said the squire.

'I'm coming to that.' Whatever I had said to William, I was not unhappy to remember my Elizabeth's first marriage as an empty one.

'I slept in the servants' quarters that night. I had to because the place was so crowded, but before dawn I woke up suddenly. You know that feeling you have, just a sense of a great noise disappearing into the night, leaving a void behind it? The void was in truth all I heard, but it was soon filled by shouts and running feet. I was freezing cold, so I threw on my clothes and I went to where the flames of torches were gathering below the curtain wall. There was a broken body lying on the stone.'

'The Baron?'

'Yes, Giles Badlesmere, twenty-four years old and not going to get any older. He had tumbled from a window forty feet above and his head was shattered by the fall.'

'How?'

'A servant shouted from the window above. He said it was Badlesmere's antechamber, where he kept his treasury, a heavy oak chest. He said the chest was open, that there was

103

a crowbar next to it and blood all over the floor. We sent to guard the gates and search the house so the robber would not escape.'

'Who did it?'

'We had no idea. All we knew at that moment was that he was dead and that someone had to tell his wife that she was a widow.'

I will remember what happened then until my dying day. We were clustered around that corpse, a puddle of blood, black and shining in the flickering light of the torches, spreading from the open head, and old Montague bending and mumbling a prayer. The crowd ahead of me parted and a young woman in a dark cloak stepped into the pool of light. She knelt to look at the man on the ground and let out a gasp and then a single sob, then she stood and as she faced her father, I saw the most wonderful face I have ever seen, dark hair flowing back from a high brow. She was focused and intent and her words had the power of sword cuts. There was never a less appropriate moment to fall in love, but I'm afraid that was the only explanation for the state of hopeless, urgent fascination in which I found myself.

'She appeared at that moment, did Elizabeth,' was all I told the squire. 'She appeared and my heart left me. "One of yours has done this, father," she said quietly.

'"No, Elizabeth, you cannot say that," Montague said. "My men are tried and true. It must have been an intruder".'

'She just stared at him, and even then, with her husband dead, she obeyed the rule that said she should never contradict her father in front of others. "I trust you will shoulder the duty of justice," she said and she turned and went back to the house.'

Here, in the modern world in our Maastricht inn, they brought us the fish, and while everyone fussed around with plates, I used the moment to go back over all that happened afterwards. We were meant to ride at dawn, but that now needed second thoughts. A messenger was sent to Dover and he was back inside an hour, having found word half-way that, as always, all aspects of the arrangements had changed. The destination was now to be Flanders, and the muster was in two days at Deal, so there was time to do what must be done here at the house. It was noticeable that there was no sudden outbreak of mourning. The niceties were observed, but I have to say that few in the house seemed to miss Giles. There was, however, a steely determination on the part of Elizabeth's household to see justice done.

In the afternoon, I was searching the antechamber again to see if anything other than the crowbar had been left behind, when I heard someone clear their throat behind me. I spun around to find Elizabeth had entered silently.

'Your pardon,' I said almost tongue-tied and quivering at her presence. I gazed at her much more closely than was suitable. 'I was only . . .'

'You don't need to explain yourself to me,' she said. 'I know who you are, Guy de Bryan, and I know your reputation. You are said to be a fine and trustworthy man.'

I bowed my head, unsure how to reply.

She came and stood so close in front of me that her face filled my eyes and I could feel her sweet breath on my cheek. Those violet eyes stared into mine and widened and something passed between us. She was nineteen years old and a full woman in her prime, and when she spoke again her voice had deepened to something richer.

'You're a member of the King's household and, I hear, a trusted friend. Will you be seeing him soon?'

'At Deal, I expect.'

'Will you give him a very private message?'

'Certainly.'

'Will you tell him my husband has been murdered and my father will do nothing about it?'

'That's a powerful accusation, Lady Elizabeth.'

'Guy,' she said, 'I know who it was and I expect you do too and I also know my father dares not take any action.'

'Who do you mean?'

'Molyns,' she said. 'I know he did it.'

'How do you know?'

'Isn't it enough that I know?'

'For me, yes of course it is, Lady. But if I must persuade the King then I should perhaps know more.'

She turned away from me and walked to the window from which her husband had been thrown after shedding so much of his blood. I was glad we had wiped it away.

'It wasn't a robbery, Guy. At least that wasn't the main crime. It was something concerning . . .' She fell silent and I waited. 'It was something concerning me.' She turned and stared straight at me. 'It was an attempt on my virtue. Do you understand now?'

All I could do was nod.

'That is how I know for certain. It was in the dark, but I know that man's shape and his smell. Molyns has been in my father's household for a long time. I have seen him watching me many times. I don't want you to tell the King that.'

'Why not? He would have to act.'

She closed her eyes and put her face in her hands for a long moment, then she shook her head.

'Please understand. Molyns has my father in his grip and he will make my father do absurd things to protect him. If he helps Molyns get away with my husband's murder, that is one thing, but if my father puts Molyns' life above my virtue, I don't know if I could stand that. Will you do me the service of telling the king what I have said and no more than what I have said?'

'Of course I will.'

I didn't tell the squire most of this last part, just the bare bones.

Anyway that was how it started. I had seen something in Elizabeth's eyes and I knew she had seen something in mine.

Fired by that, I strode back to my quarters with my head full of the image of her and a mind to find John Molyns and pre-empt the matter by taking justice on him myself. I ducked my head in through the door and there, sitting on my mattress, leaning against the wall was Molyns. Now, I had seen him from time to time at the Scottish siege, though he spent most of it away on Montague's errands, and I had seen him on the ride down, though only as you see another rider in a horse race. He looked up at me, and in those pale, blank eyes I saw the same absolute lack of pity he had displayed the very first time we met.

'Well, what's the mad bitch told you?' he said lazily.

'Who do you mean?'

'I mean that prize lay, Elizabeth Badlesmere, with whom you have just been talking, or perhaps doing more than talking.'

He was on his feet so fast I had no chance to do anything about it and the next minute, I was back against the wall with his dagger pricking the skin of my throat and those eyes staring into mine, so wide that I could see the whites all around the frozen iris.

'Don't speak of her like that.'

'Will you stop me?'

'Yes, I will, in combat, as soon as you like.'

He laughed and pricked my throat again. 'You haven't learnt anything Welsh boy. You want a fair fight, do you? Don't you understand? That's a noble idea and there are very, very many dead nobles to show for it. I am the death that comes when it isn't fair. I come in the night or I come from behind and you must always stay awake if you want to stop me.'

I tried to twist away, but he jammed the blade in through the skin and I know he just needed to twist it to let all my blood pump out.

'I loathe you, Welsh boy. You're so fucking good it turns my guts, standing there in your silly saintliness. The King thinks you're chivalry on two legs. You'll be the death of all of us. It's not men like you the King needs, it's men like me. When you're down in the mud and the blood and the blades are out, it's me who'll save the day, not you. Am I right? Go on, say it.'

He pulled the blade out and it hurt.

I shook my head, unable to speak, and he stuck it back in.

I knew he was wondering whether to push it all the way. I could see the calculation in his eyes. Would they take it for a second killing by our unknown robber, cornered in my room perhaps? We heard shouting out in the courtyard. They were calling for him and I knew at the same moment he knew that meant he would be seen coming from my room.

'I'm sent away on my Lord's business, Welsh boy,' he said. 'Just remember, Lord Montague should not be troubled with the ravings of his mad daughter and the King needs me more than he needs you. Also remember that if I stand accused of any special crime, then I may well choose to commit it again and, if so, be assured I shall tell you all the details next time we meet like this.' He gripped my throat firmly with his hand and banged my head so violently against the wall that when I woke to find myself sprawled on the floor, the blood across my throat was already drying.

By that time, Molyns was long gone.

Back in our Maastricht tavern, we began to deal with the mound of fish.

'Mine tastes of mud,' said the squire cheerfully. 'How about yours?'

'I've eaten worse things than mud,' said William. 'This is good mud.'

'Eat it and be glad there's anything on your plate,' I said. 'Now, it's time to get on with *your* version of the story, the Windsor tournament.'

'It was the year thirteen forty-four,' the young man began.

'Forty-three,' growled William, spearing a lump of fish from the lad's plate. 'Every time you get a fact wrong, I take your food.'

'Never was a man given such encouragement to lie,' said the squire drily. 'For all that, I shall try to speak the truth. The King ordered the building of a place for tournament such as had never been seen before. It was on the field below his castle and it measured a mile around.'

William speared another lump of his fish. 'Nothing like a mile,' he said. 'I was there too you know.'

The squire ignored him. 'It had stone walls and inside the seats rose in tiers to ten times a man's height so that each row of seats would have an unobstructed view.'

William raised an eyebrow and got his fork ready for another raid.

'At the two ends,' said the squire, 'east and west, there were great gates of the finest . . . what were they made of?'

'Marble,' said William sarcastically. 'What are gates usually made of?'

The squire looked at him with sudden approval. 'Marble. Yes.'

'They were wooden,' I said, but the squire was away in some reality of his own.

'The walls were decorated so that no inch was left bare of paintings and, every yard or two, there stood statues coated in gold. At twelve stations around that glittering perimeter, there stood chapels dedicated to the glory of the saints, as finely built as if they were to stand for ever. It was the wonder of the world.'

'It was a perfectly ordinary arena,' William said. 'Nicely built. Carpenter's work, nothing more.'

The squire was determined not to hear him. I preferred it that way. If he was so far from the truth in this prologue to the story, the tale itself must miss the mark by an equal distance.

'You, Sir Guy, were the lion of the lists,' he said. 'Your skill with the lance was beyond belief. You unhorsed every other knight you met.'

'I'd eat your fish myself if it were better fish,' I said, feeling almost like laughing and glad of the distraction from where my thoughts had just been. 'I had some luck that day, but I took almost as much as I gave out. That's what the sport is like. Nobody ever wins every tilt. It's not human.'

'But then it came to the final joust of the tournament and there was more at stake than the victor's garland and the King's purse.'

Abruptly, I went cold.

'There was a lady's love at stake,' he said, 'and there were two men there to dispute the issue.'

'Whose tale is that?' I said. 'I don't recognise it as mine,' but William, giving me a curious and challenging stare, reached over to my plate, speared all that remained of my fish and offered it to the squire.

'What's this?' I said and I was angry. 'I do not lie.'

'Perhaps not, but the lad has told a great truth,' said William, 'and that deserves a reward.'

I stared at him, wondering if this impudence could easily be forgiven, but long ago I learnt to recognise that tone of voice in William as beyond my power to control.

'Tell the tale,' said William to the lad. 'Tell it your way and I will answer for the consequences with Sir Guy. If it is wrong, then we shall count it as harmless entertainment. If it is right, then there may be value in hearing it.'

The poor lad. He looked as if the devil were on one side and the ocean on the other.

'Go on,' I said, because manners dictated that I, who had the power, should ease his torment.

'I intend no harm, Sir Guy,' he said. 'I see now it is a trespass on you. I was thinking of it only as a great tale.'

'Tell it,' I said, because what else could I say?

'The way I heard it from my father,' said the lad, 'you had recently been detained against your will, held by an earl without proper cause.'

The Earl, of course, was Montague, Earl of Salisbury, and at that time William had been Montague's man. He wasn't going to let that one pass.

'He thought he had proper cause,' he growled. 'You go checking an earl's honesty and there's the devil to pay if you're proved right.'

I made the cut-throat sign at him and he stopped abruptly. I had been on the King's secret business and that should be no part of this tale. The squire looked at him, curiously, and then at me. 'Please tell me if I am wrong,' he said, nervously.

'Just go on with your story,' I ordered. Molyns again. It always came back to John Molyns, and I had no wish to start debating the facts with anybody. With Molyns finally at bay and on the run from the King's wrath, I had only tried to ascertain whether the Earl was hiding him. I had been caught in the act.

'You were not alone in your captivity,' he was hesitant. We weren't an easy audience. 'I would find it simpler, Sir Guy,' he suggested, 'to tell this story as if you were not here, as if it were about someone else.' I nodded my agreement.

'This noble knight,' he went on and sounded a little more sure of himself. 'This noble knight was not alone in his tower room. The Earl held another knight in custody, this time with the King's blessing. Sir Hugh Despenser was grandson of a villain and son of a greater one, two of the men who had despoiled England during his father's terrible reign and had been executed for their treachery.'

'Don't you go leaping to judge Hugh Despenser,' I said, perhaps a little sharply. 'He was nothing like his father or his grandfather.'

'I wouldn't dream of doing such a thing,' he said in horror. 'I have the highest regard for his honour.' He looked at me

111

and at William and I thought by now he was regretting ever starting on this story. As they say in Luxembourg, it is an unwise man who tells a bear his business.

'The two men became the best of friends in the year they spent together,' he went on. It was only nine weeks, but I let that go and I'd still like to think the nub of it was true. We liked each other straight away and in that dismal place it was Hugh's humour that helped me most and perhaps my stubbornness that helped him. 'Then one day, into the lonely courtyard below their window, came the widow Elizabeth, daughter of the Earl, all unaware that she was overlooked by ardent eyes.'

'She knew perfectly well we were there,' I said, and was surprised to find I had said it out loud. The squire looked at me expectantly and I thought I had better explain.

'She had been sending notes to our cell every day for three weeks.'

The trouble was, we didn't know which of us she meant them for. It seemed she thought one man was in the tower, but as she never addressed the notes by name, neither of us could be sure which. Hugh had known her for years and confessed he had been trying to find a way to break the jesting companionship set so fast when they were both younger and start afresh with something with a hotter taste. This was not what I wanted to hear. It was five years since Giles' death, and in those five busy years I had managed to see her no more than half a dozen times, and never by ourselves. I had to make those brief moments last a long time. She was finer than ever, blossoming in full womanhood. I'd had a wife in Wales some years earlier, a Carew girl married to me at sixteen, but she had been a duty, a matter fixed by my father for the increase of his estates and the future of his bloodline. She lived her life and I lived mine once we found there was no joy in our marriage act and, when she died of a flood of black bile, I mourned her only as I should.

112

Elizabeth's notes said only that her heart was with her poor imprisoned friend and she would do all she could to secure his freedom. Her heart. That day when, with her father absent, she procured the key to the locked court and chose to take her embroidery into its unfrequented square, we both looked down on her.

My heart, squashed and dried by my incarceration, swelled to twice its size. I knew that I loved her utterly. Starved of all company bar each other and the warder, a man with no tongue, we both looked down.

'She was fairer than a lily and fresher than a rose and her golden hair was braided in a long tress.' It was the squire, intent on telling his tale, hauling me back to the here and now.

Golden? No, but the squire was set on telling his own tale, not mine so I let it go. 'It was Sir Hugh who saw her first and he gave a great sigh as if a dagger had stabbed him through the heart. Then Sir . . . I mean the other knight, startled, asked him what was wrong. "I have seen a goddess," said Sir Hugh, "and I shall die unless I have her for my own." At that, his friend looked down and he too sighed most deeply and piteously and each knew with terrible certainty that he had a rival for the lady's hand. "She is mine," said one. "Oh no," the other said, "those letters were for me." The first replied "Then let us settle it. Let us both look out and call and we shall know from her face as she returns our greeting where her affections rest." And so they did. At each window one knight stood and at a sign they both put their heads between the bars and called "Elizabeth". Startled, she looked up and turned her gaze first on Sir Hugh and then on the second knight and looked from one to the other with such joy they could not separate the depth of love she showed.'

Well, that wasn't the way it seemed to me.

'To cut my story shorter,' the squire went on, 'both knights were freed and pressed their suit before the Earl who favoured neither for his daughter's hand and told the King how matters stood. The King determined at his tournament that whichever proved the winner should have her as his prize. But as they trotted on their chargers to each end to take their lances for that final tilt, the knight, who was by far the better jouster of the two, saw all too plainly how matters stood. The lady directed such a loving look that the workings of her heart seemed all too clear. That look was not at him but at Sir Hugh, so, thus informed and with a heavy heart, he took the bravest course of all. As they clapped their visors down and spurred their horses down the sand, he aimed his lance not at Hugh's chest but past his arm and, risking death, took the other's blow full on himself.

'He fell and, lying there, heard the crowd, astonished, rise at his defeat and cheer Sir Hugh, but all three knew what he had done. When he stood, he saw their looks of gratitude.'

It sounded pretty good put like that, a noble tale of high ideals, nothing like the rough and ready reality of daily life when you're left doing the best you can on the spur of the moment in a fog of uncertainty. I had no idea how this tale could have got around, unless perhaps Hugh had told it himself. He might have done. He was never an arrogant man and it would have been just like him to make the least of his success.

The real irony was that this little man in front of me truly believed the essence of it, that I was some sort of saint who made a noble sacrifice. Perhaps I was, but what he didn't know and I did was the tragedy that lay ahead. There was a second act to this particular play and that is the reason why I can hear all the screeching devils in Purgatory reaching out for me with their irons glowing red.

That was later on, but even at the time it wasn't that simple.

What really happened was this. The night before the contest I had been sent for, summoned by the old Earl to his rooms. We had been served with wine and left alone and I remember the extreme length of the silence that followed as the man studied me. It was not for me to break that silence, and anyway I knew the game. It was his knife and I was his oyster. I played my own game to counter his, inspecting his face with care. Montague had been as close to the King as you could get, the leading member of that first loyal band who risked their necks at Nottingham Castle thirteen years earlier to get rid of the Queen's usurping bed-mate Mortimer and put young Edward firmly on his own throne. There was a scar on the side of his jaw which they said he got on that occasion. Molyns was with them there, of course, plying his sword and climbing the first rung of his ladder to favour. Montague's face was more lined than mine. He was older than me, but the weight of his position and a weariness in the way he held himself gave him more years on me than he truly had.

The tiniest flicker in his eyelid told me that he found my gaze a little disturbing. Perhaps the oyster had a knife of its own. It was more than that. He didn't know quite where he stood with me and he'd locked me in his castle, in that tower room with Hugh Despenser, hoping to discover what I was up to, whether I was there of my own accord, sniffing after Molyns, or whether the King had sent me. It made all the difference in the world to the way he played the game, and he still didn't know the answer. The King had held his cards close to his chest, leaving me locked up there for weeks and then contriving such a subtle pressure for my release that Montague never knew whose hand had opened the cell door.

Montague ran out of silence before I did. When you were with him, you always knew you were there on licence, just for the time it took for him to turn you to his predetermined will.

'You're a brave man and an honest man, Guy,' he said thoughtfully. 'Everyone knows that. Clever too, and you have the King's trust.' He rubbed his chin. 'Unfortunately, that's not all that counts. All you have of your own is a scruffy little castle in Wales and a few ragged acres elsewhere which bring in barely enough to keep you. You do bloody well in the lists for a man with only one horse.'

I'd hoped no one had spotted that. That one was a great horse and he didn't tire easily, but it was true that all the other knights had a string of chargers waiting on their choice.

'Hugh Despenser is finally forgiven his father's crimes and has had his estates restored to him. His wealth is more in keeping with my daughter's rank.'

That was not unexpected. I had never thought to be Montague's chosen suitor, but surely the Earl was not about to challenge the King's order? Edward had made it quite clear how this matter was to be settled.

Montague had read my mind. 'The King has a fancy for his tournament,' he said. 'It is to be the first of many. He has a new order of chivalry in mind, did you know that?'

I shook my head.

'You know him. He's very taken by the old tales, the knights of King Arthur, the round table. He'd like to have been Arthur, so he's planning to start a new fraternity of knights. This match of his between the two of you is part of that design.'

His expression said he thought it was all a bit silly, but his voice stayed just on the right side of loyalty to his king.

'One horse or not, you'll send Hugh flying, I'm in no doubt about that. You've got your eye in. His thoughts are all over the place when he jousts. I've watched him carefully. He's looking at the crowd half the way down the course, not at his man. He's lucky not to have broken his neck, so you'll have him in the dust, I'm sure. Then where does that leave us?'

It would leave me with Elizabeth, with my dreams, with

an entirely different life in front of me. Service had been my lot so far, service and discomfort. I had never expected warmth, overwhelming love and the enfolding of arms. The blood in my ears almost deafened me. All I had had of her in the weeks before the tournament were snatched glances in crowded rooms and the delight of four words and a touch of hands when her mother was distracted in the King's chamber. I had a softening inside me which had changed the way the whole world felt, smelt and sounded.

'I'll tell you where,' he said, surveying me sardonically. 'It would leave you very happy and me very unhappy. Now unfortunately my happiness is more important than your unhappiness. I am responsible both for my daughter's future well-being and for the prosperity of my sons and of their sons. Despenser was not my first choice, but his pardon makes a great difference, so I'll tell you what I'm going to do. The King has given you the temporary benefit of a substantial estate, I understand.'

He caught me off my guard and I stiffened. He saw it. What was this? Another test, another probe? The King had given me the charge of Stoke Trister. Something big had changed as I said. John Molyns had finally gone much too far and he was now a fugitive from the King's justice. In the meantime, Edward had given me Molyns' estate of Stoke Trister to hold for the present and to have the income.

'That is correct,' was all I said.

'Supposing I were in a position to make sure you enjoyed full title to that land in perpetuity?'

I played the simpleton. 'How could you be, my Lord? Its owner's whereabouts are unknown. The King has had a hue and cry raised for him for these past three years.' I was watching his response with care, but the very offer made it all the more likely that he really did have Molyns tucked away, an absurd risk to take, flying so directly in the face of the King's wishes.

He looked at me levelly. 'Let us just suppose it were possible, then were your aim to slip a little tomorrow, the outcome would be a happy one for everyone. You would have a soft new seat to comfort any bruises.'

That was when I found, despite my wish to remain calm, that my indignation developed a voice of its own and the words which rushed out of my mouth on its behalf heated my blood and made my whole body tremble.

'My Lord, you yourself said the King's tournament is to mark the start of a new order of chivalry. It is a place of honour. I hope I am a man of honour. I am not to be bought off with estates. Yes, I am not the richest man in England. Yes, my castle is not in the best of repair. My King's instructions are that the two of us must joust for the hand of your daughter. I am sorry that the outcome may displease you, but I follow the King.'

I bowed and swept out, and the main thought in my mind, apart from a little rather improper pleasure at coming it so high with an earl, was that living with a deeply displeased father-in-law might not be all that simple.

I never found out. The ending of the squire's story was true enough, but it did not happen exactly as he said. I did not intercept any such loving glance between Elizabeth and Hugh. I didn't need to. An hour before the time set for our match, I was kneeling in the chapel, praying for a fair outcome and no broken bones when a small hand plucked at my elbow. I cut my prayer short with an apology, opened my eyes in some irritation and saw the maid of Elizabeth's chamber at my side. No one else was there, just the two of us.

'What do you want?' I asked, thrilled at the certain knowledge that the owner of my heart had sent her trusted messenger to wish me a strong arm and a straight lance.

'My mistress says to tell you her . . . her . . .'

She had the look of one who had been told her lines over and over but never quite enough.

'Her what?'

'Her affection is with you.'

Her affection? I could have wished it more strongly phrased, but perhaps Elizabeth had spoken it more strongly than it had been repeated.

'But . . .' said the girl, frowning as she sounded my death knell.

But?

'But her love lies with another.'

The worst of it was that when I took my tumble and was helped back to the pavilions, I was met there by Montague's steward with the title deeds to Stoke Trister as if I had accepted his squalid deal. Sending them straight back to him was the only satisfaction I had that day.

Back here in Maastricht, I looked down at the table and saw a dish in front of me. I had no memory of how it got there. Somehow we had finished the fish and this looked like curds, never my favourite, especially in an inn, when you don't know how fresh it is. I pushed it away and William took it to add to his own.

# CHAPTER EIGHT

'You ask Lewis about Sir Guy. He knows,' said Eliza. 'Knows a lot of things does Lewis. Not just stone. He understands about living your life in a place and what that means and how it makes you a bit more careful about people.'

She spoke it as an accusation and Beth felt the words burrow into her skin.

'I couldn't live here,' she said.

'What? Stop mumbling.'

Eliza liked to feign deafness when she wanted to force you towards clarity. 'I said I couldn't live here, Gran.'

'Why not? Too quiet for you?'

'Too small.'

'Too small? Too small? What's the sense in that?' Eliza was staring at her eyes as if she could see behind them, and it made Beth feel deeply uncomfortable. 'You ever looked closely at anything girl? Closer you look the bigger it gets.'

'What do you mean?'

'Come with me.'

Eliza darted out into the garden where Beth could see her crouching even lower and casting around. She followed her grandmother out and watched as she picked up a jagged stone and peered at it.

'There you are. Get your eye in close.'

She handed it to Beth who looked around to make sure no one could see her before holding the stone up to peer at it.

'See?' demanded Eliza.

'I see a stone.'

'That's not a stone, not when you look close. Go on. Put it closer.'

Beth stared at the stone and its outlines broke up into ever tinier patterns of disorder.

Eliza nodded and took it back from her, 'That's a whole mountain, that is. Forget London. You put your eye up close to Slapton and there's enough to know here to keep you busy for the rest of your life. You should stay here now you're back.'

'I can't do that, Gran. My life's in London.'

'Was, don't you mean? You're a Battock. Battocks belong here. Always have.'

Beth felt anger stirring in her. It had never paid to get angry with Eliza but her time away had dulled that knowledge.

'I'm only half a Battock,' she said. 'My mother didn't belong here, did she?'

Eliza abruptly hurled the stone away and glass shattered somewhere in the bushes. She stared after it. 'Your mother? Your mother didn't belong anywhere,' she said in a freezing voice. 'Don't you go pretending to take after her. She doesn't *exist*.'

In moments of childhood rage, usually when misunderstood by her father or criticised by her grandmother, Beth had fantasised about her mother, imagining the day when a car would sweep down into Slapton and an elegant, smiling woman would step out of it, explain that it had all been some terrible mistake and waft her off to a penthouse apartment in a glamorous city.

'She took no interest in you. You take no interest in her.' It was years since she'd last heard Eliza say that.

Her father had put it more gently on the few occasions it had come up. 'No, you weren't a mistake, love, not from my point of view. As far as your mother was concerned, it was me who was the mistake.'

Beth was saved from having to find some reply by a faltering warble from the phone in her pocket. There had been no signal since she had arrived in the village, but here on the fringe, the radio waves had struggled through for a moment. She looked at the screen. The reception was marginal and all it said was 'private number calling'.

'Hello,' she said, putting it to her ear and making the automatic face of helpless apology that was second nature in her normal life, but only made Eliza scowl in puzzled affront.

A man's voice said 'Beth Battock?'

'Yes?'

It kept cutting out so that all she heard was 'private office. . .' then '. . . tary of State for Foreign and . . .' and finally, before it died completely '. . . speak to you personally on . . .' She took it from her ear and looked at it, praying for it to ring again, but the brief electronic bridge to her familiar world had collapsed again.

'Rude, I call that,' said Eliza. 'They shouldn't telephone you when you're talking to someone.'

'It was the Foreign Secretary's office, Gran.' Not one of the junior ministers. Not even Sir Robert Greenaway. The Foreign Secretary himself. Had it all got that much worse? The thought chilled her blood.

'I'll have to phone them back, Gran. There must be a signal somewhere.'

'Signals? They don't send signals these days, young lady. That was the wartime. You should know that. Everything's done on the telephone now.'

'I know, Gran. Look, I won't be long.'

'Are you going? I've hardly got started talking to you. You can't go.'

'Just up the hill to somewhere where I can phone. I'll come straight back.'

Eliza snorted and went inside the house. Beth took the other path beyond the cottage up through the wood. On the far side it angled across the slope of a big field towards the lane. Looking towards the village, she could see the square top of the Chantry tower, with its smaller corner turret pointing upwards from it and its escort of high-circling birds. She walked with her phone clutched in her hand, watching for a signal, but nothing appeared until she climbed the stile right up at the crest of the hill. Then the bars finally flashed up on the screen as if she had passed back into the world of the modern god and his ring-tone hymn-tune rang out to reassure her that she was still alive.

The voice told her she had twenty-two new messages and the part of her which needed to be important was hugely relieved. Most of the messages were from journalists all trying to sound as though they were her new best friend. One of the rest gave her a Whitehall direct line number to call and, when she steeled herself to ring it, a stern woman put her straight through.

'Is that you Beth?'

'Yes.'

'Andrew Blakiston.'

Parliamentary Private Secretary to the man himself. The Foreign Secretary's right hand. The sort of person you only get to talk to when the news is very good or very bad.

'Yes, hello,' she said, knowing this was make or break.

'You're laying low, I hope.'

'Yes, I'm trying to.' That sounded more like break than make.

'The Foreign Secretary wanted to talk to you himself, but he's gone into a meeting.'

Oh God. 'I'm sorry. There's no reception where I'm staying. I've had to climb up to the top of a hill.'

'Give me a land-line number.'

She thought for a mad moment of telling him to phone her father's neighbours and ask them to bang on the wall, but it was inconceivable.

'No, I can't. There isn't one.'

'Good heavens. You really have tucked yourself away.' He seemed to be thinking. 'I can tell you the gist of it. It seems whatever mess you may have helped stir up here, our friends over the water like you. You made a bit of a hit on that rather over-bold speaking trip of yours.'

A moment before, she had been abject and ready to confess her sins, to plead youth and ignorance and throw herself on his mercy. Those words obliterated any such thought. The oxygen of success cleared her head.

'Over-bold? I think I said what needed to be said.'

'Did you indeed? You took a big risk. If your minister hadn't sacked himself, we'd probably have had to insist he sacked you. As it is, I suppose it might be said to have paid off. I take it you've been listening to the news?'

'Well, no. No I haven't. There's . . .' Could she really admit there was no television? There hadn't even been a chance to turn on the radio.

'Beth, for God's sake. The air is full of war and the rumours of war. The PM and the Foreign Secretary have decided to back our American allies to the hilt yet again. It seems we're having another stab at the axis of evil, or perhaps just at a soft target quite near the axis. Once is not enough. The time has come for all good women to come to the aid of the party.'

'Me? You want me back in London? Sir Robert told me to stay out of the way.'

'Sir Robert was quite right. We most emphatically do *not* want you anywhere near London. There's a great deal of time and effort going into untangling the mess your man

124

Livesay's left behind him. It's going to take a while, and I have to say your neck is not yet off the block. If you turn out to be one of the other nails in Helen Livesay's cross, the PM is not going to be at all pleased with you.'

'I . . .'

'Shut up Beth. I'm not going to believe anything you say unless it's a full confession, and a confession would be very inconvenient right now. You need to persuade us that it's worth our efforts to keep your head attached to your body. Right now, we want your brain, or more particularly that part of it which can provide us with twenty minutes' worth of convincingly argued prose on why we should support a US president who half the British population regards as a criminal and the other half regards as more than mildly deranged.'

'This is about issues not personalities,' she replied, nettled by his tone.

'Oh for Christ's sake don't go all high-minded on me,' he snapped. 'I'm a simple man. I'm here to make things work for my lord and master, and I find things work so much more easily when they don't involve Armageddon.'

'This twenty minutes, what's it for?'

'A speech in the House by the Foreign Secretary in four days' time. I need your draft in three days.'

It's always darkest before the dawn, Eliza's favourite saying, delivered so regularly throughout Beth's teenage depressions that it had lost any meaning until this moment. A speech. She was being offered a speech for the Foreign Secretary himself. There would be other drafts, she knew that, and they'd cherry-pick between them, but you could count your influence by the number of words which made it through. This was gold dust.

'Shall I e-mail it?'

'Don't be bloody daft. This rates somewhere three rungs above 'most secret'. A car will pick it up at three-thirty on Thursday.

Not a minute later. Will you do it? I have so far avoided reminding you that your salary is still being paid by HMG.'

'Yes, of course I'll do it.' This was far above anything she'd done before.

'OK. Thursday, half past three. Don't screw up.'

'Wait a minute. You'll need to know where to collect it.'

'We know.' He hung up and she stared at the phone as if it had just betrayed her. How could he know? She hadn't known herself when she left London.

'Fucking hell,' she said, and Eliza, right behind her, said, 'There's no need for that sort of language.'

She spun around. 'How long have you been there, Gran?'

'Followed you up. Thought I'd better. There's been a bull in the field.'

There was no sign any animals had been in the field, and Beth knew that wasn't why she'd come.

'I heard you talking to yourself.'

'I was on the phone, Gran. I was talking to London.'

'I don't know why they think it's so clever to have telephones that make you stand in a field. Lewis has one in his office, with a nice armchair.'

'It's a . . .' Beth stopped herself, remembering how it had always been with Eliza, remembering how you could never be quite sure whether she was winding you up or not. She had a combination of feral wit and wilful ignorance of the modern world which made her constantly unpredictable.

'They want me to do some work,' she said.

'So do I,' replied Eliza. 'I got a job for you.'

'No, this is real work. Urgent stuff. I've got to write a speech for the Foreign Secretary.'

'Mine's urgent too,' said Eliza, unruffled, 'and what's more, I think you know exactly what it is.'

'I haven't the slightest idea.' Beth felt an urgent need to get on with this new task. Any odd-jobs for Eliza would have to wait. 'What needs doing?' she asked.

126

'Do you really need reminding?'

'I haven't got much time right now. I . . .' but old Eliza gave her a look of disappointment that took her right back to childhood again. Because Beth knew the old woman was the truest friend she had ever had, she sat down on the grass with her and remembered times before when they had sat and talked. Eliza had never let her down. When her father had driven her to distraction with his refusal to meet her head-on and his escapes into the solitude that his job allowed him, looking after his reed-marsh, his lake and his creatures of the wild, she had always been able to count on Eliza to restore some calm to her life. What she had started to fear on the way up the hill, smarting from the previous conversation, was that going away might have changed all that. Eliza might no longer be quite fully on her side.

Now they were sitting down, the old woman seemed in no hurry to get to any particular point.

'I came down that ditch in the war,' she said pointing across to the far side of the field, where a long furrow ran down under the hedge.

'What do you mean?'

'Oh come on Lizzie-Beth, I've told you that story. About how we all had to move out. Army chucked us out. Winter of '43. No choice. Months and months we were gone, people, animals the lot. Couldn't say no. For the war effort, they said. Had to go.'

'I know the story, Gran.' Everyone in Slapton knew the story, the story of the great evacuation, the clearing of the villages, when the powers-that-be needed a long sweep of the Devon coast to practice for the D-Day landings sealed off from spying eyes. Beth's mind was elsewhere. She had crucial work to do and she was already searching for phrases, words of certainty and justice. A rallying cry. She knew what had to be done. The task was to persuade cowards to follow the

127

brave. This was not the time to be sitting here listening to ancient, well-worn tales.

'Came back at the end of it and all the door handles had gone. Some jack-the-lad got in there before they let us back in. Everything brass gone, hinges, the lot. I had nice hinges. Pile of army rubbish in the front garden, rats everywhere *and* they'd burnt half the floorboards. Not as bad as some, mind you. Mrs Fletcher just had shell holes where her house was. Just holes, not even the stones to go around them.'

'Gran, why were you coming down the ditch?' Five minutes, thought Beth. Five minutes will be enough, then I'll explain that I've really got to go and get started.

'Had to. Only way in. They'd blocked all the roads. Sentries. You could get shot. I crawled all the way.'

'You mean you came in while the place was sealed off?'

'Oh yes.'

'What for? To check the house?'

'Oh no. A house ain't worth risking your neck for.'

Beth was intrigued despite herself. 'Was it a man?'

Eliza laughed, and the laugh seemed to come from a much younger woman. 'Not when I started down the ditch, it wasn't. You could say things had changed when I went back again.'

'You crawled down the ditch and met a man? Someone in the army?'

'That wasn't the reason I did it. That was just what happened, not what was planned.'

'What then?'

'Saint Petronella,' and Eliza said the two words as if it should be obvious, sending a deep look chasing after them as if she were quite certain Beth would know exactly what she meant.

Beth didn't and her frown made that plain.

'Guy never told you?'

'Told me what? Dad never mentioned Saint whatever.'

'Petronella,' Eliza said, with a touch of asperity. 'Saint

128

Peter's very own daughter, not "whatever". Are you really telling me he never mentioned it?'

'What?'

Eliza gave her a long look as if she suddenly understood something for the first time.

'The old duty,' she said. There was a silence while the words hung in the air like a song Beth ought to know.

'He never told you.' This time Eliza said it calmly, slowly, as a sad affirmation.

Beth shook her head. 'What is it, Gran?'

'Oh no, it's not for me to tell you. It's for Guy to do that. Has he talked to you about . . . about anything else since you got back, girl?'

'Not really.' Beth knew she hadn't given him a chance yet, and it made her wonder for the first time what had prompted his letter.

'You give him time then. He'll tell you.' And that was all Eliza would say on the subject.

'I don't know if he will. Why don't you tell me, Gran?'

'Because it's not my duty to. Father to eldest son, or daughter if there's no son, but I was the first of those there's ever been and you're the second. You better have sons, girl. It's a sight easier with sons. They can just go off unexplained. Takes more tricksy stuff for girls.'

'Go off and do what?'

'Once a year, girl, that's all. Don't get your knickers in a twist. I don't think it's enough. Once a month would be fairer to the poor old man, or four times a year at least, but that's the special day, see? Saint Petronella. That's when it really matters, so I suppose it's a whole lot better than nothing.'

Beth could feel the whole conversation slipping away from her, but Eliza clambered to her feet again. 'Come on, girl' she said.

She got up, but her grandmother had set off without her and with that fleshless wiriness of the old countrywoman, she was already following the contour of the field towards the gate.

'Where are we going?'

Eliza didn't look back. 'To see your house,' she said.

Through the gate, they were on the tarmac road which had brought Beth back down to the village only, what? A few hours ago? It seemed much, much longer.

'Tell me about the ditch and the man you met,' said Beth, catching up with difficulty.

'What ditch? What man?' said Eliza. 'Don't you go making up things, girl. Now what was that you were asking about the old house. The house you saw.'

'It's just down here,' said Beth, 'on the right. I never saw it before.'

'Whereaway?'

'Keep going. We'll come to it.' She didn't say what she thought. Nineteen years she'd lived there in Slapton. Nineteen years is too long to suddenly see a large house that was never there before. Unless they'd cut the hedges. Did she walk up this road? In her mind she did, but maybe that was only in her mind. A little mote of memory said she'd been a hurrying child who would never have walked up a hill if a faster means of transport had been on offer. The field behind the hedge to the right of the road ended, and the ground dipped into a steep and narrow valley which Beth could only glimpse from time to time through holes in the hedge. Eliza walked on until she came to a gap. 'That will be it,' she said, pointing down.

On the floor of the narrow valley, just a little below them, stood a farmhouse with two great barns in front of it. Beth felt an immediate sense of dislocation. She had seen this house before and she hadn't seen it before. From the car it had seemed much larger, much older. Her brief glimpse had fooled her. Seen on foot, standing still, it was just a farm-house, unremarkable and somewhere there in her childhood memory of the outskirts of the village.

'I suppose so,' she said. 'Funny. It didn't seem quite like that.'

There the matter would have been closed if Eliza hadn't looked at her with complete understanding and said, 'Well, that's not how you would have seen it. Of course it's not.'

'How would I have seen it?

'It's Pool, Lizzie-Beth. Guy's house.'

'Dad's house?'

'No, not little Guy. I mean *Sir* Guy. Him we were talking about. Guy de Bryan.'

'The man who built the Chantry. That was his house?'

'Back then it was. Old Pool of the many chimneys. Before they pulled all the best bits down.'

In Beth's mind's eye, there were indeed many chimneys – more, certainly than the two stacks of the house before her. She became a little irritated that she was so suggestible.

'You only see it sometimes, the way it was,' said Eliza, 'and not often in the daylight.'

# CHAPTER NINE

Oh damn. There's too much time for thought on a long journey, and the squire's incautious tale had opened up an old room which should have stayed locked.

I have spent much of my life on top of a horse. Indeed the view seems quite artificially limited when I'm on foot, so that I spend some of my time on tiptoe to see further. When I was younger, I could ride all day and all night and get off without a twinge. All day is fine with me still, but I prefer my bed at night. I've lived longer than most without falling to pieces, but I have to admit I was savouring this part of the long journey south because we were on the water again, battling our way up the Rhine. Now, I have fought my wars at sea as well as on the land. There's the land-mind and the sea-mind and too often, those who command the sea fights have only the land-mind. We've talked about Sluys and that was exactly what I mean, hardly a matter of the sea at all, just a heaving mass of close-packed decking which might as well have been a grassy field for all the difference it made.

The men of Devon taught me there was more to it than that. The pilchard fishers who have their huts on Slapton beach took me out in their nimble boats and I learnt how you get where you want to by striking your subtle bargains with the tide and the wind. That is why I built the *Michel* with two masts and the African rig, to give me a bit more choice about where I go when the wind blows. That rig attracts a few ribald comments from other shipmen, but it has stood me in good stead on many occasions, and there's a boat they're building in Dartmouth right now which is a copy of him from stem to stern.

Maybe it was because they felt they were getting nearer home, but this was where the trouble with our fine Genoese really started. Since the beginning of the journey, we had been lugging their huge packs with us, one entire horse-load. Thinking they must have some sense, I hadn't bothered to enquire whether these packs contained necessities, but I now found out the truth. They contained nothing but clothing. They were not, as you might hope, more practical working clothes, quite the reverse. Seeing the boat journey as some sort of holiday, they now delved into this tiresome mass of frippery and came out looking even more like court jesters than usual. The taller, noisier and more irritating of them, di Provan, held up something made out of yellow satin, looked me up and down and offered it to me with a remark that made his companion laugh. I took it, thanked him courteously and polished my sword with it. When I handed it back he was frowning in anger and disgust. I looked down at what I was wearing, and for just a moment I could see myself through his eyes.

I have a padded tunic made of fustian which I always wear on campaign. It fits me to perfection and, over the years, the straps and edges of my armour have pressed their pattern into it, leaving their outline in stained, dark smudges. I should get a new one, I suppose, but it is an old friend and it saves time. When I need my armour in a hurry, the plates fit into their intended places so naturally and easily that there is no room for error. Believe me, that matters. I once fought all

133

day, at Limoges I think, with a piece of plate strapped to the wrong buckle by some well-meaning idiot. It almost killed me. After an hour or two, the corner of it was carving into my flesh every time I twisted to the right, and I took a savage wound to the neck from a man I'd left for dead, all because I couldn't keep looking around.

People wear strange clothes these days and perhaps I seem very old-fashioned, but I have no wish to look like those Italians.

The boat was a bit of a risk for a winter journey, though there are always good reasons to go by river if you're on diplomatic business. It's not just the water that flows fast in a river. It's also where news flows fastest and sometimes that helps you stay ahead of the game. On the river you hear who's dead, who's out of favour and who's sided with who, and you hear it quite some time before that same news crawls off overland. We had met Wulfram and taken to the boat at the river quays of Cologne, a city which is always a fine sight as you approach, with its walls and its spires, and the great cathedral in the building, rising higher and higher above all else. The people of Cologne are the fairest in all Germany, having a fine pride about them and their city reflects that. The Genoese cocked a snook at it, but we ignored them in that as in everything else.

It is of course, not the normal thing to try to head up the Rhine when you're in a hurry. The river flows at four miles an hour for much of the time and while that carries you an effortless hundred miles between noon and noon travelling north, it usually stops you in your tracks when you're travelling south. In summer, you wouldn't think of it. In winter, with the north wind behind you, you're in with a chance, though of course the current also flows faster when there's rain. We didn't only have the north wind, we had Wulfram.

I first met Wulfram on the troop transports which took Edward's army to France, when he helmed our fat, slow trooper as prettily as I have ever seen in a difficult wind. Our paths crossed now and then until he lost his leg in a skirmish that was due more to local greed than high strategy. Like all old soldiers with damaged bodies and undamaged spirits, he sought out a different challenge. When I heard from returning pilgrims that he had a boat on the Rhine I knew he would have found ways to fight the current and I had sent messages ahead to hire him for us.

A voyage like that is a time for contemplation and for prayer. William could not refuse us mass on this boat; its motion was far too steady to endanger the Host. Sitting comfortably on deck as we passed the village of Bonn and saw the misty mountains rising, I watched these Rhine bargemen and their special ways. The boat had a square sail which carried us at a good lick through the water, with a north-westerly wind dead behind us. We tied up for the night at the old white tower, just a little short of Koblenz. It had been fine sailing, so much so that we had made sixty miles since dawn. Beyond Koblenz it was harder. At Braubach, I would have gone ashore if I could because those same pilgrims had brought back rumours of a miraculous visitation at a wayside shrine, but Wulfram was muttering and anxious to get on. He had a bonus to win if he made Basel in less than five days, and at this point the river swings west for a few miles, bringing the wind over our starboard quarter

Now I saw this crew of his come into their own, and they could not have worked faster or harder if all the galleys of Castile had been after them. They reshaped that sail of theirs into something like a lateen, hauling down the yard, rolling and lashing it into a triangle and bracing it around, very much in the style of my Egyptian foresail, so that we still got some drive from the opposing wind. That wasn't all. They poled on both sides when the bottom allowed, and when it didn't we came to a wide towpath on the side of the river. A team of eight horses waited there, bridled and yoked and ready to take our towrope. Two miles later, where the towpath ended in a narrowing cleft and the bottom went too deep for poles, Wulfram and his men bent to the sweeps, groaning with the strain as the current ran faster to oppose them, until we hauled painfully through to the far side and the widening river turned to the south east again. Then the sail was unleashed and returned to its true fat-bellied nature and we ran on at full speed as near the edge of the river as Wulfram dared, cheating the force of the current against us. It was fine work, every bit of it.

Thanks to the squire and his ruthless efforts to fan my memories, by the time we passed Saint Goar, I was back in England and wandering in the old and dusty rooms of 1343 again. The Windsor tournament was over and the victor was to take the spoils. Sprawled in the Windsor dust, I had lost my chance of bliss.

Hugh Despenser's wedding to Elizabeth was held at his abbey of Tewkesbury soon after the tournament, and I kept a smile on my face all day only by making sure I never looked straight at the bride and could pretend Hugh was marrying someone else. If I looked pale, I had a good excuse. The wound in my heart had a physical partner, the great score in my side from Hugh's lance which was proving slow to heal, a matter of the mind I think. At the end of all the interminable and painful pledging, we left the abbey and the couple stopped on its steps. I can't remember exactly what he said after all this time, but it was along the lines of how he, Hugh Despenser, had worked for a dozen years to make that great Tewkesbury edifice into an even greater testament to the glory of God and now, with the help of his beloved Elizabeth, they would finish the work together. If the words have not quite stuck, I expect it was because, just as my eyes could not bear to see Elizabeth on his arm, so my ears could not hear her name linked with his. There was not just the pain inside me, there was anger at myself, most unworthy anger at the choice

I had made and an evil worm of regret which my prayers could not suppress.

As it turned out of course, Hugh never did finish the work and I did it for him to expiate my sin, though I knew even the costliest mason's work could never make up for what I had later done.

I do remember exactly what happened straight after Hugh's speech. They had showered coins on to the Tewkesbury poor, and then the Tewkesbury rich had queued with the rest of us guests, filing in to the pavilions for the wine and the food and the toasts. Being short on small talk that day, I passed through the crowd and slipped out of the back to look across the fields and be alone with my thoughts. Though this was Hugh's land, the wedding was Montague's show, as befits the father of the bride. There was a smaller, plainer tent set up for the earl's retainers some fifty yards off, and those who weren't on duty, guarding the perimeter of the abbey and the field, were standing around it drinking.

I can remember the exact moment when I recognised one of those men. He was standing almost out of sight, around the far side of the tent with his back to me. Some woman in the pavilion behind me let out a short, sharp bray of a laugh. The first part of it sounded more like a scream, and for a moment, just the briefest moment, he turned his head, alert for danger and that was enough because, oh, I knew that face. Something flows into the senses at a moment like that to make them so much more alert. I could smell the sweetness of the stooked hay in the field and the cattle scent from beyond the hedge. A thrush sang as loud as if it perched on my shoulder, and I could see my man as plainly as if I were only half the distance from him. Sandy hair, its colour fading. Close-set eyes. It was sixteen years since that Scottish hill-top where I had first seen him take a life, five years since he had pushed his knife into my throat at Badlesmere, three years since he had gone on the run from a vengeful king.

137

Now here he was, a man on the run, the proof I had been searching for when Montague had locked me up. I was looking at a man who should not be here, hidden in the retinue of an earl, a man called John Molyns.

Then I was back on the deck of our Rhine barge again, sitting with my back against a bale of cloth. The stiffness in my legs showed I had been dreaming for too long, and the shadow of the squire across my face showed what had called me back. He was after my thoughts like a squirrel after nuts, that squire. There are one or two people you meet who find common ground in far fewer sentences than it ought to take. There are others, even rarer, who penetrate your defences with an unsettling ease and see the shape of your thoughts. Now, I had come to like the squire a great deal. He had a lion's heart in an owl's body, but I never met anyone like him for sticking his nose into other people's business. He would have been dead a hundred times over but for his ability to choose his moment and his words so well.

'May I sit with you?' he said. 'I have watched the river quite enough and one part of it looks very like another, and there are still many, many things I would very much like to know if you would be good enough to tell me.'

'You can ask. I may not answer. I have a question first.'

'Please, Sir Guy, ask anything.'

'I understand the attractions of good conversation and I appreciate your interest in the events of days long past, but I hear from William that you don't only ask, ask, ask but you also write, write, write.'

I could read of course, but my hand is much more used to the sword than the pen, and I could manage a crabbed hand at best. It was a painful business and what I had heard intrigued me. The young man had found fresh supplies of ink and parchment in Cologne to replace what had been spoiled.

'I want to write a chronicle of our time,' he said. 'I can't remember everything, so in the quiet moments I write it

138

down. There's not much time to do that when we're on horseback and there's never enough light at the inns, so I've been catching up on the boat.'

'You're not the only one with a chronicle in mind.'

'I know. I've met the Hainaulter.'

There was a man at this time who had become a bit of a standing joke in the noble households. Jean Froissart would turn up at your door and before you knew it he would have been your house guest for three months, eating your food, drinking your drink and asking the same questions over and over. He wanted to know who had struck every blow in every battle, and some of his hosts had started a secret competition amongst themselves, leading him on and seeing how much you could get him to swallow.

'I prefer your company to his,' I said, 'but will I prefer your version of events?'

'I hope you will. I have an ambition to tell the story in a different way, a new way.'

'How?'

He frowned in concentration. 'Less stiff, less formal. My story won't be all buttoned and laced up. It won't be in French, not in the language of the court. It will be as ordinary people speak, in the words they use. In plain English. It is a better language for telling stories.'

'Who'll read it?' I asked. 'At court they'd scorn it in English and most of your ordinary people can't read a word whatever tongue it's written in.'

He shrugged. 'You may be right. The King likes to use English now. I still want to try. Do you have any more questions?' He asked so politely that I couldn't help laughing.

'No, go ahead.'

'You must have fought the infidel? A man such as you, a man who sees so clearly what is right and what is wrong?'

He seemed to need me to say yes, and he'd asked me the question in his different ways at least three times already.

'I went with Henry of Lancaster to the borders of Lithuania,' I said. 'But only once.'

'I heard you were at Alexandria and Tramisene.'

'Then I'm afraid you were listening to someone who did not know.'

'Modesty is a great virtue, but . . .'

'I'm not being modest, young man. If I'd been there, I would tell you. I've seen all of England in my time, much of Scotland, some of Ireland, a bit of Spain and a whole lot more of France than I care to, but I repeat, I have never been to Alexandria or Tramisene.'

'Anatolia?'

'No.'

'But you served the Bey of Balat against the heathen Turk?'

'The Bey of Balat was a heathen Turk himself, and I didn't serve him. You're probably thinking of Guy of Brienne, who was killed by the Comte du Foix.'

'Ah! That's not you then?'

'No, one of the many differences between us is that, as you may be able to tell if you inspect me closely, I'm still alive.'

'You're happy to fight the French, and they're Christians like us,' he answered. 'Isn't it better to fight the godless?'

'I've never been happy to fight anyone,' I said. 'Fighting is what you have to do when there is no other choice, and no infidel I ever heard of is godless. They may believe in the wrong god but they still have their gods.'

He pursed his lips as if about to debate the point, but then thought better of it.

'So you fought in the dark forests of the east?'

'Lithuania? I didn't say that. We certainly went into the forests and they were certainly dark, and I suppose you might say Henry was looking for a fight, but I was charged by the King with trying to make sure he stayed alive, so that was

140

my main purpose. As it happened we were never offered a fight. They knew a lot more about their forests than we did. We made so much noise crashing around that they just melted away.'

'Do you wish you had fought them?'

I was astonished by his question. One moment he seemed to know me well, the next, not at all. 'I told you, I've never wanted to fight anyone. I fight because it is my duty and sometimes it is the only way.'

'Was it the only way at Crécy?'

'Yes.'

'Because you were being chased?'

'Yes.'

'Because you were outnumbered?'

'Yes.'

'You could move faster than the French. You could have outrun them.'

'You had to be there to understand.'

'Tell me.'

'I have told you.'

'Hardly anything. I want the whole story. Leave nothing out.'

So I told him. The relief of getting across the ford, that was the first thing and it was Hugh Despenser who won us that relief. We owed him everything. Don't think it was a simple thing, that crossing. You couldn't say with any certainty where that wide and overgrown river stopped and started. We had splashed in a long line through the marsh in the dark. A man called Gobin Agache showed us the way. I should say something about Agache because in the tales told about his part in it, he has acquired an undeserved reputation as a traitor and turncoat. Of course there were those in our army who knew of the ford at Blanchetaque without his help. It was a known crossing and, unlike the bridges, the French couldn't destroy it. What we didn't know was whether it was wide enough to get the whole army and the wagons across in the short time given to us by the low tide. Now Agache undoubtedly wanted the reward, that was why he told us, but he didn't really see himself as French or as a traitor. His mother was Breton and that put him at odds with the upstart King Phillip of France, so you might as easily say he was a patriot as a traitor for the vital information he gave us.

There was a way through the marshes to the Blanchetaque ford, but it wasn't used to the number of wagons we had with us, and what I remember most about that night is the constant wrestling and heaving to get wagons back onto the harder ground from the mud into which they would keep sliding. At dawn we came to the main stream, or at least a number of channels where the Somme flowed too fast and too deep for the reeds and the marsh plants to choke it. On the other side there was another reed-bed and then rising ground, rising into trees, rising through a horde of French soldiers sent around to head us off, one arm of their great trap. By any kind of conventional reckoning, we stood no chance at all and they thought so too, greeting our appearance with derisive shouts. The tide was ebbing and the snake of white chalk and gravel which marked the bed of the ford showed clearer and clearer as the day dawned. It wasn't wide. You might get fifteen men abreast on it and still just have elbow room, but that wasn't a lot when they'd be wading right into a mob of Frenchmen with all the room in the world and dry land under their feet.

At times like this there were always certain men who came to the fore. We paused and sent word back to the King, and in a minute or two, a couple of horses came splashing up to join us. As I could have predicted, he had sent Cobham and Chandos to take a look. Granite and Fire, that was what the men called them. Sir Reginald Cobham was the granite. I was about to call him a grizzled old man, but then I suppose

I am now just as old and just as grizzled as he was then. He was so dense, so hard-packed, that you wondered why he needed armour at all. Indeed after one little fight, an abortive ambush south of Abbeville, he had two crossbow holes in his chest plate and no visible injury, the bolts having stopped just short of his flesh, and the word spread that it was his skin which had stopped them when the steel failed. Cobham knew only one way to attack and that was head-on, advancing like a rolling boulder, roaring his head off and swinging the biggest sword you ever saw with one hand when any other man would have needed two. Chandos was his opposite, all speed and subtle motion, dancing through the fight, dazzling and feinting and luring the eye from where it should be.

Chandos reined in and looked at me. 'Well, Guy?'

'Not easy,' I said. 'We've got two hours, no more.'

'Then what?'

'Then the tide will be too high to cross.'

'Also there'll be twenty thousand Frenchmen at our back,' he said dryly. 'They're seven miles behind us.'

Cobham spat into the water. 'Better get on with it,' he said. 'Couple of hundred archers and some horses that can swim. Why are we hanging around?'

At that moment another horse came spraying through the water at a canter, a grey. I knew it well and I knew the rider better. The horse was Palamon, and my own Palamon is named for him because of that day. The rider was Hugh Despenser, and I knew from the curl of Cobham's lip that he still held that whole Despenser clan in disdain.

This one was the third to bear that name, you see. We were, after all, trying to forget the bitter and tyrannical reign of our present king's father, and it was the other Hugh Despensers, the father and the grandfather of this one, who had been the architects of that tyranny. Edward the second and his Despenser allies fled west when Edward's queen, Isabella landed in Suffolk and the country flocked to her.

143

Both Despensers were taken and put to death, in the younger's case most brutally, as the country would not forgive him for sharing the King's bed.

The third Hugh Despenser had a great deal of ground to make up. The King gave him some of his lands back to show his family was in part forgiven, and in doing so had unintentionally made him Montague's favoured candidate for Elizabeth's hand, but there was still more to do.

Hugh avoided looking at me. There was now too much between us. 'Orders from the King,' he said. 'The French are closer than we thought. We are to force the crossing.'

'Fair enough,' said Chandos, as though he had just been told to get breakfast organised. 'I'll take your men with mine, Guy. You get the archers sorted out and . . .'

'I am to lead the attack,' said Hugh. I had stayed out of his way since the wedding but, when Chandos and Cobham threw back their heads and roared with laughter, his eyes had nowhere else to go but to meet mine. I saw the anguish in them, and I remembered what it used to feel like to be his friend.

'Why?' growled Cobham when he'd stopped laughing. 'Does he hate you as much as he hated your father?'

'He had good reason to hate my father, and his father,' said Hugh with quiet determination. 'I have asked for this chance to make amends. He has agreed. That is the whole of the matter.'

'Go first then boy,' said Cobham, and for once he sounded a little abashed, knowing an inexperienced man would be as good as dead if he led the way. 'We'll be behind you.'

So we got ready. I had the archers massed twenty wide in ten ranks. That was all I had and all the geography of that wet place would allow. I reckoned there were three thousand French on the other side, with plenty of crossbows amongst them, and from where we could see them clearly, we were also well within their range. Now just try doing the

144

sums. Even with the best archers, you use ten arrows killing one man. There's always wastage. Armour saves some of them. Not every arrow finds a target and sometimes three or four arrows find the same target. So, thirty thousand arrows between two hundred men should do it, but I didn't have thirty thousand to hand, and anyway that was half an hour's constant firing. With an army behind us and a narrow ford to cross, we didn't have half an hour.

We advanced across the river. The gravel was firm underfoot for most of the way but, with the tide still just on the ebb, we were up to our waists and every now and then a cart rut would catch someone out. The ducking didn't hurt them but it was one more wet and weakened bowstring, and keeping the weapons dry was a hard, hard task. At a hundred and fifty yards, the opposition started to think it was time to try their crossbows, so we stopped and loosed the first flight to deter them. Their bolts reached us, not in sufficient quantity to do much harm, but the air was full of our yards and the whistling whine of the grey goose feather. The Frenchmen dropped, a dozen men from the first volley of twenty, ten more from the second, but their discipline was good. You can tell in that first instant. Sometimes the first arrows make them cut and run, but not these men. They had shields up for the third flight and few dropped that time.

That was the moment when a voice behind roared, 'Move right. Give us space. England!' and Palamon bounded past, more like a seal than a horse, Hugh on his back, soaking us in the spray of his passing. There were forty more horses behind him, Chandos and Cobham doing their best to back him up, but he paid no attention to them and by the time he reached dry land, he was fifty yards ahead of the rest. We had to swing our aim away to the right to miss him, so for perhaps ten seconds, he was alone and unsupported amongst a swarm of angry French. It felt much longer. However often I had rued the day Hugh was born, however often I had

145

dreamt of his death, preferably inglorious, I knew that was not what my heart demanded and I now watched the bravest action I ever saw. It can be safest to keep moving fast in such circumstances, to carve a swathe with your sword while racing ahead so that you are constantly confronting new and unprepared foes. That would have been more sensible but less effective than what Hugh did. He knew what we needed was a beachhead, and he set out to create one, whirling Palamon around and around on the spot. The horse played his own part to the full, doing that dance Hugh had taught him where he would half-rear, not high enough to make a large target, but high enough to lash out ahead with his hooves.

All the time, Hugh ducked and swayed in the saddle, sweeping his sword around him. He still wouldn't have lasted long. I set my two oldest archers to picking off anyone who raised a crossbow to fire at this demon in their midst, and they dealt with half a dozen would-be heroes. Sheer weight of numbers would still have brought him down in another second or two, but then Reginald Cobham arrived like a landslide and the affair was over. The beachhead became a battlefield as more and more of our men raced into the gap. In two minutes we had a long line of our archers standing on dry land and shooting for all they were worth, and then it was done. Those French who survived were heading over the skyline with our horsemen after them and our army was pouring across the Somme.

The very first wagon across was the green one with the Tower of London markings which Montague's men had been guarding so zealously all the way. Anyone who took too close an interest in it had been severely discouraged ever since it joined us at Lisieux soon after the Pope's cardinals arrived for another pointless peace negotiation. Whatever was in the wagon, it wasn't anything to do with peace. I knew that because John Molyns had taken charge of it. Oh yes, did I say that Molyns was back on top, forgiven by the King, pardoned in spite of everything, just because of the demands of war? It seemed to take a terribly long time to get all our other wagons across, though it can't have been much more than an hour from the end of the fighting and, before it was over, our rearguard was having to fend off the first probing assault of King Phillip's advance party. We took up the same positions our enemy had so recently occupied, ready to guard the landing place if they too tried the crossing, but it was the tide which saved us from that, not any timidity on their part. The Somme rose and rose by the minute. The last three of our men, only their heads showing above the fast-moving water, made it across the ford with French bolts splashing around them. A fourth, less lucky, was hit in the head and disappeared in a swirl of pink water. Then there was nothing more coming at us, just a swelling rank of baffled French staring in fury from the far side, a branch of red flowers drifting down on the water as the river mourned the dead, and the bird song, which seemed as if it had never stopped at all.

A man ran down the slope, casting around, then saw me and waved. 'The King wants you,' he shouted. 'Right away. Up on the ridge at the edge of the trees.'

I galloped up there, dismounted and joined a circle of men crouching on the ground around our leader. What a long way he had come since I first met him on that odd Scottish mountain. He was now thirty-five years old, the tallest of us, and his air of command had developed to unchallengeable perfection.

'Well done, Guy,' he said. 'We're all here. Now, what next? Reginald, what will Phillip do?'

'Wait for the tide or go back to Abbeville and cross on the bridge.'

'Which?'

'If it was me, I'd stay and wait. But it's not me, it's him. He'll want a fancy meal and a change of clothes. They'll all trek back to Abbeville.'

147

The King stood up and gazed ahead. 'Flat land. Not a good place for a small army to face a huge one. What's over there?' He pointed east.

'A forest.'

'And beyond the forest?'

'Villages, rivers, valleys, the way north to Boulogne and Calais and the Dover straits.'

'Then that's the way we'll go.' He looked around. 'I want three scouting parties. One to ride straight ahead, that's you Guy. One to branch towards the right. Montague send that man of yours. He knows what to look for. One to the left. Despenser, you've done well today. Do one more service for me. That little port, Le Crotoy. Take it so our ships can bring in supplies. Raise a beacon there. They've been told to look for a blazing fire. If you find a likely battleground along the way, send word fast.'

'We're going to fight?' asked Montague.

Edward stared at the plain ahead and the distant trees. 'Not here, and only if the signs are right.'

I took only ten men for speed, all with fresh horses, and we ran down the distance to the looming wood, staring ahead to see what the dark trees might hide. There was a wide track running into it and in the normal way I would have shunned the obvious path, but we had no time for considerations of safety that day and I needed to see if that track could take an army. The wood was oak and chestnut, wide enough spaced to give us a good view on both sides for most of our way, but from time to time, the underbrush filled the gaps in lethal clumps of cover and my eyes were standing out ahead of me as I tried to see who might lie in wait behind them.

We saw only one man as we went and he was harmless, an old woodsman with a donkey laden with bundles of the faggots he had been cutting. He was too old and too lame to run away, and we reined in around him in a flurry of hooves and dust. In those days, of course, we all spoke as much French around the court as we did English. Edward's promotion of the English tongue had barely started to take effect. The French of the Normandy fringes was only a small and civilised variation on the court French I was used to.

'What's ahead, old man?' I asked. 'Don't be afraid. We won't hurt you.'

'The edge of the wood,' he said, with a painful anxiety to please.

'I guessed that. What's beyond the wood?'

'My town.'

'Which is?'

'Crécy-en-Ponthieu, my Lord, on the river Maye.'

'It lies in the river valley?'

'Oh yes.'

I could have cheered when the wood came to an end. It was more than a wood, it was a good-sized forest and if the worst came to the worst there was a place in it where our whole army could spend the night, protected by a small ravine on one side and a maze of thorns on the other. There was even more to cheer about out in the open. The track dipped into a valley and crossed an eminently defensible bridge, then it curved back and forth up the hill into our woodman's town, which was little more than a village in reality. I had ridden ahead, because one man going fast can often be in and out of trouble again before his enemies have noticed, but there were no soldiers to be seen – in fact almost nobody at all except two old women who dived into a house as I came by. I turned back, gave the loud shout of the all-clear and dismounted to let the horse drink from a trough at the place where the village began. Then I straightened up. Next to the trough was a tall monument. It was a fine piece of work of columns and arches in glazed red brick, tapering upwards to the sky, layered and decorated with bands of grey stone. High above me on its summit was a tall cross, with

149

one of its arms broken off. It was very old, this cross. The glazing on the bricks was starting to flake.

I looked at it once and then I looked at it twice, not just because it was ancient and of quality, but because I realised I had seen it many, many times before.

# CHAPTER TEN

'You'll be needing a typewriter,' said Eliza as they walked back down the hill together. Beth barely heard what she said. Consciously, she wasn't in Devon at all, but back in her own world, thinking about the tremendous opportunity she had just been given. It was heady stuff. The drums of war were beating and they needed her to rouse the nation. Why had these hard, pragmatic men taken the risk of calling her back from the edge of disgrace? Had someone in America, someone in the Pentagon or the State Department forced their hand? Beth knew how these big speeches worked, how one draft would be in favour, then another, then some mongrel combination. Her words would have to fight their way in. Their logic would have to dominate. Phrases and snatches of phrases began to assemble themselves, and the first phrases came straight from Christie Kilfillan, 'In an age of unseen adversaries, we must sometimes strike first and strike hard', and 'our democratic responsibility to protect our people may conflict with outmoded notions of chivalrous warfare'. You could say those things plainly in America. She needed to coat the pill with English sugar.

'Did you hear what I said?' Eliza demanded, tugging her sleeve.

'A typewriter? You said I'd need a typewriter?'

'After that. I said do you remember the picnic we had when you won the prize?'

'Picnic?'

'Over there, under the tree. You and your dad and me.'

Eliza had been the curator of Beth's school prizes, all the engraved wooden shields with their brass names. She'd polished them until you couldn't read the engraved inscriptions.

Beth found that she did remember picnics. She smiled.

Going around by the lanes, their route back to Eliza's cottage brought them again to the gates of the quarry and Lewis's truck was already back there. Beth walked on along the path, but after a few steps, she realised she was alone and looked around to see Eliza disappearing in through the quarry gate. A little exasperated, aware of time ticking by, she followed. Lewis was standing just inside the shed, looking down at the remains of the old stone slab. Eliza, ahead of her, hailed him.

'Lewis! Are you free a minute?'

He looked up and smiled vaguely at them. 'Hello. What can I do for you?'

'Nothing. Not for me,' said the old woman 'It's for Lizzie-Beth. She needs a typewriter.'

'Gran, what are you talking about?' Beth asked.

'You said, didn't you. Up there,' said the old woman, 'you said you had work to do. Work needs a typewriter. You got to write a speech haven't you? They might not be able to read your handwriting. Be much better if you typed it.'

'I'm afraid I haven't got a typewriter,' said Lewis, 'I've got a computer if that's any use to you.'

'I've got my laptop, thanks,' said Beth and realised as she said it, that she didn't have her laptop at all, that in the rush to leave London, it was still sitting on the floor beside her bed. 'Ah,' she said, 'then again, maybe I haven't.'

'There you are, you see,' said Eliza. 'Just as well I asked.'

'You're welcome to use it,' said Lewis. 'I'm only in the office now and then. I spend most of the time in the sheds.'

In the office? He expected her to sit in his office and write? But then again, where else was there? She couldn't imagine trying to write this speech in her father's house.

'Come and have a look,' he suggested, 'it's up to you.'

Eliza waved her hand. 'I'll be off then,' she said. 'Don't forget what I said, Lizzie-Beth.'

'About what?'

'About talking to your father.'

Beth looked blank.

'You know,' Eliza prompted, 'about what I said,' then turned and trotted off through the trees like some fairy-tale creature returning to her lair.

'This way,' said Lewis, and he showed her into the office which was little more than a timber lean-to attached to the side of the bigger shed. It was spartan in the extreme, with a dented khaki filing cabinet, a cork notice board impaled with sheaves of curling papers, and an old pine table with a computer on it.

'I'm sorry, I'm sure it's not what you're used to. There's a chair somewhere. I'll go and find it.'

She looked at the computer. Its cream casing had been yellowed by the sun on one side and the buttons were as unfashionably ugly as a ten-year-old dress. She pushed the power button and waited and then waited some more. Lewis and what he had become, disconcerted her. She had got away, he had let himself be pulled back, an awful example to her of how things could have been if she hadn't held on to her ambition. He was as he had always been, annoyingly at peace with himself. How dare he look so good when he'd patently given up on everything the wider world had to offer.

By the time Lewis came back with a wooden kitchen chair, the machine was still booting-up. They looked at it in silence and finally the screen came to life.

'It seems to take longer and longer, I'm afraid,' said Lewis. 'I don't really need to use it for anything very clever.' He

153

clicked on the word processor icon and they settled in for another long wait.

'Have you tried defragging it?' asked Beth.

'Not knowingly. What's that?'

'It gets the hard drive working faster. Shall I show you?' She did. The display showed the hard drive was in a terrible state and the machine slowly began sorting itself out.

'It's going to take a while,' she said. 'Maybe I'll come back later.'

'How long?'

'Fifteen minutes, maybe twenty.'

'Why don't I show you around properly?'

She still wanted to understand why this energetic boy she had known had given up, to find what tied him to this neolithic life. 'All right,' she said.

He smiled. 'It's good to see you. I'm glad you came.'

'I'm not really here by choice.'

'Then we must make the best of it. Come and see the stone.'

The quarry was not at all as she had expected. He took her past all the machinery and out of the back door of the shed where, instead of a rock face, they came to the entrance to a wide cavern.

'You're about to see a rare sight,' he said, 'a working free-stone seam.'

'I have no idea what that means. You'll have to explain.'

'I was about to,' he said mildly. 'Even a geologist would be out of their depth here. This is a place for historians. There's no need to get snappy straight away.'

'I wasn't snapping.' God, she thought, if he had any idea what real life was like, he'd know that was just what passed for efficient communication in the corridors of government. If someone tried to bullshit you with jargon, you let them know, quickly. You had to. All the same, she felt a bit better, knowing that ignorance was expected.

'Good,' he said, 'I'm glad to hear it,' and she thought she detected a touch of irony. 'The thing is, this is like a little island of its own. It's the same strata as you find away off to the east at Purbeck, just another tiny patch of the same rock. It's a lot smaller of course, too small to be much of a commercial proposition. That's why everyone's heard of Purbeck and no one's heard of this place.'

'But I thought you said it's been going for centuries.'

'It has one way or another. I'll show you the older workings later. This bit's only been open a short while.'

'What did you call it?'

'The freestone. That's what they always called the good easy stone. At Purbeck, they pretty much finished it off a hundred years ago.'

'But what is it?'

'Come in and see.'

They went in through an entrance that was a little over head height and maybe twelve feet wide, a rectangle as straight-cut overhead as if it had a concrete lintel. Lewis flicked a switch and two floodlights came on. The rock floor and the ceiling were both flat and even, and the height was the same right through the wide space ahead of them. The proportions made the roof seem lower so that Beth found herself bending her head unnecessarily. Here and there, narrow columns of stone blocks were wedged under the ceiling as supports.

'This is the freestone, you see,' said Lewis. 'It was laid down in beds two or three feet thick and between each bed there's a couple of inches of clay to separate it from the next one.'

'Why did they do that?'

'They? No, I mean that's the way it comes. Nature did it. It's a sandstone, deposited by the sea and I suppose once every half a million years or so, the sea did something else for a while and that's why you get the seams of clay. Anyway, the beauty of it is that nature already formed it in slabs for us.' He had lowered his voice almost to a whisper and the rock amplified it. There was a loud plop as a drip of water fell into a small pool in the floor. 'All you have to do is pick out the clay above and below, and out it comes, do you see?'

She did. She could see that the whole bed was divided into flat rectangles a few feet long.

'We leave two beds undisturbed to make the floor and a few more up top for the ceiling. The blocks are tight together here you see, so it stays up if you don't mess about with it. When we find a block with loose seams round it we put a leg up under it to keep it in place.' He pointed at the wedged-in stone columns.

'It looks like hard work.'

'Oh, it is, but none the worse for it.' He glanced at her. 'You don't really get it, do you?'

'I wonder why you do it.'

'The old men had names for every bed,' he said as if that should be an explanation. 'Look at the floor. They called that the white horse. It's good stone, but if you lift that you find the dun cow under it and that's useless stuff, soft and brown and it doesn't make a good bottom at all. The top beds in the seam, they're called the grub, then there's the roach. You get a lot of fish fossils in the roach, so maybe that's why it got its name. Under that, there's the grey-bit and the thorn-back, then there's the whitstone and then finally you get to the freestone, and that's mostly what we're after here.'

'And you like all this because . . .?'

He shot her a doubtful look. 'What do you mean?'

'I mean, why do you like labouring with your hands down here, instead of using your brain?'

'I do have to put a bit of thought into it, you know,' he said, and once again she couldn't quite tell if he was teasing.

'You were going places.'

156

'I did. As it happens, I was doing rather well. Joined a big company. I was the flavour of the month, you know. I got promoted twice in a year.'

'What sort of company?'

'Defence procurement, that sort of thing. Anyway the point is I knew I didn't want to go on with that. The letter came about the quarry and I came back.'

'Because of the quarry?'

'Not just that.' He looked at her evenly. 'If you really want to know, there were other reasons. I'd fallen in love.'

'Oh. With . . . with someone back here?'

'No, with a married woman, married to my boss. Anyway that's not the point. When I got back here I found I liked it because it's in my blood.'

She laughed.

'Listen to me, Beth,' he said. 'I mean it. My family has been doing this for generation after generation.'

'What is it then? What do you like?'

He paused a moment before replying and looked around him at the stone. 'When you lever out a slab of freestone, you're seeing behind it for the first time ever. You're doing it the way the old men did it hundreds of years ago. Do you know what happened? When I first came in here and started work on the back face, and I was getting depressed because it was all surly stone, I needed a longer paddle to cut out the clay and when I sat down to think about it, I found I was sitting on a hard iron bar, and there it was, the very paddle I needed, left there the last time someone worked on that bed maybe a hundred years ago. That's why I like it.'

'All right,' Beth said, taken aback by the length and the certainty of his answer. 'What's surly stone?'

'It's just like surly people. It's hard and difficult. When you first cut stone that's been covered in, it's sweet stone, full of the quarry sap, easy to shape. When it gets exposed to the

157

air it dries out and gets harder. Leave it long enough and it turns surly, then it's the devil to work with.'

'I thought rock was rock, end of story.'

'Oh no,' he said, 'stone's a living thing. It gets harder once it's out and some say it even shrinks a bit. You know Michelangelo's *David*?'

'Of course I do.'

'What made that a real miracle wasn't just that it's so well carved, it's the fact that the marble he used had been lying around for years and years. It was cut for a job that never got done. How he managed to carve those legs with stone like that is a complete mystery to me.'

She looked around, 'So where did that other stuff come from, that dark green stuff you showed me before?'

'The Purbeck marble? Oh, that's not in here. That comes higher up by the lannen vein. It's a bit of a walk from here and it's down a deep hole, so you'd really need overalls.'

'Are you still in touch with her?'

'Who?'

'Your boss's wife?'

'No,' he said curtly. 'I reckon the computer's probably ready for you by now.'

She followed him back out into the daylight, still wondering at this tiny world of his. The monitor showed a fully defragged disk and even if it didn't exactly leap into life under her fingers, there was serviceable word processing and that was all she needed.

'I keep the key under that stone,' he said. 'Lock up when you're finished. Apart from that, help yourself. I've got a couple of jobs to do.'

'Thanks, Lewis,' she said, then, because she suddenly wanted to give him something back, she said, 'if you're not in too much of a hurry, there's something I wanted to ask you.'

He glanced at his watch. 'I've got a minute or two.'

'You mentioned Guy de Bryan, then Eliza started talking about him. I don't know anything about him.'

'Guy de Bryan? You never had much time for history, did you? You always preferred politics.'

'We never did modern history and I couldn't see the point of all that ancient stuff.'

'You wrote a project about him in primary school. We all had to.'

'Did we?' Faint memories of drawing shields and helmets came back to her. 'I don't remember any of it.'

'It would take more time than we've got right now.'

'It's a long story is it?'

'Not really. There are fragments here and fragments there. I've been gathering them together for years.'

'When exactly did he live? Eliza talked about him as if she'd known him.'

Lewis laughed. 'She does that. He was born in 1307 and he died at the grand old age of eighty-three in the year 1390. A bit before even Eliza's time. He built the Chantry when he was in his sixties.'

'And a Chantry is what exactly?'

'I suppose you'd say it was a private chapel. People built them to have prayers said for their souls. More often than not they were just side chapels in churches. This one was a whole lot more. It wasn't just the tower, although that's just about all that's left. It was more like a small monastery once.'

'So the house by the tower is part of it?'

'No, that came much later. The tower just happens to be in its garden.'

'Why's de Bryan so famous?'

'I'm not sure he is, except to those who take the trouble. He's one of the many that history forgot. Maybe he *should* be famous.'

'Because?' Lewis went out through the door and beckoned her to follow.

'Because of a whole lot of things but mostly because of this.' He stood by the workshop and she followed him. They stood by the broken stone tablet on the bench and both looked down at it. 'These are the words he left behind him for all to see, except someone took exception to them.'

'In what way?'

'It might have fallen off by itself, but I don't think so. Someone took the trouble to climb up the Chantry tower and knock it down. You can still see where it used to be and it's quite high up.'

'When?'

He shrugged. 'No idea. Maybe in the sixteenth century when Henry the eighth had them all shut down. They dug up the bits from the earth around the tower where they fell.'

'What does it say?'

'I'm not sure yet. I know what the first bit says, but I've only got a rough idea of the rest.'

'Tell me.'

'It's in Latin and it's very worn. I've been over and over it. I know how a mason uses a chisel, so maybe I can make more sense out of what's left of the marks than most. Do you remember George Samuels?'

'Mr Samuels.' The Latin teacher at the grammar school. A thin man with large, damp eyes.

'He's retired to Dartmouth and he's helping me with it. It's not even very good Latin, so it's difficult. I've got a rough translation of some of it, but there's a bit missing, see?'

Laid out as if it were a jigsaw, Beth looked and saw the triangular gap, a few inches wide.

'Tell me what the rest says.'

'It's too rough. It doesn't flow. George says Latin's like that. The ideas behind the words sometimes don't translate literally. It needs a poetic mind to convey what it was meant to say when you turn it into English. He's working on it. He's a bit of a poet himself. That's where I've just been. I went to see him and he's almost finished.'

'Except for the missing bit.'

'Yes, except for that. We'll have to do some guessing.'

Because Beth liked information for its own sake and disliked others having information that she didn't, she wouldn't drop the subject.

'You said you know how it starts?'

'I kept on at him until he gave me the first line.'

'Which is?'

'It's funny,' he said. 'It made me think about you and what you're doing. All the way back from Dartmouth, I wondered how you'd take to it. It might stick in your throat.'

The idea that anything written in the fourteenth century might have any bearing on her own opinions seemed so absurd that Beth had to stop herself laughing. 'Well tell me anyway. I promise not to take offence.'

'If you're sure.'

He turned and stared at the stone, running a finger slowly along the faint grooves. 'We wrote it all down, but George has got the piece of paper. I think it starts "Senes" or is it "Senesci" then it's "qui domi manent, nolite juvenes verbis belli . . ."'

'I've forgotten my Latin,' she broke in, feeling time pressing even harder on her. 'Just tell me what it means.'

His voice was deliberate and self-consciously neutral. 'According to George it means something like, "Old men, do not stir up the young with your exhortations to battle. The ruin that results should not be theirs but yours."'

Anger rose in her like a red tide, anger that he should be making assumptions about what she would or wouldn't agree with.

'Is that what you think I do?' she said. 'Is that what you think I am, some bloodthirsty manipulator playing with people's lives?'

161

He looked at her steadily. 'That promise didn't last long, did it?' he observed.

'What prom . . . ah.'

'I don't know what you are, Beth,' he said calmly. 'I'd like to find out because I know what you used to be and I was very fond of at least half of you. Maybe more.'

'Half of me? And I suppose you're perfect, are you?'

'No, I'm not. Maybe we might both learn a bit from old Sir Guy.'

'Oh really?' snapped Beth, 'well tell me then, if he was so bloody good why did he need to have prayers said for him?'

'That's just what I'd like to know,' said Lewis. He looked at his watch. 'I'm going. Don't forget to lock up.'

After he had left, she avoided looking out of the office door at the slab, just visible inside the shed, and when she began to type, she closed the connecting door. Half an hour went by, but it didn't work. The words would hardly dribble out on to the screen, and when they did, they sat there, dull and flickering like a poor attempt at an indignant justification. In the end she switched off and locked the door.

When she closed the yard gate behind her there were only two places to go and for once, it was harder to face Eliza again than it was to go back to Carrick Cottage and her father. That was what it was, Carrick Cottage. It wasn't 'home' even if she had lived there for the first nineteen years of her life. As she walked slowly back into the village, she glanced up at the old hulk of the Chantry tower and looked for a moment to see if she could see the place the tablet had fallen from. As she approached the house, slowing down even more, the door opened. Her father came out, turned to pin a sign on it and caught sight of her as he did so.

'Oh Beth, good timing,' he said. 'I was just off for a walk. Will you join me?'

She looked at the piece of paper. It said '6.35 p.m. Gone

down to the Ley. I'll be along the Line by the Royal Sands. Hope to see you. Love Pa.'

'I'm quite tired,' she said.

He looked at her with his head a little on one side and put a hand out to touch her shoulder. The touch irritated her, but she had to look back at him and she saw clearly how old he had become, those clear eyes turning milky and the flesh of his face starting to fall inwards.

'I'll go slowly,' he said. 'I would very much like you to come.'

So they went off down the road, father and daughter, walking together but separately. He stuck to neutral things, telling her slowly of all the people she had gone out of her way to forget around the village and what had become of them, which was generally not much.

'Ryan Woolcombe, you remember him from school? He's got a boat out of Dartmouth now. Does charter fishing trips. Had to be rescued last year when his propeller fell off. That caused a bit of a stink with the powers that be. They're doing a lot of safety checks on him this year.'

Ryan Woolcombe to her was eleven years old, a pink boy, apt to cry, who had ratted on her several times when she'd been defending herself in the playground.

'Angela's done well. Angela Broom? Did her degree in Bristol and now she's in publishing. She was down last week.'

Beth heard a criticism in that. 'Well, I'm down now,' she said. 'I'm sorry I haven't been before, but I can't tell you how little time I have.'

He stepped into the hedge and waited as a car went by, then climbed the bank onto a high pavement that ran along above the road and held out a hand to help her up. She ignored it.

'I didn't mean that,' he said. 'You're here now and that's the main thing. Were you coming anyway or was it my letter?'

'I only read your letter when I was half-way here.'

163

He nodded, considering that. 'Are you all right?' he asked. 'Sounds like they've been giving you a hard time.'

'It's the job,' she said. 'It makes you a bit of an Aunt Sally. There are always people gunning for the advisers.'

'You could do something else,' he said.

'Dad, I'm in politics. That's what I do.'

'I never really thought of you as political,' he said, and she had to suppress a sigh. 'I mean, before all this I couldn't really have told anyone which side you'd vote for,' he went on. 'I never really heard you say what you thought about education or the health service or taxes.'

'I'm dealing with foreign affairs. It's not like that.'

'You mean it's just a job? Haven't you nailed your colours to the mast? Don't you have to support them in all the other ways too?'

His tone was mild and he sounded genuinely interested, but as she had so often felt with him, she feared he was probing down towards somewhere she didn't want him to go, that suddenly he would turn up some illogicality in her that she hadn't even thought of. She didn't want to feel fifteen again.

'I concentrate on what I do, Dad. I'm a specialist. That's the way it works.'

He stopped by a field gate. 'There was a big old brock badger in here this morning, early. He didn't mind me a bit. Noisy old thing. They sound like a regiment on the march.'

Oh come on, Dad, she thought. What are you building up to?

'I suppose I'm just a bit puzzled how it must be in your world,' he observed, when he'd done with staring at the absent badger. 'Seems like in foreign policy the only choices are right-wing or even more right wing at the moment. Isn't that a bit hard for you?'

'Do you know, I'd really rather talk about something else,' she said. 'What about you? Are you still playing snooker with Jeff on Thursdays?'

'No,' he said. 'I stopped that.'

'Why? I thought you loved it.'

'Well, it wasn't by choice. I'm afraid Jeff died.'

'Oh. I'm sorry.'

'It was a couple of years ago now.'

That took them on in silence until they crested the final gentle hill, and there below them was the Ley stretching out to the west and beyond it the Line, the thin defence, with its roadway and the sparkling sea beyond.

'You heard about the storm?' he said. 'The one that washed away the road.'

She had seen pictures on the news, where? At a seaside conference. Someone asked her why she was so interested and she'd made a joke of it.

'The memorial went,' he said. 'You should have seen the waves. We thought they'd breach the Line. You get too much sea-water coming through into the Ley and it does any amount of damage. It cut great chunks out of the road. Do you see there? They've built a new bit further inshore.'

There was a kink, where the narrow road running its mile length between the salt water and the fresh had once been straight. The memorial had stood between the sea and the road, in the car-park where the Royal Sands Hotel had once been, a long time ago.

'They're going to put it back together again,' he said. 'They've got all the bits. Your friend Lewis is very hot on getting it all done right.'

'Lewis. You and Gran go on and on about Lewis.'

'That's the first time I've mentioned him,' said her father. 'What's Eliza been going on about?'

'Lewis this and Lewis that. It's as if he had the secrets of life in his pocket, when all he's done is throw away his education to hack lumps of stone.'

'He's done a bit more than that. He's called in by all the top people when they have problems restoring ancient

165

buildings. Did you know he's an adviser to English Heritage? They tell me you see him on television sometimes, being interviewed about this and that. He knows his stuff.'

'He still could have done a lot more.'

Her father shrugged.

They came down to the junction where the road inland to Slapton met the Line, and there was no traffic to be seen anywhere. The tide was high and every hundred yards or so a fisherman stood with his long beach rod propped up on a tripod, its tip dipping and rising as each wave crest sucked at the invisible filament stretching from it.

'Shall we sit?' her father pointed to some squared stones, tumbled into the shingle. 'The storm did some good. They're comfortable, these.'

'Gran says there's something you have to tell me,' said Beth when the silence stretched out too far for her, and that was when he misunderstood her completely.

# CHAPTER ELEVEN

'I have heard it said at court,' the squire suggested rather carefully, 'that the King decided to make his stand at Crécy because of an insult, something concerning a heron? Is there any truth in that?'

I realised how long I had been talking about our old battle by the cramps in my legs and I hadn't even got to the fighting yet, but the lad seemed to have an insatiable appetite for details.

'The heron?' I said. 'I've heard it said he fought the whole war because of the heron.'

I suppose the episode of the heron had made him more alert to signs, portents and how legends spread among fighting men. I could still remember the moment my reconnaissance party arrived back at the camp with complete clarity. The King was walking up and down outside his tent. Not pacing, walking. I'm sure he knew that every eye was upon him, and he was careful to show deliberation, not anxiety. In private, just to myself, I can recognise some of his faults after all these years. He was guided far more by his heart than his head, if that is a fault. He could be more cruel than was warranted by circumstance, although that was often done for effect, knowing others would restrain him. It helped to build the legend without the need for blood.

I would say he knew more about the subtleties of command than anyone else I ever met. None of his commanders could hold a candle to him for attention to detail. He had many changes of clothes with him on this campaign, I knew that for a fact, but he was careful to be seen wearing an outfit that was just as stained, damp and uncomfortable as those his men were wearing after their struggle through the Somme. Finer, yes, but just as damp.

He took no apparent notice of my arrival, not wanting to give any appearance of concern. The army was spread out through a few hundred yards of the forest, not a clearing exactly, but the place I had found where the trees were larger and further apart and the bank of thorns protected us. Though they were getting on with cooking and all the other stuff of military life, there wasn't an eye that didn't flick past the King every minute or two, just to check how things stood. I tethered my horse and he ducked into his tent with hardly a glance in my direction. Cobham stumped up to me and slapped me on the back with a guffaw. Being slapped by Sir Reginald Cobham was like being hit by a falling tree. I had seen him coming and braced myself.

'Follow me,' he said quietly. 'He's waiting.'

Inside the tent, Edward was sitting on a stool with the Bishop next to him, and Northampton fiddling with his sword strap. I bowed to each of them. They were talking and I waited for them to stop.

'Shoes,' said Edward. 'What about shoes?'

That took me back to a misty Scottish hilltop. He shot me a quick look and I knew he was remembering it too.

'Not good,' said Northampton. 'No more than a hundred spares left and many of the ones on their feet are nearly worn through. It's going to slow us down.'

'We need to make a stand,' opined the Bishop. 'The very worst outcome is to be overtaken and picked off.'

'Numbers,' objected Northampton. 'There are four of them for every one of us.'

'No,' said Edward firmly. 'You know how they move. They straggled out of Abbeville like a ball of wool unravelling. They don't know how to keep together. We need to surprise them so we can deal with the front ranks before the rear even knows we're there. We need to stop before they're expecting us to stop.' He fell silent, but he clearly hadn't finished and nobody else spoke. 'This isn't just about tactics,' he said. 'We need to find the right place, for sure, but we also need a sign.'

The Bishop nodded, but Cobham gave a badly suppressed snort and Edward glared at him. 'You don't believe in signs, Reginald?'

'When it comes to fighting I believe in things I can see, Lord. Things with sharp edges.'

Edward smiled at him and his reply was soft, but that was only his way of heightening the power of his words. 'This whole affair is about signs, Reginald. You know very well how it began. Phillip wanted me, the King of England, to kneel to him, the so-called King of France, in homage for lands to which he has no right. How would that be for a sign, me kneeling in front of him? Now he marches after us with the Oriflamme at the head of his army. Now there's a potent sign for you. What's special about a scarlet banner?'

Everyone who'd fought on campaign in France knew what it meant when the French king took the Oriflamme. When it was taken from its resting place at the Abbey of Saint Denis, it was usually safe to bet there would be a battle sooner or later. Now, of course, the saving grace of battle, if you were of high birth, was that the enemy had a cash incentive for capturing you alive. Fortunes were made and lost on the battlefield through ransoms, but not when the Oriflamme was waving. It was the sign that no prisoners were to be taken, and it was the colour of blood.

Edward looked around him. No one answered. 'Whatever men believe – that's what's special about it, and what French

169

soldiers believe is that the unfurling of the Oriflamme puts God on their side. They invest that banner of theirs with all the stolen power of righteousness. You know what else it means. Reginald? Do you?' His voice was less soft now and Cobham looked as uncomfortable as I had ever seen him.

'Of course I do, Lord. It means no quarter will be given.'

'No ransoms, Reginald. That's what it means. No hard cash, no cosy protection for the rich while the poor die. No Frenchman will take you prisoner for the increase of his personal fortune while that bloody flag is flying in their midst. It'll be the sword in the ribs for you and they have a lot more swords than we have. I want our men to know that we have a sign as potent as the Oriflamme, even if we have to invent it here and now between us and spread the story ourselves. What shall it be, a vision? The holy Madonna coming to me in the full glare of daylight to assure us of her blessing? We need something like that to turn the tale our way. Do you know, there's a song they're singing in France now. Have any of you heard it? It's called the "Vow of the Heron".'

I'd heard it. We'd all heard it. Nobody wanted to be the first to say so, not knowing how he'd take it.

'Do you know what it says? It says I was too much of a coward to stand up to the French. It says I was such a coward that I got down on bended knee and paid homage to the King of France for his permission to be in Aquitaine, while I claimed it for England only under my breath. Well, have you heard it?'

Reginald Cobham had recovered himself. 'I've heard it,' he said. 'You're doing yourself an injustice, Lord.'

'You think so, do you? It says I only took arms because a Frenchman served me up a roasted heron.'

'I remember the occasion, Lord,' put in the Bishop. 'It wasn't really a heron. I'm sure it was a peacock, and it's only the French who think the heron is a cowardly bird.'

170

The atmosphere inside the tent had become extremely uncomfortable, as though Edward had decided we had somehow got together and written the song between us. He could be unreasonable at times. His gaze swung round them all, passed them and alighted on me, and I decided it was time to speak.

'My Lord, I think I may have found your sign.'

Another man entered the tent at that moment, noisy and intrusive, unable to contain himself. 'My Lord,' he said in a nasal, high-pitched whine of a voice. I swung around to look at him, knowing that voice. Montague's man, the other scout. 'I have found you your killing ground. A place where we may use the . . .'

'Be quiet,' said the King and I thrilled at the hard fury in his voice. John Molyns flushed as far as his sallow complexion allowed. He might be back in favour, but that favour clearly had strict limits to it.

'Speak, Guy,' Edward said.

It was just before noon the following day, the twenty-fifth day of August, in that potent year of 1346, that I stood next to the King at the top of the hill that led up from the river to Crécy village. Here, at the first division of the road, Edward knelt in front of the old brick cross and said a prayer for victory, a prayer of remembrance and a prayer of thanks. All the while, while I was trying to pray, I was struggling unsuccessfully to crush the resentment in me, unable to stop my memory re-enacting the day before at the Blanchetaque ford when Hugh Despenser became a true hero and set the seal on my sinful treachery. I hoped God wasn't listening, but I know he was because within hours he set me a test and in failing it, I committed my second sin.

At the end of his prayers, Edward got to his feet and gave me a grateful look. 'How did you know it for what it was, Guy?'

I was embarrassed to admit it. 'I . . . I spent my childhood staring at it, Lord.'

'Not here?'

'No, no. At home in Wales.'

'How?'

'We had it embroidered on a tablecloth.'

'This cross?' He sounded understandably astonished.

'The cloth was embroidered by my father's grandmother. She was in the court of Queen Eleanor. I knew she lived in Ponthieu for some of her life, so she must have been here often. When I realised what it might be, I went looking for the priest here and persuaded him to tell me the story.'

'Tell me in exactly the words with which he told you.'

'He said Queen Eleanor put up the cross in the year 1189 as an offering for the safe return of her two sons when they rode off to the Crusades.'

Edward nodded, considered and then turned to the half-circle of his commanders waiting behind.

'Gentlemen. There could be no more fitting place for our coming fight than this. Behind me, you see the great cross built by Queen Eleanor, wife of our former king, Henry the second, my grandfather's great-grandfather. She built this cross in honour of her two brave sons, two more kings of England, John, and Richard Coeur de Lion, the Lionheart, a man with the courage of King Arthur before him, a warrior who struck fear into his enemies wherever he went. More than that, she built it here because this marked the boundary of her ancestral lands of Ponthieu, because she was not only Queen of England and of our province of Aquitaine, but also she was Countess of Ponthieu, our own lands, of which we have been deprived by the false declaration of this so-called King of France. Beyond this cross, we are in those English ancestral lands. This is where we shall stand, this is where we shall fight with God on our side and our feet on English earth, and this is where we shall win. Go and tell your men we have been given a sign, and Crécy is where we shall make our stand.'

He turned to me, smiled and lowered his voice again. 'And you're telling me that all this is because of a tablecloth?'

'Well, I thought it must be the same one, Lord. It's quite unusual. That's why I started asking questions.'

'It must have been well-embroidered.'

'My father didn't like me to raise my head when I was eating, Lord. He thought it was disrespectful for me to look at him when my mouth was full. He kept a rod next to him to hit me if I looked up. I had a great deal of time to look at that picture.'

The King laughed. 'Poor Guy. You and your mad father.' He looked at me and frowned. 'Have I done you a disservice?'

Oh, the emotions that leapt up in me, emotions I had left behind in England, emotions suppressed until that moment by the minute to minute pressures of the campaign. I jumped to the entirely wrong conclusion.

'No, no. You tried to do me a service,' I said. 'I know that. I lost Elizabeth to Hugh Despenser by my own performance in the joust. Without you, I would never have had the chance of her hand at all.'

His look of astonishment told me I had missed the mark by a mile.

'My dear Guy,' he said wonderingly. 'You still dream of Elizabeth Montague? I had no idea. I thought she was a passing fancy of yours. We must find you a wife at once. No, I see by your face that even that would be a bad idea. You poor man. Damn. I would have tried a more certain method to secure your happiness if I had known the stakes were so high. And now Despenser has her.' He frowned. 'Well, if he keeps up his deeds of derring-do, you may find the fair Elizabeth is once again a widow. Cheer up. He may not have survived the attack on Crotoy.'

I could not bear to hear him say that because I had thought the very same thing at the ford.

173

'Sir, Hugh Despenser was my friend. I could not for a moment wish for that.'

'Was? You said "was"? No, of course you couldn't wish for that,' said Edward absently, 'but he's out to prove himself in a way that seems quite unwise.'

The commanders had ridden back down the hill to spread the word amongst the army and only his guard were left, spread out around the junction of the roads, vigilant and watching us curiously.

I carried an ache of unbearable loss and an even greater ache of unbearable guilt about Elizabeth and Hugh, for things done and things undone, so I was anxious to move to firmer ground. 'If you did not mean that, Lord, may I ask what you did mean?'

'I meant Molyns.'

The sun grew dimmer. 'What of him?'

'You had custody of his land while he was a fugitive. I gave you Stoke Trister in care for your own, to enjoy the benefit of the estate.'

'You did, sire, and I am grateful.'

'But then I took it back.'

'You did that too, sire.'

'Drop the sire and the lord, Guy. There's no one close enough to hear. I want to tell you why I did it.'

'You don't need to.'

'But I do. I'm sure you felt slighted by it. I know you hate the man and I also know you have good reason to hate him, and if I had to make all my choices from the point of view of what is good and what is bad, he would have been on the gallows long ago. We hunted for him hard enough.' He caught my look. 'Well, all right. You know better. We hunted for him until we knew whose protection he was under, and then the stakes became a little too high to take the game further. A king may not always do everything he wants. He needs his earls behind him, and preferably not holding daggers.'

174

I was flattered and disturbed. It was further than he had ever gone with me before.

'Oh, for the Lord's sake, Guy,' he said, 'take a part in this conversation. I'm talking to you man to man. Do me the honour of answering in the same fashion.'

'Why did Montague shelter him?' I said. 'He's a sensible man. He must know Molyns for what he is.'

'Old Montague was always in debt,' said the King, drily. The old Earl had died the year before, and I for one had not felt more sorry than anyone should feel for a Christian soul bound for torment. 'Molyns made money in a hundred different dirty ways and lent a lot of it to him. Young Montague is a bit more biddable as far as I'm concerned, but I suspect Molyns is already enmeshing him in the same trap.'

'All the more reason for the old Earl to surrender him to justice and wipe out his debts,' I answered and Edward laughed.

'That's as near to an unworthy thought as I have ever heard you come.' He looked all around and then up at the sun, reckoning the time and seemed to find himself still in no great hurry. 'John Molyns has the blackest soul of any man I know,' he went on. 'He belongs to a past time, before this more enlightened age of ours. He understands the power of arms and not much more. He uses violence with the skill of a torturer and he knows no limits. You know why I stripped him of his lands?'

I did, by heart. 'The murders at Stoke Poges and the terror he spread afterwards.'

Edward shook his head. 'Others have done worse. It was what followed. He lost sight of his allegiance to me. His natural state lies inside the narrow confines of war, and I thought I could trust him there. Cast your mind back six years. You were with me at the siege of Tournai, weren't you?'

'No,' I felt a little hurt that he didn't remember. 'You sent me to Scotland.'

'Oh yes. Sorry. Well, you didn't miss anything, I promise. We were starving – far hungrier than they were inside the town. I was short of men, short of food and short of money. Allies don't come cheap, you know. I owed Ludwig's Germans a small fortune, not to mention the Brabanters, and they were threatening to break ranks and go home at any moment.'

I had heard rumours, but this was stuff normally kept only for the ears of great lords. 'Why didn't they send you what you needed?'

'Parliament? The Council? Because when a king is out of sight, he can be conveniently out of mind and the narrow English Channel suddenly becomes a very wide ocean. I sent Molyns back as my right-hand man to get them moving. All I needed was two months' money and twenty ships of men and food, and do you know what happened?'

I shook my head.

'Absolutely nothing,' he said. 'Not a word. At the end of September, I was forced into peace talks at that little chapel with the bowed roof. What's it called?' I didn't know, but it seemed to matter to him. 'Esplechin,' he said. 'That's the place. All their top men and some of ours. King Phillip knew he held the whip hand and he forced a truce.' There was anguish in his eyes.

'Was that so bad?' I asked, and he whirled on me.

'Don't be a bloody fool,' he said. 'I couldn't leave. I was too much in debt. We went to Ghent and I owed so much money I had to promise to stay there. I couldn't go home. I was as good as a hostage for the money I owed to all our allies of the coalition. I had trouble borrowing a hundred pounds to feed my archers, and after that even the humblest baker wouldn't give us credit. I had to send the horses back to England because there was no money for fodder. I jousted on a borrowed horse. Those bloody bankers had me by the balls. The Archbishop of Trier even took the crown, the Great Crown of England. It was all I could do to stop him breaking it up for scrap. I told them I would pay in wool, and they said no, they would only take gold. I was sending messengers back to London and all that came back to me was silence. No word from Molyns, no word from anyone. Do you know who came to my aid in the end? Not England, not Brabant. The Italians. Italian money men, the Bardis and their friends. I said I would leave four knights and two of them, two of the Bardis, but the men of Ghent still wouldn't let me go. I had to pretend to go riding with my queen to escape.'

I knew this part of the story well, but I wanted to hear it from him.

'We went with Northampton and Walter Mauny,' he said grimly. 'Mauny's another of those men. He's a lot straighter than Molyns, but he's what you need when things get hard. He got us a small, smelly boat from Sluys to Zeeland and there, in the islands, we found a ship for England. Three days of storms and we came to the Tower of London in the middle of the night and do you know what we found? Darkness and our children left unguarded. No Constable or Treasurer to be seen.'

The story of the bankrupt King's wrath was legendary.

'John Molyns, the man I trusted to act for me, had been the worst of them. He was living high off the hog in the Tower of London with his cronies, doing nothing to help.' He stared at me. 'He is a strange man, Guy. He's like a pack wolf. When the leader of the pack is there, he'll obey the rules, but give him a sniff of power, take the leader out of his sight and there is no knowing what he'll try to do. He and his friends had set the Council against me. They thought they could ignore me. I showed them they could not. He had stolen from me. I found his gold, my gold, hidden at St Albans. I took it back. I sent Montague to seize him, and you know the rest.'

'And now you have forgiven him and given him his lands back and he is here riding at your right hand,' I said, 'so that's all right now, is it?'

'I have not forgiven him, I have pardoned him, which is a very different thing.'

'But why?'

'Quieter,' said the King looking around and up at the sun again. 'It's time we were busy. Why? You don't know why?' He pointed back the way we had come. 'Because we are at war for the honour of our country. Because we are outnumbered by a margin that makes me break out in a sweat when I think about it. Because they have unwrapped the Oriflamme and if it goes against us tomorrow we will all die and Phillip of France will be King of England. Because in a war such as this it is my duty to win, and to win I need the wolves on my side.'

'And one man makes a difference?'

'That man makes a difference. He came to me with an idea, a plan to help defeat the French.'

'What plan?'

He opened his mouth, closed it, then opened it again. 'You will see, Guy. You will see. You have done me great service today and I shall not forget that. You were the best of squires and now you have been the best of men-at-arms, but I'm afraid, Guy, that from today, you will no longer serve me as man-at-arms.'

I stared at him, unable to believe that he might be sending me away.

'No,' he said. 'Tomorrow you shall serve me not as man-at-arms, but as a knight of my household. This evening I shall make you *Sir* Guy de Bryan, and I promise you that you will have estates to replace Stoke Trister if we survive the battle.'

'We will survive it.'

'Perhaps. We will discuss it this evening.'

He looked at the cross in silence for a moment then looked back at me. 'This evening we will discuss Molyns' plan, and if you, Guy, if you tell me it should not be done then it will not be done. Oh, and one more thing I can promise you, Hugh Despenser will be sent to the thickest part of the fray.'

That diverted me. I wanted to say that we would survive it without Molyns' plan, whatever it was. I would have taken the risk of calling my king's judgement into question. Instead, I said. 'Not for me. I couldn't live with that on my conscience.'

I could hardly live with myself as it was.

'That's why I need you, Guy, for your friendship and your good sense, but above all for your conscience, but now, on the eve of battle, I need your strong right hand.'

All I knew for certain at that moment was that I had no ambition to be a king.

# CHAPTER TWELVE

Wulfram had won his bonus. We tied up at Basle two hours before his five day target was up, though his men looked as if they would need a week or two to recover from their exertions. For much of the last twelve hours, they had been working at the sweeps, rowing their fat barge into the open mouth of an increasingly freezing gale. It didn't bode well for the Alpine passes. Winter was showing his teeth.

It was a good many years since I had last been through Basle, but I didn't realise just how long at first. When we left the boat and loaded the horses, the men from Genoa were being difficult.

'They want a good inn tonight,' said the squire after listening to an absurdly passionate speech from di Provan. 'I can hardly be bothered to pass this on, but they say conditions on the boat and on the journey up to this point have not been anything near the standard they expect.'

I had been saying a brief farewell to Wulfram, ever a gruff man, who was aching to get off to the riverside taverns to sniff out some business for his return journey northwards. I mounted my horse and looked down at the squire. These people just did not understand that the trick of travelling is always to give up any expectation of comfort. If you can get through a long journey without losing a limb or contracting a major disease then you're doing well. I have been told by priests that I must think of travelling as time partly suspended because, while travelling, I do not get the chance to protect my soul with any dependable regularity. As I've said, I made use of such wayside shrines and chapels as fitted in with our brief rest breaks. William led our daily prayers, but knowing he was only paying lip-service to my soul's concerns took some of the comfort away from that. I got up early in the morning and stayed up late at night to pray and to search out more certificates wherever I could find them, but I knew I was in danger of losing ground and there was not much I could do about it. I stared down at the squire and wondered whether it was time to bring these absurd men to their senses, but I did nothing. I think I just wanted a bit of peace and quiet, and I already knew where we were going to stay.

'You can tell them they're in luck. I have in mind a place for the night which is entirely in keeping with their status.'

The Gentian was in a village ten minutes' riding from the City walls of Basle, but you didn't stay inside those City walls unless you had very long pockets. The Baslers thought travellers were just wandering purses, there to be helped by taxes to make those purses lighter. Even pilgrims had a hard time finding a cheap enough floor to lie on. Outside the walls it was different, and the Gentian was a place of surprising beauty, grace and even a measure of luxury. As I remembered it, they had more rooms than travellers and the beds were the warmest and softest anywhere. I was in some sort of dream because as we rode down that lane in the dusk, the circumstances of a previous visit began to come back to me. There's a crossroads in a clump of trees just by a bridge where you turn left to the inn, and the road was a lot worse than I remembered. Little Dafydd rode ahead to check the trees, then whistled the all clear.

It was only when we'd ridden for another minute or two

down the side road that I fully woke up to what was around us.

The neat hedges I remembered had gone. They had fronted each of the small, stone-built houses which had been remarkable for their immaculate order and the squared-off firewood piles which sat under the wide eaves, always so perfect that you could run a ruler down the front of them. There had been chickens, ducks and geese, but instead of running in the road, as they would anywhere in England, they had been penned up beside the houses in neat enclosures of woven hurdle. Now, where the hedges had been, there were unkempt tangles of trees and bushes. I slowed Arcite to a gentle walk and nudged him towards a gap in the hedge. Beyond it, what had been a house was now a ruined sprawl of stone with old, burnt timbers heaped in the centre. I stopped and the whole train of them behind me stopped too, and all I could hear to break the utter silence was the harsh cry of crows in the trees beyond.

I nudged him on, all my senses abruptly alight. Up a gentle slope, threading through saplings growing out of the broken road, we came into what had been the square, and there was the great ruin of the Gentian, the walls still standing, but the roof bowed in and creepers growing in profusion all over it, intent on their slow prying of stone from stone. I dismounted thoughtfully and ducked through the threshold where the door had once been. Inside was what had been the great parlour of the inn, and I took another step and another, puzzled in the gloom by the look of the floor, the heaps of ivory white which caught the last of the daylight, then I stopped abruptly.

Outside, none of them had dismounted, and my archers had fanned out around the company, bows ready, though from their faces I would say they were more concerned with the supernatural than the natural.

I walked out into the middle of that puzzled company. 'It

is a charnel house,' I said. 'They filled it with the dead and left them here to rot.'

Di Provan was muttering away, frowning, and now he got down and strode inside.

The squire was staring around him wide-eyed. 'Was there a battle?' he asked, and then he answered his own question. 'No, of course not. It was the Death, wasn't it?'

I nodded.

'Twenty-five years ago?' He sounded surprised. 'So have you not been here for twenty-five years?'

It made me sound like the worst of journey planners, but in truth I hadn't. Until that moment, I would have said it was ten years at the most, but I worked it out and it was even longer. It must have been in the year 1344, because it was after the joust for Elizabeth's hand and before the truce was broken and the war restarted. I had passed through here on a royal errand, combined as best as I could with a pilgrimage. Oh, how often that had happened. How was a man supposed to balance the requirements of his king and his God? I had been taught that the King embodies God's divinity and that the King's service was part of one's service to God, but close experience of my king had soon made me realise this theory was more likely to have been dreamt up by a king than by a god.

I had been sent to Avignon, to the Pope's Palace, under the dubious protection of a French safe passage document, with a sealed packet to deliver and then on to Rodez with a letter ultimately intended for one of the King's bankers. It was strictly diplomatic business, but it was hard not to use my soldier's eye to note the typical mess they had made of that town. I could remember it now – the usual thing, an old fortress village on the hill, still with sound walls, a new town down at the bottom with its own set of walls and nothing connecting the two but a sprawl of unprotected houses and hovels. Any decent commander could have reduced them to abject surrender in two days.

183

As I pictured it in my mind, I knew my memory was doing its best to protect me with distractions and irrelevancies because something else was spreading alarming tendrils out towards me. What had happened next? What happened after Rodez? That huge brute memory was coming shuffling around the corner of my mind just as my men were shuffling, anxious to leave this terrible place. Then di Provan strode out of the remains of the inn and began to shout in fury.

'What's he saying?' I asked the squire, glad to come back to the present whatever it might contain.

'He says you have insulted him and his party. You said you would bring them to an inn fitting to their status and he takes the gravest offence at this extremely bad joke. He says he demands an immediate apology in front of everyone.'

'Then he's the stupidest man I have ever met. No wait. You don't need to translate that. Tell him he is entirely mistaken and I did not know the fate that had overtaken this place. Tell him we will return to Basle without delay before it gets any darker, and there we will find suitable lodgings.'

It made no difference, perhaps because his friend di Mari seemed to have understood my comment about stupidity and whispered something to his compatriot which deepened the flush on his cheeks. Di Provan shouted at me.

The squire sighed. 'He says he demands for the sake of honour that you apologise or fight him here and now in this place, and then your own bones may be left here with the others.'

'Look, tell him that normally nothing would give me greater pleasure than to fight him, but sadly I am charged by my king with the responsibility for his personal safety as far as his own country, and if I killed him on the way, I suspect that would be regarded as treason.'

More shouting.

'What's he saying now?'

'Oh, nothing,' said the squire.

'Come on. You have to tell me.'

'He says you are a coward and an ignoble buffoon.'

I climbed down off dear Arcite thinking it might be easier to make di Provan see sense from ground level, but he misunderstood, drew his sword and rushed at me. King's instructions or no king's instructions, I really didn't have any choice. I pulled out my dagger, caught his sword blade on it and twisted it out of his hand. The bloody fool picked it up and came at me again, so this time, having had enough, I drew my own sword and sent his blade flying out of his hand so that it cartwheeled through the air. Well, blow me down if he didn't pick it up a third time.

I know it wasn't very gentlemanly, but this time, after I disarmed him, I booted him up the backside as he turned to find it again, and when he fell over on his face, I stood on him until he stopped struggling. That caused a bit of fidgeting among his pals, but my archers were up to that. It was hard to see an easy way out because I was fairly sure that once I let him get up he would just go for me all over again. I respect determination even if it is extremely stupid.

William Batokewaye solved the problem. He had taken little interest in the proceedings, seeming to be very far away in his own thoughts. Now he got off his horse and came down to kneel by di Provan's head. He began to address the prostrated Italian very earnestly and quietly in what seemed to be Latin judging from the odd word I could make out. When he got up, he looked at me, nodded, and said 'I think you can get off him now.'

'What did you say to him?'

'I told him I was under no instructions from our king and was therefore free to fight him whenever I chose. I told him I would enjoy severing his head from his body and I was only looking for an excuse. Oh, and I also mentioned that I'd always been a better swordsman than you were, even with only one arm.'

'That's a bit of an exaggeration.'

'You may think so. I don't.'

We both walked away, and di Provan was immediately surrounded by his solicitous friends. He scrambled up and talked to them intently while William and I got back on our horses.

'Does the disease still live in places like this?' asked the squire, apprehensively.

'Who knows?' I said. 'Best not to find out.'

'Are there places like this in England? I've never seen one.'

'There were some, but wooden houses rot fast and stone doesn't stay empty long in our country,' William told him, 'Are you not old enough to remember the Death?'

'I was five when it came first time,' he answered. 'My father took us away out of London. I don't remember it at all. I was eighteen the second time. I remember that all right.'

'It came for the poor people first time,' I said, turning Arcite and giving the signal to follow, 'and it came back for the rich.'

'Did you go to a safe place or were you close to it?' the squire asked, bringing his pony up on my right.

'A safe place? Were there any? I suppose there were. When did it reach London? The end of '48? I was in Calais. It didn't hit us too badly there. I was in a new-built house, clean and airy. That helped.'

'So you missed it.'

'In a sense.'

William, riding on my left, snorted so loudly I thought for a moment the sound came from his horse. 'Missed it?' he said to the squire, 'You've no idea. The King sent him right to the middle of it. Bristol and Gloucester in '49. Then Cardiff. It's a miracle he's still here. King's special commissioner to find out why the townsfolk weren't burying their dead. Simple answer. There weren't enough of them left. Sir Guy here, he got them organised.'

'So that must have been a truly terrible year, '49,' observed the squire.

'England before the Death and England after the Death?' William mused. 'They were two different countries. One crowded, the other desolate. It was indeed a terrible year.'

I thought to myself just how wrong he was. For me, '49 was probably the best year of my life.

The other Italian, di Mari, galloped up from the party trailing behind. He addressed the squire in a flood of Italian, delivered in a haughty tone, then turned and trotted back again.

'Lord Bryan, Signor di Mari proposes a solution to the present difficulty,' said the squire, very formally.

'It hadn't struck me there was a difficulty,' I said, 'unless I left footprints on di Provan's cloak.'

'He suggests that the matters of honour raised today are put to one side for the remainder of this journey but that on reaching his own city, they be resolved in the lists.'

William burst out laughing. 'He wants to joust! This I must see.'

The squire frowned. 'I think you need to take this one seriously. They told me he has quite a reputation with a lance. He says there will be no coronals.'

The coronal is the main reason more people didn't die in the lists. Its three-pointed crown fits over the end of the lance and dulls the impact.

'He wants plain wooden tips?' I asked.

'No he doesn't. He wants steel blades,' said the squire. 'He wants blood.'

'It will be his own blood,' said William.

'It won't be anyone's blood,' I said angrily. 'I cannot accept.'

'I don't see why not,' said the big priest. 'He thoroughly deserves it.'

'He may, but I'm afraid it makes no difference. It's not just my duty to the king. I swore an oath I would never joust again.'

William looked at me curiously. 'You never told me that.'

'There may be many things I haven't told you.' I knew as I said it that it would not pass any rigorous test of truth. There was only one that mattered. He knew the rest.

It wasn't quite a lie, but perhaps it contributed to my uneasy night, There was another, much bigger, reason for my restlessness. Back in Basle I needed a church badly and the one I found that evening gave a thirty-day certificate for prayers made to their relic. That completed the process of unlocking old memories which had begun in front of the charnel inn because the relic just had to be a relic of Saint Foy. The old memory brought the screaming demons into my dreams and woke me so that I sprang out of bed, fending off their tridents in a sweat, and then stood looking out onto the misty midnight streets of Basle, loath to run the risk of sleeping again.

How could I not have remembered that I had stayed at the Gentian on *that* journey of all journeys?

Saint Foy is a very powerful saint, and her main church is, of course, at Conques in the hills to the north of the valley of the Aveyron.

I seem to be dwelling more and more on the past, but I must get it all right and ordered in my head. The year I went to Conques was the year that I was so utterly consumed by guilt, so burnt up by it that in the gaps left for thinking, I could think of nothing else. None of that guilt has gone. It lives in the back of my head, unassuaged, but now it has the horrid comfort of an old accustomed pain to it.

In that year, 1344, the seventeenth year of Edward's reign, just after the Windsor tournament and Hugh Despenser's marriage to Elizabeth, Edward had given me charge of Abergavenny Priory. By that time, he had started to use me as a safe lodging for any property or money or responsibility which was in dispute between one or other of his nobles. I was generally trusted, it seemed. On this occasion he coupled with it a tricky little bit of business concerning his oldest son,

Prince Edward of Woodstock. Now, I know it is becoming the custom to call Prince Edward 'the Black', after the figure he cut in his black armour at the great tournaments, armour, by the way, that worked rather well in the twilight of the final and most crucial jousts of the day, making it very hard to hit him accurately. I did hit him though, and he often became quite annoyed when the coronal left bright metal scratches through the black paint. It has also been the habit of many to call him Edward the fourth, in anticipation of his future reign, which feels presumptuous to me. Now that he is an ill and enfeebled man, unlikely to return to full health since he caught the dropsy in Spain, that feels an even more dangerous assumption. Anyway, I still think of him as Prince Edward. This one was a complicated deal involving a loan to the Prince from Montague, and the King sent me off to see if Montague was claiming more out of the deal than he deserved. Somehow, I'd been persuaded to guarantee the loan, so if I didn't succeed, I could easily have been left out of pocket. The King's service was rarely simple.

I went to see Montague at his castle, the very same place where I had been locked up the previous year. This was old Montague still, in the last year or two of his life, though I have to say old Montague and young Montague turned out to be two from the same root. It's as if the King kept a mould somewhere in his palace marked 'Earl of Salisbury' and when he needed another one, he just poured in the wax. The old man still thought that he had persuaded me to let Hugh have Elizabeth's hand and that then, out of pride, I had accepted nothing from him in exchange. I could tell he was unsure whether to regard me principally as an honest man or as a fool and I was determined, with the King's delegated authority on my side, to take a firm line with him in the matter of this money.

I arrived unheralded and unexpected, late in the day. That was unmannerly, but I had been given no option and I had also been delayed on the road by an absurd attempt at robbery. Dinner had already begun, and they made an extra space for me in the great hall. It was quite an occasion. I think Bohun was there and Mowbray and many others, though what happened later has clouded that part of my memory. I was right down at the far end of the table and I was starving after riding flat-out all day. It was some way into the meal before I looked up from my food and that was when I saw a woman's face leaning forward between the men up near the head. She was leaning and looking towards me, and as our eyes met, I saw it was Elizabeth, my dear Elizabeth, Elizabeth Montague who was now Elizabeth Despenser, and who still held the high ground of my heart however much I tried to think as I should. As our eyes met, she turned her head away as though my look had burnt her, but I knew she had been watching me, watching and waiting for me to look up.

I went to bed in the west tower that night in a room which had not been warmed. Anxious about my business and intensely disturbed by my first sight of Elizabeth since her marriage, I walked backwards and forwards in the dark wishing I was anywhere else in the realm and on any other business. I should have bolted the door.

# CHAPTER THIRTEEN

'Gran says there's something you have to tell me,' said Beth when the silence stretched out too far for her, and that was when he misunderstood her completely.

He nodded. 'That's right, there is. Did she say anything about it?'

For a moment, Beth couldn't remember the phrase Eliza had used. Was it 'the old duty'? It was something like that. 'Not really,' she said.

'It's not very complicated,' he said after another long silence. 'You just don't expect it. Particularly when you feel quite well in yourself.'

'What?'

'To hear the words.'

He glanced at her, but she was looking mystified. 'So Gran wasn't talking about my problem?' he said.

'She was talking about some family duty. I don't know what she meant.'

'Oh right, I'd better explain.'

'No you hadn't. You'd better tell me what *you're* talking about. It sounds far more important. Are you ill?'

'I was having a spot of pain in the gut. Indigestion. It's been going on for quite a while. I went in for a check-up and now the doc tells me it's a little bit worse than that.'

Beth could find no proper reaction to his words. She could find no clue in his face as he looked impassively at her and then back at the sea. What did this have to do with Eliza's old mysteries? She just shook her head and he went on.

'I thought they'd do another operation, you see, but it turned out it was a bit too late.'

'You've got *cancer*?'

'Yes.'

'And it's too late to operate?'

'There's a sort of cancer that spreads very fast, Beth. A bit like a bushfire. That's the image he used. The good thing is you don't know much about it until pretty far on.'

She thought of the letter. 'So that's why you wrote to me?'

'Yes. That's right. I'm sorry.'

She thought she could look at him and just see this as an intellectual problem, a puzzle to sort out, the sort of thing that might have come up at work.

'Why are you sorry?'

'Springing it on you like this. I thought Gran might have hinted at it, you see? Softened the blow a bit.'

'How bad is it?'

'Oh it's been all right up to now, poppet. I'm starting to notice it now. It's beginning to get uncomfortable. They've got very good stuff for pain.'

'How long?'

He looked up at a gull which hung in the air for a moment before them.

'A few weeks, they think. Maybe a couple of months, but maybe less.'

She'd expected him to say a year or two. Even six months would have been a shock. Her first thought was that she wouldn't know how to miss him, that she'd written him out of her official life so long ago that there was no space for loss, but that was just on the surface. Somewhere in the middle of her, a great hollow cavern was beginning to form in the rock. In the suppressed, unaddressed core of her, down where the little girl's anger lived, she had always thought one day they would be close again. It was something she was saving up, something inevitable for the time when he was older and she was kind enough to forgive him. Three or four weeks wasn't nearly long enough to deal with this.

'I know we haven't got along,' he said, 'not for the past ten years anyway. I know I haven't been everything you needed. A girl needs a mother. Eliza did what she could, but between us, I don't know . . .'

He stared down the beach where a middle-aged man was weaving up and down, fanning a metal detector in front of him. They both watched him bend to dig in the shingle.

'You always did your best,' she said, as kindly as she could.

'Yes, I did,' he answered with surprising firmness. 'I'm not apologising, Beth. I'm just talking about the circumstances.'

For the first time in her whole life, it seemed absurd to Beth that they never talked about her mother.

'I've probably been a bit hard on you,' she said.

'Yes, you have,' he replied, and when he saw her face, he said, 'there's only time for the truth now. Doesn't mean I don't love you.'

The way was open for her to say the same, but it was all rushing at her way, way too fast. 'I don't think you approve of me,' she said after a time.

'I approve of you. That doesn't mean I approve of what you're doing. I don't have to. I don't think you approve of what I'm doing either. You think anyone still down here is wasting their life. That's plain.'

'Why don't you approve of what I'm doing?'

'I'm not sure it's for the right reasons, if you want to know.'

'So tell me why I'm doing it, then.'

He nodded. 'I suppose I asked for that. Did you see what they called you in the *News of the World*?'

'No. I didn't know you read it.'

'I don't. A man in the pub showed me. It said you were England's Joan of Arc. It said you had Winston Churchill's brain in, I don't know, some actress's body.'

'Jennifer Lopez?'

'I think that was it. Is she pretty?'

'Very.'

'So you did read it.'

'No, I just heard that part of it before.'

'You shouldn't look so happy about it,' he suggested. 'The rest of what it said wasn't quite so flattering. The personal stuff about you and this horrid man, Livesay.'

'He's not horrid,' she said automatically. 'Look, Dad. I need a bit of time to get used to what you're telling me.'

'So do I, Beth. So do I. Didn't you guess when you read the letter? I thought you might.'

'No, I expected it to be something about Gran.'

'It is really, isn't it? I see her every day. Often three or four times. I haven't the faintest idea what to do about that. I worry about her and her heart. Who's going to look after her? She's been, oh I don't know, very *wise*, I suppose you might say, since I told her. She knows how to help me keep my chin up and she hasn't said a word about where it leaves her.'

They stared at the sea. Both of them, Beth was thinking. I'm going to lose both of them and where does that leave me? In this fiction I've invented of having no family. For the first time she knew what that would really be like in fact, not fantasy.

'She told me I had to get you to tell me something, but it wasn't anything to do with this. She called it the old duty.'

'Oh Beth,' said her father, frowning. 'It's got *everything* to do with this,' then she saw he had tears running silently down his cheeks and she found she was crying too, but they didn't reach out to hold each other because they were both so out of practice.

That moment of weakness was short-lived. The man with the metal detector was walking up the beach towards them, his boots crunching into the shingle. Beth dried her eyes with the back of her hand.

'Hello mate,' he said as he came up to them. He nodded at Beth. 'Hi there.'

Beth's father levered himself to his feet. 'Hello Ronnie, found something?'

'Yeah. Dog tag on a bit of chain. Couple of rounds of three-oh-three. I buried them, kept the tag.' He held it out for their inspection. The chain was a rusty ball and the ID tag was bleached and scraped by the waves and the shingle.

'American?'

'Reckon so,' said Ronnie. 'I'll send it off to the Yanks. Doubt they'll be able to read it. See you soon.'

'Year after year after year,' her father said as he watched the other man make his way, splay footed in the loose stones, up the last steep rise of shingle behind them, 'it goes on turning up. All that stuff left behind, and the sea slowly brings it back.'

'What are you talking about?' Beth said.

'Oh come on. I told you about it often enough. You wrote an essay about it. The 1944 exercises.'

'Yes. One went wrong, didn't it?'

'More than one.' He stared out to sea as if he expected to find something bad coming out of it. 'Exercise Tiger. Six hundred and thirty-nine men died out there, heading for this beach. April twenty-eighth 1944, early in the morning. They were men on exercise, men not expecting to meet their maker, not expecting to be machine gunned by German E-boats, but that tag's not one of theirs. They died way out there to sea.'

'Who's is it then?'

'There was a lot of blood spilt right here. Friendly fire. That's what they call it now, isn't it? The ships firing short while the men were landing. Just practising. Bang, and all that's ever found is a rusty dog tag sixty years later.'

'Men, as I remember, practising for the D-Day invasion which rescued Europe from Hitler, Dad. It happens in war.'

'Beth, it happens *because* of war.'

'And wars happen because of evil men who have to be stopped.'

'Evil? Now there's a big word. Isn't it like "infidel"? Just something you say about people on the other side?'

'Hitler?'

'Yes, he's the easy example, isn't he? But it's not always like that. Sometimes it's just men's pride, and a little insult that grows and grows into a war which kills thousands and thousands of people who didn't give a toss about the insult in the first place.' A big bird flew overhead, gliding towards the reeds around the Ley. 'You take that fellow,' said her father, 'he was used to start a war once. Some French lord served up a roasted heron to our King Edward. It was an insult you see, the French thought the heron was a cowardly bird, so our king swore an oath for revenge and we were fighting the French for the next hundred years.'

'I've never heard that one.'

'Lewis told me. I forget the details. You should ask him.'

'Lewis, Lewis, Lewis. I'm always being told to ask Lewis. What is he? Brain of Britain? Why do you and Gran have this thing about Lewis?'

He sighed, 'He's been very good to both of us. I always thought you liked him.'

'Dad, we went to school together, that's all.'

'You went out with him.'

'When I was eighteen. That was a mistake. Anyway, that was a lifetime ago.'

'You were a beautiful couple.'

'Oh God.'

'I didn't mean to offend you,' he said, and once again it

sounded like a statement of the facts rather than an apology.

His face was grey, and this seemed to Beth to be the wrong moment to sink back into the disagreement that always waited just below the surface when they were together.

'What happens next?' she said.

'A bit of supper? We could go to the pub.'

'I meant about you and your . . . your illness.'

'So did I,' he said, getting up. 'I've only got a few suppers left, so let's make the most of them.'

The Chantry tower rose on the far side of the wall, looming over the pub. Lewis was the very first person Beth saw as she walked in to the bar behind her father. She would have ignored him, but he didn't give her the chance.

'Evening you two,' he said, nodding at them. 'Did you get much done Beth?'

'A bit.'

'Use it any time you want.'

They sat in a corner and people she had not bothered to think about for several years came up one after another and welcomed her home with a simple friendliness which had her groping for the right response. Their food came and they were left alone to eat. She had chosen duck, her father had a small salad and showed no great interest in eating it.

'The old business,' she said, 'or did Eliza say "duty", I forget. Anyway, it's time to tell me, I think.'

'In here?'

She rolled her eyes and made a show of inspecting the walls. 'No microphones, no spies. I think we're all right.'

'All right. If you like. I suppose it's the right place really.'

'Why?'

'Did you know, apart from the tower, this is probably all that's left of the Chantry? It was probably the part where the priests lived. If you go outside, you can see it all lines up.

197

No one's ever done any proper digging here. You'd think they would have done.'

'Come on, Dad,' she said, a little irritated. 'Cut to the chase. I want to know about this duty thing.'

'I'm telling you,' he said sharply. 'I'm telling you in my own way. There's a lot of history to this and you'd be as well to listen.'

She blinked and, looking down, cut a pink slice from the duck.

'Before we were Battocks,' he said, 'we were Battockways, and before that we were Batokewayes. If you look in the history of the village, you'll see that the very first priest put in charge of Slapton Chantry was William Batokewaye.'

Despite herself, somehow that got to her. For the first time in her life a bony finger reached right out of the past and poked her. Discomforted, she had to fall back on the distancing tool of logic.

'If he was a priest, we can't be his *direct* descendants, can we? Weren't priests celibate?'

'We are,' he said firmly. 'There were priests and priests, and maybe this was a priest who didn't take his chastity too seriously.'

'How can you possibly know? When are we talking about? Thirteen hundred and something?'

'We've still got the old back page of the family bible. That's where it's all been written down.'

'From the 1300s?'

'No, of course not. From about 1680, but they copied it all out very carefully with a note saying it was written down in the year 1547.'

He looked at her as though the date ought to mean something, and she shook her head.

'Don't you remember your history?' he asked. 'Didn't they teach you about the dissolution of the monasteries? Henry the Eighth and all that?'

'Yes they did, but I've been a bit too busy with the present day to bother too much about Henry the Eighth.'

'That's a pity, I'd say. Everyone should know their history. You know what they say, don't you? "Those who don't know their history are doomed to repeat its mistakes."'

'Yes, Dad, I do know they say that. They also say the only thing you learn from history is that no one learns anything from history. Somehow I don't think British foreign policy and our attitude to the growth of the invisible terrorist state crucially depends on my understanding what Henry did to a bunch of Catholic monks in 1547.'

She'd said it too loudly and too harshly, and his face fell. She knew other people had heard and that she had embarrassed him.

'Eat your salad,' she suggested.

'I've no appetite,' he answered, and she felt the reality of the dwindling number of meals he had left to eat.

'I'm sorry,' she said. 'I didn't mean it to come out like that. You tell me what you want to tell me and I'll listen.'

'I know this is all going to sound very odd,' he said quietly. He cut a tiny triangle off the end of a slice of tomato and put it in his mouth. 'After he got rid of the monasteries, Henry got rid of the chantries too, and nobody could stop him,' he explained when he'd chewed a few times. 'Outside the church, not that many people cared any more. All those rich men had built chantries because they were terrified they would be tormented in purgatory if they didn't. Well, they say Thomas More was the last man brave enough to stand up for those old ideas, and Henry sent him to the Tower. After that, they said relics and purgatory and all those things were nothing more than superstition.'

He chased a piece of cucumber around his plate for a few moments then left it. Beth felt a little embarrassed by her own appetite.

'Henry wanted the money,' her father went on. 'A chantry

like this one had a lot of it. Land and precious bits and pieces. They had endowments so there would always be money to employ the priests and have the masses sung. He had them shut down and he retired the priests and he sold the lead off the roofs and he flogged the buildings to his cronies. That was what happened.'

'And nobody cared?'

'No, or perhaps nobody dared. Except here. Slapton was different. There was a man here who still cared. They'd been singing the masses for Sir Guy de Bryan for a hundred and seventy-five years, and he wasn't about to see that stop.'

'Was he the priest?'

'No he wasn't. We don't know exactly what he was. It's just his name, written down in the family bible, and the line that says what he decided. He was Guy Battockway, and what he wrote down in the bible is still as clear as day.'

'And it says?'

'It says, "From this day forth it is the sworn duty of this, the Battockway family, to say prayers for the soul of Sir Guy de Bryan on his day from now until this family shall last."'

She might have laughed if she hadn't already seen what that did to him and she had a suspicion that Lewis was keeping an eye on them over his glass from the far end of the bar.

'So why haven't *you* been doing this?' she asked gently.

'I have,' he answered, surprised. 'Of course I have. That's the point. I've done it for the past five years. That was only when Eliza got a bit too unsteady to go climbing over walls. She always thought it should be a man really, but I didn't like to take over until I had to. I always went with her before that, ever since I was a boy.'

'You never took me,' she said, astonished. 'You went and did this and I never knew?'

'I tried to once. You must have been about eight or nine. You wouldn't have it.'

200

The slimmest of memories came back to Beth of unreasonable requests and childish rebellion.

'Did you explain?'

'You didn't give me much chance to.'

'What walls were you talking about? You said Eliza couldn't go on climbing over walls?'

'We say the prayers in the Chantry,' he said, seeming puzzled that it shouldn't be obvious. 'His Chantry. We do it in Sir Guy's old tower.'

'But that's private, isn't it?'

'That's why we have to climb over the walls.'

'How often?'

'Just once a year. On his special day.'

'That's the day Eliza was talking about, saint someone's day.'

'That's right. Saint Petronella's Day.'

'When is it?'

'May the thirty-first.'

'That's in a month's time,' she said.

'Yes. That's the whole point. Eliza wants you to come with me.'

'I don't mind doing that. If I'm here, that is. A month seems a long way away. Why does she . . . Oh.'

He was looking hard at her and he nodded. 'That's right. So you'll know what to do next time.'

'Me? That's what it's all about? Me taking over? What? You think I'm going to come back down here every year and do it? Have you any idea what you're saying? I don't even believe in God. I don't say prayers. This bloke's been dead for six centuries. What do I care about him?'

'Please be a bit quieter. People are looking. I told you it would sound very odd.'

'More than odd,' she hissed. 'It sounds completely bloody mad.' She swallowed another mouthful of duck and didn't notice the taste. 'I've got a life,' she went on. 'Do you really think I can drop what I'm doing and come down every May just to say words I don't believe for a man I know nothing about?'

'That's the point. I want to tell you about him, Beth. We've always known about him. The story gets passed down. Eliza does it because of the story. I've done it because of Eliza. If I tell you, you might understand.'

She shook her head.

'Don't you even have a feeling for the tradition of it?' he asked her. 'All those generations of Battocks stubbornly keeping it going, refusing to let a king tell them what to do? Doesn't that appeal to you? You're always preaching about freedom.' He stopped himself. 'Sorry, I didn't mean to say preaching,' but it was too late. She had lost patience with him.

'Don't tell me what I believe,' she said. 'You don't understand me. Just think about it, Dad. This is some stupid old story of Gran's and she's been spinning you along with it. I don't care what you say to her. Tell her I came with you if it makes everyone feel better. I've got better things to do.'

She took a twenty pound note out of her wallet and put it on the table.

He looked down at it then back at her. 'Do you have the right to make that decision? All those people, your family, stretching back so long, keeping it all alive? Do you have the right to cancel out everything they've done?'

'Yes, I do. I have the choice, that's the great thing about life. I don't have to subscribe to someone else's fantasy.'

He shook his head.

'I'm going for a walk,' she said more gently as she took in his forlorn face. 'Don't lock the door if you go to bed. I'll let myself in.'

'I never lock it.'

She walked through the bar concentrating on the path ahead and resolutely refusing to look at the faces. She got half-way across the yard outside, dodging around the parked cars, when she heard the door open and shut and rapid footsteps behind her. Then a hand touched her arm and a voice said, 'Hold on a minute,' and she swung around in fury to find herself face-to-face with Lewis.

'Let me go,' she said, and he held up both hands.

'I'm not touching you,' he said. 'I can guess what happened in there. I just want to talk.'

'Guess away, Lewis. It was between him and me.'

'Beth, I know about it. I know about the Petronella mass. Eliza told me about it ages ago.'

'You and Eliza, you're pretty pally, aren't you?'

'There's no need to be jealous. We talk to each other a lot. She's your Gran, not mine. Listen, there's no reason to get mad at your dad. He was going to let it all drop. Eliza forced him. She said if he didn't tell you, she would.'

'Is this what you do for a life, Lewis? Is it the most important thing? Plotting with old people about mad prayers in a ruin full of brambles?'

'There's a bit more to it than that,' he said, and his calmness made her want to get under his skin, to hit him in any way she could.

'You've just given up, haven't you?' she said. 'You've come back here and you've just stopped. Well, I'm not making that mistake. I hate this bloody place. Eliza's the only part of it I give a toss about. I wouldn't be here now if I'd had anywhere else to go.' She wished she hadn't admitted that as soon as she said it.

'You didn't come back because of Guy's letter?'

It came as a shock to hear her father called Guy. She never thought of him as Guy.

'Is he called after this bloody old knight of yours?' she asked incredulously.

'I expect so. There've been Guys in your family for years.'

'Lewis, I don't know my family history. I don't want to

know my family history, and I certainly don't want to know it from you.'

'Fair enough.'

'Why don't you get my father to adopt you?' she said with heavy sarcasm. 'Eliza would love it, then you can sing in the tower to your heart's content. That's if your parents wouldn't mind.'

'My parents died. You obviously didn't hear.' It was a simple flat statement.

'Christ almighty. I go away and everyone dies. How am I to know?'

He was silent.

'I'm sorry,' she said, but it sounded entirely empty. She had gone too far and as her anger started to leave her, guilt was pushing its way in. She tried to hold onto the anger because it felt better than guilt.

'I'd really like to know what makes you so upset,' he said.

'Oh really. Do you want the list? Coming back here and finding the whole bloody place still in the middle of the last century. Thinking people here just might be a little interested in the wider world and realising all they can think about is ancient history. Finding you stuck down a hole with a hammer and chisel.'

'Beth, I'm completely happy doing what I'm doing.'

'More fool you.'

'Why do you have to take it out on Guy?'

'Oh just stay out of it will you?'

'No. He's in a bad way and he's being very brave. You've bullied him since you were tiny. It's time to stop.'

'Bullied him?' she snapped. 'What the hell do you mean by that?'

'Well, since you ask Beth, you've never been fair to him. I used to see you doing it at school. You were always imagining insults before anyone said them. You'd go for people before there was any reason. You're still doing it now, in fact it sounds like you're making a profession out of it.'

Her blood ran ice cold then. 'What are you saying?'

'I read the papers. I've read about you and your ideas. It reminds me of the playground all over again. Same problem, same solution.'

'Listen to me Lewis fucking Tucker, I come back here after seven years and you dare say things like that. You are a fucking Devon peasant and you don't have the first idea what you're talking about. My father is my business not yours.'

She expected him to turn and go, but he stood his ground. 'You've had a hard day,' he said. 'I shouldn't have put it like that. I love your dad and your gran and you may not believe it, but I'm on your side too. I don't change, you know. If there's anything I can do to help, I will,' and then he walked rapidly off into the darkness before she could find anything at all to say in reply.

Too angry to think about going back inside, she waited until he was out of sight and walked slowly down the lane to her father's cottage, intending to go straight to bed so that the night could wipe the slate clean. As she went to turn the handle a voice spoke from the gloom beside the door and she realised that the darker lump against the wall was a person.

'Hello Lizzie-Beth,' said the voice. 'Are you by yourself?'

'Gran?'

'Lewis just came by, going like a steam train. Never seen him go so fast. I thought you wouldn't be far behind.'

'Were you waiting for me?'

'You or Guy or both of you. I reckoned there'd be some putting right to do tonight.'

The edge of the moon showed above the cottage opposite, and the shape that was old Eliza seemed to shrink.

'Aren't you cold?' asked Beth. 'Wouldn't you like a cup of tea?'

'Later. I don't get cold any more.'

'Shall we go inside?'

'No. I want you to come with me.'

'Where?'

'Just upalong. A little walk. Not far.'

'Isn't it a bit late for you to be going walking?'

In the growing silver moonlight, Eliza's eyes gleamed.

'It'll be a bit late for everything if we don't.'

Disorientated by the darkness, Beth found it quite hard to keep Eliza's small, dim figure in sight as the old lady set off. It was an extremely roundabout route which first took them out to the outskirts of the village, then through a gate into a field of soft, sticky earth, recently tilled, then along a hedge uphill and through a gap in it towards the top. Eliza never slackened for a moment. They came back down on the village as if ambushing it, climbing through holes in fences, bending down to slide between wires and, finally, levering themselves over a stone wall into a flower bed full of shrubs.

Here, Beth finally caught up with Eliza. 'What are you doing? This must be private property, isn't it?'

'Quieten down girl. Just stay quiet and walk behind me,' Eliza whispered, and Beth's only other choice was to accept abandonment there in unknown territory. And that was when they came out from a copse of small trees and she knew what she should have known from the very first, that they were in someone's garden and that Eliza's objective was the Chantry tower, rising right in front of them with silver moonlight on its ivy-covered stones.

'We'll stop here,' said Eliza in a low voice. 'We won't go in. I haven't got the puff to say a mass and you shouldn't go in there without saying one.' She turned around and felt in the shadows with her arms outstretched. 'There's a bench here. Sit down.'

'Have you brought me here to tell me about this business of the duty, Gran? I've had quite a bit of it today you know.

First Dad then Lewis telling me what I've got to do. I have to tell you, I'm not really in the right mood for any more.'

'Shut up girl and listen. You're as spitty as you ever were. I'm not telling you a damned thing about the old duty unless you choose to ask. If it wasn't for the old duty, you wouldn't even be here, and before there's no one left to tell you, I thought I'd better.'

# CHAPTER FOURTEEN

The facts are simple enough. I was pacing around my bedroom in the west tower of the castle and I was a long way from sleep. There was business going on in the castle that night, men talking loudly in a room below which echoed up the stairs, and sentries laughing on the battlements. I would have come down hard on them had they been my men. Even in the middle of the longest peace, even in the middle of the safest country, a sentry is a sentry and if he's having a joke he's not doing his job. This wasn't a time of true peace, just flimsy French truces and the constant threat from Scotland.

They weren't my men.

Because it was a cold night, I put on enough of my clothes to keep me warm and sat on the sill looking down at the moat. To limit the path of my thoughts I set myself a mental exercise, working out a means of attack. This wasn't too hard because they'd been very sloppy. They had foolishly let a copse of small trees grow up on the ridge, allowing a concealed approach. Worse than that, the moat itself was partly blocked below me by a pile of timber which must have been thrown down from the roof. A well trained band could have been inside the castle in minutes. I was at the far side of the castle from the cell where I had been imprisoned, and perhaps it was the memories of that imprisonment which prompted such thoughts.

All I was trying to do was stop myself thinking of Elizabeth, but that was very hard in this place where Hugh and I had been incarcerated together, where she had walked in the yard below us and prepared the ground for all that followed. There aren't good words to describe how I had felt at the meal table when I had met her eyes. In the moment before that, I had been only dully aware of where I was and who I was. My mind had been preoccupied by the business I had to do. I was half in my memory, listening to the King explain his wishes, and half in the future, imagining the path my discussions might take the following day as I tried to put those wishes into practice with an unwilling Montague. In the moment I looked up and saw her, I remembered who I was, as if my true self had been let out to rejoin me and there was no past and no future. It seemed amazing that no one at the table in between us had flinched from the scorching passage of that momentary glance. The force between us was stronger than ever.

Then I thought of her maid's message before the joust, and of the Tewkesbury wedding, and I resigned myself to the fact that the force had travelled in only one direction. I had come full circle back to this castle where I had first thought we might be one, only to be reminded that we were two.

The castle gradually quietened and the moon set. Even the sentries became so silent that I was sure they had fallen asleep at their posts. In the end I think I fell asleep myself sitting there by the window, because at first the opening of my door had the quality of a dream about it. Somewhere down below, on the spiral stair, there was a lantern still burning and a faint light from behind showed me my visitor had empty hands. Asleep or not, my hand had reached out towards my sword which stood in its scabbard against the wall close by, but then the visitor whispered, turning towards the bed, 'Sir, sir. Are you awake?'

The voice was female, with the burr of the local accent.

'I am,' I said, puzzled, and she whipped her head back towards me, startled. I realised that, coming from the lighter passages, she had not seen me in the dark window.

'Oh sir, I have a message for you.'

'Who is your message from?'

'From my lady Despenser whom I serve.'

From Elizabeth? A second message delivered by a maid-servant? I hoped it would be gentler than the first.

'Then please deliver it.'

'She said I must be sure not to be overheard.' The girl looked around at the stairwell.

'Step in and close the door.'

'And she said that you must not come close.' There was anxiety in her voice and I thought perhaps she had made that one up herself, knowing the hazards any young servant might face when caught alone with a man of unassailable rank.

'Then I will stay here. You can sit down over there.'

It was pitch dark now, but I heard her feeling around and then she sat on what I took to be the edge of the bed. There was a silence.

'You can give me your message,' I said encouragingly.

'My lady says that once before she sent you a message.'

'She did.'

'She says that she would like to know for certain and for her heart's ease that the message you were given was the same message that she sent.'

My first response was that Elizabeth had been angered by my glance at table. Did she want to be reassured that I had no remaining hopes of her?

'I am sure it was,' I answered.

'Was it delivered to you with a token?'

'What token?'

'A flower, sewn from silk for you to wear.' Why would

she have sent me a token? A token is a favour for a lady's champion. 'Was it?'

'No, it was not.'

'Then what was the message you were given?'

The maid's voice had changed a little. It had a touch of eagerness about it.

'Is this a proper thing for me to tell you?'

'My lady says to say to you that I have her complete trust and you may speak to me as if I were her.'

'Then I shall tell you for her ears what the message said. It said that your mistress's affection was with me but that her love was with another.'

There was a sigh in the darkness. 'She wants to know this then. Did you lose the joust for that reason?'

'What else could I do? I would not have stolen her love from my friend and I would not have condemned two lovers to misery.'

There was a silence and I thought I heard a suppressed sob. Every one of my senses was focused on the bed and the woman sitting on it. When she spoke again, her voice sounded thick.

'My mistress will be very sad to hear this. It is not what she would have wished.'

'It is what her message said.'

'It did not. It said the reverse. It said her affection was with Hugh Despenser but she loved you and you entirely.'

'What? How could it have? How can you know that? Were you with her at the time?'

'I was close to her as she gave the instruction.'

Then I was certain. 'Elizabeth, I know it's you. You can drop the accent.'

At the moment when I called her bluff and let myself speak her name, a dam burst inside me and all the dry wreckage of the past months was swept away. The world shrank to the two of us, sweet Elizabeth there, in my room, in the dark, on my bed, me four strides from her and no one else to serve as chaperone.

'I'm not Lady Elizabeth,' said the woman on the bed with an attempt at a laugh. 'I'm Meg, her maid.'

There was an edge of panic in her voice and, understanding the risk she was taking with Montague and a dozen other nobles in the house, I went along with it though it was not easy.

'Well then, Meg. That is the way it was.'

'You must listen to me sir. It was done by another man. He persuaded Alison the maid to say the opposite of what our mistress intended. All else has followed from that.'

'And is your mistress happy, Meg?'

'It is still as it was. Her husband has her affection, though that is not enough for him and he is apt to show his unhappiness with the state of things.'

'And who has her love?'

'The same man who always had it.'

There was nothing to be done and that room became a stretched cord of misery between the two of us, alone together and alone separately in the darkness of knowledge, and I thought then that it would have been better not to have known.

She broke the long silence with a faltering question, 'My mistress wishes to know if that man feels the same?'

'Tell her that man feels exactly the same. Go. Go away and tell her that now.' A tide of emotion was sweeping through that room. It was not a safe place for a man and a woman to be together when they had both found out that they had made the worst mistake in their lives.

Another long silence and then Meg's voice spoke again, the accent stronger than before.

'I don't need to go.'

'You do. You mustn't stay.'

'Sir, if I were a lady, a married lady, it would be most

improper, but I am a serving girl and you must know that serving girls sometimes comfort gentlemen on a cold night like this one, when the house is asleep and there's no one to know.'

There was nothing coquettish in her tone. She spoke simply as if it were the obvious truth, and this time she spoke in Elizabeth's own voice.

I got up from my window seat and I was moving towards her as if swimming against a fast flowing river. I still couldn't see her, but I could smell her scent and as I got nearer, I could feel a growing power in the air between us.

I make no excuses. I was as fully aware of sin as I am now, and I lived my life by moral rules, so what was it that let me move? It was the knowledge that Hugh had won her by fraud, by so dishonourably subverting her messenger. A man who had been my friend had tricked me out of the thing I most wanted, the transformation of my whole life. That allowed me to suspend all normal rules.

I sat down on the bed next to her and her hands found mine. Just holding them was the headiest experience imaginable. I felt her breath on my cheek and then her lips on mine and after that I was lost in the sweetest, warmest meeting of my life. She led me all the way, and as she slid my clothes from me and covered me with her body she said over and over again, 'I am Meg, I am Meg,' but it was still Elizabeth's voice.

When sanity came back to us, I was lying there in that blessed bed with my arms holding her as tightly to me as it was possible to hold her while she slept. My fingers traced the shape of her shoulders and her back and I was so happy that I knew I must find a way to hold on to it, a way to change this fate of ours. It seemed to me there was a way. The tournament was that way. The rules of chivalry had been broken by the man I had fought in clean combat. Hugh Despenser had gone against the King's own wishes, the King's own rules. If I could explain that to Edward he might annul the marriage and call for the joust to be taken again. Would he though? He might hear me or he might not. If he did, would he do anything about it? He might just as easily regard my own actions as a breach of chivalry, for no one should ever give less than his best in the tiltyard. But surely he would take Hugh's breach more seriously?

I kissed her cheek and she stirred. I kissed her again and I felt her eyes open by her eyelashes moving softly against my face.

'I knew you let Hugh win,' she murmured.

'How did you know? My lance was no more than a hand's width from where it should have been.'

'I knew by the way you held yourself as you came into the lists. I could feel a hurt in your mind.'

'Why did you think I would do such a thing? Did your maid admit what she had done?'

'No.'

She was silent.

'So why then?' I insisted.

'I was told my father made you an offer of money and estates and that you had accepted it.'

'I threw it in his face.'

'I know that now. I learnt that part by chance at the table tonight. Until that moment I had not even known you were here. Thomas Holland was disputing with the others over whether they could name a truly honest man and he said he knew a man who had refused every bribe ever offered, and then he named you. They talked of Stoke Trister, though they kept their voices low so my father wouldn't hear. I have keener ears than they supposed then all at once Holland said, "By heaven he's with us, right down there with the commoners'," she took off his deep voice to perfection. 'I looked down the table and saw you and I kept on looking until you looked back, and then I

214

knew what I had to do. I knew I had to find out why you did not fight for me.'

'How could you have believed that?'

She sighed again. 'I've lived all my life with intrigue. My family never does anything by the straightest way. I knew I loved you but I didn't *know* you.'

'I thought I knew Hugh,' I whispered in the dark. 'I always trusted Hugh. I cannot believe he did such a thing.'

'Did what?' she asked, her breath warm on my face.

'Told your maid to say what she did.'

She stiffened in my arms, 'Oh no, Guy,' she said and I froze, 'it wasn't Hugh. Hugh wouldn't have done that.'

'Then who was it?' I asked in a voice I could scarcely master.

'It was Molyns,' she said, as if that should be obvious.

I could not move a single muscle for a moment, paralysed by the terrible implications of what she had just said. I still held her, though I knew I had no right to do so, no right at all. I forced myself to let her go and sprang from the bed.

'Molyns?' I demanded. 'Why Molyns?'

'Come back here,' she said gently. 'Because Molyns wanted me . . . wanted my lady.'

'No more of that. *Molyns* wanted you?'

'You must have known that, Guy. You knew he killed Badlesmere. He tried to force himself on me and Badlesmere came in. An hour later Badlesmere was dead. Since then I have had to beat off Molyns' intentions two or three times every year.'

'He has a wife.'

'Gill? Gill Molyns would not live five minutes if he thought he could have me instead.'

'Have you told anyone else? Have you told your father?'

'Molyns has him in thrall. He would not go against Molyns.'

'So Molyns tricked me into giving you up to Hugh? But how did that help?'

'He thought he could deal with Hugh more easily than he

could deal with you. He is much more afraid of you. Oh, and he hates you. That's just another small part of it.'

Well, I knew that, but I seized on it to delay the moment of facing the horrifying truth of what had just happened.

'Why?'

'Guy, for many reasons. Because you've got his lands and he has to hide. Because you have the King's ear where he used to. Above all, because you are day and he is night.'

'Is he here?'

'Not in this castle, but he is never far from the Earl.'

Then the demons came howling into my head and I saw the awful shape of what I had done, a towering thunder-head of betrayal. 'Hugh was my friend,' I said. 'I have betrayed him in mortal and venial defiance of all the laws of God and man. I have committed the greatest sin imaginable.'

She was silent, staring at me as if I had somehow changed.

'You must go immediately,' I said. 'We must both go straight to find a priest and confess and do penance.'

'There's no priest here I can trust,' she sounded horrified at the idea. 'They'd go to my father. You mustn't confess here either.'

'We can't leave it.'

She got off the bed and stood next to me, pulling her robe around, and I had to step away from her.

'Perhaps it was a sin,' she said quietly and sadly, 'but I don't believe God would think so. He knows the truth of all actions and he must know that the truth is you are my real husband, not Hugh.'

There was just that one step's distance between us and there was just a heartbeat of time, and it could have gone one way or the other. I stood there too long. She left the room without another word. The cold night closed in around me with the crushing awareness of the great sin we had committed, filling my head so fully that I could not even move from where I stood for fear of the bed where we had committed it. I stood there until dawn came up and showed me the crumpled sheets.

I did my business badly that next day, and Montague looked at me in curiosity. I know I should have made confession straight away, but I thought of what she said and I did not trust his priest. I rode and rode for the rest of the day on smaller tracks until I found a church in a village I had never passed before. There I confessed the full story of my sin, omitting only the names, to a priest who looked at me in what I thought was too much pity. He gave me such slight penance that I argued with him for more. You know inside you when you're freed of your sin, and I wasn't. It pressed me down so hard that I could feel the floor beneath my feet dent with the weight of it. I told him so and he seemed unsure what to say or do, then a look of inspiration came into his eyes and he told me the story of the martyrdom of Saint Foy, or Saint Faith as people call her in England. He suggested that she was the saint who could help me best and that, if these troubled times allowed, I should visit her relics at the church of Conques for a fuller expiation.

Thinking back, I have no idea if his intentions were kind or cruel because he told me only of the relics and didn't make the slightest mention of what else I was to find in that place. He was not a clever man and I had the sense that he had clutched at a vague memory of Conques to get me out of his way, but that makes it worse, not better. That means he was led by divine inspiration to send me there.

It was on that journey that I had last stayed in the Gentian, that charnel inn of ours, on my way to Conques. I could not wait to go, being unable to sleep properly, constantly tricked by my dreams into remembering that night over and over and over again. The opportunity came quickly. At court they were casting around for someone for an Avignon errand, to take a letter to the Pope, but the King was very reluctant to let me do it.

'It's a job for a messenger, Guy, not for you,' he said. 'I may need you. This truce isn't going to last. We'll be back in France within months with swords, not messages. This Pope claims to be a peacemaker but I don't trust him. He's French through and through.'

I got my way in the end. I told him I had personal business.

'What is this business that troubles you so much?' he asked. 'I see I mustn't press you. Go on then, but take the Rhine route, then travel by Grenoble and Sisteron. You have a messenger's safe pass, but I don't want you taking any risks and I want you back soon.'

'They say there's a letter to go to Rodez too, my Lord.'

I knew Rodez was near Conques.

'Rodez? Is there? Ah yes, perhaps there is. You have an appetite for that too, have you? What a mystery.' He was having his beard cut and he waved the barber away, dropping his voice. 'I don't want you away for any longer than you have to, but I see I mustn't get in your way. They like dealing with you, these Frenchmen. If there's anything honourable to be gained from parley then you're a good man to have around. I doubt there will be, but you never know. Don't delay.'

I went as he said. It was mid-summer and I had a fast passage. My business at Avignon was so menial that once I had handed over my document and received rather cursory blessing from a cardinal, they didn't even offer me food or board and I had to find a lodging for the night in the town.

I don't now remember the journey from Avignon to Rodez, except that when I arrived, the man I sought wasn't there and I had to ride half a day more to find him at Estang. I left my pair of horses in the care of an inn there, squeezed between the desire to act as a proper penitent pilgrim should and the need to fit in with my king's tight timetable. From Estang, I took to my feet to climb out of the steep valley of

218

the Lot Gorge, up the winding trail to the ridge above. I was on the pilgrim route that ends at Santiago de Compostella and I was not alone. Determined to drive myself to exhaustion, to make up in effort for what my pilgrimage lacked in distance, I overtook men every mile on that route, all with the staff, the hat and scallop shell badges of the true pilgrim, and they looked at my soldier's garb with curiosity because it was the wrong clothing for that path. It was a stout walk and it felt as if I were travelling through land that stood a little above the rest of the world, so that the occasional views between the trees down on to the plateau were clear and wide and pure. I craved purity. My skin itched with sin and I had scrubbed myself to rawness.

I came down a steep and wooded hillside to Conques in the middle of the afternoon. It was a village laid out along the eastern contours of a winding valley, half way up the side, and I looked down beyond it to the narrow stone span of the pilgrims' bridge crossing the Dourdou stream taking the path on the next leg of its journey to Spain.

I walked through the village towards the great church of Saint Foy, pilgrims everywhere around me. I swung downhill into the square at its end and approached the building, prepared for proper penitence and proper absolution, and then I saw the carvings.

# CHAPTER FIFTEEN

A pilgrimage should not be easy or pleasant, though I know many people these days make such journeys as much to get away from the troubles of home as from any proper concern about their souls. High up on the hills, I passed one like that, a man wearing the scallop shell but with both arms up under the tunic of a giggling farm girl, whispering and nibbling at her ear. He had no shame at all and I thought him likely to return home with many more sins to his name than he had left with.

But the worm inside me envied him and made me remember and sin again in remembering. I hurried even faster towards penance.

I had a sense of certainty that something was waiting for me. I pushed my way down the crowded street that led into Conques, past a goat, lying on a wall, lifting its head and languidly scratching its back with the end of one curled horn. The abbey church was built of a warm yellow stone capped with small stone tiles which looked at first sight like wooden shingles. A stubby tower rose from the transept, surmounted by a large dome. I came into the cobbled square and the doorway in the west end stood before me. Above the double doors, a huge and intricate carving filled the semicircular space under the archway over the doors. I glanced at it and was about to go inside, intending to make my offering to Sainte Foy as soon as possible, when the ebb and flow of the crowd produced a momentary clearing around me and a lanky man in rags came bounding across the square, stopped in front of me and stared into my face from far too close. His hair was long and knotted, his teeth were few and far between and his breath stank. What he was wearing looked more than anything else like the remains of a shroud, and I recoiled from him as you might from a risen corpse. He laughed, and in the French patois of the region, which I could follow easily enough, he said, 'I see the colours of your sin.'

'What colour is it?' I said uneasily.

He just studied me closely, moving his head from side to side and darting it at me as if he were a beast deciding which part of me to bite.

'A fresh colour,' he said. 'Your sin is new. A burning colour too. Your sin is great.'

'I have come here as a penitent,' I began to say, 'I . . .'

He put his face closer than ever, 'Silence,' he said. 'Before you enter this church you must understand what has been put here for such as you. Give me money.'

I tried to turn away, a little relieved that he was just a beggar.

'Not for me,' he said, 'for the lepers. I am charged with showing you *this*,' he hissed the last word, spraying me with his spit, and flung his hand up at the carving over the door, 'and for that service, your sin obliges you to be *generous*.'

I reached into my purse and gave him my heaviest gold coin and he put it away in some fold of his grave clothes without even looking at it.

'Now listen to me very carefully and despair,' he said. 'What you see above you is the Last Judgement, carved under instruction from Saint Foy herself more than two centuries ago by the hand of the divine and blessed Begon. Look up

221

at the fate which faces you!' He had turned to the church and his voice had risen almost to a shout, but I looked and once I had looked, I could not look away because what was carved there in the stone went straight to the root of my sin and told me there would be no easy escape from what I had done.

I didn't need his description, but as my eyes wandered, appalled, all over that vision of my soul's future, his voice hammered home the images like nails into my skull.

'On the *left*,' he intoned, 'are the righteous and the blessed. On the *right* are the damned, and *you*,' he said, swinging back to crane his face into mine, 'are one of them. You are a knight, I think, yes? Yes?'

I nodded.

'A man practised in war. You have killed men, yes?'

I nodded again.

'And pretended while you killed them that God was only on *your* side? Yes?'

I could only nod again.

'But that is not your greatest sin. Look, sir knight. There *you* are, do you see?' and he pointed to the lowest of the three bands of carving and there I was indeed, me in stone armour with my stone horse, swallowed by the gaping beast's mouth of hell, tumbling down, prodded by pitchforks down into the fire.

'Your greatest sin is flaming in you and you will not put out that flame easily because it is a mirror of the flames that will consume you when you *die*. Look up there and see your certain fate.'

In the middle of that terrible stone sat an angel and a demon weighing souls in the balance, and the demon's finger was pressing down on the scales to make quite sure that sin received its full weight and more. The crowds of the pious and the righteous were lined up in the safety of the left hand half, where all was ordered under the watchful gaze of protecting angels, but I could find no comfort in that for I had left their ranks that night in Montague's castle, and I knew I now belonged on the right, beyond the realm of the seated Christ at the centre of it all. On that side of the divide, devils were hanging sinners upside down to flay the flesh from their bones, roasting them on a spit over searing flames. I could not take my eyes away and even when the corpse-man stopped his intonation, gave up on me and loped away to a fresh victim, I stood there, staring and staring at the old carving until there was no detail I had not carved equally deeply into my own memory. There was a man bent over under the weight of the demon on his back. The demon was eating his brains while the sinner plunged a knife into his own throat in a hopeless attempt to escape by a death that was no longer at his own command.

I stood there so long that I did not notice the crowd around me gradually lessen and the light begin to fade, and when I came out of my trance and stepped inside the church on stiff-ened legs, I found the famous relic of Saint Foy already shut away, locked in safekeeping for the night. An old priest stood by the transept, his arms folded, watching me as I lit a candle.

'You must come back in the morning,' he said. 'No confessions now, no access to the relics, not unless you have an offering.'

'I have brought gold with me,' I said.

'As indeed you should, for it is a great guarantee of your intent,' he said. 'But have you brought a precious stone, an emerald perhaps or a sapphire?'

I shook my head.

'We are decorating her image with precious stones,' he said, 'and those that bring them may see her when they want.'

'I will give you gold to buy a precious stone.'

'It is not in the giving but in the bringing. You must come back in the morning.'

'Please. I cannot wait.'

He laughed as if he didn't really care. 'You'll have to. Just don't die tonight, that's all, or Purgatory will have you. Otherwise your confession will be as good in the morning.'

I had not studied Purgatory at this stage in my life. 'Is that Purgatory, carved outside?' I asked him.

'That is Heaven and Hell,' said the priest. 'There was no space for the horrors of Purgatory, and no chisel sharp enough to reveal it.'

The truth, as I now know, is different. It was carved before the horrors of Purgatory were fully revealed to those of us alive on earth.

There was dust in the air, filtering down from the dome in the evening light, and as he spoke there came a faint groan from somewhere up in the dome as if the church itself were complaining at my presence.

He walked off. 'Go away,' he said over his shoulder. 'Come back tomorrow,' and as I reached the door and turned to genuflect, it seemed to me that the last rays of the sun made a curtain across the dusty transept too thick to see through, depriving me of a last sight of the altar.

I tried the pilgrims' hall which stood behind the abbey-church, but it was so full that they had put up the sign for no more admittance. There was an inn in the square, but it was the same story and, where in England they would have always made space for a gentleman or a knight, here they had no such sensitivities. I went from pillar to post, to less and less likely places and then in a house that was no better than a tavern, they told me to try the pathway down to the bridge, and knock at the first door on the right after the rowan trees. There was laughter as I left, but I did not know that it was directed at me.

I walked for some way down the hill below the village and found a large shambles of a house just beyond the grove of trees. I knocked at the door and it was opened by a dirty woman of some age in a state of drunkenness. I told her I needed a bed and she said something quite incoherent. Then I held up some coins, said it again slowly and loudly and she hiccuped, raised her eyebrows and told me fairly plainly that I could have her finest room.

'Would you like refreshment?' she asked, but I could now see that the room behind her contained several men in the same state as her, being served by two pot-girls with wild hair and painted faces. Why they were allowed to behave like this in a place of pilgrimage was quite beyond me but perhaps, being so far down the hill, they were out of the abbey's immediate control.

I went up to my room and if that was the finest, I had no wish to see the rest. There was a wooden balcony where I could sit, ignoring the singing and the yells from down below, looking out at the valley with the lanterns of Conques gleaming through the trees above me. Knowing that I must leave in the morning, I decided that I would be up at first light to make my offering to the relic of Saint Foy and tell the story of our downfall to the priest. Her whole body was there in the abbey, I had been told. A sliver from her skull, sliced away at her martyrdom by her killer's blow was preserved inside the head of the seated golden statue, the Majesty of Saint Foy, and the rest of her bones were kept in their reliquary, rediscovered by the monks five hundred years ago.

Sitting on the balcony, preparing myself for what was to come, I suddenly understood what I must do. I knew that I must take the sole responsibility for the sin. It had after all been me who crossed the room to her, and if I had only stood still, she would have gone away. If Elizabeth refused to accept there was a sin then I must take both shares, hers and mine. I knelt and prayed to Saint Foy on that balcony until my legs were shaking with tiredness, and when it was dark and the house below had quietened, I levered myself to my feet, stripped off my clothes and lowered myself onto the bed. It was the usual biting bed that you find in all but the best inns, full of tiny pain, and I knew in the morning my body would be covered in red swellings, but I was in the mood for a hair shirt and I did not mind at all.

I was hoping for an answer as I lay in that bed, moving slowly into that gentler state between sleep and waking, and as I lay there, I had what I took to be the first vision of my life. White sparks rushed across my vision, circling into the centre and then, in the gloom of the wooden roof beams above me, I found I could make out the shape of a face in the rough lime plaster between them, the face of the saint above me, looking down. She had a huge head with wide eyes, and she told me in a deep, deep silent voice that I was right to come to her.

'If you are truly sorry,' she said, 'you will be forgiven. You must kneel before my bones tomorrow and do them honour. Forgiveness will only be yours if you confess in honesty the full and detailed extent of your sin and decide in your heart that you will never, ever repeat it.'

I asked her a question in my head. It had no precise words but it meant how will I be sure? How, when I have gone away from here and my mind flails my soul with the nail-tipped lash of conscience, how will I still know for certain that I am forgiven?

Her face dissolved, but I felt her presence there, under the roof, and I heard her words.

'I will send you a sign,' she said.

'A sign that will leave me in no possible doubt? I am a great doubter.'

'A sign that will leave you in no possible doubt. Now tell me what you have done.'

The room was dark and it was easy to relive it, to imagine once again the door quietly opening, the quiet footfalls to the bedside. There was a potential for further sin just in

226

remembering it. This time I was on the bed, not sitting on the windowsill, but I smelt Elizabeth as she stood next to the bed, felt her weight as she sat down on the edge of it, saw the profile of her against the starlit window and then knew again just how it had been to be carried away from conscious choice by the silky touch of skin as she slid over me. I was trying to explain it all carefully to Saint Foy in my head, trying not to enjoy the memory of the sweet, close heat of it. I knew all over again that I had not been strong enough, that no man with red blood flowing in his veins could ever have been strong enough to resist the rising, all embracing, boiling passion of that ever-faster act of love, and I was searching for a way to explain that to the saint when I was woken fully by a laugh and a loud profanity and found myself on the bed under the pumping, arching figure of one of the pot-girls from down below, her long hair flying backwards and forwards over her head as she drained me of my final chance of salvation.

I threw her off me and she fell on the floor, cursing and shrieking in the dark room.

'Pay me,' she said, then louder, 'are you too good for me? Pay me. Pay me or I'll wake the house.'

'I didn't ask you to come to my bed.'

She laughed derisively. 'What else did you come here for?'

What could I do? I opened the door, threw coins onto the landing outside and pushed her out, then I sat in horror on the edge of the bed and tried to find some lurking trace of my saint in a corner of the roof. She was gone as if she had never been. A full confession, that was what she had demanded, that and a promise never to repeat my sin, and there I was, repeating it even as I tried to confess.

I scrubbed at myself in the bowl, put on clothes and sat in complete misery out on the balcony while I tried to clear my head. I heard more laughter downstairs, as if my succubus was sharing her tale and my blood ran chill. Then I got down on my knees to pray, determined to go on praying until daylight and then to pray at her bones whether she would hear me or not. I had my eyes fixed on the dark loom of the abbey church up the hillside far above, and was mumbling words of contrition when I heard her church make that same groan again, the groan I had heard as the dust fell from its great dome.

That is her rejection of my prayer, I thought. She knew when I first entered her church that I would only sin again, and that was the sign of her displeasure.

I wish it had been only that.

The groan came again, and then a third time and that time it didn't stop. I kept on trying to pray, louder and louder above the rising roar, but the words I spoke were drowned by the immense thunder from above which filled the whole echoing valley. It was the stone-sound of a mountain falling. It chased the words out of my head and I stared up the hill expecting to see my death coming in a rock-slide through the trees, but then the noise abated into individual bangs and crashes. That was when the shouting began from the houses above and the lanterns began to flicker until a choking cloud of dust swirled down the hill in the wind and blotted them out.

A man raced down the path, shouting the news of what had happened as he ran, and I prayed in terror right through the rest of that night.

At first light, I climbed up to the village again as if going to my execution. I came to the abbey church from the south, through a side-alley as the road to the square was entirely blocked by people. I saw in the first pale rays of the sun coming up over the plateau behind that the dome on the transept tower had utterly disappeared and that in its fall, it had taken with it a large part of the roof and a slice of one wall of the church. The west end however, still stood undamaged, with the awful carving accusing me of my doubled and trebled sin.

The priest I had met the day before was toiling away in a group of men, hauling shattered timber and blocks of stone out of the collapsed remains of that wall.

'Are the relics safe?' I asked him and he looked at me as if I were mad.

'I have to make my offering. I have to pray to her relics,' I explained and perhaps I was a bit strange in the head after that night of mine.

'What do you think we're doing?' he said angrily. 'Do you think we're doing this for fun? We're searching for them. Give us a hand. You can say all the prayers you like after we find them, but the treasury chamber's under here somewhere, so come on, get to it.'

I bent with a will and started to heave at a large stone, and then I heard the priest say, 'Wait a minute. Stand up. Let me look at you.'

He peered into my face. 'I've seen you before, haven't I?' he said.

I nodded. 'Yesterday evening.'

'You asked about the relics. The church made a sound as if it hurt. That was its first sound. It was you. You made this happen. Who are you? What are you? How did you do it?' He had begun to shout and the other men were looking up from their task. He turned and started to denounce me to the crowd.

'He made the church groan. I heard it. He wanted to see the relics.'

A man near him, covered in stone dust and bleeding from a gashed arm, stared at me. 'The saint stopped him. She brought the dome down to protect her bones from him.'

'I'm a pilgrim,' I protested.

'You don't look like one,' he snapped. 'You don't sound like one. You're English aren't you? He's an Englishman.'

I turned and ran because there was no choice.

# CHAPTER SIXTEEN

'He was sorry for what he'd done, poor old man. That's why he built it.'

Eliza was looking up at the tower and Beth couldn't suppress a sigh of exasperation.

'It was something about his wife and it was something about fighting wars. Guilt and more guilt. That's why he put his words up there on the side. That was the war part of it and that's why we keep up with the old duty.'

'It wasn't your war, Gran.'

'It *was* my war, you stupid tart.'

'That's not very nice,' Beth said weakly.

'Not trying to be nice,' the old woman said. 'I'm trying to get into your thick head. Always quick to say what *you* think. Time to shut up and listen, I'd say.'

'Hang on. You said you weren't going to talk about all that ancient stuff. You said you were going to talk about something else.'

'I'm going to tell you about what war does. What it did to me. Then maybe you might think twice before you go out and start another one.'

'I'm not trying to . . .'

'Shut up, I said.'

Eliza had always had the capacity to dominate Beth, all the more so because it happened so rarely and mostly on those occasions when Beth had a niggling suspicion that she deserved it.

'I told you about how I came down the ditches that time. We'd all had to leave. They told us in November. Sir John Daw, that was him. He was a bigwig from the County Council and he came down here and called us all together in the village hall and then he told us for the good of our country we had to pack up and go and not ask any questions nor tell people anything. Well, we guessed what it was all about you see. Very secret they were, but there'd already been exercises. Back in September, these Yank soldiers had come up the beach. We all turned out to watch them. Wasn't much like real war. They didn't even get their feet wet. The navy unloaded them on the beach and they strolled up the sand, cool as you like, and that was that. They'd have dropped in at the Royal Sands Hotel for a cocktail if it hadn't already been blown up. You know that story, don't you? That old dog, old Pincher, he stepped on a mine and set them all off.'

That was the way the whole story had come down to Beth, not from her father nor from Eliza, neither of whom ever talked much about the past in any form, but from school and from the old folk of Slapton. It was as if the whole of the Second World War could be summed up in the story of the local dog who had set off a minefield and utterly destroyed the village's main source of income and the only landmark on that long expanse of shingle.

'Nice hotel, that was, up 'til then,' Eliza went on. 'The Prince of Wales, he used to stay there.' She tailed off for a moment, dreaming of old times and, possibly for the first time in her life, Beth felt a twinge of curiosity about young Eliza.

'I was up back, staying with the aunts, helping with the farming with all the men away. We took the cows up there when we got thrown off. There was only me, you see. Your great-grandfather never came back from Burma. He'd made me promise before he went that I'd do the you-know-what on the right day at the right time.'

'The mass.'

She saw Eliza nod in the darkness.

'We weren't allowed back in, you see? It was a huge bit they closed off, all along the bay and then backalong as well. I was going mad with worry. I'd given my solemn promise I'd keep it up while he was gone. Never thought he might not be back. I'd done it in '41 and '42 and '43, but come '44, they wouldn't let me through. I went to the barricades to tell them I had a job to do in Slapton, and they said they'd do it for me if I told them what it was. Well, I couldn't, could I? I know they had to keep it all tight. Thing is, they were practising for the invasion, for Normandy. Landings and that. Blowing everything up. If the Germans got to know, well then, they'd have wondered why Slapton? Then they might just have put two and two together, see, and thought, well blow me down, there's beaches in Normandy just like this with a lake behind them, and marshes. Then it wouldn't have been no secret no more. Anyway . . .' she fidgeted a bit. 'I was in my overalls. Dark brown and they didn't show up and I had my hair in a black scarf and mud on my cheeks. Proper commando, I was. Scared stiff, 'cause they said anyone caught inside the area would be shot on sight, you see, and I believed them. I think that was true. There was road blocks on all the roads and patrols in all the fields, but I wriggled along under the hedges and I hid when I had to and they didn't stand a chance of finding me, those poor little soldiers. It was a strange land to them. Now I knew what was up cause old uncle Timothy, the one with the bad lungs, he was on Coast Watch and he had to spend night after night sitting up there beyond Beesands with his binoculars which wasn't that much good because one of his eyes got gassed at Wipers in the first lot. Nineteen eighteen. Two weeks before the end of the war, poor old sod. Anyway, he'd seen what was going on and though he wasn't meant to, he told us after he'd had a pint or two of cider. He knew it was big. They were up there one day right by the start of the forbidden bit and they heard two men talking the other side of the hedge so they jumped on them. Do you know who it was?' Eliza was chuckling.

Laurel and Hardy? Abbot and Costello? Beth could only think of comic duos. 'No.'

'Montgomery and Eisenhower, come to watch the show. Monty and Ike, imagine. They told old Timothy to go away and forget he'd seen 'em. Some chance. Anyway, we could hear it all going on. Over the New Year, then right through March, you'd hear the guns all banging away and he told us they were ships, shelling the beaches, then the men would come ashore, like it was for real. Told us some of the houses were getting knocked about a bit and one of the sentries told him the bridge over the Ley was gone and the old limekilns on the beach. Then come April, he walks in one morning with a face like curdled milk and he says how it's all gone wrong and there's ships exploding way out east across the bay.'

'Exercise Tiger,' said Beth.

'You don't always have to know the answer.'

'Sorry.'

'I was there, not you.'

'I know.'

'Germans got them, didn't they? Those fast little boats of theirs, they got in among them out to sea, out there in the dark with guns and torpedoes and all that. Killed hundreds. Mind you, the Germans never realised what was going on, just thought they'd struck it lucky. Wasn't just the Germans. Then there was another big go after that. Lots of shells and gunfire. You could lie down on the ground where we were

233

and feel the earth shake. I used to sit there by our gate staring this way, staring at the hills, wondering if we'd have anything left to come back to and if the whole village would be flattened, tower and all. Anyway, you don't want to be hearing all this.'

Beth didn't say anything, not sure how to respond.

'Well, you're going to whether you want to or not,' Eliza went on. 'You see what happened was, I came crawling down the ditch. Got past the last of the sentries and then I was very careful, see? I came around this way 'cause you can stay out of sight easier and I waited back of here until it was well dark, then I came into the tower. We always sang it at midnight, see, so I waited and waited. I listened out and there wasn't anyone around and I thought I'd sing it really quiet to be safe. Anyway, I started off with the song just like my dad taught me. Sang it right through, and I was about to say the words, the Latin, when this voice spoke to me. I nearly died. This man, he was standing there just by the doorway on the outside and he said, "Are you an angel?" He had this deep voice and I knew he was a Yank and the thing is, he didn't sound like he was teasing, he sounded like he meant it.'

'Go on.'

'I'm going to. Got to get my voice back.' There was a catch of tears in Eliza's words.

Beth reached out to take her hand and the old woman flinched away for a moment, then her thin fingers came stealing back again, not quite sure what they were doing, and took comfort inside Beth's.

'"I've got a lantern here," he said. "Shall I light it? I don't want to scare you," so he did and then I could see him. He made a fine sight. "I'm a sergeant," he said, "First Engineer Special Brigade. Sergeant Jimmy Kimber at your service."'

'"You're not going to shoot me, are you?" I asked him. "Why would I do that?" he asked. "Because I'm not meant to be here," I told him. And he said, "I'm not either, not really."

234

'Well that surprised me, because he was a soldier so I asked him why not and he told me how he'd been with a unit on the last landing.

'"You know what's going on, don't you?" he asked me and I told him I did. "No secret to keep then," he said, "but there'll be one big secret if we get through this lot." "What's that?" I asked, and he told me about how the firing had gone all wrong and the shells from the ships and the tanks and all that had landed short and they'd landed in the men as they tried to get up the beach and how a whole lot more had been killed. He knew what had happened before, with that Tiger thing, but this was something new. This had only just happened that day.

'"I'm supposed to go back," he said, "back to Dartmouth and help get it all straightened out but I couldn't go." Then he sat down all of a sudden against the wall and he said, "Please go on singing. I need an angel."

'"Are you running away?" I asked.

'"I don't know. I guess not. It's crazy out there. They won't miss me for a while. I'll be back by daylight. Go on."

'So I sang some more of the mass, the way I'd been taught and I looked at him and in the light of the lantern I saw he was crying, so I stopped and knelt down by him.

'"Don't look at me," he said, "I'm a tough guy. Tough guys don't cry."

'"What happened to you?" I asked, gently as I could.

'"I joined the army," he said, but he didn't say it quite like that. There was a bit of a swear word in there too. So then he told me about what happened that day on the beach. Not details, just feelings. Anger that someone could make a stupid mistake and kill his friends.

'"Not even the other side," he said, "our guys did it."

'"Have you been in the fighting before?" I asked.

'"I've been in plenty of fighting," he said, "but not this sort."

235

'Do you know what he told me? He poured it out like he was confessing, like he was bringing up everything inside him to get rid of it, to clean himself out. He told me he'd been in a gang in Chicago where the gangsters come from. He said if you're born where he was and when he was you had a choice. You could starve on the street with no job or you could get in with a gang. He told me he'd done more than his share of shooting and being shot at. He rolled up his sleeve and he showed me the scar of a bullet hole right through his forearm, all puckered up.

'Then he asked me to sing again, so I sang that last bit, you know, the lovely sad bit.'

She seemed to have forgotten that Beth didn't know, and that feeling of exclusion, of not knowing, gave Beth a desire to know in a way that nothing else could have done.

'Then he asked me what it was all about, the singing, and I told him the story of Sir Guy and how we'd kept it going. He had a blanket and to keep warm, he put it around me and he sat against that wall over there and I sat against this one here and we told each other all about our lives, except he had a lot more to tell than I did because I'd never been anywhere and I'd never done anything much. I had to tell him something, so I told him more about Sir Guy and about what he had to say for himself about how wars start and what it does to people. I showed him.'

'What did you show him?'

'I was sitting by a bit of the stone, lying on the ground and I picked it up and I showed him the old lettering.'

'The stone that's up at the quarry?' She almost said up at Lewis's quarry, but she didn't want to let Lewis and his opinions into this private place.

'That's the one. It was just lying around in bits in the grass in those days.'

'Did you know what it said?'

'I'd always known. It was one of the things your dad has

to tell you when he passes it on. Not the exact words, not the Latin, but I know what it says.'

'Will you tell me?'

'No.'

There was no arguing with that flat answer. In the silence after it a fox called for a mate on the hillside behind them. Eliza seemed to relent a little.

'He was a good, loyal soldier, Sir Guy. But he knew that wars don't solve the problem. He knew wars are as often about pride as anything else. He'd had to swear the vow of the heron so he'd seen close up how it all starts.'

'What's the vow of the heron?' Asking Eliza meant not having to ask Lewis.

Eliza thought. 'I used to know it all once,' she said sadly. 'It was King Edward and he had these lands in France but he wasn't standing up for himself. He had to go and kneel in front of the King of France for permission or something so some Lord or Duke or Earl or something who wanted to stir it up a bit served him up with a roast heron. It was saying he was a coward, see? Funny way of saying it. I'd have gone straight up to him and said, "King Edward, you're a coward," but he didn't. Anyway, the king, he was so angry at it that he went and started a war with the French to show he wasn't one. Funny thing, eh? If they'd served him up a chicken, it would never have happened.'

'Go on. You told the sergeant that story. Sergeant Kimber.'

'Jimmy Kimber,' the words came slowly. 'Jimmy Kimber. Oh yes, I told him and he said his mother was German, imagine that. He said he might be fighting his cousins and they were decent people. It wasn't their fault they had Hitler in charge. I said maybe it was, and he said they'd been desperate. That's why they chose Hitler. Well, we agreed to differ on that. His lamp ran out of batteries but by that time it was starting to get a little bit light and we just went on talking and talking. Then he asked me if I'd sing the mass

237

again for him. "You're not dead," I said. "It's for the dead."
'"I soon will be,' he said. "Believe me, I soon will be."

'I said, "You don't know that."

'Then he said, "I do. I thought I was dead today when the shells started landing. I got down on the sand and the major was next to me and he got hit. He just twitched once and died, and another shell came down right next to us but it was on his side and it blew him right over my head. First good thing he ever did for me." That was what he said. Then he said he knew he wasn't going to make it through the landings. He'd seen his own death.'

Eliza turned her head towards the tower and her eyes stayed fixed on it as if she could use it as a landmark to find her way back to her sergeant. 'I wish you could have seen him there. He was such a fine-looking man. I sang him a requiem we'd learnt at school when the teacher got the TB and died, and I looked at him and I saw tears pouring down his cheeks and I had to comfort him.' She looked back at Beth. 'You must know how it is, Lizzie-Beth. There weren't any rules, not that night. There was me and him and I might be the last woman he ever touched and after talking all night like that, how could I not love him?'

Beth stared at her in dawning realisation of what Eliza was saying, not sure she wanted to hear this from her grandmother. Eliza seemed to sense her unease.

'I've only got you to tell and I'm telling you woman to woman before I die. You'll let me, won't you?'

And then something shifted inside Beth. She looked at the old woman and saw the girl of her own age looking back at her with something she had to say. Eliza's hand was still in her own and she squeezed it gently.

'Tell me whatever you want,' she whispered.

Eliza nodded and looked down at their hands. 'It was my idea, not his. He might have been a gangster but he was a gentleman. I went over to where he was sitting and put the

238

blanket around both of us and then I kissed him and I didn't have any thought of being careful or being sinful or anything like that, and I knew Sir Guy would have understood, knowing war like he did.' She looked up at Beth again. 'How many men have you slept with, Beth?' she asked.

Shocked, Beth tried to think. 'Why?'

'Don't be coy. I want to know.'

'Five.'

Eliza nodded. 'Five. What was it like the first time?'

The first time? Damn. She'd missed out Lewis. 'Six,' she said hurriedly.

'Well, what was it like?'

'I can't remember.'

'Don't give me that. Course you can. How could a girl forget that?'

And of course that was right. It was just that she had wanted to forget it, needed to forget it because her distaste about everything that was Slapton was imperilled by it. There could be no strings when she left this place, as she had been about to do. The trouble was, this bizarre night-time conversation with Eliza required total honesty.

'It was very sweet,' she said. 'Not the sort of thing you see in the movies, but very sweet.'

'How old were you?'

If she told Eliza that, the old woman would work out who it was. 'Old enough,' she said. 'Why do you want to know?'

'Because I can't imagine it ever being better than that time,' Eliza said. 'Oh, I didn't know anything and I suppose he did because it wasn't like anything else you could ever imagine. That made it all right, you see, because I've had my whole life to remember it and nothing else to get in the way.'

It took Beth a moment to understand what her grandmother was saying.

'You mean . . . You mean that was the *only time*?'

239

She saw the old woman nod once in the darkness and for a moment all she could think of was what her life must have been like in all the years since then.

'Did you ever hear from him?'

Eliza shook her head and she realised the old woman didn't trust herself to speak. Beth threw her arms around her and found she was sobbing herself and then the extraordinary, obvious conclusion finally dawned on her. This American sergeant, finding solace on the way to his death was the only person who could possibly have been her own grandfather.

# CHAPTER SEVENTEEN

Moving through the soft borderland between sleep and waking, Beth's hand was up by her cheek, fingering the familiar patch on the old candlewick bedspread which had been worn smooth by those fingers over the years. For a moment as she surfaced, she thought she was late for the school bus, then she smiled when she realised just how late and stretched out luxuriously. Bacon was frying downstairs and it was years since she had last smelt bacon like that, years since she had last slept in this bed.

The comfort of sleep's amnesia lasted only until her eyes were fully open, then, as she looked around her untouched room, it was washed out of her head by the wave of yesterday's revelation. The cardboard box of books she had brought back from university was still in the corner of the room. An old blouse was still on its hanger, hooked on the handle of the cupboard door. Nothing had changed and absolutely everything had changed. She unhooked the hanger and opened the cupboard, and there were all the other clothes of the former Beth, hanging there, bringing with them little darts of association. Down in the bottom of the cupboard an entire generation of shoes waited for nothing. She picked up her first high heels, the straps stiffened by a decade of disuse, and then quickly put them back down again, ambushed by disturbingly pleasant memories.

Her father had heard her movements on the old floor-boards and he called up to her.

'There's breakfast, Beth. Whenever you're ready.'

The only bathroom in the cottage was downstairs, out through the kitchen in the lean-to. She opened the cupboard again and there was her pink towelling dressing-gown with the hood she used to put over her head when she didn't want to talk to him. She put it on again now and it felt stiff too.

In the kitchen, he looked around at her from the hotplate.

'You must have been late back in,' he said and for a moment she took it for the old criticism, which it wasn't now and never had been.

'I was with Gran,' she said. 'Did I wake you up?'

'No, love,' he said. 'I've got sleeping pills that knock me out completely. I didn't hear a thing. Do you want one fried egg or two?'

So the scene in the pub was to be forgotten.

It was on the tip of her tongue to say she never ate fried breakfasts these days but she held it back, noticing how his arm shook a little with the effort of picking up the heavy frying pan.

'One please.'

'Kettle's just boiled. The coffee's over there.'

Instant coffee. Another forgotten taste.

'Would you like one?' she asked.

'No, I'm off coffee. I'm taking these homoeopathic tablets and you're not meant to have coffee with them.'

She had forgotten his fads.

'Tea then?'

'There's some fruit teabags in the jar. Can I have one of those?'

He put a plate in front of her and sat down opposite her.

'Dad?'

'Yes love?'

'Gran told me a story last night.'

He frowned at her. He seemed a little on edge, she thought.

'What was it?'

'It was about her. In the war.'

He said nothing.

'She told me how she met her American sergeant.'

'Oh yes?'

Just that. Oh yes.

'Dad?' Beth wasn't sure how to put it. 'Was he your father?'

'Yes, I expect so.'

'So I'm a quarter American?'

He sipped his tea and smiled.

She pressed him. 'Sergeant Jimmy Kimber was your father?'

His eyes widened a little. 'Was that his name?'

'Didn't you know?'

'She never told me.'

'What about your birth certificate?'

'It's a wartime certificate, love. It just says "unknown" in the father bit.'

'Doesn't that matter?'

'Well, I've wondered, but there's not much point.'

'Why do you say that?'

'Your gran says he would have come back if he'd liked, and really I don't think she knew anything else about him that she hasn't said. I thought I'd let his name be her secret if that's the way she wanted it.'

'Oh. Until I came blundering in.'

He shook his head. 'No, I'm quite glad I know actually.'

'But you never asked her?'

'You know how it is.'

'I know how it is in *this* family. Now we've started, is there anything else I should know about my mother?'

She'd grown up knowing the barest facts as if they had been implanted there at birth. Someone must have told her. Her mother had been called Tina McLennon and when Beth was only six months old, she had gone away and left them. That was all. Tina had gone away and never come back and her father and her grandmother had got on with bringing her up.

'I was wondering if you'd say that. I'll tell you anything else you want to know.'

'Yes, I think that would be good.' Looking at his drawn face, she saw something else in it.

'What's the matter, Dad?'

'I'm afraid there's a bit of bad news,' he said. 'You're in the papers again. Next door get theirs delivered. They came and told me.'

'What does it say?'

'I can get it if you like.'

'No, just tell me.'

'The headline said something along the lines of "mystery grows over Livesay girl's absence". It says you've gone to ground and no one's admitting where you are and there's growing speculation – that sort of thing.'

'Oh God.'

'I'm surprised they haven't been banging on my door already.'

What could she say? Nobody knows you exist? I airbrushed you out of my life?

'They will soon enough,' she said. 'If I'm the story, someone here stands to make a few quid by tipping off the papers.'

'They're not like that around here, Beth.'

'Everyone's like that, everywhere.'

'In London maybe, but not down here. I can put the word around if you like. I can explain you don't want anyone to know.'

'Dad, that would double the chances of someone picking up the phone.'

'These are people you know, people you've always known. They wouldn't do that.' He looked at her. 'I expect you've had a hard time in London, but remember this place has always been a bit of a sanctuary.'

'What do you mean?'

'Oh don't you think it has that feeling? It's got the Ley to keep the sea away on one side and miles of narrow lanes to keep people away on the other. You have to try hard to get here.'

'I suppose so.'

'Have you ever looked at the old ring on the church door? That's what they call a sanctuary ring. There's a long, long history to that old thing. If you got as far as that, and gripped it with your hand, nobody could touch you whatever you'd done. So long as you stayed inside the church, you were safe from the law.'

'I'll bet that wouldn't cut any ice today.'

'Maybe not, but maybe we're the poorer for it. What else did Eliza say last night? Did she talk about the Petronella mass?'

'We touched on it.'

'I just want you to know,' he said, 'that you don't have to do it.'

'Oh stop it, Dad. That's your oldest trick.'

'What do you mean?'

'That's what you always used to say about anything I didn't want to do. Homework, swimming lessons, piano. You knew I'd do it if you said that.'

He looked at her with genuine surprise and interest. 'No I didn't. I've always believed you should have the choice.'

'Who are you kidding?'

'No,' he said, 'I'm not kidding. I knew I had to be careful, bringing you up by myself. I had to give you a bit of scope. You didn't have anyone else to be on your side, except Eliza of course, and she was sometimes a bit too strict.'

245

'But you must have known I'd take it that way.'

He was shaking his head. 'Oh dear,' he said. 'How very perverse life can be.'

He was looking at his watch. 'I've got to be off in a minute. There's a school coming in to the Centre and I'm taking them around the Ley.'

'Should you be working, Dad? You don't look very strong to me.'

He put a hand on her shoulder and looked down at her. 'What would you have me do, Beth? It's what I like best. Every day that I can still get up and go down there is an unexpected blessing. I take them one at a time. Would you have me sit here and wait? I expect it will come to that, but I'm not going to give up until it does.'

After he'd gone out, she found there were tears in her eyes.


Lewis was in the shed when she got to the quarry.

'All right to use the computer?' she shouted over the noise of the machinery.

'I don't know. Am I still a fucking Devon peasant?' He was smiling as he said it and she couldn't help smiling back.

'Well, you're definitely from Devon and in those overalls you look pretty like a peasant.'

'Then my very latest technology is at your disposal.'

For over an hour, she sat there with her fingers on the keyboard, but the words wouldn't come. She wrote a paragraph and tried it out loud, doing her best to get somewhere near the Foreign Secretary's mixture of coaxing reasonableness and schoolmasterly imperatives. It just didn't work. She started again, forgetting about his style and just trying to get her own ideas straight, but Slapton got in her way. Somewhere in her head Eliza wagged her finger at her and undermined the certainty she needed. At eleven o' clock, Lewis put his head in through the door.

'Cup of tea?' he asked.

'Yes.'

'That's not a happy yes.'

'No.'

He brought in a mug for her a couple of minutes later and she noticed with a touch of irritation that he had his own tea in the other hand.

'I'm not up for any lectures,' she said, 'or any amateur psychology.'

'Just tea,' he said, smiling. 'Well, tea and an invitation actually.'

'Invitation?'

'If you've got writer's block, I thought a short walk might help.'

'Where to?'

'Where the Purbeck marble comes from, the green stuff. An even older bit of local history. Are you up for that?'

'Is that all? No more telling me I'm a bloodthirsty bully?'

'No, just the stone. You'll need overalls. There are some hanging up in the loo and I found a pair of boots that should fit you.'

The boots did fit, which was just as well because the way to the marble lay uphill through two fields and a wood. Lewis strode along with a toolbag in his hand and he pointed out the hollows of old workings in the grass.

'You've been up this way before, haven't you?' he asked.

'Only once.' She wasn't sure if he was teasing her.

He looked around at her as he walked. 'You were never much of a one for exploring. Was it by yourself?'

'You know very well it wasn't, Lewis.'

He nodded. 'I just wanted to make sure you remembered, that's all.'

In the middle of the wood, he pulled aside a sheet of tin and showed her a small tunnel, diving down into the earth at a forty-five degree incline.

'That's one of them,' he said, 'but it's not the right one for this.'

At the top of the hill was a small paddock, well fenced in. A sign said 'Keep Out, Dangerous Shafts'. Lewis unlocked a gate and held it open for her to go through.

'Is this yours?' she asked, looking around.

'This and the wood. It came with the quarry. They knew it might be useful again one day. See here? In the old days there would have been a windlass here, with a horse walking it round and round to haul up the stone.'

She could see a flattened circular area, and to one side of it, another shaft, angling down into the ground.

'There are steps cut,' he said. 'but they're very rough. Come down after me, then if you slip, I can stop you. Put one of these on.' He got two lamps fixed to elastic headbands out of his bag and handed her one.

'How far down is it?'

'Not that far.'

She crept down into the cramped tunnel just behind him, using her hands to steady her. The steps were just rough flats cut into the muddy rock and she kept looking behind her to make sure she could still see the daylight. When she reached the bottom, the tunnel entrance was the size of a coin held at arm's length and the temperature had dropped sharply.

These workings were much smaller and much darker than the quarry she had seen earlier, with a sense of oppressive weight above them. In three places, the roof was held up by more shaky pillars of stone slabs, piled on top of each other in columns less than a foot in diameter, wedged together. The roof itself was only just above her head, and Lewis was having to stoop.

'It's a bit claustrophobic,' she said.

'Do you need to go back up?'

'No, I'm all right for a bit.'

'Come and see down here.' He knelt on the stone floor at

the furthest end of the workings away from the narrow beam of daylight, and got something out of his bag. 'Look at this.' It was the damaged piece of the church column he had shown her before.

'I reckon this is where they cut it from,' he said and held it out, next to a squared off hollow in the rock. 'I think they cut the block just here all those years ago, and this column is what they got out of it, so I'm going to cut the next one from just behind it.'

'So there's more good stone here? Why did they stop quarrying it?'

'It's easier for us now because this stuff is different to all the other stone. The seam's too narrow and in the old days, you needed a good, big block because otherwise you could ruin it easily.' He half turned, brushing against her and showed her the piece he was holding. 'If you don't have enough to play with, you have to pinch every little bit. There's waste rock around the good marble, see? Normally when you're working stone, you punch down the waste with a chisel until you're almost there, then you work sideways with the chisel to make a smooth face. Now this stuff doesn't take kindly to too much of that. You punch down too hard and you put a bruise in the marble. You don't see it until you put a polish on it, then you get a little cloudy spot and that's where it'll start crumbling, given time.'

'So what's changed? You can do it without bruising it, can you?'

He laughed. 'Me and my machines. We've got diamond cutting blades now that'll cut it to size without damaging it at all. Mind you, you look at some of the work the old men did way back then and it's as good as anything we can do with our machines now.'

She reached out and ran her fingers around the cut where the block of marble had been taken, then took the damaged section from Lewis's hands and imagined all those years in

249

between. What he was doing began to make some kind of sense for the first time.

They both stood up and she turned around and he was looking at her intently only inches away from her. A shaft of daylight lit the other end of the cave and he was grey and silver, the same stuff as the rock and all there was to hear was the dripping and her own pulse.

'You really do remember last time we were up here, don't you Beth?' he asked. Because she had been remembering just that, and because she was embarrassed to be caught in mid-memory, she said, 'Oh stop it,' and pushed him in the chest. She was horrified when his feet went from under him on the wet stone, sending him backwards into the nearest stone pillar.

His shoulders and the back of his head hit the stones about half way up the pillar and Beth thought it was all right, that the pillar had broken his fall. Then she saw, just for a second, that the middle stones had been bowed out sideways, before the pillar buckled and Lewis fell, rolling on the floor to one side, his light going out as the glass of the lens cracked. For a few moments, the workings were full of the sound of the falling rocks. Lewis groaned and she went to him but he waved her away.

'Get back,' he said urgently, 'Get to the shaft.' He scrambled painfully to his feet and came after her, and just as he moved, a slab of rock some four feet across, fell from the ceiling of the chamber with a thud that set the whole place vibrating.

'OUT,' he shouted. 'Get up there,' and she shot up the steps with him right behind her.

Up in daylight, she tore off the head torch and turned to look at him.

'Oh God, Lewis. I'm so, so sorry,' she said. 'Sit down. Let me look at you.'

He did as she said and she took her packet of tissues from

the overalls pocket and began wiping stone dust and blood off his face. The blood kept on trickling down the right side of his forehead.

'We should get you to hospital.'

He laughed. 'If I went to hospital every time I ran into a piece of rock, I'd never get any work done at all. Scalp wounds always bleed. Don't worry. I'll live.'

'I don't know.'

'I do,' he said firmly. 'I know when I'm hurt and this barely counts.'

She held a wad of tissues against his head.

'I can't bear it. I never meant to do that.'

'Oh, that's a relief. I thought you might have done.'

'Don't tease me. I feel completely sick about it.'

'Beth. It happens. Nothing sudden underground, that's what they say. Think twice then three times, then make your move. Nothing sudden.' He lay back, propped on one elbow and looked at her. 'Anyway, I suppose I asked for it.'

'You did.'

'But you do remember?'

'I wouldn't have pushed you if I hadn't.'

'Was it that bad?'

'Don't be unfair. It was a long time ago. Everything was different then.'

'Seven years ten months and four days,' he said, then looked at her and added 'very roughly.'

'What a memory.'

'You don't forget your first time.'

'Hey, get over it, Lewis. We're different people now. You go on like this and I'll have to go.'

'I suppose we both should,' he said and began to get up, but she stopped him.

'No. Wait for it to stop bleeding first.' She looked back at the shaft. 'Have I wrecked it down there?'

'Course not. That leg was just holding up a patch they

251

didn't like the look of, but now that's dropped out it's probably fine. I'll build the leg up again next time I'm down there if it needs it.'

She found she didn't want to leave this spot. 'What are you doing this afternoon?' she asked.

'I've got a spare hour or two. I thought I'd do some more cleaning up on the Bryan inscription. George keeps going on at me for the rest of the text.'

The inscription took her back to Eliza and her sergeant, down there in wartime. She wondered if Eliza might have told Lewis any of that story.

'Do you know much about my family history?' she asked elliptically, and Lewis, not guessing her meaning, missed the mark by more than six hundred years.

'A bit. I mean obviously there was Guy Battockway, the one who wrote in your family bible. He's not listed as having been rector or vicar or anything like that, but then there was William, who must have been his ancestor.'

'William?'

'William Batokewaye,' he spelt it out for her. 'That's the earliest version of the name. Now he *was* in at the start. He was the first rector of the Chantry, so he was pretty close to Sir Guy. Just think. He would have been there when they first put up the inscription on the tower.'

'Does anybody else have any idea what it says?'

'Not that I know of,' he said, and Beth felt pleased that Eliza had clearly kept that secret to herself.

'So old Sir Guy was a pacifist. You don't think he might have been a bit of a coward do you?' she said provocatively.

'Coward? No, I don't. A man who fought at Crécy?'

'A one-sided battle where the French never got near us if I remember my history.'

'Well, he did a lot more than that. He was always in the thick of it. Never stopped.'

'Such as?'

'There was Calais. Do you know that story?' he asked.

'Tell me,' she said, 'then I'd better get back to work.' It sounded like what she needed, a tale of war, not a plea for peace.

# CHAPTER EIGHTEEN

From Basle, it should take five days to the high Alps in winter, but that requires determined travelling, not the sort these Genoese were capable of understanding. They didn't like riding in the dark and they still expected me to find them hot meals three times a day. Oh, and they weren't very good at getting up early either. I did the calculation and realised we'd be lucky to get to the Saint Gotthard pass in nine days. Nine days to the test which would determine whether we got through to Italy or died on the way. I was not at all happy about the route we were taking but with France barred to us there was little choice. There is a better winter pass, a much lower crossing place far to the east, but it would add a month to our journey and we did not have a month.

Then I became unhappier still. The news from the mountains was that the Saint Gotthard was impassable, utterly blocked by great slides of snow and rock. That was appalling news. Normally, one would take the track up to the hospice at the top, a track which has been much improved in recent years, but the way there lies through two narrow valleys and we learnt from returning travellers that there was no way through.

The Great Saint Bernard was the only alternative, if it was passable.

Once, that had been the main route through the Alps, but for many, many years now it had been shunned since the Saint Gotthard improvements made that a far safer way to go. People said they thought there was still a track, but no one could tell us for certain if the monks still lived in their monastery at the top of the pass.

With that to think about as well as the brooding thoughts of Basle, I was a silent rider for the next day until I discovered that the reason for my silence had been misunderstood. We stopped for the night at Moutier, in something little more than a farmhouse where we all had to sleep together in one open room. The far end of the room contained a low haystack and over this was spread coarse cloth. That was all we had for beds. I was out in the stable with Palamon, making sure his feet were standing up to the journey because we had crossed several freezing streams that day and he never liked that.

I was walking back to the farmhouse when I heard two men talking on the other side of the yard wall and I stopped in my tracks because I heard my own name spoken.

'It's not fair,' said one of them, and I knew it was the squire. 'A man of forty, challenging a man of sixty-five to joust. If I had any experience at arms, I would offer myself in his place.'

'If I had *more* arms, I might do the same,' said William's voice in reply, 'You need two for jousting, but you can spare your concern. He's as strong now as he ever was. He's more than a match for a whole troop of di Provans.'

I could have stopped listening right there and gone on my way. It is not honourable to overhear another's conversation without them knowing, but then it's not very honourable to discuss another in their absence, so I stayed.

'Well then, why is he so quiet today? It seemed to me he must be worrying about it.'

'He's worrying about something, but I can tell you it's not

255

that. You keep right on asking him questions, like I said. It's the best medicine for him. Men like that, they forget all the good things they did as soon as they've done them. All they ever remember is the bad.'

I didn't like that much.

'I want to write a song about him, or perhaps a poem,' said the squire, 'but I don't know where to start. There's so much.'

'Ask him about Calais,' William suggested, 'but above all, keep asking about John Molyns. Ask him about Stoke Trister. Ask him about what happened to Molyns in the end. It's a poison that's got to be let out if he's ever going to heal.'

That was quite enough from them. I walked quietly back a few paces, then contrived a coughing fit and walked straight to the farmhouse, hearing them scramble to their feet as I did so.

The following morning there was a lot of complaining about the hay bed. Everyone said everyone else had been snoring, except little Dafydd who had been sleeping next to the Italians and proudly owned up to me that he'd snored as loudly as he could even when he wasn't asleep. Then there was another time-wasting piece of nonsense by one of the Genoese crossbowmen who was convinced his purse had been stolen, until we found it tucked under the edge of the hay bed, smelling strangely of urine. All my archers were suddenly looking very innocent, but I decided to have a word with them when circumstances allowed. The Alps demand team work. It would be suicide to climb the pass unless we were all pulling together by that time. It seemed to me that it might well be suicide anyway, but orders were orders.

On the fifteenth day we were jogging along towards Biel, coming over the top of those lower hills which are nothing but a gentle reminder of what is to come. I was relishing the next part of the journey because I hadn't done it before, and it felt like a last interlude before the Alpine barrier ahead. The

256

way I knew, the normal Saint Gotthard route, bends off further east from Biel by Bern, to the Thuner lake, and I loved that lake. This time, heading for the Grand Saint Bernard, we were on new territory for me and much larger lakes lay on our path. Two days down the Biel lake, then over the hills and another two days along the shore of Leman. That, I'd been told, is usually where you see the mountains ahead if the air is clear, and the lake itself is said to be one of the most beautiful places you could ever see. We were riding along and I had been giving Dafydd a bit of a lecture, in Welsh of course so no one would overhear. I told him how I wanted it to go with the Genoese, and then I waved a hand for the squire to join me and asked him to find a good moment and say much the same thing to di Provan to pass on to his men.

'We have to think of the Alps as a battle,' I said. 'If your forces are fighting each other and not the enemy, you always lose. Tell him that. Not now, maybe sometime this evening when he's fed and warm and all is quiet.'

'I'll do my best,' said the squire and then he didn't pull away, but went jogging on beside me. 'If you've a mind to talk, would you tell me about Calais? I've always wanted to hear about it from someone who was there.'

It was all I could do to hold back a laugh. 'Always' was a bit of an exaggeration. 'Calais in '47 or in '50? They're entirely different stories.'

He didn't know. William hadn't told him. 'Both?' he said hopefully.

'Are you sure? It's a lot of words to say, and I fear they'll be like specks of dust in the wind. By tomorrow, they'll be scattered along the road and forgotten.'

'I haven't forgotten anything you've said, Lord Bryan,' he answered and he seemed to mean what he said. 'I write it down.'

'Writing is a great trick to have, but it tires out the wrist and it takes a great deal of time.'

'Calais?'

'Ah yes, Calais. *That* was how warfare is meant to be, not the first part, not '47, but certainly what happened in 1350.'

'When did you get there?'

'In May of '47, I think. Is that right? Let's see. Yes, I was back in England. The King asked me to sort out some dispute over an estate in Surrey. He wanted it nipped in the bud because he didn't want any of his noblemen falling out at a time like that.'

'Was it such a bad time?'

'Oh yes, it certainly looked like it. King Phillip of France had taken the Oriflamme in March. That started a panic. Nothing much happened until May, but then he gathered his army and the drums started beating. We weren't really ready. All this time, you see, we'd had an army sitting outside the walls of Calais. We'd been laying siege to it for so long that we'd had time to build a pretty fair town of our own. We even gave it a grand and slightly mocking French name, Villeneuve-la-Hardie. Do you know, it was just as cosy as home. Fine houses, built of timber, proper markets which was just as well as twelve thousand of us had to live there for nearly a year. War was never so comfortable before or since.'

'It sounds pretty good. The perfect siege.'

'In a way. I was back and forth, doing this and that for the King. I spent some of the time patrolling at sea, trying to blockade their port but we didn't have enough ships to do the job properly. The French had hired Genoese galleys from the Grimaldis and they had the legs of us. Two out of three of them got past us, and they kept the town supplied. It could have gone on for years except for the money.'

'The money?'

I looked around to check nobody else was close enough to hear. 'The King has great strengths, but they don't include a good head for business. We'd had all that fuss after the failure of the siege of Cambrai, and Edward's furious return home; not just furious, but absolutely ignominious, in debt up to his eyeballs. We'd even had the humiliation of having to pawn the crown. Well, that started all over again. We had to pay for a lot of ships and a lot of men and the bankers were getting pretty difficult. The French were in much the same state. King Phillip was blaming everyone in sight for what had happened at Crécy. They were so short of money, they had to go around forcing the churches to hand over their gold and silver. They even stopped paying the Grimaldis for the galleys half-way through the winter, so the Genoese sailed away and that made my life a bit easier. Calais began to starve after that. Anyway, Edward followed their lead. Everything he could get out of the churches and the monasteries back in England was turned into cash, put straight on to packhorses and sent down the Dover road. He was always a bit too late when it came to finance, you know, and it cost him very dear.'

'You'd fallen out with him, hadn't you?'

'Who told you that?'

He looked all innocent. 'Oh, I'm sorry. I didn't mean to annoy you. Maybe I'm wrong. One forgets where one hears these things.'

Behind a wall from William Batokewaye was my guess.

'We'd had a little disagreement. The King pardoned the debts of someone I knew. It put me at a bit of a disadvantage.'

'Was that Sir John Molyns?'

'Yes, it was. Anyway, where were we? Calais. It was June when it all came to a head.'

There was no need to pay much attention to the road for this part of the journey. The land we were passing through was a byword for safety, and I could see that my men were in the right positions and as vigilant as ever. As I told him the story it all came back to me so clearly.

259

I spent much of that June cruising up and down off the entrance to Calais. We'd taken the sand spit which covered the south flank of the harbour, and we had them almost bottled up. Only if they ran the blockade could they possibly keep going, and at the end of June, that's exactly what they tried to do. We were keeping our eyes open and saw them coming up from the mouth of the Somme. Fifty ships at least. They could have slaughtered us, but what cowards they turned out to be. They scattered when they saw us coming. It never even came to a fight. Their galleys ran away and the crews abandoned the merchant ships to drift ashore. Shame on them.

What will stay in my mind for ever is what happened the following day. The French commander in Calais was a man called Jean de Vienne and he knew this was likely to be the end. I was up early that morning and at first light I took a little boat and five good men to poke our noses into the entrance to Calais harbour. I wanted to make absolutely sure that no boat had sneaked in that night while we'd been busy sorting out the drifting Frenchmen. It's hard to see until you're almost inside the port, so we were creeping carefully in, drifting up to the harbour entrance on a breath of a westerly with an early-morning sea fog curling and billowing around us. Then I heard something. I signed to the men for utter silence and held on to the boom to stop the sail slatting, and then we all heard it, the creaking of oars on tholepins. The fog was rolling all around us, but then it swirled away, just for a moment, so that we lay in a clear, small pool of sea and I looked up and saw the tops of two masts moving past us, sticking out of the top of the fog bank.

We bent to our oars then and flew after them to head them off from the sea and as we did, the fog blew away entirely and we saw, between us and the beach, two boats the same size as us, four men in each, rowing out to sea for their dear lives. They should have turned and fought us. It was two to one after all, but they tried to slip between us and the shore, right where the sandbank lies and, on a falling tide, both boats ran aground. They did their best to get off again, back-watering their oars and then the men jumping over the side to push off, but we were on them in a moment. That was when I saw one of them do a most curious thing. He reached into the boat, took something out of it and hurled it as far as he could out into the sea. I marked the splash and as soon as we had them subdued, which took a moment or two, I called to the soldiers who were running up the beach from our lines to bring two spears, and I set them up in the sand as sighting poles to give the line of the place. We sat there on the sand and when the tide was far enough down, we walked out along the line and there, in a little pool, we found a leather pouch, sealed up and lashed to an axe-head.

I sent word to the King and was commanded to bring it straight to his house. It was the first time I had been alone with him for some while. He greeted me courteously, alone in his solar, an airy room which ran the width of the house, looking out onto the marshland on one side and the great grey walls of Calais on the other. Taking the bag, he cut the seals, pulled out a rolled parchment and read the contents carefully. A smile spread across his face and he poured me a beaker of wine. It was the first and only time I ever saw Edward pour wine for anybody else.

'Guy, you've done me good service many times and now, it seems, you have excelled yourself. In this letter, meant for King Phillip himself, Jean de Vienne says that the town is entirely out of food, that they will soon have to start eating dead men's flesh. He says if no help comes, he and his men have decided they will come out of their gates in one final charge and certainly die in the attempt.' He looked at me hard, 'I know you think I've taken bad counsel,' he said and waved away my attempt at answering, 'and I know you think

261

I've thrown in my lot with the odd villain, but I want you to know that I value your service most highly. You will always have my ear and you will always be my right hand.' Fine words. 'Always' has its own sense when it's used by a king. It means 'for the time being'.

I told the squire parts of that, glossing over the personal bits, and of course he knew much of the rest because it was one of the best-known war stories of our time, though some parts had been changed in the telling. He knew that Jean de Vienne had immediately expelled the useless mouths. The gates opened and we watched as five hundred people, the women, the children, the old men and the sick, were herded out, protesting. The squire believed the nonsense version. He really thought King Edward had ordered them to be fed and shod and sent on their way with a blanket each, which was what I had suggested at the time. In fact Edward had forgotten that I 'had his ear' almost immediately, and those five hundred miserable souls huddled together below Calais' walls in plain sight of our lines until they all died. That apparently made more sense militarily.

The squire also knew the somewhat truer story of how the French army finally arrived behind us at the end of July, spreading out on the sand dunes of Sangatte. The Pope's two cardinals appeared with them, and I was sent off with Lancaster and Northampton to meet them for parlay at the bridge. One of the cardinals was not a man you'd ever really trust, but the other one, Etienne Aubert, was a man I took to immediately, a man who was driven by a clearly genuine passion to avoid warfare at almost any cost. He lived a simple life, that man. He had a face like a starving hermit and he drove himself hard for a man who was far from well, but there was a look in his eyes of the purest honesty, and I took every chance I could to help him find a way out. In the end there wasn't one to be found. They were always odd occasions, such meetings, full of circling and suspicion. We had

Reginald Cobham and Bartholomew Burgersh with us, another English oak of a man in Cobham's mould, around whom French scheming washed unnoticed, like ripples around a rock. Phillip offered an unacceptable solution. He knew Calais was lost. The talks ended and we were back as we were before, the town surrounded, our position behind the marshes completely impregnable and the French army standing well back out of the way. That night, the poor men of Calais lit a bonfire on their battlements as if to kindle their distant army into action. The next night, as I came back in from patrol, there was the bonfire burning again, but only half as big. On the third night, they lit the fire again but this time it was a tiny affair, little more than a glow. The towns-folk had found a poignant and vivid way to tell their distant brothers just how fast their spirits and their strength were dying, and there was nobody in the English camp who was not affected by that terrible sight, except perhaps for the King.

On that third night it seemed the French army was answering them with a message of hope. A hundred fires were lit on the dunes of Sangatte as if to say, 'hold on, we're coming to save you'. It was a cruel deceit. In the morning when Cobham's scouts went to look, they found it was the end of hope for the people of Calais. The French army had burnt their tents and their stores and crept off to their homes.

The squire knew almost all there was to know about the final surrender of Calais – how Edward showed his harshest side, offering no quarter at first. I was one of the three who went with Walter Mauny to the gates of the town to nego-tiate that surrender, and all we were allowed to offer was that the men should leave at once and take nothing with them. It was to be a wholesale change of nationality. Edward had English families lined up across the Channel to come and make this town a part of England, and no Frenchman was to be allowed to stay. The squire also knew how they were told to choose six of their leaders to come out with the town keys and with nooses around their necks to meet whatever fate the King should determine. The men who volunteered for that job were brave. They had every reason to believe our King was as angry at their defence of their town as he pretended. As they stood outside, surrounded by all our knights, we went through a charade in which he ordered them hanged and only gave in when his queen begged for mercy on their behalf. I knew it for what it was. Edward wanted the story to spread, to let the French people know they'd better surrender their towns quickly if an English army came to call.

'Are you sure that was why?' the squire said when I told him.

'I was there when they discussed it. Every moment of it was planned, who should say what and when. The King arranged it himself.'

'Was it effective?'

'Very.'

'But he nearly lost Calais in 1349, didn't he?'

William must have primed him, must have told him to get me talking about that year.

What a terrible year '49 had turned out to be for almost everyone. I spent part of it in Calais, helping with its transition into an English town, and we kept Villeneuve-la-Hardie going as we'd got used to it and it made more sense to live there while we installed our new English settlers into the old town. I suppose it was the end of '47 when we first heard rumours from Avignon of a plague on that south coast of France. In the next six months it swept up to Paris, and late in the autumn of '48 we heard the Death had leapt past us to the coast of England. It was brought to Melcombe Regis by a Gascon trading ship and it killed almost everyone in the town. After that it set off on its terrible course around the country, and through '49 it destroyed a third part at least of every town and village it came to. In my mind, there are two different Englands, England before the Death and England after it. The first now seems like a lost world in which the ordinary people were content with their simple lot, in which small hamlets thrived, in which cows were milked and crops were harvested. England after the Death was a landscape of tragedy, sorrow and horror, its hamlets deserted, its fields reverting to wilderness and animals dying of neglect because there was nobody left to care for them. It stank, that landscape, and where it was populated at all, it was populated by people who now questioned everything they had once taken for granted.

For years, deep inside me, I have believed that we brought the Death on ourselves by the hole we blew in heaven, by our wilful destruction of the finest rules of chivalry.

It is true that the Death focused its attention quite disproportionately on the poor, but there was sorrow to spare in the houses of the rich. The King's youngest daughter was one, cut down on her way to marry the heir of Castile. In France, King Phillip's queen also died, though he married a very young replacement soon afterwards. We got away quite lightly in Villeneuve-la-Hardie, and some reckoned it was because our wooden houses were new and well-aired, but I was sent hither and thither in England throughout that year on the King's service, doing my best to organise those few that were still healthy to keep our ports working. We quickly set up a quarantine system for the Calais settlers, and that was quite easy, because they lived in isolated huts for a week when they arrived and if they were still alive after that, it was safe to let them into the town.

The King and his eldest son, Prince Edward, arrived in Calais with an élite party of the very best soldiers in great secrecy one night just after Christmas. The first I knew of it was when there was a knock on my door, and to my amazement, I opened it to find the King himself standing there smiling broadly.

I explained all this to the squire, and he said, 'Well? What did you do?'

'I bowed, of course, then I opened it wide and he came rushing in, followed by his son, who was even bigger now than when he had fought so well at Crécy.' I liked the Prince a lot at that time of his life, particularly when we'd found ourselves on the same side in the shouting match that followed Crécy. 'The Earl of March came in after them, dressed in plainer clothes than I'd ever seen him before, then I looked back with fresh eyes at the first two and saw that they too were in ordinary soldier's gear. "We've no time to lose Guy," said the King, "there's treachery afoot and we've got three days to stop it. It's that wily old bastard de Charny." I woke servants and heated spiced wine and the King told me Geoffrey de Charny, always one of our trickier enemies, had tried to bribe our Italian galley-master, Aimeric. He offered the Italian a huge fortune to open the gate and let de Charny's army into Calais at night, but Aimeric had gone straight to the King with the plan.'

I stopped talking then because one of my men, the larger of the two Owens, rode back to say there was a roadblock ahead with the local militia stopping everyone who passed. Rhys rode ahead with my papers, and when we came around the corner, they had pulled the log out of the way and were standing with swords raised at the salute for us.

'Go on,' said the squire. 'What happened?'

'They'd made plans on the journey over and it was a very clever plan indeed. They decided to teach de Charny a lesson, so in great secrecy, we got to work. We built a false wall out of small stone across the entrance to a side-yard by the main gate. Then we carefully weakened the drawbridge until it would just bear the weight of half a dozen horses. When it was all ready we waited, hidden behind our wall. The King was in disguise, pretending to be a knight of Walter Mauny's household. I bore his standard, but I was commanded to hold it up only once we were in the midst of battle. "That will show them the full error of their ways," said the King. The Prince was disguised as well. He wore ordinary plate instead of his black armour, and a plain helm without his ostrich feathers. We knew de Charny was coming on the first of January and we had men watching the road from St-Omer all night. No one got in their way as they came across the bridge through the marshland. There were five thousand at least I should say, far more than we expected, and they formed up on the flat land outside the gate with the marshes at their back.'

'Were they suspicious?'

'Yes, of course, but it all looked fairly convincing. Aimeric played his part perfectly. He went out of the gate to meet them. The portcullis was up, the drawbridge was down and he took de Charny's flag and raised it from the gate tower. De Charny and his commanders trotted over the bridge into the courtyard to enter the town, and that was when the King gave the signal. The portcullis dropped in front of them. They rolled a rock off the wall and caved in the drawbridge behind them and there was de Charny trapped in the entrance court starting to realise it was all going wrong. Then we all burst through the wall to one side of them on our horses and laid into them. Half of them fled. The other half fought as well as they could, scrambling back down through the ditch to join the rest of their men outside with us after them, but the Prince and his men came tearing out of the other gate, the sea-gate, and went at them from behind. The few who got away went into the marshes because they had no choice, and most of those never came out again.'

'You liked that fight, didn't you?' said the squire, 'I can tell by your face.'

'It was brave and bold and chivalrous.'

'Hiding behind a wall?'

'Yes, when there's treachery afoot and you're outnumbered five-to-one, that's perfectly allowable.'

267

'And the King made you a baron?'

'My father died that same year. That's what made me a baron.'

Of course the other thing that happened in the middle of all that time, despite the horror and the fear of the Death, was the King's next great tournament at Windsor, but I certainly wasn't going to tell the squire about that. It was a gaudy affair and everyone behaved as if this was their last chance for pleasure, and the women mocked death with their wild and scanty fashions. It was also where I compounded my sin most dreadfully and very probably destroyed my hope of redemption. As if he read my mind again, he looked at me and said, 'Now, please would you be so kind as to tell me why you've sworn never to joust again?'

# CHAPTER NINETEEN

'That's a private story,' I told the squire, 'and not one I choose to share.' He looked crestfallen, so I threw him a bone. 'I'll tell you all else there is to tell about Molyns,' I offered. 'I've been thinking about him and I never want to do so again.'

'If you tell me, I'll think about him instead,' said the squire, 'and relieve you of the burden of that task.'

I looked at him. He'd lost some weight on the journey. His face had leaned up to show the bones. I rather wished he'd been a son of mine.

'I'm not joking,' he said. 'Did you ever come to blows with him?'

I swung around in my saddle. I was riding Arcite, and Palamon was walking behind, enjoying the rest. Back there, behind the packhorses, William was busy trying not to look at us.

'Why do you ask?'

He'd seen my look. 'Your priest says that if I want to understand the extremities of good and evil on this earth, which I do, then I should study Sir Guy de Bryan and Sir John Molyns as the examples of those two extremes.'

'Does he now? Well for a start, he's not my priest any more than that cloud up there is my cloud.'

269

'I don't think it is a cloud,' the squire replied, peering ahead. 'I think it's a mountain.'

He was quite right. The air cleared as we both stared, and the Alps showed themselves to us with that trick that makes them appear to have come from nowhere almost to touching distance. There was a great deal of snow on them.

We both stared at it for quite some time.

'How does your heart stand up to that sight?' I asked.

'I find it hard to be afraid of it,' said the squire.

'That's good.'

'No, it's not good at all. It is a failure of my imagination, Sir Guy. I should be able to project my mind ahead of us, up there into the wild. I should be able to reduce myself to abject terror by the power of that imagination.'

'Why on earth would you want to do that?'

'A poet should not be limited by his immediate surroundings.'

'What's stopping you?'

'You and your men. You're all so . . . so capable.'

'My apologies for interfering with your muse, young man. I will try to frighten you more. What were we talking about?'

'Molyns?'

'Oh yes, Molyns. William Batokewaye, it's true, has been my companion for many years and is to have the running of my chantry, but he is sometimes given to romantic over-statement. The answer to your question is that I came to blows with Molyns on only two occasions, if you don't include our rather one-sided encounter at Badlesmere, though there were many others when we came close.'

I was going to leave it at that, but he kept his silence and forced me to say more.

'This is all a long time ago, boy. The first time was when he was in hiding, so that would have been after the year '40. It was very soon after the King gave me Molyns' estate of Stoke Trister to hold. Let's see it must have been '42. I was at the manor. Have you ever been in that part of the world?'

'I don't even know where it is.'

'You would have come past it on the way to Slapton. It's on the way through Selwood Forest, south of Penselwood, a beautiful place. Of course, that's just a little to the west of the Montague lands and I already suspected Molyns was hiding somewhere under Montague's cloak.'

'So it still *belonged* to Molyns?'

'Oh yes, and I knew my duty. The estate was merely in my care. If the King chose to grant it to me in full, then that was a different matter, but for the moment, I was its custodian and could enjoy only such income as it gave me after I had invested in its upkeep. Until then, there hadn't *been* much upkeep and I was having to spend my own money.'

'It sounds like the sort of present it's better not to be given.'

'The King was making a point, I think. He was showing his displeasure to Molyns, and perhaps to Montague, in the most direct way. Anyway, that day, I was out on my horse, riding up along the ridge beyond Penselwood into the end of the Stoke Trister lands. I had been to visit a tenant of the estate, to arrange repairs to his house, and he was a man after my own heart, a simple fellow in appearance, but a man who turned out to know all the old stories of the place and the wars it had seen. He'd told me of an old castle on that ridge, a castle built of earth long before they first used stone. It has high banks in a great circle and the local people call it Canny Welkin's camp. He suggested I go to see it, and as the sun was out and my horse, my good mare Emily, had waited patiently for me all that time, I took his advice. Now once, of course, that ridge must have been kept bare of trees, because nobody would build their fortress in a forest, but now the trees had grown thickly around it.

I rode in through a gap in the earth rampart and the next moment my dear horse Emily collapsed to the ground, dead

271

with an arrow in her, and four men came at me with swords. Two of them were poorly skilled with a blade and I disposed of them in my fury, but the other two were harder work and kept me going for fully half an hour without advantage on either side. They both wore brigands' cloths around their faces below the eyes, but as I fought, I realised I knew the eyes of one of them. They were pale eyes, pale and close-set.'

'Molyns!' said the squire.

'Molyns indeed. In the end, I cut the other deep across the arm and he ran off, but at the same time Molyns pricked me in the shoulder from the side which hampered me considerably. After that, he knew he could wear me down, so he tried me out with fancy swordplay. He tore off the cloth and he taunted me. "Have you been enjoying my lands? Are all my tenants pleased to have such a *nice* landlord at their beck and call? Are their daughters safe now, you milksop? This is the end of your tenure, young Guy. The King will have to find a new ear for his conscience." He had a steel breastplate on and all I had was cloth. I was losing blood and my vision was blurring.'

I stopped for a moment, remembering because the scene was very vivid in my mind and I wanted to get it right. Memory is so dangerous. You take it out and use it, but if you misuse it, that memory is changed for ever when you put it back.

'But you beat him in the end?' asked the squire anxiously. 'You must have done because you're here.'

'It wasn't me who beat him,' I answered. 'As I say, I could hardly see clearly any more, but as I tried to keep his sword out of my body, I was looking back beyond him, down the track which had brought me there and I seemed to see a man coming up behind him. At first, I thought it was his henchman back again, but then I saw it was the tenant who had directed me there in the first place.'

'Was he Molyns' man too? Had he sent you to a trap?'

'That was my own first thought. He held a thick staff in his hand and it looked as if he were coming to join in. Molyns saw me looking past him and laughed. "You don't fool me," he said. "There's no one coming to rescue you, Guy." The man behind him raised his stick in the air and brought it down hard on Molyns' head.'

'Good man. Why?'

'Afterwards, when he got me back to his cottage and his wife dressed my wound, he said it was pure self-interest and he'd rather have me as a landlord than John Molyns any day. In fact, I learnt from his wife that it was no mere chance. She had been walking home and she had seen Molyns and his men racing across the fields to cut me off. They had been watching for me. She ran home as fast as she could to tell her husband, and he set off after them with an anger she said she had rarely seen before.'

'Excellent. Molyns got away? Why didn't you kill him?'

'Unconscious? On the ground?'

'You just left him there?'

'I was fainting and in no state to do anything else. He went back into hiding. Well, I've told you some of what happened next, haven't I? The King forgave him three years later when he thought he needed him back at his side for the war. Edward even took Stoke Trister back from me and returned it to Molyns. Then there was Crécy.'

'Yes, Crécy. I don't think I fully understand Crécy. What exactly it was that happened between you and Molyns there? There was something, wasn't there, that set you even more on opposite sides?'

I wasn't ready to tackle that one. 'Later,' I said. 'We've still got a long way to go. There'll be time for that part later.'

'But he fell from the King's favour in the end, didn't he?'

'Oh yes he did. He flouted the King again. You don't do that twice and get away with it.'

'When was that?'

'Let's see. It was after that pointless peace conference, so it must have been about '54? We all trooped off to Avignon, summoned by the new Pope, Innocent the Sixth, and do you know who it turned out to be? None other than my old friend from Calais, the peacemaker Cardinal Etienne Aubert, worn even thinner by his troubles, but even more determined to stop Christians fighting each other. It's hard to keep your loyalty polished when you no longer quite believe your own king has the right approach and you meet someone else who does.'

'Is that what you believed?'

I reined in Arcite in surprise at what I'd said and Palamon, who wasn't paying attention, ran into the back of us.

'That slipped out,' I said. 'I certainly shouldn't have said anything of the kind.'

'Everything you say is in utter confidence,' the squire promised.

'Anyway, things did go better after that. When I got back, the Queen was complaining at the top of her voice about Molyns. For some unaccountable reason, the King had made him master of the Queen's household and, of course, he'd been caught creaming off the money. Things suddenly seemed to be going in the right direction. Were you at the battle of Poitiers by any chance?'

'No,' said the squire, 'I was thirteen.'

'Oh, of course. Well it was a much finer affair than Crécy.'

'Just as much of a slaughter, surely?'

'Yes, but a chivalrous one.' I realised we were getting into dangerous ground again so I went quickly on. 'Of course, we captured their king at Poitiers and that was the end of open warfare for a while. Anyway the result was that the King started paying a bit more attention to what went on at home. He had Molyns charged with treason, felony and conspiracy, then he threw in a few more charges, from giving refuge to murderers, all the way to the theft of firewood and decapitating swans.'

'What?'

'Oh yes. Do you know, I think Edward was more annoyed about that than any of the murders.'

'Really?'

'It was so completely disrespectful, a direct challenge to the King. You know all swans are royal birds. They belong to the King and to him alone. No one else may take one. Molyns was eating almost nothing else.'

'Why?'

'It was almost as if he were doing it to contrive the most direct insult possible, some sort of symbol that no one had power over him, not even the sovereign. He'd have them plucked, then chop off the necks and pretend they were bustards. Do you know, he even served one to the King himself? There was something in him by that time that carried confrontation to a mad extreme.'

'Better than a heron.'

'Not in the King's eyes. In fact, very much the same. The heron helped start a war. The swan helped start the process of justice and, I have to say, it had been delayed far too long.'

'So they arrested him?'

'They tried to, but he gave them the slip and do you know what he did next? He came for me. I was in Slapton. It was before the Chantry was built of course, and I was at my house of Pool. Oh that was a fine house in those days. Of all my houses, that was the one I enjoyed the most while I had my wife to share it with.'

'Isn't it still a fine house?'

I started to answer, and all at once I couldn't speak, and he saw that and looked away, taking a sudden keen interest in the scenery. In terms of stone and mortar, yes, Pool was still a fine house, but not in any of the ways that really mattered. It now lacks all the warmth Elizabeth had brought to it and I now inhabit it, as a soldier finds shelter in a ruin, gathering around me only what I need at that moment.

Elizabeth and I were married at Slapton in that plague year of 1349. She was thirty years old that year and I was forty-two, but it was better late than never, much better. Few came to our wedding because few dared leave their country retreats while the towns were dying, but that did not matter at all. Pool was our first home together and always seemed the first of all our houses, though Elizabeth had many, and by that time, I already had three or four.

When the King arranged matters so that we could marry, he encouraged me to make the most of my new happiness and to look only forwards. For the years of our marriage, I did my very best to obey him and it was not too difficult because there are some foods that gain in flavour if you are prevented from eating and can only watch. The circumstances of war and plague kept me away all that year on the King's business, and when I passed by her house at Tewkesbury, charged by the King as commissioner of his enquiry for Cardiff, Gloucester and Bristol into the scale of the damage the Death had wrought, I had been too close to the disease to risk her life by going in. When she came to Slapton, I had not seen her for a long age. It was five years since our blessed, cursed night in Montague's castle. She contrived it that we did not meet until she entered the church, and then I saw that she had somehow become younger in those five years. I can remember that moment when we looked at each other again with absolute clarity, but I cannot describe it except to say that a complete peace came over me for perhaps the first time in my life, and I saw a soft comfort there that I did not ever expect to have.

We didn't sleep for most of that sweet wedding night, not until dawn broke, but it was not just acts of love that kept us awake, but also the hungry need to talk and talk and fill the gaps in all the intervening years with our words. In the morning, I woke to a different sort of touch, and found Elizabeth examining me carefully and smoothing oil from a vial over the worst of my scars.

'It's time someone looked after you,' she said. 'I need you to last at least another fifty years. You're not to get old before I do.'

I didn't, I suppose, but I wish she had grown old. We had only ten years, Elizabeth and I. They were ten years in which I still served my King, but was allowed off the leash for half the year to spend that time at home. They were ten years of extraordinary happiness and for all of those ten years, I was able to follow my King's command, to push away my terrible doubts about what had gone before, helped by Elizabeth's unwavering certainty that we had done nothing wrong. It was only after she died that my doubts redoubled, because then I had to worry about the safety of her soul as well as mine.

The squire respected my silence for a while, and when I knew I could speak again with a strong voice, I told him the rest of it. 'We had built a side-altar in the village church, Elizabeth and I. It was nothing as great as the Chantry, but it was a start. William Batokewaye had come down from his other business to dedicate it for our prayers, and we decided to take a week away from all business to pray there every day. In between our prayers, we would walk on the edge of the Ley and along the line of shingle that holds back the sea, or we would sit in our garden in the sun. There was a day when Elizabeth had gone down to the village before me, to visit a woman who was sick. I said I would join her at the church. I was sitting in the garden, talking to William, when I heard racing feet coming up the hill and a man yelling. Then my steward came to us and told us there was a madman in the church and the verger had sent for help.'

The scene lay before me. 'I had gone to the church with no idea that it was anything other than the sort of wandering lunatic who would occasionally appear, create his nuisance and wander off again when he needed a new audience. I took no weapon, and when I went into the church and saw

277

my dear Elizabeth lying sprawled over a pew with her blood dripping onto the tiles, I still had no idea of the truth of it. A man was standing in our chapel by our altar, using the crucifix to club everything in his reach to fragments, just as he had already used it to club my wife. It was only when he turned that I saw who he was, older and madder, but unmistakeably Molyns. Then I rushed at him, but he sprang over the rail with a yell, hurled the cross at my head and ran for the door. There he came to a halt, seeing his way blocked by the men of the village gathering on the pathway outside and, as I seized him from behind, he grasped the iron ring on the door.

'"You can't take me!" he shouted. "This is a sanctuary ring and I claim sanctuary. There, Sir Guy. You're too holy to break the rule of sanctuary, surely."'

Now there was an absurd turn of events, all the more absurd if I could have explained to the squire what that ring was, something Molyns knew all too well as he had been there when I had it made.

'"He has attacked Lady Bryan," I shouted at the men. "Don't let him get away," and I turned back fearing to find her dead, but she was breathing and starting to move her head. I tore my shirt to bandage the wound and did what I could to make her comfortable, and then I heard a new commotion start at the door.

'I went quickly to it and saw the crowd part for William, who came through them like a warhorse through a riot. Molyns saw him coming.

'"Don't let him near me," he shouted. "I shan't let go of the ring."

'"You won't have to," said William, and putting his hand right around Molyns' own, he squeezed hard and pulled the ring, nails and all, right out of the door, still in Molyns' grip, then he cuffed Molyns around the head to render him insensible and hoisted him over his shoulder.

'"Where do you want him?" he asked me.'

The squire liked that tale. 'Then he stood trial?'

'He did, though would you believe he appeared at the last dressed as a priest and tried to prove he could read the holy scriptures out loud so as to claim immunity through benefit of clergy? They locked him up in Nottingham Castle which he richly deserved.'

'Did you see him again?'

'I did,' I admitted, but I wasn't altogether sure I wanted to remember our final encounter.

'When?'

'He sent for me three years later in '61. It was the time of the second visitation of the Death and I was on the King's business. That was the year that the Death changed its clothes and came knocking on the doors of the rich. Many great people died that year, Henry of Lancaster among them. Well indeed, you said you remember it. Anyway, I was at Warwick when a messenger came to beg me for the sake of Molyns' soul to go to see him in Nottingham on his deathbed, so he could ask my forgiveness.'

'You went?'

'I had to.'

'Why?'

'I believe every man has the right to repentance and soul's ease.'

'What was it like?'

'It was . . . unexpected.'

It was worse than that. The room he occupied was little worse than a dungeon, and the jailer was strangely willing to usher me in. I thought afterwards he must have been bribed. Molyns lay on a thin mattress, barely able to move, and beckoned me near. He had the corpse look.

I bent over him, stooping down into a miasma of decay and listened. I had my words of forgiveness prepared because I had time on my journey there to go over the grim coupling

279

of our lives and all that had fallen out from that. It had seemed to me that he had to be forgiven just as a wild beast had to be forgiven for attacking you.

'I defiled your altar,' he whispered.

'You did,' I said. 'I forgive you for it.'

'Wait until I request it. Did I also defile your wife? Ask yourself that?'

I stared at him.

'*My* soul is safe,' he said, and it sounded like a hiss. 'For thirty years they have been saying prayers for me in the chantries I built. I can do what I like now because of that. I hope your soul burns in Purgatory and then rots in Hell.'

'Whether you ask it or not, I forgive you,' I said. 'May your death be easy and your judgement swift,' and as I made the sign of the cross, he ripped open his shirt, showing the black buboes under his arms.

'You're coming with me,' he shouted with the last of his breath and he spat at me as I sprang back from him.

'He had the Death?' the squire asked, shocked.

'He did, and he died of it that same night.'

'And you did not take your own death.'

'I left the castle straightaway and I went into the countryside and there I sheltered in an empty barn for an entire week until I was certain I had escaped it. It was not for my sake. I had no great will to live by then, but I did not want anyone else to die if I were infected. While I was in the woods, I had time to reflect on Purgatory and on what Molyns had said, and I realised our altar at Slapton had indeed been defiled. I decided then to build a proper Chantry, and I knew I had to stay alive for long enough to arrange for that to secure the safety of my wife's soul.'

'Was she dead?' asked the squire, then added, 'I'm sorry. That came out harshly.'

'My Elizabeth never fully recovered from his blow. She was apt to trip if left to herself, and sometimes wandered in her wits. She died on the last day of May of the year 1359, on Saint Petronella's Day, by falling from the window of our fair house of Pool while I was at prayer.'

The squire had the look about him of someone who knows he is about to venture into soft ground. 'And this is the same Elizabeth?' he asked softly. 'The same one who married Hugh Despenser?'

'It is,' I said, remembering her protestations against my intentions, 'and when she died, I had her buried with him.'

# CHAPTER TWENTY

The cut on Lewis's head had finally stopped bleeding by the time he finished telling the story of the Calais ambush. To Beth's surprise he told it well.

'All right, I accept it. He was no coward. Is there a book about him?' Beth asked, lying back in the grass.

'No, you have to glean bits here and there. He's a footnote in the history of lots of other people. There was a short article published years ago and there's quite a bit on the Chantry itself, but I keep digging away. It's surprising what comes up. He gets mentioned in the history of Tewkesbury Abbey as well.'

'Why Tewkesbury Abbey?'

'He's buried there.'

'Is there a gravestone?'

'Better than that. There's a fantastic marble tomb inside the abbey on the south aisle. His effigy is carved on top of it.'

'You mean you can still see what he looked like?'

'Sort of. He's got his armour on. He's wearing a helmet and chain mail, so that just leaves part of his face showing. He's got rather a fine moustache. There's only one arm left, but it looks as though he was reaching across with his hand on his sword. They think it shows he was the king's faithful protector. Do you know the saddest thing?'

'Tell me.'

'Just across the aisle, almost in touching distance, there's an almost identical tomb and his wife Elizabeth is buried there.'

'Separately? Did they split up?'

'No. She died in 1359 when she was about forty. He was fifty-two, and they'd been married ten years. He had her buried with her previous husband, Hugh Despenser.'

'Why?'

'No one knows. Sometimes women were buried with their first husbands by the custom of the time, but that's not what happened here because Sir Guy was her third, and Despenser her second, not the first.'

'She got around a bit.'

'It was a hard time. Death was always around the corner. She was a Montague. Loads of money, loads of land. There always had to be a husband to sort out the estates.'

'So it was a marriage of convenience? She and Sir Guy didn't necessarily love each other?'

He looked at her, smiling. 'Do you want them to have done?'

She found she did, but she wasn't going to say so. 'I just wondered.'

'We don't know anything much about their story. We do know he'd been married once before, years earlier, but I think he must have loved her.'

'Is that because *you* want it that way?'

'No, not at all. I base it on solid fact. We know from the records that Elizabeth died on May the thirty-first of 1359, which is of course?'

He was sitting up, and now he looked down at Beth expectantly. It was a moment before she got it. 'Saint Petronella's Day,' she said. 'So he chose the day she died as his special day for the mass,' and at that moment that old finger reached out of the past again and made her jump at its touch.

'How did she die?'

'There's no record, but there is a ghost story which might have something to do with it. It's an old story in your family,' he said. 'Has Eliza told you? It's about Sir Guy's old house.'

'Pool?'

'That's it.'

'She did say some funny things about it. She called it "Pool of the many chimneys."'

'What else did she say?'

'Nothing much. We were walking past the farm. It only came up because I thought I'd caught a glimpse of something a bit different when I drove down the hill.'

'What did you think you'd seen?' he asked mildly.

'Something much bigger. A grand old house. It was only out of the corner of my eye. What's the story?'

'*That's* the story,' he said. 'The Battocks who sing the mass can still sometimes see Pool as it once was, usually in the spring, in the time before the mass.'

'I saw a ghost house? Is that what you're saying?'

'No, I'm just telling you the story.'

'Well, I'm not one of the Battocks who sings the mass,' she said, getting up. 'I'm one of the Battocks who has a life to lead which doesn't include spending the rest of it in Slapton.'

'Are you going on with your speech?'

'In a while,' she said. 'I've got a few things to do first.' This was not strictly true, but irritation had flared up in her again at the way he was telling her family's story to her and all its implications, and she didn't want to walk back down the hill with him.

Lewis got up, shrugged and disappeared down the edge of the field back towards the quarry, and Beth cut across the fields until she met the road down into the village. Ten minutes' hard walking brought her to the place where she and Eliza had looked down on the farmhouse which now stood where Pool had once been. She stopped again and inspected it, and then a rational explanation for her mistake began to dawn on her. The two stone barns in front of the farm house formed two sides of a farmyard with the farmhouse itself making the third. With her eyes half-closed, Beth could see all three buildings almost as one, a great house with two wings coming forward from its ends. That was what she had glimpsed from the car, glimpsed and misunderstood. Looking harder, she wondered if maybe the barns were the remains of the old wings, built from the surviving stone walls of the old building. As she drove past, with the sun right up there, it would have been an easy mistake to make. There was no ghost house, there was no special vision for the Battock family, and by extension, there was no good reason to carry on with the Petronella mass.

A car came down the hill and she pressed herself into the hedge, but instead of passing her, it stopped. The man who wound down the window was large, tanned and lost.

'Could you help us?' he said. 'We're trying to get to a place called Torcross, and we don't know where we are.' He was American.

'You're going in the right direction,' said Beth. 'It's down this way. I'm going down to Slapton which is on the way. Shall I come with you? Then I can put you on the right road.'

'Hop in,' he said, and she got in the back seat.

'It's a rental,' said the woman in the other front seat. 'Joe's not used to a stick shift.'

'It's not a problem,' said the man at the wheel as they moved off. 'That's Leona. I'm Joe Rushton. These lanes are kinda confusing. There's not too many signs.'

'Are you staying at Torcross?' Beth asked politely with only half her attention, thinking about the barely-begun speech waiting for her on Lewis's computer.

'Just visiting,' Leona answered. She and Joe looked around sixty, but her hair looked thirty years younger. 'Paying our respects for Joe's daddy, Joe senior. He was in Force "U".'

'Force "U"?'

'You don't know about it?' Joe sounded mildly disapproving. 'Force "U" was the army group that landed on Utah Beach, Normandy.'

'Your father was in that?'

'Sure. He was in LST 507.' He glanced back and saw her blank face. 'Landing Ship Tanks 507. She was sunk by German torpedoes from their E-boats. Two hundred killed, two hundred and fifty rescued. He was one of the lucky ones. It was worse for 531. They lost four hundred plus.'

'Is he still alive?'

'Hell no. My old man died of the big C, but I promised I'd come back here for him. He'd been over four, maybe five times.'

They came down into the village and they crept through its narrow twists and turns in second gear.

She thanked them for the ride and got out by her father's cottage. 'Keep straight on,' she said. When you get to the Ley, that's the big lake, turn right and you just follow the sea along to the next village. That's Torcross.'

Leona was looking around her. 'I would love to take a walk around your beautiful village,' she said.

Joe shook his head. 'There's no time. We're late enough as it is. The ceremony will have started.'

Beth had started to turn away but that caught her. 'What ceremony is that?'

'It's the anniversary commemoration,' he said. 'The wartime operation. You know? Exercise Tiger?'

'Today?'

'Yes indeed, today.'

She changed her mind. 'Do you mind if I come too?'

On the way there, she rationalised it. The heroes of the

D-Day invasion might summon up some echo for her, something to fuel the fires of her speech. It would be time well spent.

The Torcross car park was almost full.

'Look, I think there's still something going on over there if you're quick,' said Beth, pointing at a crowd on the beach. She suddenly felt herself an intruder and she hung back as the Americans strode away.

At the end of the car-park stood the memorial to the invasion exercises, a Sherman tank hauled out of the sea. She could remember standing among the onlookers on the beach in the late evening years before, watching and hearing the cheers as its turret broke water and it was pulled slowly up to the water's edge, covered in forty years' growth of barnacles, a final relic of those ancient manoeuvres. It stood now on a low ramp in the car-park, but on this day it was covered in bouquets of flowers. She walked over to it and looked more closely.

There were wreaths and American flags all over the dark hull of the old tank, propped against it and taped on wherever they had found space. The nearest, a circle of lilies, said 'For Jacko, who carved his initials on a window ledge overlooking this spot and died soon after D-Day'. And so it ran, heartfelt messages of remembrance, bouquets left by remote control, delivered by English friends of Americans who could not be there, a note saying, 'The daughters of PFC Murdoch Pierce ask any of his comrades with knowledge of the manner of his death to contact us collect'. There was an American number. Then, Beth twisted around the label on a bunch of yellow roses and read 'To the memory of Sergeant James Kimber from his daughter Eleanor'. She let it go and turned to the next and then the name shouted inside her head and she reached out with a shaking hand to read it again. Sergeant James Kimber.

She stood up so quickly that she felt momentarily faint

and looked around her. Eliza's lover was dead, but had somehow come back here out of oblivion. Someone had put the flowers there that day. They were fresh, recent. The story of Jimmy Kimber was alive and that meant it might yet have an ending.

The tail end of the day's events on the beach was still in progress. She crossed the road to the row of buildings which stood between the car park and the beach and looked out towards Start Bay. Forty or fifty people were making their way back to their cars. Whatever had been happening, it was over. She scanned their faces with no idea how to find the person who had put the flowers there. Kimber's *daughter?* If her own father was Kimber's son, Kimber's daughter must be a roughly similar age. There were a dozen women among the men. She went up to the first one.

'Do you know Eleanor Kimber?' she demanded. The woman looked at her, surprised, shook her head and went on by.

'Eleanor Kimber,' she shouted at the top of her voice. 'Is Eleanor Kimber here?' No one took any notice except Leona who appeared with Joe in tow and came, frowning, up to her.

'This is a very dignified event,' she said. 'What's with the shouting?'

'Do you know someone called Eleanor Kimber? It's important.'

'What does she look like?'

'I don't know. She's left some flowers here.'

'Dear, a whole lot of people have left flowers here. They're meant to stay here. Doesn't mean you have to go looking for her.'

Joe tried to be helpful. 'We don't know anybody. Maybe the flowers were delivered in a truck. Maybe she never was here. Do you want a ride back to that place of yours?'

'No, thank you.'

Drenched in failure, thinking it would have been better not to have seen the label, Beth sat on the wall by the little slipway, looking at the boats on the beach and the waves breaking, every wave eroding the chance of sorting this out. The fishermen were spread out, watching their floats or winding in their spinners. Two couples were throwing sticks for prancing dogs and a woman was walking up the beach towards the car park from the water's edge, a woman who looked so exactly like Beth's father that she could hardly believe it.

She walked across to intercept her and the woman looked towards her curiously.

'Excuse me,' Beth called. 'Wait a minute.'

The woman stopped, frowning uncertainly. She wore a light scarf around her neck, one end blowing in the wind, and a cotton jacket.

'Can I help you?' she said, and she was indeed American.

'I think you must be Eleanor Kimber,' Beth said.

'Good God. It's a very long time since anyone called me that. I'm Eleanor Sempleman by marriage, but I have to admit that my maiden name was Kimber. How did you reach that conclusion?'

'I'm Beth Battock. I saw the bunch of roses you put on the tank and I just had to find you.'

'But why? And come to that, how did you know it was me?'

'Well, I'm sorry if this comes as a bit of a shock, but you look just like my dad.'

'Who's your dad for heaven's sake?'

'Guy Battock.' She waved an arm in the direction of Slapton. 'He lives just over there.'

The American woman was shaking her head. 'It's not a shock, but that's because I don't come from anywhere around here. I think you may have got the wrong person and I simply don't have any idea what you're talking about.'

Beth liked the way she looked. There was intelligence in her eyes and laughter lines on her face.

'Can I tell you about it?' she suggested meekly.

The other woman was looking hard at her. 'This wouldn't have anything to do with someone called Eliza, would it?' she asked.

Beth nodded. 'Yes, it would.'

'Then it's starting to get interesting, so why don't we go right over there to that public house behind us and sit down and discuss this over a large drink?'

Once inside, Beth bought two glasses of wine and followed Eleanor to a quiet table in the corner, trying to work out how to start explaining, but Eleanor beat her to it.

'While you were getting the drinks, I was having a think,' she said, 'and it seems to me that you might just have the key to the little mystery that brought me here, so before you go on, let me try this out on you. I do love to see if I can work out a mystery.'

'Please do,' said Beth, a little relieved.

'I don't remember my father at all,' said the other woman. 'I was born in forty-three and he went away to Europe around about that time and anyway, I think he and my ma had pretty much come to the end of their particular road. I don't know for sure because they never divorced. They didn't have to. He went and got himself killed over here in Europe.'

So Eliza was right. 'How did he die?'

'Second day of the invasion. Back of Utah Beach. I only know this because of recent events so I'm shaky on the details.'

'Go on.'

'It seems his friend Eddie looked after his gear when Jimmy was killed and he brought it back home without looking at it, I guess, and he gave it to my ma, Susie, which was not wise, and she put it away in a trunk. You with me so far?'

'Yes.'

'Susie married Rick, then she married Josh, then she

290

married another Jimmy and then finally she married Obadiah who was a minister in the seventh church of something or other in Pennsylvania and he buried her last year.'

'She's dead?'

Eleanor gave her a level look. 'Yes, that's traditionally the order we do things in over there.'

'I'm sorry.'

The other woman smiled. 'I'm kidding. She had a good life. No regrets. Then just a few weeks back, Obadiah sent me a heavy package with a letter, asking me if I was saved and luckily I opened the package instead of binning it with the letter and it was from Jimmy.'

'The first Jimmy?'

'That's the one. My dad. But it wasn't to me or to Susie. It was to Eliza at Slapton. I'd say it was a love letter. Eddie never delivered it and Susie might have burnt it, but maybe she was keeping it for evidence in case he ever popped up from the dead. Anyway, I finally decided to bring it. Now from the way you're looking, I guess you know who Eliza is?'

'Eliza's my grandmother.'

'Oh. Wow. And she's alive?'

'Yes.'

'Married?'

'No. Guy is her only child. He's my father.'

'And you say Guy looks just like me?'

Beth nodded.

'So, let me think. He was born in, let's see, in about January nineteen forty-five?'

'January the second.'

Eleanor stared at Beth. 'I've just got to count to ten and take this all in. Do you mind if I count slowly?'

Beth shook her head and they stared at each, other then Eleanor smiled. 'You know, I always wanted a brother.'

'I always wanted an aunt.'

'Jesus, one minute I'm feeling lonely on a beach. The next minute, I have a family and about ten million questions I want to ask. What's Guy like? Are you two close?'

'Oh. Not very. Well, we haven't been, but I suppose that might be more my fault than his. He's a good man. Very quiet. A countryman. He's been a nature warden all his life, down here on the Ley.' She wanted to say he's not well at the moment, he hasn't got long, but she couldn't take away Eleanor's new brother just as she'd found him.

'So is Eliza anywhere near?'

'Yes. She still lives in Slapton.'

'And that's close by?'

'A couple of miles.'

'It's about time she got her letter then.' She reached in her bag and got out a cardboard folder which protected a small, brown, faded envelope. 'Maybe you should hear it first.'

'It sounds very personal.'

'Well, yes it is, but she must be a fine old age now. I'm guessing what, eighty odd?'

'She's seventy-nine.'

'Well I think you should hear it. Then you'll know how she'll take it. I wouldn't want her passing out on us. Shall I read it to you? I've deciphered the handwriting.'

'Please.'

Eleanor carefully took the old brown envelope out of the folder. Inside was a single sheet of dry old paper, closely written in tiny letters. She put on a pair of scarlet reading glasses and turned the letter to catch the light behind her.

'OK, here goes. "We came ashore soon after dawn near Saint-Vaast-la-Hougue,"' she began.

# CHAPTER TWENTY ONE

'We came ashore soon after dawn near Saint-Vaast-la-Hougue, on the beach running to the south. I waded through the surf holding my weapons above my head with tendrils of mist swirling around me. My company had been quite silent all the way in to the shore, every man of them, I am certain, thinking ahead to the fight we faced, but it was not like that at all. A dozen French ships, the ships which should have met us at sea to oppose our landing were beached on the sand and we burnt them straight away. The town itself was deserted, the people having fled into the marshes. One man we saw and one man only, an English prisoner set free from a cellar when our soldiers heard his shouts. He told us what he knew from his jailers, how Robert Bertrand, the Marshall of the region, has summoned men to gather that day to fight our fleet, but none had yet come. He was right, they made a brief appearance later, but they were a handful, and by that time we had thousands on shore. King Edward landed at noon and knighted his son and Montague, and then we set-to to land the wagons, heading, though we did not yet know it, for Crécy and the valley of the clerks.

There among all the others, I saw that same green wagon

with the markings of the Tower of London armoury and there I heard the first rumours of its cargo.'

I stopped to get my breath. We had to stay awake, the squire and I. We had volunteered to take the watch, or rather I had exercised my right of leadership and he had insisted on joining me. If we all slept, I feared that none of us would ever wake up again.

I crumbled some more of the soaking, rotten wood around the fringe of the fire. The only way to burn it was to dry it first and then feed it into the centre, replacing it immediately with more wet crumbs of wood. On that fire, our lives hung.

The leader makes the choice and the safety of his men hangs on his choice, but what of the times when he has no choice? No other route to Italy was possible, we knew that. This one might also be impassable, but none could tell us one way or the other, and with a royal instruction which allowed no failure, it was my duty to do all I could.

So far it had been a bad day. Three days ago we'd left the Lake Leman behind and started up the lower hills. I had found a good place for prayer every day and one chapel had yielded a certificate for sixty days. Past Orsieres, we'd had our first tussle with the snow and I was not reassured by the response. My Welshmen were fine of course. I never saw the place that could provoke in them anything except a wry resilience and a knowing smile. William was noisier in complaint, but equally determined, and the squire? The squire was a revelation. It was as if he craved extremity, seeking to milk every experience dry for some purpose of his own. No one would say he was yet in fighting trim, but he had lost a lot of flesh along the way and it suited him. No, my concern again was the Genoese. The crossbowmen could manage, but their two proud lords were equally faint in heart and wind.

At Bourg Saint Pierre, we spent a last night in some sort of comfort. The innkeeper there told us no one ever used the pass in winter, and we would be mad to take the horses up it. He knew there was a hospice still at the top and that there were refuge huts on the way up to it, but whether the monks remained there in the winter was a question with no answer.

'It's another world up there,' he said. 'I have no knowledge of it and little that's good ever comes down from that direction. My guess is they scuttle off southwards when the snow starts. Are you determined to go? Have you made your wills?'

I knew I wasn't nearly ready to contemplate death.

We decided we had to leave all the horses and most of the packs and take only what we could easily carry in saddlebags slung across our shoulders. The track was bad enough at the best of times, and in winter it would not do. I charged the man to care especially for Palamon and Arcite. I paid him well, but it worried me greatly because I could tell he never expected to see me again and I was not the least bit sure of his honesty. We told him that as we were on the King of England's business, he would send soldiers there to enquire after us if we did not return, and they would know our horses. The first light was in the sky as we left, having levered di Provan out of bed by brute force, but we had only gone a short way up the valley from the inn when a commotion broke out below us, crashing hooves and splintering timber. A moment later my two horses appeared, racing up the track. William and I calmed them down and led them back, then we had words with the innkeeper and made sure this time they were tied securely to a stout tree. I could hear Palamon complaining all the way up that first valley, and I didn't like it because that horse always seemed to have an extra sense for the future.

It was a hard, hard day, but before it was dark, we saw the first refuge hut up above us with the peaks towering up around us against a mercifully clear sky. It got colder and colder with every yard we climbed, and on much of the track ice was more of a problem than snow. For the last mile or so, the snowdrifts had been increasing in depth and I had to help the Genoese through every deep patch, breaking a path for them, then encouraging and scolding them in equal quantities. They had refused sensible clothes at the inn, simply adding layers of absurd silks to what they already wore and the loose clothing hampered them constantly, but they seemed to gain a little extra strength when we saw the hut far ahead. They asked the squire constant questions.

'Will it have beds? Will it have a fire?'

Through him I told them what I knew from my own experience and from travellers' tales that, in the mountains, the monks who kept the passes open made sure the refuge huts had firewood and blankets. I was keeping my doubts to myself because as we got nearer and nearer, the sky in the cleft ahead turning from the brightest blue gradually to silver-grey, it dawned on me that there was something wrong with the look of the hut. Its roof was not as it should be, straight against the sky. We turned a final corner to come to it and from that new angle we could see the huge hole right through the central part. I climbed through a patch of deep snow, came to the door and pushed it open with great difficulty. Inside was devastation, and the boulder that had tumbled down the mountain to cause all the damage stood there in the middle of the floor for all to see. I thought in that moment that it had killed us as surely as if it had fallen on us.

Di Provan and di Mari came in behind me, and I could tell immediately from the indignant clamour of their voices and from some of the words I had come to know all too well that they were blaming me for what they saw.

I turned on them. 'Be quiet,' I said, or perhaps it was a little louder than that word implies. 'Get to work. We have a short time before the sun sets to try to make this roof weather-tight, and every man must play his part.'

My men did everything they could, but in a landscape made of frozen rubble, where even the stones were gummed together by the ice, there was a limit to what they could achieve. The roof had been made from wooden beams and great flat stones, cunningly set on top. We did what we could with the one beam that hadn't been smashed by the boulder's fall, then we lashed broken ends of the other beams across it and tried our best to place the shattered slates to fill the gaps. There were still more gaps than slates when we ran out of materials and it was the wrong time of year to find the moss or whatever it was they had used to seal the cracks.

'What's di Provan saying now?' I asked the squire when we stopped. The absurd man had barely ceased talking for the whole time.

'He says you promised there would be firewood but it's soaking wet. He also says you promised there would be blankets.'

'It wasn't exactly a promise. Tell him the blankets are underneath that,' I indicated the boulder which filled up a quarter of the space in the middle of the hut. 'If he can get them out, he's welcome to them.'

Dafydd got the fire going by taking his knife and peeling a precious arrow into slivers of wood, lighting them with tinder from his pouch, then taking the only faggot from the hut's pile that was even half-way dry and shredding it around the edge of the flames. We nursed that fire and as the darkness fell and the air sharpened, we sat close together around it.

William organised the sleeping, the same way we did it in France in that foul winter of '60 when men's eyelids froze shut and the hailstones were so big that they killed twelve men. You sleep on your side, all of you stacked like spoons in a drawer, stretching away from the fire, sharing what covering you can, and when the man furthest from the fire can stand it no longer, he comes and takes the position at the front. So it goes on. We had two racks of men, ours and theirs, on either side of the fire, and it became an article of faith with my men that they stood the cold spot for longer than seemed reasonable, whereas the Genoese were springing up at every other moment to claim the warmth, disturbing each other's sleep.

The squire and I fed the fire and he found it so hard to stay awake that I almost let him sleep, but I knew without him to check on me, the danger was too great, for I was exhausted too.

'Shall I tell you a tale I know?' he suggested.

'Why not?' I said, 'then if you stop talking I shall wake you and if I stop listening you will know to wake me.'

He launched into it and got my attention straight away because he described a poor widow's house on the edge of a village, and it sounded more and more like my Slapton until I saw him watching me and smiling and knew that was what it was meant to be. It was Slapton as he had first seen it looking down at my Chantry from the hillside where I had marked him on that day of its dedication. I don't know if I started nodding off, but the story did seem to veer away from its subject from time to time. At the start it was about a cock and his seven hens, then it suddenly seemed to be about a murder and a body hidden in a dung-cart, then next it was about a dream foretelling a shipwreck at sea, and finally we were back with the cock again. That was the bit I liked the most, of how the cockerel was snatched by a wily fox. He described it so well that I could see it in my mind with its coal-tipped tail. Being a story of course, the fox used flattery instead of teeth to overpower the cockerel, but all ended well when the cockerel bested the fox with its own wits. He even gave the cockerel its own name, Chanticleer, which was not the name its owner called it, but the name by which its wives the hens knew it, a funny idea indeed but, I suppose, no funnier than a cockerel which talks. I never had tales like that in our cold castle when I was a boy. I wish I had.

When he finished the story, I judged it was still not time to wake the next pair because it would surely be a very long night.

'Will you tell me a tale now?' he asled.

'I don't have your way with my tongue,' I said. 'I have no stories like that.'

'You have the true story of Crécy,' he said.

'I've told you that at least twice.'

'And missed out all the most important parts, if I'm any judge,' he said. 'Don't you think maybe it's time for you to tell it all, right from the very start, right from when you came ashore and stepped on the soil of France? Where was that exactly? What time of day? What did it feel like? Don't leave anything out.'

'All right,' I said, 'if you insist,' because I knew it would be a relief to finally tell the whole story, and I was starting to fear there might never be another chance.

'We came ashore soon after dawn near Saint-Vaast-la-Hougue, on the beach running to the south.' I told him about the rest of that first day, with the green wagon coming off the ship and the rumours that it contained something akin to magic, something to match the power of the Oriflamme. Fool that I was, I thought perhaps it was nothing more than new and finer flags, battle standards to rally our men.

'The King issued a command that night that no one in his army should molest civilians or steal their property or burn any building.'

The squire made a derisive noise. 'That would have been a new kind of war. How long did it last?'

'By that night, there were fires burning in the dark all around the horizon. That army started as a mob. Discipline only came later, on the march. It took us five days to get the supplies ashore. We marched through an almost empty country, though

299

our scouts said the roads south were choked with refugees. We razed Cherbourg, where at least their soldiers put up a fight, but to our shame, our men burned the abbey there. The fleet was keeping abreast coming down the coast of the peninsula, and we moved on to Caen where the enemy was stronger and we took the town in a crazy attack, led by some hotheads long before the commanders were ready.'

'And the green wagon?'

He was on to me, that boy. 'I didn't see it again until the Blanchetaque crossing and Hugh Despenser's feat of arms.'

'All right,' he said, 'I know about the next bit. You found the Lionheart monument at Crécy-en-Ponthieu and that's where the King decided to make his stand and there, in that valley, our bowmen made their slaughterhouse, but what of the wagon? What of Molyns?'

Finally, up there, up against the freezing stars, in a place we might well never leave and where there was only space left for trust, I found I could tell him.

'All right. I'll tell you all of it, every bit, then you'll understand my whole life because what happened that night before the battle, that night was at the heart of everything that's happened to me.

'When we passed through Crécy village and arrived on the high ground by the windmill, I took the first opportunity to make for the wagons. I wanted to see what was in the green wagon with the Tower markings. Four soldiers were guarding it, but they knew me and they didn't try to stop me. I unlaced the canvas cover along one side and lifted it up and what I saw there, lying on the wagon's wooden bed, were four tubes of thick, black iron, each one of them longer than a man's height. With them were a dozen small wooden barrels, well-sealed, and a pair of open tubs, and the tubs were full of heavy round balls, some of stone and some of iron. I picked one out. It was bigger than my fist and I tried it for fit in the nearest of the iron tubes. It was made for it.'

'A cannon and its cannon balls,' suggested the squire.

'Yes of course, and you can say it as if it should be obvious now, but it wasn't then. I had never seen one before. I didn't know we had such a thing. No one did. I was trying to work out what use this thing could possibly be put to when a hand gripped my shoulder and I turned to find John Molyns glaring at me.

'"You're not allowed here," he said.

'"By whose order?" I answered.

'"By mine," he said, "I am in absolute charge of the cannon, entitled to protect them by any means I find necessary," and before I could move out of the way, he clubbed me on the head with his fist, sending me to my knees. The thing about Molyns was he always resorted to violence a few moments before anyone else would have done so, and I was never ready for him. I heard him draw his sword and I sprang backwards into the gap between the rows of the other wagons, drawing mine. Then he came at me with murder in every cut. I was limited by my wish to do no more than defend myself. It wasn't for me to kill another of the King's knights on the eve of battle, but he clearly didn't see the need for any such nicety.

'"Have you seen your Montague bitch?" he said as he slashed at my head. "I'll have her before you do. Despenser will never be enough for her." I was being forced back down the line of wagons and it was dangerous work keeping him away. He lunged again and his sword tip tore through my tunic and I felt the sting of cut flesh, then I heard a voice roar behind me with enormous power.

'"Put up your swords!" and I recognised it as the King.

'That stopped even Molyns, and Edward strode up to us with Burgersh and Chandos following him.

'"Molyns," he said, "present yourself at my tent and wait outside it on my convenience. Leave your sword behind you." Molyns stalked off and Edward turned to me. "Are you hurt?"

301

he asked, seeing the blood. I told him I wasn't. "Then walk with me," he murmured and sent the other two away.

'He demanded that I account for our fight, how it began and why and I told him everything about the wagon. "That's why I need to talk to you," he said, "but before that, there is something else. What you said to me at the Lionheart's memorial has been weighing on my mind. I have asked Chandos who knows more about jousting than any man in England and he tells me he knows for a fact that you let Despenser beat you in that joust. I take that very ill, Guy. It is your choice whether you fight by the full rules of chivalry for the woman you love, but I dislike it when you put on a sad face at the outcome. I want an explanation."

'I gave him one. I told him the whole story of the double-dealings which brought the serving-girl to me and turned my life away from happiness and I saw in his face and his response that he had suspected something of the sort and had used the threat of his displeasure to force it out of me.

'"And what does Elizabeth feel?" he asked at the end.

'"The same as I do," I said.

He saw it in my face, "Guy have you and she . . . have you . . .? Guy de Bryan, you dog, have you fallen to the level of us mortal men? Ah, I see again I mustn't tease you. Well, let me think about it. Now, I have another pressing matter to discuss. When we have finished talking, we are going back to my tent when we will meet with all my captains and make a momentous decision about the conduct of the battle ahead. You have seen what is in the wagon?" I nodded. "They're for killing Frenchmen," he said, "twenty at a time at a distance longer than the longest bowshot. They use a black powder which has the power of thunder in it, and all they need to make them work is a man with a lighted match. I need your approval to use them."

'"No you don't," I protested. "You need nobody's approval but your own. You're the King."

'"They have caused a small stir among my Lords," he said. "There are some who think they are a direct and flagrant breach of all the rules of chivalry. There are others who think the longbow did away with the need to stand toe-to-toe, and these are nothing more than a more extreme version of the same thing. I can think of only one way of resolving it to everyone's satisfaction."

'I looked at him and I had to ask him what he meant.

'"I mean you must give your opinion, Guy. Like it or not, you have become the watchword of what is fair. If you approve the use of these smoky, noisy tubes of ours, the others will follow." He looked hard at me. "I see you are not sure," he said.

'"How can I be sure?" I replied. "What you describe is something I abhor. Even a bowman has to stand exposed to the enemy's aim. He has to show skill. He has to show deter-mination. He has to stand fast when the horsemen ride at him. Can you tell me the same is true of the man with the match?"

'"No, I can't," he said simply. "He can send a thunderbolt through the ranks of the enemy at no greater risk to himself than the risk of the tube bursting, which to be fair, they have done many times in the testing, then, if the enemy attack he can run away."

'"How can you approve of this?" I demanded. "Don't you see where this will go?"

'"There is one simple reason why I can approve of it," he said, and he sounded equally angry. "Because tomorrow I have to find a way to defeat a French army which is over-whelmingly larger than our own, and if I do not defeat it then I may die or I may be taken prisoner. In either case, my country and yours, Guy, will be under the French yoke. I am asking you to help me make sure that does not happen. Do you understand the position I am in?"

'"Yes."

'"Then come with me and tell the others what you think. It is maybe two hundred paces to my tent. You have two hundred paces to make up your mind and I will not try to sway you any further. I will tell you this though. Whatever you decide, if we win tomorrow I shall announce the annulment of the marriage and your rematch in the Windsor lists with Hugh Despenser who, by the way, has inconveniently returned intact and even more glorious from the sack of Crotoy. If you win then you shall have Elizabeth's hand, and I think anything you may have done in the past will be sanctified by that marriage, don't you?"

'We walked in silence to his tent and just before we got there, he said, "It will not have escaped your notice that the chances of my being alive to make such an announcement will be affected by your decision."

'I wish he hadn't said that. It was twisting the knife and I had already decided, not for myself, but for him, because I recognised that I could not be the means by which the King failed his nation.'

The squire fed the fire a few more chippings, rubbed his hands in front of it and said, 'I hope I may never be caught in such a trap. You approved his plan because you had to.'

I nodded.

'So what happened? I never heard that they were used in the battle.'

'That was because of the shame that followed,' I said. 'How far did I get before? We were on that little ridge by the windmill. I was with the King. It gave us the best view and we held our reserve there, such as it was, to throw into any breach. It was also just above the Prince's position, which gave the King comfort because his young son was holding that flank against heavy odds. Northampton and the Bishop were to our left. That was when a silence came across the whole of the field of battle, a holy moment, an angel passing. That was when a gap opened in the French ranks and they fell back in awe at the inspiring sight of the blind king galloping to save his men.'

'John of Bohemia.'

'Blind John, lashed to his two friends, tearing through the ranks on those three great horses, their bridles tied together.'

'No one touched them.'

'Men moved aside for them. They rode right through their own men, towards our first line and I think our men would have moved aside too. I spurred my horse to meet them because they would have reached the King and someone had to stop them, but Molyns beat me to it. I saw him down below me bend to his work, bend to his black iron tubes, and then a sound was heard that was never heard before on any field of battle. That was when we heard blind fury roar. A jet of flame belched out, black smoke rushed after it and ahead men fell with no assailant near them, fell as if they had been struck down by the Death. That was the first tube. Three more tubes erupted together in a doubled gout of fire and this time, I saw their missiles tear into the men ahead, tear into Blind John and his companions. For just a moment, I thought I saw a jagged hole appear in the shining armour of his breastplate, then all three horses and their brave burden plunged to the ground, smoke swept over the scene and the battle swallowed up the awful sight. In that moment, I knew that chivalry lay dying with them and that we had unleashed a beast upon the battlefield.'

Daffyd stirred and sat up, then shook Rhys awake.

'Our turn now,' he said in Welsh. 'You and the talker, you get some shuteye now. We'll keep you warm.'

# CHAPTER TWENTY-TWO

'"We came ashore soon after dawn near Saint-Vaast-la-Hougue, on the beach running to the south. I waded through the surf holding my weapons above my head. My company had been pretty silent all the way in to the shore. Every man of them, I am certain, was thinking ahead to the fight we faced." Am I going too fast for you?' Eleanor was sitting in one of Eliza's armchairs. Eliza was on a hard chair, her own choice, half turned away, staring out of the window at the encroaching woodland.

'You go on.'

'"I call it Saint-Vaast, because I can see that written on the map, though we're supposed to say Utah Beach. The way I see it, this is France we're invading not the US of A, so I'd sooner call it by a French name. We're not where we were meant to be. We were designated for what they called the northern assault sector, but it all fouled up right away which turned out to be a good thing. I was in a landing craft full of tanks and the one right next to us hit a mine, and that was the end of their big day. Then two of the boats which were meant to be leading us did exactly the same and we had no idea where to go. In the end we landed way down the beach and that was where I say it was a good thing, because there weren't so many German guns right there and most of us got ashore. You would have been right at home there Eliza. Beyond the dunes, there was water, just like your Ley and a neat causeway right across it.

'"Do you know, I never saw a German soldier until we were ashore, I just felt the wind of the lumps of iron he was throwing at us. Well, like I say, we got on shore and I guess the best you can say is that it could have been worse. The main thing is, to my great surprise, I'm still alive.

'"I'm writing you this because I decided something on the boat. I had plenty of time to think about it because after we went aboard in Dartmouth, we sat in those tubs for day after day while the gold-braid brigade made up their mind. When this is over, which could yet be a long time, I'm coming back to our tower and I'm going to sit there and wait for you to arrive and then I'm going to ask you to sing me those songs again, and then I'm going to see if you might let me stay a while.

'"I'm writing this now because we're sitting on the outskirts of a little place called Pouppeville where the 101st Airborne dropped their paratroops yesterday and we don't want to go no further case we get a mix-up with friendlies. I have no objection to lying here in this hole, letting some other folk do the fighting. Maybe the supplies will catch up with us."'

Eleanor looked up.

'That's where it ends, I'm afraid.'

'What happened?' Eliza's voice was almost timid.

'There's a note from Eddie with it. He didn't write too well. He says Jimmy dropped his helmet and it rolled down the slope and when he went to get it, he was shot. I'm sorry.'

'He was coming back,' said Eliza. 'He was coming back. I knew he would if he could.'

'It's in an envelope and on the outside of the envelope, he wrote, "To Eliza the beautiful girl with the beautiful voice. Slapton with the tower. Devon south coast. England."'

'Please let me see?' Eliza took it, and gazed at it then she lifted her head again. 'I used to sit on the bank by the road, you know, after the war. Every car that came, I thought it might be him.' Her eyes were shining. 'Oh dear.' She bent forward, dropped the envelope and put her head in her hands and Beth went to put her arms around her grandmother. For a moment, the old woman was a vibrating hairpin of misery, then she gave a sigh and went limp, as if she were being poured out through Beth's grasp.

Eleanor was with her in a moment and together they cradled Eliza as she folded up.

'Has she fainted?'

'I think so.'

'Put her head down.'

They held her carefully.

'It's not making any difference,' said Beth, desperate. 'What do we do?'

'Phone an ambulance,' answered Eleanor. 'Come on. Let's lay her on the sofa. She's breathing fine.'

'There's no phone.'

'Use my cell phone.'

'There's no signal down here. I'll go and call from the quarry. It's the nearest phone.'

Beth ran down the path which seemed so much longer, thinking if there was no one there, she could unlock the office and use the phone, hoping there would be someone there. Lewis was there. He saw her coming.

'Is it Eliza?' he said.

She nodded, out of breath. 'She's collapsed.'

'I'll phone for help,' he said. 'Go back. Look in the right-hand drawer of the dresser. There's a bottle of capsules with a red lid. Break one and put it in her mouth. Have you got that? Go. I'll be right there.'

He was there in five minutes and he brought with him Doctor Morrison, the retired GP who lived at the end of the lane.

Beth and Eleanor, who seemed just as anxious, hovered behind him while he inspected her, and then Eliza's eyes opened and she stared at the old doctor.

'Bugger off,' she said, and he laughed.

'I think she's on the mend. She ought to go in for a check-up. Would you like me to phone for you?'

'Yes please,' Beth smiled at him in relief. 'That's very kind.'

He went out and Eliza tried to sit up.

Eleanor knelt down by her. 'Just take it easy,' she said. 'Shall I make a cup of tea?'

'There's a bottle of mead on the dresser,' said Eliza. 'That's better than tea.'

Lewis stood there, looking questioningly at Beth and she realised what she had forgotten to do. 'Lewis, this is Eleanor. I found her down at Torcross, at the Tiger ceremony.' He put out a hand and Eleanor shook it.

'This will come as a surprise,' Beth said, 'but it turns out that Eleanor is a relation.'

'A relation of yours?' Lewis asked.

'Yes, she's Dad's half-sister.' She watched Lewis working it out and knew that Eliza had never told him the story of Jimmy Kimber and the Chantry tower. That pleased her.

'Right,' said Lewis. 'That certainly is a surprise. A very nice one.'

'We all need to get used to it,' said Eleanor. 'Shall I get that tea?'

'I'll do it,' said Lewis quickly. 'It sounds as if you've got plenty to talk about.'

'Eleanor,' Eliza said weakly. 'You come and sit by me so I can hear you. Do you have a photograph of Jimmy?'

'Not with me. I have one back home. He's in uniform and it was taken just before he came over here.'

'I would like to have a copy of that picture,' said Eliza. 'I might be remembering him wrong. He was a fine man. Very fine.'

'I'll send it to you the minute I get back.'

'I suppose you must be Beth's half-aunt,' said Eliza. 'Is there such a thing?'

'No, I think there's only aunts,' Eleanor answered, turning to look at Beth, 'and I'd be very pleased to be her proper aunt, if that's all right.'

'Gran, I'm not sure you should be talking. Just take it easy.'

'Nonsense girl. How do I know I'm alive if I can't talk?'

'You sound OK to me,' said Eleanor. 'Just as long as you lie still.'

Beth was still wrestling with the idea that she now had three relations, not just two, but on another level the matter was already settled. There was something undeniably family about Eleanor, and that seemed to carry the promise of a fresh start. It suddenly struck her that Eleanor might have sisters and brothers of her own.

As if Eleanor guessed what she was thinking, she said, 'You wait until I tell you about all your cousins. I didn't like being an only child so I made sure my children never suffered from *that* problem. And just think, I wasn't an only child after all.'

Lewis came in with the tea and Beth was relieved to see that he'd ignored Eliza's request for mead.

'Does Guy know about this?' he asked.

'Not yet.'

'Do you want me to go and find him? You'll be going with Eliza, will you?'

'Oh, yes, I suppose so.' The speech would have to wait even longer. 'Lewis, don't tell him about Eleanor, will you. I think I ought to do that.'

'Yes, I think you should. Do it carefully.'

'Of course I will,' she said, but she didn't yet have any idea how she would go about it.

It was another fifteen minutes before the ambulance came.

'Phone me if you need a lift back,' Lewis told her. 'They'll probably keep her in.'

'I'll be at the hotel,' said Eleanor. 'Give me a call there, will you? I've written the number down.'

Eliza spent the first half of the slow journey in the ambulance complaining about all the fuss. 'I've got my tablets,' she said. 'I'm perfectly all right. Lewis always goes on so.'

'Has this happened before, Gran?'

'Once or twice. It's nothing to get bothered about. Lewis keeps an eye on me.'

'Well it bothered me,' said Beth. 'I was so glad he was there, I was terrified.'

'He's a good boy, Lewis. You should have treated him better.'

'Me? Oh Gran, that was ages ago.'

Eliza changed the subject. 'I think she's very like her father. I hope she remembers to send me the photograph.'

Beth smiled. 'She looks like Dad, so that means Dad must look like Jimmy, I suppose.' Before this day, her only relations had been two people surrounded by their own walls of silence, two people with no known history. That had made it easier to start her life again, to break contact with her childhood. Now she felt as if she were a tree, sending roots down into the soil with bewildering speed.

'I don't think Guy looks like Jimmy, not really. You can look like two people without them having to look like each other.' The old woman reached out and squeezed Beth's hand.

'I thought you said you were worried that you might have forgotten what Jimmy really looked like?'

'I've always kept his face there in my head,' said Eliza, 'but I suppose I might have kept changing it and course, it was mostly in the dark. Looking at Eleanor has sort of freshened it up. I'm glad you found her. It was meant to be, you coming back here. Finding her and being here in time to sing the mass as well,' and Beth kept quiet because it didn't seem the moment to say that nothing had changed in that respect.

*　　　*　　　*

311

They decided to keep Eliza in overnight at the hospital, and Lewis came, as he had promised, to pick up Beth in his truck.

'I couldn't find Guy,' he said as they drove back to Slapton. 'They said he's off somewhere around the Ley, but I couldn't see him.'

'I'll find him when I get back.'

'Break it to him gently. He's not as strong as Eliza.'

'Not as strong as Eliza?' She thought of Eliza's feather-weight body crumpling in her arms and that seemed absurd, then she knew what Lewis said was true for all that. There'd soon be nothing left to tie her to Slapton, nothing left to cause those occasional twinges of guilt. A momentary feeling of relief inverted itself into utter bleakness and she quickly turned to stare out of the window.

'Are you all right?' he said.

'Me? Why wouldn't I be?'

'You've had a pretty momentous day.'

She nodded. 'I suppose I have. You know, if I hadn't come back down, none of this would have happened. You wouldn't have hurt your head and I wouldn't have found Eleanor. Eliza wouldn't be in hospital. Life would have gone on quietly and easily the way it always does in Slapton.'

'No,' he said, 'you're wrong there. Life may have been going on quietly but it wasn't going on easily, not with your dad in the state he is and Eliza worrying about it every second of the day. I like the look of Eleanor, don't you? Finding her could just be the best thing for both of them. Oh, and for the record, I'm not at all sorry that I hurt my head.'

She looked at him and looked quickly away. In the silence, he put a tape in the cassette player and all the way back to Slapton they listened to Grieg.

Lewis stopped in the road in front of her father's cottage. 'He usually comes home about now,' he said, 'I sometimes pass him on the road, but he never wants a lift.'

312

'I'll walk down and meet him.' She felt it would be easier to talk in the open air than in that constricted house of his.

'I forgot. Eleanor meant to give you this.' He reached under the seat of the truck and brought out a package the size of a book, done up with bubble wrap. She took it. It was much heavier than a book.

'It was with the letter, something else from Jimmy Kimber's gear. She thought you ought to have it.'

'What is it?'

'I don't know.'

The bubble wrap was very thoroughly taped up. Lewis offered her a knife and she slit it down the side.

'It's a piece of stone,' she said, 'a stone triangle. Why would he have carried that through an invasion?'

'Turn it over.' Lewis's voice was urgent.

She did so, and when she saw the faint grooves on the other side, she understood. 'It's from the inscription, isn't it? From Guy de Bryan's inscription. It's the missing piece.'

'Why did he have it?'

'Eliza told me,' she said. 'They sat in the tower all night, her and Jimmy Kimber. It was lying in the grass and she told him what the inscription said.'

Lewis looked completely astonished. 'One thing at a time,' he said. 'I'm having to do a lot of guessing. Eliza met this man Jimmy at the Chantry?'

'Yes, on Saint Petronella's Day.'

'When she sang the mass?'

'Yes.'

'And they got together.'

'It was just that night. A wartime thing, but she's carried the torch all this time.'

'And, hang on, you said she told him what the stone said. *She knows* what the inscription says?'

'Roughly.'

'And she never told me?'

'Lewis, she probably thinks it's our family's business, not yours.'

'Beth, are you by any chance starting to feel it *is* your business?'

She was. Damn. 'No,' she said, 'of course not.'

'What do you want to do with this?' he hefted the stone in one hand, feeling the marks on it with his fingers.

'I think you'd better have it to go with the rest, don't you? Listen, Lewis, sorry. I'm sorry.'

'What for?'

'For being so scratchy. I've got no right to be.'

'That's all right. You've got a lot on your plate.'

'I was so relieved when I saw you, Thank you for coming to the rescue.'

'I told you before, I love your old gran,' he said, 'and your dad. They're the best.' Then, quite unexpectedly, he leant over and gave her a kiss on the cheek. 'Go on,' he said, 'I'm blocking the road. I'll see you at the quarry. I assume you've still got a speech to write?'

'A speech? Oh God, I'd forgotten about it.'

Beth walked down the road towards the Ley. There was no sign of Guy, but she followed her instincts, taking the path that ran along the back of the Ley, and she saw him ahead, sitting on a bench, staring out over the lake.

She sat down next to him.

'How's Eliza?' he asked. 'Have they sorted her out?'

'You *know*? How?'

'By a sort of miracle,' he said. 'Maybe it was an angel. She sounded quite like an angel. I was putting a notice up on the board back there and a car drove past. It stopped and backed up and this very nice American woman said, "your daughter says you look just like me."'

'You met Eleanor?'

'I did.'

314

'And she explained everything?'

'She did. We had a long talk. She's coming back this evening and she says she's going to cook us all spaghetti.'

'All?'

'You, and Lewis too. Her special bolognese.'

'Dad, stop talking about spaghetti. You've just met a sister you didn't know you had. How are you feeling?'

'Pretty good. My biggest regret is that I didn't meet her a long, long time ago. Look, see the heron?'

'Yes. Do you like her?'

'I feel I've known her all my life, so perhaps it doesn't really matter that she's only just appeared. Still, it's quite a lot to take on board. Enough for one day, I should say.'

He stopped as Beth's phone beeped and she took it out with some sort of presentiment that it might have been better left switched off.

'Sorry,' she said, 'I won't be a moment.' She got up and moved a little away from the bench.

The screen said Blakiston. Andrew Blakiston's direct line number was calling her, the Foreign Secretary's right-hand man. It felt like an intrusion, a visitation from a distant planet.

'Is that Beth?'

'Yes Andrew.'

'Beth, we just wanted to know how the old speech is getting along?'

'Fine, Andrew. I'm working on it. It's very nearly finished,' a harmless lie.

'Thing is, old girl, the Foreign Sec's been given a dossier on your friend and mine. Details of all his little escapades. It does seem he was much more your friend than mine, if you know what I mean?'

'No need for innuendo.' Beth looked at her father, still staring at the Ley, watching the circles where the fish were rising. She took a few more paces away. 'I had an affair with him.'

'Well, you know the Foreign Sec. He's a bit of a prude. He's not best pleased. If you want to get your feet back under this table you'd better make that speech a humdinger.'

'I'll do my best, Andrew.'

'My advice, old girl, is you should definitely err on the side of bloodthirstiness, you know? Make it something your mother would approve of.'

'Yes, understood. What? What did you say?'

'Bloodthirsty. I said be bloodthirsty.'

'No, after that?'

'That was all.' He sounded defensive.

'What did you say about my *mother*?'

'Slip of the tongue. Don't forget to have it ready for collection. You'll be at your father's place tomorrow, won't you?'

'No. What do you mean tomorrow?' Tomorrow was Wednesday. They were meant to be picking it up on Thursday.

'Didn't you get the message? Been brought forward. If it's nearly finished, that won't be a problem, will it?'

Caught by her lie, she thought desperately. She'd have to work up to the very last minute. 'I'm borrowing an office.' She gave directions to the quarry, switched the phone off completely and went back to sit down.

'Problems?' asked her father.

'Not exactly, just time pressure. Well that and something rather odd. That was a senior man in the Foreign Office telling me to write a bloodthirsty speech.'

'Is that so odd?'

'What's odd is that he said I should make it something my *mother* would approve of.'

Then he looked at her, and he didn't say, 'how strange', or 'what could he have meant?' He said 'Oh don't do that, Beth. Please don't do that.'

# CHAPTER TWENTY-THREE

The taller of the two Genoese crossbowmen died at about
midday and I wouldn't have minded that much if little Dafydd
hadn't also died trying to save him. We were moving at the
slowest pace imaginable up and up that twisting mountain-
side and now, for much of the time, we couldn't really be
sure we were even *on* the track. It is the custom in the Alps
for travellers to pile rocks up beside the path to mark the
way, but either the snow had covered these cairns or it was
so long since anyone had last passed this way that the wind
of the years had tumbled them. I preferred to think it was
the former, and certainly the depth of the drifts through which
we stumbled made that quite likely.

All I could do was study the lie of the land to work out a
likely route between the rocks, and hope it was the right
one. If it wasn't, then we would all die that night because
the cold, even now the sun was up, was harsh enough to
stop the heart. We had to reach some sort of shelter and any
shelter would lie on the track, not off it.

My men spent their strength on others that day and those
they helped showed no gratitude for it. At noon, we clustered together in the lee of a low rock cliff to make what we
could of our food. I broke the biscuit I was carrying and

passed it all around, and the squire cut his cheese into equal slices for each man. Unbelievably, di Provan then produced a fat sausage, sliced it four ways and gave it only to his fellow Genoese. That turned out to be a waste of one quarter.

I heard the noise as we got up to move off again. It had been a silent world, that black-and-white landscape, but up to our left, somewhere beyond the cliff, there was a far-off rustle which quickly rose to a rumble.

'Stay down,' I shouted as loudly as I could, 'get in under the cliff.'

The rumble had now grown to a roar and I gestured to the Italians, flattening my hand down towards the ground as we dived under cover. I had never seen the snow slide called avalanche, but travellers had told me, and you stay alive by picking the brains of travellers for what they have seen and what might be yet to come for you.

One of the crossbowmen laughed at us, stood up and stepped away to look over the cliff and was immediately engulfed by the charging mountain-side of snow which swept over us. Dafydd sprang to grab his legs and got one arm around them. Then the huge force of that torrent swept the damned crossbowman, I never knew his name, away down the mountain-side taking Dafydd with him, and I *did* know Dafydd's name, had known it since he was born, the first son of my most loyal Gwynn.

We stood up when it was over and looked down on what had been a deep cleft below and was now a rough snow-field. Gwynn plunged down the slope before I could stop him, sank up to his knees at the bottom and began desperately shovelling snow with his hands.

We scrambled down to join him, the squire the first to go, then both the Owens, Llewellyn, Rhys, even the other crossbowman, though his masters stayed huddling under the cliff. We searched the surface of that jumbled calamity, but in the end I knew that Dafydd had run out of time and so had we.

318

'Gwynn,' I spoke in Welsh because this was for my men's ears only, 'he is gone.'

It was as we climbed back up that I saw William's foot slip ahead of me. I broke his slide as best I could, but he bounced off my shoulder and I heard the impact of his body against the rock which stopped him.

'Are you all right?' I called and went down again as fast as I could.

'Yes,' he said testily, then, 'no,' as he stood up. 'My ankle's twisted.'

We got him up to the top again, but he needed support and as we came back up to the other two Genoese, I could feel all the dice falling against us.

'Let us say a prayer for Dafydd,' I said, 'because now we must save ourselves.'

I had sweated down there, kicking and delving into the snow. Now I could feel it freezing deep in the wool of my jerkin. I came to the end of my prayer and as I said 'amen', di Provan struck me in the face. Grabbing his wrist, I held him there and spoke to the squire.

'Ask him why he did that?'

'He says you have killed his man.'

'The snow killed his man.'

'He says your route killed his man.'

'There is no other route.'

'He says your lance can debate this against his own when we arrive.'

'Tell him if we arrive, I am still bound by my vow. I will not joust. Tell him also it is only my command from the King that stops me settling this now with swords or fists or daggers as he chooses. When we arrive, I'll fight him with a sword or anything else he prefers, but I will not joust.'

I flung the man's arm down and he spat at me.

'Translate this,' I said to the squire, and I addressed them all. 'There is no time for this,' I said as loudly as I could and

319

my voice echoed in the valley. 'We have lost friends, but we will join them if we do not act together. The next stage of our journey is the steepest, but at the top, God willing, we will find the hospice of Saint Bernard. Stay together, work together and we will get there.'

We plunged on into the afternoon and it was hard, hard going. William showed the quality of his heart, but he could not take a step without someone to lean on and we were desperately slow. I gathered my band around me and we kept together, with the Genoese coming up behind in the broad path we made with our bodies. It was the only way.

'Go on with your story,' said the squire. 'If we're going to die, I'd rather hear the rest of it first.' I could find no reason not to.

'This part is William's story too,' I said and the priest grunted. 'He'll put me right if I get any of it wrong. Remember that night, William? That night when the King burnt the windmill and we found blind John's body under his horse.'

'I've remembered it every day of my life,' said the priest as he heaved himself another foot forward, waist-deep. 'Not because of blind John, but because that was where I met you and I seem to have been in trouble ever since. If I'd left you to root through that heap by yourself, I'd be at home in front of the fire right now.'

My Welshmen liked that. They pressed forward to hear more.

'Thank you William,' I said, 'I don't remember inviting you.' I looked at the others 'Whatever he says, it was half his idea. I'm talking about Crécy, right? The night after the battle. We pulled the body out of that pile, you see, and we knew for certain it was King John of Bohemia. There was his helmet with the ostrich feathers and when we took it off, we both recognised him by his face. Then we looked at his chest, with the plate armour still on him. We looked at the wound which had killed him. William, tell them, lest I exaggerate.'

'There was a hole the size of a hand right through the plate, its edges buckled in with tremendous force. The ball from Molyns' cannon had passed through him and when we turned him over, there was nothing there.'

'No hole?' said the squire.

'You mistake me. There was nothing there, just a crater of flesh where his back had been as if the ball had gathered up everything inside him and taken it along.'

'We carried him back between us,' I said. 'We carried him back to where the King sat with his knights in front of his tent, staring out at what we had done that day.

'I said, "Lord, I have found King John of Bohemia and I am ashamed," and we laid him on the grass.

'I saw the King cross himself and stare down at the hole in blind John's breastplate. He crouched by the body of the brave old king and touched the torn edge of the metal, then he started to turn him over until he saw what we had already seen and let him go abruptly.

'Get Molyns,' he said, and someone went running.

At last, I thought. At last he has realised the price you pay for giving that thug his head. Now he has seen what this new instrument really does. He has seen the moment of the very highest chivalry dissolved into the most squalid murder.

'Prince Edward appeared first, diverted from his vigil, still wearing his black armour plate and still with the stain of battle on him. The young man was only sixteen, and he had fought two men's battle that day. He had not been present at the discussion of the cannon, excluded perhaps because his father knew what he would say. He too knelt by blind John's body and inspected the wound. We stood watching in silence, William and I.

'Molyns came and it was clear he had not been making

any sort of vigil. He smelt of drink and he was clothed for sleep.

'"I'm here, Lord," he said, bowing to the King and sneering at me. "What further service may I provide?"

'"This is the crop you have harvested, Sir John," said the King. "Look at it and tell me how it seems to you."

'Molyns stirred the body with his toe, and if William hadn't caught my arm, I might have struck him.

'"It's as I told you, Lord," he said. "Even the best steel plate is no protection. It goes straight through. Did you note that after the first firing, they did not press their attack home against my part of the line, but veered away to either side?"

'"I did," said the King. "The effect was remarkable."

'Then I could not restrain myself and I opened my mouth to speak words which might have been my last on this earth, but the good Prince was there before me.

'"This is John of Bohemia lying here, emptied like a drawn chicken," he said in horror, "Blind John of Bohemia who has done the bravest deed I ever saw and we have killed him by the most vile means, and you *condone* it? This was an unforgivable thing."

'The King gave him the coldest of looks and turned to me. "Well Guy, tell him. You approved their use."

'I had approved it, and I could already feel the multiplying evil of what I had done and the cold hand of appalling responsibility clutching my neck.

'"I wish I had not," I said. "I gave you my approval to save us from defeat, but at that moment we were not threatened by defeat. I approved their use, but the method of their use was unforgivable."

'The King's face turned white. "Do not speak to me in such a way ever again, Guy de Bryan. Down on your knees and show respect," and I remember then, I saw the king in him overwhelm the man, the friend. He turned to William here and said, "Down, or I chop your legs from under you," and do you know what William said? He said, "Let us pray, for I am a priest in holy orders and the time is right."'

William nodded at the memory.

'Go on,' said the squire. 'What happened next?' and all my company were pressing up behind us, anxious to hear the outcome.

'You should tell it, William,' I suggested, but he shook his head.

'Not enough memory, not enough breath,' he said.

'He said a prayer he made up on the spot. I can't remember it exactly, but it went something like this, "Our father, give us the wisdom to know that when we seek for advantage against our enemy, they may seek double the advantage in reply. Remind us that your peace was before war, and will come again after war and help us design our actions so that we do not delay that coming. Let us always remember the difference between men and beasts, Amen."'

'Was that what I said? I'm no longer quite so sure there is any difference,' said William, taking another painful step. He was leaning on the squire's arm now and we were taking it in turns.

'A prayer to lose your head for,' the squire said, and I noticed he was now gasping for breath with the exertion of moving.

'Perhaps, but William had the protection of his office. Anyway, as soon as the prayer ended, the Prince claimed the King's full attention. "This man will be my watchword for gallantry," he said, turning back to blind John's body. "I intend to take his crest and wear it as my own," which of course he did, with his three ostrich feathers.

'When the counting had been done in the valley of the clerks, we carried the bodies of the nobles down a sunken pathway to a cleft in the earth where we could bury them. We dug blind John a grave a little above them, and later, when they disinterred his body and took it back to Luxemburg for proper ceremonies, a cross was made to mark that spot. I went to Luxemburg later to take part in a service in his memory though even that was against the King's wishes.'

'And what of the man Molyns and his cannon?' The question came from Rhys who was not as good in the English as he was in the Welsh, but had clearly been listening closely to every word.

'You can judge by the result. Five days later Molyns and the King conferred again and orders were sent back to the Tower of London that every cannon being made at the foundry should be finished, readied for use and despatched to us in France immediately. Shall I tell you the greatest irony? The cannon which killed blind John was cracked in the firing. It only ever fired one ball. I had its mouth cut off, a ring of iron, and I had it fastened to the door of Slapton Church.'

'The sanctuary ring?' asked the squire.

'The same ring that Molyns grasped.'

They talked among themselves when the story ended.

'Look at that,' said the squire. 'We've come a long way while that was going on. Your story gave them something to think about instead of bitter wind and freezing limbs.'

I looked down to where the Genoese were trailing behind, even though they had our flattened trail to help them. 'And now we'll have to wait for them.'

The squire glanced towards the sun and up at the heights ahead. 'Will we make it?' he asked.

I didn't want to answer, but in the end I just shook my head once. 'Not at the speed we're going.'

'Then,' said the squire, 'with your permission, I have an idea.'

# CHAPTER TWENTY-FOUR

'I never meant it to be a secret,' said Guy. 'It just grew that way. Can you imagine what it was like for Gran in the forties, having me? She just brazened it out, wouldn't tell anyone at all what had happened. I bet she just gave them that look of hers and they gave up asking. That's the way I was brought up.'

'You don't have to tell me if you don't want to.'

'I think I do. Like it or not, it seems to be the day for filling in family trees. When you get a phone call like that, it's definitely time. Anyway, I wouldn't want to die without telling you.'

'That's morbid.'

'No, that's accurate, Beth. I'm afraid it's a simple description of what has to be. I really must tell you. It feels a bit like a confession really.'

'What do you have to confess?' asked Beth.

'What do you know about Tina? Has Eliza told you anything I haven't?'

'No, she's never told me anything at all really. Just that Tina wasn't made for motherhood. I think that's how she put it. Dad, both of you closed up like clams if anyone ever got near the subject.'

'All right.' He stared at the water again and she saw his hands were knotted tightly together, the fingers white with pressure. 'I did try and tell you once, when you were quite little, but you didn't really want to know.'

'Let's not get into an argument about who did and who didn't.'

'No, you're right. Trouble is, now I don't really know where to start.'

'How about when you first met?'

'That's easy. It was down on the beach along to the left a bit, towards the cliff. Summer of 1974. There was a dying seal washed up and we were down there seeing if there was anything we could do for it. I saw this flashy cabin cruiser come in and drop its anchor a bit off the beach. There were people shouting on the deck. You often get that you know. They can't hear themselves over the engine, and they don't realise we can hear them perfectly well on shore because the human voice carries further than the engine noise. I was looking at the boat because there's a big kelp bed there and I thought they might end up with a fouled anchor.'

She knew he was working his way back into his memory, and though she was aware of time pressing, she let him go on.

'It wasn't ordinary shouting. I soon realised that because they went on shouting after they'd cut the engine. They were having a row on board, a real old ding-dong, three or four of them at it, then this girl came up out of the cockpit, dived over the side and swam ashore. She wasn't in a swimming costume, she was in shorts and a shirt, and she came out of the sea dripping wet, like Ursula Andress in that Bond film. I thought she was absolutely beautiful.'

'That's really romantic,' Beth said, taken aback by the image. She had always assumed Tina was a local girl from the village, someone of limited horizons.

'Oh, I didn't go up to her and say so, or anything like that.

I wasn't really that sort,' said her father. 'I just looked at her every now and then because she sat down on the beach and did absolutely nothing, while the men in the boat pulled up the anchor and sailed away.'

'She sat there, soaking wet?'

'She looked as if she was drying herself out by the heat of her own anger. I've never seen anyone radiate such fury.'

'But you went up to her in the end?'

'No, no. She came up to me. We'd loaded the seal in a van, and Jerry drove it off to the sanctuary, and I came back down to the beach to pick up my bag of stuff. I remember I took one last look at her and she turned around at that exact moment.

'"What are you looking at?" she said.

'"I was wondering if you were all right," I answered.

'"No I'm effing, blinding not," she said.

'Well, to get to the heart of it, I took her back up to the cottage. I'd only just bought it, 'cause I'd been living with Eliza up to then, but I felt I needed a bit of my own space. I ran her a bath and I put her clothes to dry on the stove.'

He looked at Beth hopelessly. 'I can't exactly tell you what happened next, but one thing led to another and she wound up staying. She made the running.'

'She must have fallen for you.'

'I'm not sure that was the main thing. I think it must have been some sort of revenge.'

'Against who? You?'

'No, against her family, I think. She wanted to lose herself in a far away place.'

'And you got married and then she had me?'

'That was more or less the order. It was one of those things when you know you love someone before you have a chance to find out whether you like them. We were complete opposites, your mother and I. We believed in opposite things. She carried this terrible anger with her everywhere she went, and she was so ambitious. If it hadn't been for getting pregnant, she would have gone even sooner.'

'Why was she so angry?'

'I don't really know the answer to that. She hated her father and everything he stood for.'

'What did he stand for?'

'Oh I don't know,' he said vaguely. 'I never met him.'

Beth smelt evasion. 'You must know something.'

'I think he was much more liberal than she was. She had very strong opinions for someone of her age in the seventies. She used to say she'd fallen out with all her friends back home because they all had bleeding hearts and she didn't. I thought it was just some sort of front she put on, but I don't think I was right. It was more about her childhood than anything else.'

She smelt more than evasion now. This wasn't just about her mother. 'You're trying to tell me that I'm like her, aren't you? What you're saying is that everything I believe in might just come from my genes not from my own brain. Is that it?'

He shrugged. 'Doesn't your brain come from your genes? Oh look, there's the heron again.'

'Forget the fucking heron. No, I'm sorry.' She took a breath. 'Look, I'm not just a blob of irrational DNA which is pre-programmed to take certain attitudes whether they fit the world situation or not. I've studied, Dad. I've read and I've written and I've debated, and everything I believe in has come to me because I've analysed and weighed up the thoughts of generations of political analysts.'

'And how did you know which of those to believe in, Beth? Isn't that still a choice you make, and might not your genes have something to do with that choice?'

'It was obvious.' She took another breath and decided he deserved a rational, unemotional answer. 'No wait. It's just that you read one person's work and there are doubts niggling at you all the way through. Then you read someone else and

328

it's almost right, but it's not quite there, and then finally, you find *the* book, *the* writer who's got it just right. You just know.'

'Who was that writer as far as you were concerned?'

'An American political commentator.'

'Man or woman?'

'A woman as it happens.'

'What's she called?'

'You've heard of her. There's one of her books on your shelf. I saw it. She's called Christie Kilfillan.'

'Yes, I've read it. I know what she thinks. I see that you think the same way, but maybe that's not just because of all those things you said, rational analysis and all that.'

'What else could it possibly be?'

'Beth, Tina *is* Christie Kilfillan.'

Supper proved to be a strange business. Eleanor was clearly puzzled by the odd atmosphere between father and daughter and seemed, Beth thought, to be blaming herself as if she had shaken their world too hard. Lewis arrived late, probably to give them some time together, and left early, making excuses. Beth wondered why her father had invited him at all. The spaghetti was probably very good, but she hadn't tasted it. When they'd washed up and they were sitting down around the fire, Eleanor took the bull by the horns.

'Look, I think I've upset a few things. I'm so sorry I had that effect on Eliza. I'm feeling terrible about it. Maybe I shouldn't have read that letter. It was a case of blundering in too fast.'

'No,' said Guy, 'why do you say that?'

'You two look like you've really been through it today.'

Guy shook his head. 'It's not that. Anyway, it wasn't your idea, was it? It was the happy accident of Beth finding you. It's not really that at all. It's just . . .' he looked at Beth. 'Is it all right to say this?'

She shrugged.

'It wasn't just you. I'm afraid there's been more than one secret in this family. Beth found out who her mother was today.'

He explained carefully and deliberately, and at the end Eleanor looked sympathetically at Beth and whistled.

'What a tough day *you've* had,' she said. 'I'll bet you don't know quite *who* you are after a day like that.'

'That's true.'

'It happens to all of us, though I guess that story's more dramatic than most. We all get to the point where we have to see what's us and what's our parents. I've been through that too.'

'Have you?'

'Yes, I have. I didn't know too much about Jimmy until I started on finding out, but I really hoped I didn't take after my mom.' She studied Beth. 'My guess is you're an independent-minded girl and you'll puzzle your way through this. I don't know your mother, though I have to admit I've seen her talking on the TV shows, but it seems to me you definitely take after your grandmother, from what I've seen of her.' She turned to Guy. 'If you don't mind my asking, how did your wife get on with Eliza?'

'Chalk and cheese,' said Guy. 'Acid and water. Eliza pretended she liked her for the first two days, then gave up on it. It was a fight with Eliza that finally persuaded Tina to pack up her bags and go.'

This was new information. 'What sort of fight?' Beth asked quickly.

Guy looked embarrassed and addressed his answer to Eleanor. 'There's a little ceremony we do every year for someone who used to live here. Tina hated it. She didn't want me to go. She tried to stop me, and Eliza came down and told her it was none of her business.'

'I don't suppose it *was* her business,' said Eleanor, 'not if it was for an old friend of yours.'

330

Guy looked at her. 'No, that's right,' he said, then he and Beth shared a complicitous look.

Eleanor was looking at both of them. 'Hey, Beth, do you realise that makes you three-quarters American?'

The next day, sitting staring at a computer screen that had no more than two hundred words on it, Beth went over everything she knew about Christie Kilfillan. Daughter of an ex-soldier, James McLennan, who had later served as a democratic senator. He'd stood against the Korean War and opposed the McCarthyites. Of course, Tina McLennan, *Christi*na McLennan. It had never crossed her mind. Married to Rosko Kilfillan, the head of a huge manufacturing conglomerate who funded her think-tank. Come on, she said to herself. Put this away for later. Get on with the speech. The jacket notes on the book in her father's shelves said nothing about a previous marriage. Then she remembered her mother's reaction when she'd tried to talk to her in New York, the reaction of someone who clearly didn't want contact. Impossible to think of her as a mother.

She *had* to start writing this speech. Time was dribbling away fast. How had Blakiston *known*? Well of course, they knew everything. She'd been vetted. It wasn't a mystery after all. Tina McClennan. Christina Kilfillan. Maybe everyone had known except her. Obviously Christie Kilfillan knew. 'This is Beth Battock.' What an absurd introduction. Why had Blakiston mentioned her? Because he assumed she knew?

She wrote a sentence, 'The elected leader of a democratic nation who shies from pre-emptive action against the organisers of terror betrays the voters who put him there.' Then she looked at it and shuddered, and pressed the delete key until it had run backwards into the same void from which it had come. That was the problem. It hadn't come from a void. Those words came straight from Christie Kilfillan's books. Or perhaps they didn't. Worse, perhaps they came straight

331

from her mother's genes. It was a terrible moment to be told, because it forced her to look twice at everything she believed and there wasn't time for that.

At midday, with just four hours to go before the scheduled arrival of the ministry car, Beth had half an hour's worth of prose saved on the screen, but she knew it was dull and clichéd, lacking energy and passion. She stared around at the walls of the office with bitter frustration. The dead hand of Slapton had reached out and engulfed her and turned off her muse.

Lewis opened the door. 'Are you all right?' he asked.

She didn't answer.

'Clearly not,' he said. 'I'm going up the hill. Can you do me a favour? Rob's due in soon. I'll be back by one o'clock at the latest. Tell him not to start on the cutting until I'm back, would you? I've got some ideas for him.'

'Right,' she said, and she stopped herself saying, of course I've got nothing better to do than to pass on messages, though she wanted to.

Her next visitor, to her surprise, was Eliza.

'Hello Gran,' she said, getting up out of her chair. 'I thought Dad was fetching you this evening.'

'They needed my bed,' said the old woman. 'Sent me home in a hospital car. It was lovely. Smelt all fresh and flowery.'

'Are you feeling all right?'

'Never better. What's the matter with you?'

'Why should anything be the matter?'

'Saw you scowling as I came in. It's the rays coming off that screen thing if you ask me.'

'No, it's not. I'm just having a hard time with this speech.'

'Maybe you shouldn't be writing it. It's not the sort of thing a young girl should be writing if you ask me, which you haven't. All those nasty ideas.'

'Gran, I know you didn't like Tina.'

The old lady lifted her head, fox-like. 'What's she got to do with it?'

'Dad finally got around to telling me who Tina was last night. I'm me. I have my own ideas. I'm not Tina.'

Eliza looked hard at her. 'You're very like her,' she said. 'You've got her hair and her mouth and your father's eyes.'

'That leaves my nose.'

'They got that in the Harrods sale,' Eliza said, and began to laugh so hard that she started coughing and Beth had to sit her down.

'Look, I must get on with this now,' Beth said when she'd stopped. 'Shall I come up and see you later? They're coming to collect it at four o'clock. I'll come after that.'

'I'll have the kettle on,' Eliza said.

After another half hour of tinkering with the keyboard and doubting the originality of every word that had come crawling on to the screen, there was another interruption. This time it was Rob, Lewis's part-time assistant in the quarry.

'Have you seen him?' he said, coming into the office without any form of greeting. Beth looked at him. He clearly had no idea who she was, and in the intervening years since primary school he had gained about two hundred pounds. It didn't suit him.

'Yes, he said . . .' What had he said? 'He said don't do anything until he gets back. He's got some instructions or something.'

'Instructions? What do I need with fucking instructions?' the man said, and went outside leaving the door open.

Beth stared at the screen with increasing desperation as the hands of the clock speeded up. Make it tougher, she thought. That has to be the way, that should get some power into it. When she tried, she found it had taken on the flavour of Hitler's rants at the Nuremberg rallies.

Two hours went by and Rob appeared at the door again. 'I've got better things to do. If he can't be buggered, nor can I. Tell him to ring me when he gets his act together.'

'Sod off then,' said Beth to his disappearing back, but he didn't seem to hear.

She tried again, and fifteen more minutes went by as she began to think laterally. If she took out the first section and went straight in to the analysis of how the world had changed, of how the pressures had built up, then she might have something that worked. Another five minutes and she knew she was getting down to the good part and discarded the dross, like cutting marble.

Like cutting marble.

She looked at the clock and it said five to three. 'I'll be back by one,' he'd said, 'one at the latest.' What else had he said? 'I'm going . . .' where? 'I'm going up the hill.'

Up the hill could only mean the marble workings, couldn't it? There wasn't anything else up the hill except the workings where she had knocked down the pillar, the leg he'd called it. He was going to put the leg back up and he wasn't here. He was two hours late. Lewis had always been meticulous in everything he did. Lewis was never late.

God almighty, she thought. He's up there under a rockfall and as she thought it, the thought had a horrid feeling of certainty. She reached for the phone, but stopped with her hand hovering over the handset. Who was she calling, the police, the fire brigade? What could she possibly say? That she had a horrible feeling? They'd laugh at her.

The speech needed another hour's work and there only was one more hour. She decided to finish it, see it on its way, and then go up the hill. That decision lasted all of five seconds.

'Damn,' she said, getting to her feet. There was nobody else she could call, and though the speech had seemed the most important thing in her life, the thought of what might be happening in the old workings up on the hill was shouldering it aside. She read through what she had written at lightning speed, made a couple of quick changes, then printed it out, agonising over the sloth of the old printer. She copied it onto a disk for good measure and put both into an envelope. She could be back by four o'clock she thought, but then what if she wasn't? Eliza, she could leave it with Eliza. Writing a quick note giving directions for the ministry driver, she taped it onto the quarry gate and ran down the track to Eliza's cottage.

The old woman was in the kitchen. 'It's not tea-time yet is it?' she said as Beth burst in. 'You look awfully thirsty.'

Beth explained as fast as she could. 'It's probably all right Gran, but I'm just going up there to check,' she said. 'I'm sure it's fine and I'll be straight back down, but if the man comes before I get back, give him this, will you? It's really important.'

'Lewis is more important. You get up that hill, girl.'

She went up through the fields as fast as she could, only slowing when the slope got too much for her and her breath started to rasp in her throat. As she came into sight of the paddock around the shaft she was horrified to see a cloud of dust hanging in the air outside it, then even more horrified to see that the gate in the fence was unlocked.

'Lewis,' she shouted into the tunnel entrance through the thick dust. 'Are you there?'

There was no answer. Wishing she had brought a head-torch, she wriggled into the entrance and crept down the slippery steps into the thicker and thicker darkness, more scared and more desperate with every inch of the way. At the bottom, in the dim light from the shaft, she saw what she most feared through the swirling dust. A big section of the roof had come down and a mound of shattered rock now filled the floor in the centre of the workings, up against a single surviving vertical leg. She crept around the pile, feeling the rocks, trying to find any sign of him

'Lewis!' she shouted again, and there was no answer. She leant across the pile, heaving at a rock which seemed beyond

335

her power to move, breathing in the dust which caked her throat and made her cough. Trying to fight down panic, she thought perhaps she should go for help straight away, but then she looked at the pile and knew that if he was still alive, it wouldn't be for long. She heaved again at the rock and it slid a little to one side. One at a time, she thought, one at a time. Every rock I shift is one less rock to crush him. She heaved again and the rock slipped, pinning her left hand under it, then, as she pushed hard at it with her other hand, it tilted and crashed over, away from her clutching fingers, down the sloping pile. In slow motion, she saw it turn over once, then twice, then collide with the bottom of the other roof support. In the next instant, the world changed. Something hit her very hard on the leg, and she was hurled forward in a rain of rock and an immense noise.

She was in some sort of half dream for a long time, where Eliza was scolding her for carelessness and Lewis was telling her to think carefully before she moved. Then she came out of her daze to find she couldn't move if she wanted to. Her legs were under a pile of stone, and where the round reassuring daylight of the tunnel had been, there was now only a narrow crescent of light.

# CHAPTER TWENTY-FIVE

'You can *use* the story,' said the squire. 'Use it to keep us alive. Tell us all the story of why you won't fight di Provan.' He was radiating heat and passion, becoming, as some men do, the purest essence of himself as adversity increased around him.

'How can that help?'

'Do it like this. Every ten paces, tell us one more part of it. Ration it out, sentence by sentence. Keep the suspense up and everyone will keep going. They won't want to miss it, even that lot.' He nodded towards di Provan and di Mari who were wandering up towards us with expressions of anguish on their faces, as if the flattened path they trod was just as arduous as the snow we had ploughed for them. Even their surviving crossbowman was now doing his best to speed them up, as if he had suddenly realised his own life depended on it.

'They won't understand it.'

'They will when I translate. They'll have to keep close.'

'It will slow us down.'

'It will speed us up. They'll keep going if they're following your bait.'

'You're putting a lot of faith in my story, young man, and

in my ability to tell, it *if* I want to. What makes you think I have such a story?'

'Don't try to fool me, Sir Guy, not up here. The air's too thin for that and I'm too cold to be polite. Listen to me. I know about men's stories. I know there is another part to it, and I think you haven't told anyone.' He shot a glance at William, but William, his face drawn tight with pain, was giving nothing away. 'It's the part you haven't told me,' he went on. 'I've heard the story of the cannon. I understand you feel the guilt of your decision, though anyone would say you only did your duty to your king. Now I want to hear how you won Elizabeth and why that joyful moment now seems to cause you so much pain.'

I thought about it. 'And if it's a story I would rather not tell?'

'Ah! You don't deny that there is such a story. If you would rather not tell it then we will all depend on your leadership to get us to safety tonight.' He was looking at me, studying me closely, and he leant towards me to whisper his next words. 'I see your doubt as to that. If we all die, then you will go to your death with that story still inside you, unconfessed and unshriven, because I believe you have not confessed it, have you?'

I didn't answer, and he swung around on William and spoke again in a full voice. 'He'd confess his tale to you if anyone,' he said, 'Has he?'

'The confessional is a secret place,' said William through his pain, 'but then so is this if we're going to die here so, no, he hasn't.' He heard my sigh and looked at me, 'Oh come on Guy,' he said, 'the boy's right. For all your fat bundle of daft certificates, you're still bound for aeons in Purgatory, if there is such a place. In any case, it's better to die with a clear conscience, that's what I say.'

The truth is my conscience wasn't clear, not at all clear, but what was far more important was that I was instructed by the King to do anything I could to preserve the safety of these people, and I had simply run out of any other ideas.

'We will try. Tell the Genoese what we're going to do.'

He did, and they appeared puzzled, but then the squire added some further explanation of his and they actually clustered closer.

'Almost twenty-five years ago, I jousted for the last time and swore never to joust again, and now I will tell you why,' I shouted so they could all hear, and the squire burst into his own version of it. I turned and we moved forward, forcing our way for ten hard paces up through the snow-bank. I stopped and they were all close on my heels.

'I had sinned. I will make no secret of that,' and for the next two hundred paces, I told them the story of my sin in twenty instalments. Of course, I was gentlemanly. I missed out the fuller details because there was Elizabeth to consider, but I told them enough to explain what was to come, and by the questions they began to ask, I saw they took it as a fitting tale of love.

It was a soaking wet summer of violent storms and there was fear everywhere because we knew the Death was creeping through France towards us. In August, word came that it had stepped onto our island. Two Gascon ships came in to the little port of Melcombe Regis down on the Dorset coast and the whole town died. By September it was advancing towards London, and the rich were retreating ahead of it. Edward called me to Windsor. I thought he would want to discuss the Death to make plans for it, but he had an altogether different matter in mind.

I was shown into the old chapel at the castle, the chapel built by another Edward more than three hundred years earlier. It was an extraordinary mess, not at all as I had last seen it. There were wooden scaffolds and builders' tools everywhere. The old panelling had gone and huge changes were afoot wherever I looked. The King was sitting alone in the front pews and he waved an arm for me to join him. I knelt in front of him, but he banged the seat next to him, so I sat down. He looked around to make sure we were alone.

'Edward the Confessor built this place,' he said. 'Edward the third is rebuilding it.'

In the year after Crécy and the confrontation over blind John's body, he had stayed cold and distant, and I learnt what it was to be the subject of a powerful king's displeasure, but in the following twelve months he had favoured me in various ways. He had made me keeper of the Great Seal of England which was an unexpected honour, and gone out of his way to grant me odd estates here and there. What he had not done was to say anything further about Hugh and Elizabeth, and his proposal to set the results of the last joust aside. If it was forgotten, then perhaps that was for the best. It had been part of a devil's bargain and it had the power to scorch my soul. The King's mind appeared to be on other matters.

'The Death is coming,' he said, 'People are dying in their hundreds and thousands and I greatly fear that I have had a hand in bringing it. Do you have any idea what I mean?'

'I think I do, because I share the same fear,' I told him. 'The firmament of Heaven, it seems to me, is kept intact by the rules of chivalry.'

'Yes,' he said. 'It was the cannon, wasn't it? I fear that was what we did at Crécy when we unleashed that blind fury. We tore a hole in the fabric of Heaven and through that hole the Death has come sliding in.'

'You had to make that decision,' I said. 'As you said, we were hugely outnumbered.'

'Guy, don't fool yourself and don't fool me. We would have beaten them anyway. Our bowmen were slaughtering them. The cannon made no difference to the outcome. All they did was tarnish our victory. I was about to send down to Molyns to tell him not to use them, but I was a moment too late.'

I wasn't sure I believed this, but I pushed my doubt aside.

'I am going to do something to make up for it,' Edward said. 'That's why I am rebuilding this place. It will become the chapel of my new order of chivalry, a society of the most chivalrous knights, the finest fighters in the land. It will be King Arthur's Camelot reborn, and I intend to call it the Order of the Garter. At the end of this month, there will be another tournament here to mark its inauguration, and if we show we are returning to the highest standards of the code of chivalry, perhaps we will yet be spared.'

I gave them the gist of this and then had to wait while the squire translated into Italian something that I presumed was an overblown account of my long history with Molyns, because I kept hearing his name, and the Genoese kept looking at me with more respect than they were wont to show.

We came to a place where the wind had carved the snow in a curving bank hanging over our path to give us shelter, and there, I was delighted to see, sticking up through the snow on the other side, what was unmistakably a cairn of stones, piled one on another.

I was about to announce that we were indeed on the path, when I realised in time that I had never admitted I was unsure of that fact.

There are times, I have found, when the voice may tell a tale but the mind roams on ahead to pick its way through the parts the voice has not yet come to, and that was what I did despite the cold, despite the enormous physical effort we were having to make.

That dreadful summer of '48 got even worse as the tournament approached. It had rained for months on end. The harvest was ruined in the fields. Indeed it didn't just rain, the sky was split day and night by lightning bolts, and the rain was driven sideways by tempest-blasts of wind. The stricter priests started preaching that we were being punished for our sins, and that there were better examples to be set by the nobility than spending their energy on fine clothes and jousting.

We levered William up for the next section of our journey, and this time, the surviving crossbowman came to take his other arm, probably, I thought, to be nearer to the squire's translation.

I told them of the tournament all the way up that next part, of how the lists were muddy and treacherous, and that between every joust they spread straw and sand to little effect. Under the mud was hard stone, and when the horses' hooves hit that, anything could happen. Finally I had told them all the stories I could remember and I could no longer avoid the moment when I entered the lists on the tournament's final day. It was a fancy of the King's that we were to represent knights of Arthur's table. I was billed as Sir Lancelot and my opponent was, if memory serves me right after twenty-four years, Sir Gawaine. I met the King's gaze and he bowed his head to me just ever so slightly, then I looked down the lists to see 'Sir Gawaine' emerging, and there was Hugh Despenser riding that same superb horse with which he had forced the crossing at Blanchetaque. It was Palamon the magnificent, after whom my own Palamon is named.

I rode straight to him. 'What? Are we to meet?'

'The King says so,' he answered in the curtest way imaginable. 'Before the rain starts again.'

'It's too late for that.' The light was fading as the next storm cloud swept over the castle and spread its shadow on us. A new spatter of raindrops had the crowds in the seats reaching for their canvas.

'We'll get on with it then, Guy.' He spoke to me so coldly. 'Unless you'd rather wait for the sun to come out? You haven't forgotten the outcome of our last meeting, I hope?'

He wheeled Palamon away. Then he was gone, rearing Palamon in the air, which was a risk in that mud, and charging off to the other end.

342

The bitterness of his words broke around me. I cantered back towards my place, and as I did so, I saw Elizabeth, sitting to one side of the King's box, looking from one to the other of us with a drawn, white face. The King was staring at me intently. On impulse, I pulled my horse up in front of him and raised my visor.

'Sire,' I said, 'Sir Lancelot shall fight Sir Gawaine with no other goal in mind than the display of the fullest chivalry and no other reward expected.'

He nodded. 'That is the purpose of this tournament.'

I took my place with some relief, but it didn't last long. That first pass was a revelation. I have never met such a determined foe in my whole life. This was not the Hugh Despenser I had met last time, even when the fierce competition between us had spurred him on. There is a conscious difference between jousting and true battle in the way you hold a lance. For some years, since the earliest days of the campaign in France, we had had very few mounted charges, having adopted the King's tactics of fighting mostly dismounted, but there had been a few occasions when a determined assault on horseback had still been necessary, and one or two of those had been with lances rather than swords. At times like that, the grip on the lance is different, a tighter, harder grip to make sure that the thrust of the lance does not abate at the moment of impact. That is not the grip you use when jousting, not unless you want to kill your opponent, rather than simply unhorse him.

Hugh Despenser had the death-grip on his lance for certain, and he never wavered an inch. My hand was looser. We met with a crash that shattered both our lances and I was lucky to stay in the saddle.

We took our places with new lances for the second run, and I found whatever I did, that my hand hardened its grip. The rain had started coming harder. Watching Hugh circling at the far end, I knew he had decided to show no quarter. I wondered for a moment if the King had told *him* that Elizabeth was at stake, because surely this was more than a matter of pride. There was hatred here.

My time to think ran out because we were called to position and the flag was dropped. Then there was only battle-time, that strange state of the highest alertness when every moment draws out to twice its length and you have time to observe the tiniest detail in the middle of the carnage. I saw Hugh Despenser accelerating towards me in a tighter stance than I had ever seen him before. He was tucked and curled as far as armour allows into a lethal ball of fury, coming at me with the tip of his lance rock-steady and every fibre of his being intent on killing me.

What could I do? Pull up? Concede the fight? Breach the King's instructions and hazard the purpose and reputation of his tournament? I couldn't. The only way to meet such an attack is to match the way it is delivered. I tightened my grip and aimed my lance. Hitting the shoulder will spin a knight from his horse. Hitting the neck may kill him. I aimed for the shoulder, and Hugh aimed for the neck. Neither of us died, but only because our lances clashed and deflected each other, unhorsing us both in the process. I was back on my horse quickly, but Hugh was winded and it took some time before he even got to his feet. In that time, I rode to the King again.

We looked at each other. I said, 'Sire, my opponent has taken a hard hit. Might the requirements of chivalry have been met?'

He glared at me. 'Three passes, knight. That is the rule. Go to it,' and he turned his head away.

On my way back to the end, I looked back at Edward again. He was staring at me. Then I knew for certain what was happening here as surely as if he had told me. Knowing my objections to a straightforward challenge, the King had sought a conclusion to our business by roundabout means.

I knew that Edward had told Hugh Despenser of my sin with Elizabeth and that this fury I was facing stemmed from that.

The flags dropped for the last time, and as we began the long gallop, my mind was still swirling with possibilities. I forced my fingers looser, but they tightened again. I shifted the focus of my aim from his neck to his shoulder and back again. One of us was going to die on this field. Hugh was coming at me with murder in mind and, at the doubled speed of two horses galloping, there was no time left to sort out the rights and wrongs of it and then, at the very last moment, I remembered Palamon's blind spot.

I had seen that horse in battle at Blanchetaque, and I had seen him in the lists, and I knew he was above all a warhorse, not a jouster. The one thing, the single thing that could make him jink from his rider's chosen course, was a spear coming for his own eyes, straight at him. It was a good gift to have in battle, but a bad one in the lists and I thought it might just save the day for both of us.

At the last possible moment, I moved my point down at him, then lifted it again as he swerved, taking Hugh's lance and mine harmlessly past each other.

I should have done anything else but that.

I stopped telling my story then because I was suddenly aware that we had spread out again and the translation had been interrupted. The squire and Rhys had stopped five paces back and were crouched over di Mari who was face down in the snow. We all went back.

'He's had it,' said Rhys. 'Look at the colour of him.'

It was true. The man's face was blue. His breathing was shallow and his eyes were closed.

'It's the bone-cold,' Rhys suggested. 'He needs heat or he's dead.'

'We'll have to carry him.'

'What's he saying?' asked the squire. I had forgotten we were speaking the Welsh.

'We'll try carrying him.'

'We'll all die if we do that.'

'We must try.'

So we did. I could see a ridge up ahead, maybe two or three hundred paces away, and it struck me that it might well be the summit of the pass.

'We'll get him up to the top there. That's where the hospice must be. Come on, two of us can manage him, and when we get to the top, I'll tell you the whole of the rest of the story and then William, I'll ask you for God's forgiveness.'

Oh, that was a slow and dreadful business. We half carried and half dragged the man, for he was a well-built, heavy fellow. Di Provan fussed around him and even helped as much as he could, which was not much, while William made do with only one man to lean on and swallowed his own pain. I wondered if we should send someone on ahead to get help, but all the time, I knew only too well that we would probably find at best an abandoned building. Our time was running out very fast. The sky was darker every moment, with a purplish tinge to it.

The ridge ahead was sharp against the sky, and as we inched nearer and nearer, it looked more and more like the summit which is why, when I finally took the last two or three steps and came on to it, what I saw hit me with devastating finality.

It was a false ridge, and on that, all our hopes broke. Ahead I could see the real summit of the pass, across miles of snow and rock, but it was impossibly far away.

I knew then that at least two of us would die here, William and the man from Genoa, and I knew my duty must now be to save the rest.

'You must all go on ahead,' I said. 'I will bring William up behind. If you find help there, send it back for di Mari. We will cover him with what we can.'

I knew it was a sentence of death for him and probably for William and me as well.

346

'Go on,' I said. 'Go now and go as fast as you can. Up there, you will find a roof and walls.'

'Tell us the end of the tale,' said the squire. 'Then we'll decide whether we obey you or not.'

'I lead this party. You will obey me.'

The squire looked around. 'No, we won't. Not until you tell us what happened next.'

'We're wasting time.'

'*You're* wasting it. Tell us.'

So I did, simply because it was the fastest way to get them moving.

'As I said, Palamon swerved and we missed each other, but as I reigned in and turned my head I saw the consequences of what I'd done. In swerving, Palamon lost his footing on the stone below the mud. One front leg twisted under him. I saw Hugh Despenser, clutching at his bridle, fly forwards over the horse's shoulder to the ground, then saw the horse, unable to do anything to stop himself, roll over on his master.

'I ran to Hugh and we hauled him from under his dying horse, and for a moment I thought he was all right.

'Then he coughed and blood came from his mouth. "You killed me Guy," he said. "You killed me with a trick," and that was the last sentence he spoke.'

'And for *that* you have punished yourself all these years?' barked William. 'Are you as stupid as that? You were trying to *save* him. Lord, you've even called your best horse after his.'

The squire was still translating.

'The King gave us no choice. He had us married the next year. I told him I was undeserving, that I had been the instrument of Hugh's death, and he wouldn't listen. He said God knew what he was doing when he first made the chain of love. He said all men had their predestined hour in this wretched world which they could not go beyond.'

347

'And you chose to ignore that,' said William. 'Why?'

'No. For ten years I let his judgement sway me. For ten, years Elizabeth and I lived as happily as it was possible to be, so wrapped in our love that we did not look beyond it. Then she died, and that was when I began to think, and I knew I had been given my sign. You well know what happened next, what came at the end of that year? The great new order of chivalry made no difference. Despite the tournament, the Death came to silence our towns and villages, and it was my sin, my corruption of the rules of chivalry which helped open the door to it.'

'That was your sign?' The old priest stared down the valley.

'I am sure of it.'

'You believe in signs do you?' he demanded. 'If you had another sign right now, a sign of the same weight and significance, a sign to match that fatal swerve of Palamon, then would you start to believe it's all right to live?'

'There won't be any such sign, William.'

'But if there were,' he said, 'then will you promise me to forgive yourself?'

'Yes,' I said, as much to stop him wasting time as anything else. 'but I don't know what you mean.'

'I mean you should look back down there. There's your sign.'

I turned to look where he pointed and could not at first understand what I saw. Two dark shapes were plunging and leaping up the trail behind us, like dolphins in the snow, and then I saw them for what they were, Palamon and Arcite, broken once again from their captivity, following the path we had flattened as we went.

348

# CHAPTER TWENTY-SIX

Beth gulped for air and there was only dust, coating her throat and choking her. She forced herself to breathe slowly through her nose. The dust swirled round her head, strangling the faint light from the shaft. Fifty feet above her were the green Devon fields, but that fifty feet hung over her in the darkness, a vast mass of rock held above her poised to squash her as casually as a human boot might crush a bug. She found she could only move her body from her hips up. Her legs, trapped in the mass of fallen stone, were starting to hurt badly. She tried to shout but her throat seemed to stick and the dust muffled the small, desperate noise she made and even then, more fragments of rock came cascading down as if she had caused them to. A drop of water fell on her cheek but the dust silently absorbed any others.

Beth did what she could to hang onto hope. She twisted round, reaching out to try to pry the mound of stones apart but she hadn't the strength and could barely get a purchase on them. How long would it be before someone came? Would the roof stay up that long? Lewis would come. Lewis would get her out. Then the most awful knowledge of all hit her with the returning memory of why she was here. Lewis wouldn't come. Lewis was in here with her. The gate had been unlocked. He hadn't come back to the quarry. He must be here under these rocks and her carelessness had killed him.

The sorrow which overwhelmed her astonished her at the same time because she couldn't tell whether it was for her own helpless state or because Lewis was dead. There had never before been a moment when she could get a clear focus on him. The village boy who'd vied with her for top of the class. The boy who'd stood up for her at grammar school. The seventeen-year-old she had suddenly found disconcertingly attractive one summer's day here at the top of this hill, when they had each lost their virginity in the same moment and discovered something unsaid. He was the only thing that could have kept her here. She had to turn her back on him to break away from Slapton, there being no place in her future for her past. She had to invent ways to despise him. It was only possible to admit all this to herself because she knew she had lost the chance of ever putting that right somewhere under this pile of stone.

One of her legs was going numb and the other was hurting even more. She twisted herself up as far as she could go and managed to pull one small rock loose, but it slid towards her and she had to push it away with her hands as it tipped and fell towards her face. She lay very still after that, trying to breathe through her nose but her nostrils were blocking up with the dust and every breath she took through her almost-closed lips added more dust to the choking layer in her throat. She heard a drip from the roof falling on to stone somewhere where it had washed the dust clean. There was no time left to put anything right. There would be no time to tell her father that she would miss him, no time to hug Eliza as she hadn't hugged her for years, no time to get to know Eleanor better, and no time for Lewis. The thought of dying here with him, of leaving all that ragged mess behind, filled her with anguish.

She closed her eyes, imagining the mass, imagining Eliza and her father singing it in the Chantry tower, singing it for her, imagining it ending forever. Another piece fell from the roof to her right and the echo filled the workings and in that echo, covered up by it, there was a new sound. She heard it again. A voice. A man's voice calling from up there, echoing down the tunnel.

'Is there anyone down there?'

She tried to answer but the dust choked her.

It called again. 'Is there anybody down there?'

She still couldn't make a sound.

'Hello?' it said again. 'Can anyone hear me?'

Reaching out, her fingers found a lump of rock she could hold and she lifted it and banged it down on the floor, again and again.

The man shouted to her once more. 'All right, I can hear you. Stay still. I'm coming down.' The echo rolled over her.

It seemed to take ages. She heard stones moving. 'Knock again,' he called. 'I need to know you're there.'

She banged the stone hard, hoping he'd say something else, straining to hear the precise shape of his voice through the echo and the dust. Another drip fell on her cheek and then another, and she turned her head sideways to catch the drops of water. There was a sudden run of five or six drips together and she spread the meagre liquid around her mouth with her tongue.

'Hello?' she said and it came out so faintly she wasn't sure he would hear, but he did. The noise of stones being moved stopped.

'Beth?'

'Lewis?'

'Are you hurt?'

'Yes,' she whispered. 'My legs . . .'

'Can you move your toes?'

'No.' She choked again.

'I'm coming to you as fast as I can.' He sounded like a desperate man trying to be calm. 'I'm putting up some supports as I go.'

She wanted to explain, to tell him she'd thought he was here, that the gate was unlocked, that she had been trying to get *him* out.

'I'll be with you in a minute. I've got a water bottle.'

Something else fell and a broken piece of rock skipped across the floor and hit her arm.

'Hurry.'

'Beth. I'm going to get you out. I'm not losing you now.'

'What?'

'I said I'm going to get you out. OK, the tunnel's nearly clear.'

She heard him working faster, the sound of rock on rock, and in what could equally have been five minutes or an hour, she was aware that he was kneeling by her side, dribbling water into her mouth. She spat it out and he gave her more, then he wiped her face and her eyes clean.

'I'm going to start moving the rocks off you, love. Just be patient.'

More rock fell to her right.

'Wait,' he said. 'I'll need to put another support in over there. It won't take long.'

'I don't want you to go away.'

'I'm not going far. I'll talk to you.'

He moved away and she turned her head to watch him as he started piling slabs of stone under the place where the rocks had been falling.

'What happened was, I came up here,' he said, 'and I saw there'd been a fall, so I started back down to get a prop from my house.' He had the support pillar half-way up to the ceiling now. 'The phone was ringing when I got there. It was George calling from Dartmouth. He'd finished the translation. You know? Guy de Bryan's inscription?'

'Yes.'

He cast around for another stone of the right size and heaved it up to chest height.

'I went right over there to pick it up. I couldn't wait. I'm so sorry. I wish I hadn't.'

'I thought you were dead.'

'I thought you were too.'

She watched him as he struggled to raise three more stones to complete the pillar. All she could hear was his breathing and she needed his voice again.

'Talk to me, Lewis.'

'OK. I went to Eliza's when I saw your note and she said you'd come up here. I ran all the way, Beth. I was bloody terrified.'

'So was I.'

He shoved and heaved the final stone into place then jammed smaller stones into the gaps to wedge it, looking carefully at the rock ceiling. 'That should hold it,' he said and he came back to her. 'Now let's get that stuff off you.'

He started moving stones and Beth yelped in pain. 'OK,' he said in a tone of relief. 'It's not too bad. There's a big slab across you, but it's supported at one end. It's keeping most of the weight of the rocks off you. Once I've got them out of the way, the rest is small stuff. There's a bar over here. I can do it.'

'You said, you're not losing me now?'

He grunted with effort as he levered the large block to one side, then delved into the stone pile again, scattering smaller rocks.

'Well, you don't deserve it but I never stopped thinking about you.'

He pushed the bar in under another slab.

'Careful, that hurts. Thinking what about me?'

'Thinking you're worth it in spite of everything.'

'Ow, Jesus.' There was a crash and the weight went from her legs, then a grunt from Lewis.

353

'That's got it,' he said. 'Let's have a look.'

'It bloody hurts.'

'I'm not surprised, but I think that big rock saved you. Don't try and move your legs. I'll see if I can pick you up. Let me just roll you over.'

He had his arms underneath her and he half straightened, cradling her in the narrow space. He stopped and looked at her and in the dim, dusty light, she saw the look on his face, then he bent his head and kissed her quickly on the forehead.

A faint and familiar voice called down from above. 'Are you down there, Lewis?' it said.

'Eliza?'

'That's right. I hope you can come up because I don't fancy my stockings down there. Is Beth down there with you?'

'Yes, we're coming up.'

'I should think so too. That's a funny place to be carrying on.'

'She's hurt her legs.'

Lewis got Beth to the base of the shaft and began inching his way up it, crawling backwards with her held tightly to his chest with one arm. Every foot lifted the fear a little further.

'Eliza, are you by yourself?' he called when they were half-way up.

'No. Eleanor's here too.'

'Has she got her mobile phone?'

Eleanor's voice called down. 'Yes. What do you want?'

'Call Rob. He's got a Land Rover. Tell him to get it up here right now.' He gave her the number.

As the mouth of the tunnel opened up and the blue sky greeted them with sweet air, Eleanor was waiting to help get Beth out and on to the grass. They laid her down gently. Eleanor inspected her while Eliza sat by her, dabbing her face with a damp handkerchief.

'It's not a very pretty sight. Your legs took a hammering. You've lost quite a bit of skin,' said Eleanor, 'and you're going to be black and blue from the crushing. We'd better get you to hospital.'

'What time is it?' Beth asked. It was hurting more and more but she had suddenly remembered all that had happened before she got trapped.

'Close on six,' said Eliza.

'Gran, did the man come for my speech?'

'I gave him what he needed. He didn't look like a foreign minister to me.'

'No, he wouldn't, Gran.'

'Here's Rob,' said Lewis, staring down the hill. Eleanor glanced at him, then looked again.

'You're bleeding all over the place, Lewis,' she said. 'The back of your head's a mess. That shirt's going to take a bit of washing.'

'Always happens when you take Beth underground,' he said, 'but it's worth it.'

They held Beth between them in the back of the Land Rover and Rob took them straight down to Lewis's cottage. They carried her inside and for a moment she felt a surge of panic, wanting to be out under an open sky. The house soothed her immediately. It was full of light and white paint and carved stone.

'Hospital for you two,' said Eleanor. 'I'll drive you. At least my rental car's got springs.'

'I don't need the hospital,' replied Beth. 'I can move all my toes now.'

'Oh yes, you do.' Eliza wasn't having any argument. 'No question. Anyway, we've got to go anyway 'cause we need to go and see Guy. They've taken him in there. Two birds with one stone.'

'Dad's there?'

'He was took bad this afternoon, just before we came up.

That nice old doctor drove him there. Said he'd be staying in.'

'Oh no.'

'Well, you can go and see him but you'd better let them give you a bit of a clean-up first or you'll frighten the life out of him.'

In Accident and Emergency they put Beth on a trolley and they waited with all the other miscellaneous wreckage of the day. Eleanor came back from her enquiries with a set expression on her face.

'Guy's in a ward upstairs,' she said, sitting down next to Beth, 'but I'm afraid they're not very happy about him.'

'He was fine this morning,' said Beth, gripping her hand.

'They say there's a few things all going wrong at once, Beth. I talked to one of the specialists. He didn't want to talk to me at first, then he asked me if I was a close relation. Funny. I suddenly realised I was. He said they need to get Guy's pain relief sorted out, so they're planning to keep him in for a bit. Did you know he refused to have chemo when they offered it?'

'He didn't want it,' said Eliza. 'Said he needed to keep his hair on 'cause you get cold winds around the Ley.'

For the next hour, Beth was processed slowly through the X-ray department and once they'd found a great deal of crushing and bruising but no actual breaks, they dressed her wounds. She kept saying she wanted to see her father and in the end they gave in, wheeling her bed into a small room on the next floor. Guy's bed was already in there and he seemed to be asleep. Eliza sat down next to him. Eleanor had followed them in and stood there uncertainly. Lewis was still having his head attended to.

'Would you two like to be left alone?' Eleanor asked. 'I don't mind. Whatever you want.'

'No,' said Beth. 'I'd like you to stay here. I think we both need you.'

356

She looked across at the other bed. 'Dad?' she said. There was no answer.

'You know Lewis loves you, don't you?' Eleanor asked Beth.

'How do you know that?'

'The same way I know the sea is wet and grass is green, by looking at it. It's about as clear as it could be.'

She didn't answer.

'He's such a nice man,' said Eleanor, 'and he's quite a hunk. Isn't he?'

Beth hadn't allowed herself to think like that. 'Is he?' she asked.

'He'll look after you,' said Guy with a thick slow voice, without opening his eyes.

'Dad? Were you awake all the time?'

'They've given me a shot of something. Can't tell when I'm awake and when I'm not.' He turned his head to one side and managed to open his eyes.

'Are you tired love, or what?' he said at the sight of her in bed. His voice was weak.

'I hurt my legs. It's all right.'

'No, it's not all right at all. What happened?'

'Some rock fell on me. Don't worry. It's fine.'

'It's not fine at all,' he said, looking at Beth and Eleanor. 'I'm not doing too well, Beth. I know it. I know it better than these doctors do. I wish I'd had a bit more time with you two.'

'What about me?' said Eliza.

'No, I've had quite enough time with you, Ma,' he said, then he looked at her and smiled. 'Joke,' he added.

Eleanor spoke softly. 'I'm staying Guy. I'm in no hurry to go anywhere. I thought your three girls ought to stick together.'

'That's good to know,' he said. 'Beth, I realise there's no point.'

'No point in what, Dad?'

'No point asking you to do the mass, no point telling you that you don't have to do it because that's even worse, you say. So I'm telling you *not* to do it, because that's the only other thing I can do.'

Beth just stared at the bed, unable to answer.

'Thing is, someone, some day might feel different so what I've done, I've written it out and I've recorded it on tape so you know how it goes. It's in my desk drawer. Will you keep it carefully, just in case?'

'Can I sing it too, Guy? Eliza's told me a bit about it,' said Eleanor. 'I sing OK.'

Silence still from Beth who wasn't sure she wanted her aunt to step in like that.

'Well, that would be a weight off my mind,' said Guy. There was a silence which spread out into a network of invisible duties stretched across the room. Guy broke it, his voice slower and fainter than before. 'Eleanor. Tell us all about you, about you and your family.'

So Eleanor told them about her life and about her children and long before the end of it, Guy had gone off to sleep. She went on quietly into the evening with her tale until she noticed that Eliza's head was drooping.

'I'll take her home,' she said. 'I'll get her to bed then I'll come back again and see how you guys are going.'

'Don't worry,' said Lewis. 'I'll stay with Beth.'

He sat in an armchair next to her bed, holding her hand in his. Her throat felt raw and he told her not to talk. Instead he went on where Eleanor had left off but his stories were their stories and he painted in all her missing memories of how life had really been in Slapton, of the small things she had forgotten and the big things she had chosen to forget. A nurse came to give Beth more painkillers and she drifted in and out of a comfortable doze on the pillow of Lewis's voice. She woke once, later on, and found he was still holding her hand but he was asleep in the chair. She could hear his breathing and Guy's breathing, almost in time. Sleeping again, she woke at four a.m. by the clock on the wall and this time, there was only Lewis's breathing. She lay absolutely still until she was sure, but then she knew that her father had gone, that there had been no further wakening, no last words to hear. He had gone as if he had decided it was quicker and kinder for everyone that way.

They took Beth back to Eliza's house the next day and they were all in that state of near exaltation that can follow a death. The mead bottle was on the table and Eliza had had several glasses.

'Your children should never die before you do,' she said with a measure of unsteadiness in her voice. 'That's not right. What shall we say about him? Who's going to speak at the funeral? He wouldn't have wanted much fuss.'

'Lewis, where are the words?' Beth asked.

'What words?'

'The translation. You said you had all the words of the inscription.'

'Yes. It's here somewhere,' he said. 'I'd forgotten all about it. Where is it? It must be here. I left it on the sideboard when Eliza told me you'd gone up to the workings. Eliza, what did you do with it?'

'Dunno,' said the old woman, a little truculently.

Lewis delved among the stack of papers. 'This looks like it,' he said in the end, holding up an envelope, then he opened it. 'That's funny. What's this disk? It wasn't on disk.' He unfolded the paper that was with the disk and Beth recognised it with horror.

'What is it?' he asked a little faintly and looked at Beth as if he knew the answer.

'It's my speech,' she said, aghast. 'It's my bloody speech.'

'Language,' said Eliza.

'Gran, what have you done? You said you gave it to the driver.'

Eliza stared at her and hiccupped. 'I said I gave him what he bloody needed.'

'What was it? What could you possibly have given him?'

'I read your speech, you see.' Eliza poured herself another glass with irritating slowness. 'Wasn't right for the world. There was a better one, that's what I reckoned.'

'What did you give him?'

'Don't you sound like that, Lizzie-Beth. It was a sign, you see, Lewis turning up just then with the old inscription. I thought that's it, that's just the ticket.'

'You gave the de Bryan inscription to the Foreign Secretary?' asked Beth, feeling her future collapsing inwards.

'He didn't look foreign. Anyway, I corrected it a bit first. Your fancy clever Latin man had got some of the words wrong. Didn't sound right at all but I sorted it out and I sent it off.' She looked at Beth with her head on one side. 'Yes,' she said, 'that was it, that's what I did.'

Beth looked at Lewis and then at Eleanor. They both seemed to be struggling with some hidden emotion.

'And I'm not sorry. Not a bit,' added Eliza.

'Good God,' said Beth. 'I need to call them. What will they be thinking?' She glared at her grandmother who looked defiantly back at her as if she didn't care what the fuss was all about. 'What did it say, Gran? If you know it so well, can you tell me how it went by the time you'd finished with it?'

'Yes.' Eliza frowned in concentration, then in a voice filled with new purpose she declaimed it there and then in her kitchen and when she had come to the end, Beth put her head in her hands.

'Oh my God,' she said. 'That's done for me then.'

# CHAPTER TWENTY-SEVEN

With William on Palamon and di Mari lashed over Arcite's back, there was room for hope again. Those horses knew they'd done something clever and they were determined to go on in the same vein. We took turns to lead them, and the path they made was broad enough for the others to get their breath back while they scrambled up behind. I was pleased to see the whole party filled with new energy, but I still said constant prayers to myself because I knew we were a very long way from being safe. It was getting colder with every moment. Even with our brave horses, it was quite clear that we now depended utterly on finding shelter at the summit of the pass because the last of the light was draining away in the west.

I called a halt to adjust the ropes holding di Mari, who was entirely unconscious, and was just turning away when William said, 'Silence!'

That produced immediate wariness among my men who, like me, strained their ears fearing the rumble of another snow-fall. It also produced a hubbub of Italian between the two Genoese who were still capable of talking.

'*Silenzio*,' said the squire, which had the desired effect, but was so similar to what William had said that I wondered why it had been necessary.

I could hear nothing. Then I could hear something, just. An animal, up above us baying.

'Wolves?' I asked.

William shook his head, still listening. 'That wasn't the first noise I heard. Listen, there it is again.'

'Barking. It's dogs. The monks keep dogs. They *must* be up there.'

What new energy that gave us. As we got nearer, the dogs which had surely heard Palamon and Arcite, set up a frenzied noise and then, in the last of the twilight, we saw lanterns coming down towards us.

How warm and comfortable that bare, bleak hospice seemed. Four monks and twenty great hounds were its only inhabitants until we arrived, and they seemed to live their life without fires or any comforts, but our arrival granted them permission to soften that rule. The stables were dry and the horses had hay, and by the time we got inside after seeing to them, tinder was doing its job in their fireplaces and split wood was smoking, then burning, then roaring. They had pans on the grate as soon as there was enough heat, and what wonderful food they produced for us from their locked storerooms.

Two of them set about di Mari, pummelling him and rubbing his limbs with rough towelling cloth, then they put him in a bed, heated by a warming pan, and piled it high with sheepskins.

One of them, the oldest, spoke excellent English.

'You've come the hard way, lord,' he said. 'The pass to the south is a kinder place. The sunlight reaches it for so much longer. We still travel up and down it to Saint Rhémy and on to Aosta when we have to. The dogs help us.'

Di Provan was sitting beside di Mari in the next room. My archers were huddled together around the refectory fire composing a dirge for Dafydd. William was propped up in a cushioned chair with a warm poultice bandaged to his leg, and the squire and I sat on a bench together near him, content to soak up the heat. I knew he wanted to say something, but I had noticed some degree of formality had returned to our relationship since survival was no longer an issue. I decided to put him at his ease with some informality of my own.

'Go on, Geoffrey. What's eating you?'

'Your story was what saved us, Lord Bryan.' The squire sounded tentative. 'I have it by heart. I wonder whether you would mind if I wrote it down?'

'Yes, I certainly would mind,' I said. 'It was told as a confession. It should have the protection of the confessional.'

'It wasn't a confession,' William rumbled from a state of half-sleep. 'You had nothing to confess. You didn't make the bloody horse fall over. You were trying *not* to hit him. It doesn't count. I absolve you of it, but I warn you if you go on insisting that was a sin, I might withdraw your absolution just for wasting my time.'

I was weary of thinking about it. It could wait for the end of the journey. 'In any case, it's not a tale for other ears.'

'That's a great waste of a good story.' The squire wasn't going to give up easily. 'I'm collecting good stories and it's the best I've heard yet. Supposing I change the names?'

'People will guess it's me.'

'Not if I set it in ancient Athens. That will work. It can all take place under the rule of great King Theseus.'

'What will you call your knights?' asked William.

'I know,' said the squire. 'If I can't honour Sir Guy, I'll honour today's other heroes.'

'Who are they?'

'The horses. Palamon and Arcite,' said the squire in delight. 'That even sounds like ancient Greek.'

I would have told him that was nonsense but just then, di Provan came in from the other room, a greatly changed di Provan, to tell me through the squire that his friend had opened his eyes, that he, di Provan, had been greatly moved by my story to which he felt he owed his life. He desired that I forget all about his foolish offer to fight me and wished to offer me the hospitality of his country in thanks for my splendid leadership.

The squire finished translating and William said, 'Or to put it another way, he's finally realised he would have ended up like a lamb on a spit and he's taken the easy way out.'

The squire didn't bother to translate that.

That night I slept better than I had for years.

We rested there for three days until both William and di Mari were fit for travel again. I prayed with the monks five times a day, and I have to say that the quality of that prayer felt different, more joyful, less burdensome.

On the last morning, the squire and I sat outside waiting for the Genoese to get themselves ready. There was a little warmth in the sun and the way down to Italy lay in front of us in the clearest, brightest air imaginable.

'Ah, Zephyrus, with his sweet breath,' said the squire, sniffing that gentle south wind. 'Now, Sir Guy, would you tell me one last thing?'

I looked at the young man with deep affection. 'Anything you like.'

'What exactly will your inscription say?'

In the last three days, I had spent many hours polishing it in my mind.

'You want all of it? It's quite long.'

'Yes.'

'If you must.'

He nodded and sat back.

'Old men who stay behind, do not inflame the young with words of war. The ruin that you risk should be your own, not theirs. Young men beware, to make you . . .'

Then everyone came piling out of the door of the hospice, anxious to get on the way.

'Later,' I said, and looked towards the warm south, enjoying the day.

# CHAPTER TWENTY-EIGHT

Late on Thursday afternoon, Beth had had enough of being fussed over by Eliza and decided it was time she moved back into Guy's house so that she could think and grieve. She bullied Eleanor into driving her to the top of the hill on the way and when they got up there, she dialled Andrew Blakiston's number on her mobile, full of trepidation. It was answered by his secretary.

'It's Beth Battock,' she said. 'Can I . . .'

'I'm sorry, he's not available.' There was not the slightest hint of sorrow in the secretary's voice.

'No, I really must have a quick word with him, I just want to . . .'

The woman broke in again, openly snapping at her this time. 'Look, have you any idea what's going on here? He's far too busy to talk to you.'

'Bad news?' asked Eleanor sympathetically as Beth put the phone away.

'Just the final nail in the coffin of my career,' said Beth, but she found the idea had no substance to it, as though the whole of the other end of the conversation had taken place inside the phone, not in a real office in a real city. Slapton and the hospital seemed to have claimed all the reality that was available.

There were flowers everywhere at Carrick Cottage, all around the house and more kept arriving, brought, it seemed, by just about everyone who lived in the village.

'You come and lie down,' said Eliza, fussing over her at the door. 'I've made you a bed in the sitting room so you don't have to go upstairs on those legs of yours. Lewis says he'll be over at the end of work, just as soon as he can.'

'I'm all right,' said Beth, 'I can get around if I lean on someone.'

'Well, you can lean on me anytime you like,' said Eliza. 'Lewis says I've got to do some apologising.'

'Oh?' Beth wasn't used to the idea of Eliza apologising.

'Yes, he says it was wrong.'

'What was?'

'Not giving them your speech. He said it meant a lot to you.'

The old lady was doing her best to look contrite though Beth wasn't completely sure it was genuine.

'Well, Gran. You probably did what you thought was right.'

'Right for me. Not for you. Not for him either, the bloke that needed it, your Foreign Secretary man. I suppose he'll have to think up something to say all by himself. Is he good at that sort of thing?'

'I'm sure someone else will help him.' Someone else who would profit by the big fat political opportunity which had just fallen into their lap. 'But yes, he is good. He's a clear thinker, one of the best. Whatever he says it'll be worth hearing.' She looked at the clock. 'If we listen to the six o'clock news, we'll probably catch it.'

'Will it be on the news?' Eliza said with her eyes widening.

'I should think so. It's a big event.'

'Oh dear,' said Eliza. 'I didn't know it was as serious as that. I didn't know you were going to be on the news. I might not have done it if I'd known that.'

'Not me, Gran. It wasn't going to be me on the news. Maybe just some of the words I'd written.'

At six o'clock, they listened in anyway. On the radio, Big Ben chimed and the opening headline said, 'The Foreign Secretary resigns. He condemns the path to further military action . . .'

Beth would have leapt up if she could. 'What did he say?' She waited out the other headlines with her attention glued to the radio. 'The Foreign Secretary, Robert Baker, walked out of this morning's Cabinet meeting to announce his immediate resignation. Mr Baker said he was utterly opposed to the government's decision to prepare for fresh military action without seeking further United Nations approval. Mr Baker was due to deliver a major speech in the Commons this afternoon which was expected to be a rallying cry to the House and the country in support of the Prime Minister's tough stance. Instead he used his speech to explain the reasons for his resignation, which, he said, he had been considering for some time.'

Robert Baker's voice came on the air. 'In making my decision, I was greatly moved by words of which I have recently become aware. They take the form of an inscription placed in a Devon church dating from the fourteenth century. I would like to read it to you. It goes like this:

"Old men who stay behind, do not inflame the young with words of war. The ruin that you risk should be your own, not theirs.

"Young men beware; to make you fight, they first must make you fear then out of that, mould hate.

"Take arms when all else fails, but mark you this: before the battle's joined, remember what it is to see friends bleed. In the battle's midst, remember peace is both behind you and ahead. Once the battle's won, remember how it is that wars begin.

"Kings and captains, you who order war, know that your people, left alone, would choose to eat not fight, would choose to love not hate, would choose to sleep not die. Take care what

367

you may say to turn them to your will. Tell them that you fight for God, not gain, and know your enemy is saying the same.

"You who read this, pray for me. I have heard blind fury roar and sow the seeds of future war and I have wept as heroes died."

'That,' he said, 'expresses my present feelings perfectly.'

'Lord almighty,' said Eliza, as Lewis knocked at the door. 'Did I do that?'

When Lewis came in, he stared at Beth. 'Has something happened?'

Beth could only shake her head as if trying to clear her thoughts.

'It's her man, wotsisname,' said Eliza. 'Her boss. He read out old Guy's words. Right there.' She pointed at the radio. 'Now everyone's heard 'em. 'Bout time too, if you ask me.'

Guy's funeral was held five days later and in those five days, a part of Beth came back to life. A stream of visitors came to the cottage, people she had chosen to forget and whom she now chose to remember again. Lewis was in and out several times a day and she looked forward to hearing him at the door. After three days resting, she found she could walk with the help of her father's stick, her hand where his had been, and she walked slowly round the village lanes, finding fragments of her old self wherever she went. When the time for the funeral came, she insisted on standing at the front of the church to deliver the words she had written about her father's life in Slapton and when she had finished, Lewis read out the text of Guy de Bryan's declaration. By that time, its words were familiar to everyone in the church. The inscription had been printed in full in every newspaper in the country in their coverage of Baker's resignation and it had caught the public mood of disenchantment.

In the graveyard, when the coffin had been covered, Lewis took Beth's arm and she was grateful for the support.

'I'm going tomorrow,' she said.

'Going where? London?'

'I've got to.'

'Are you all right to drive?'

'Don't be so practical, Lewis,' she said. 'I've got to go back and face the music. They'll get rid of me now and I need to find another job.'

He stared hard at her. 'The same sort of thing?'

'It's what I do.'

He looked around him and then up towards the top of the Chantry tower. 'I want to know something,' he said. 'I want to know what you thought when you heard the words of the declaration. I want to know if they got home to you?'

Beth squeezed his arm. 'Lewis, you mustn't hope for a happy-ever-after ending. I'm still me.'

'You've got your dad's cottage now. And there's Eliza. Will you be coming back?'

'Yes, I will.'

'How soon?'

'I don't know. It depends on my plans.'

'Is there any space for *me* in your plans?' he asked, and felt her stiffen.

'I don't know that either,' she said, but what she was feeling inside was a sudden strong memory of that time before, the time when he had been the bond to Slapton, the bond she had to break. Lewis didn't press her.

Beth left for London at ten o'clock the next morning and they couldn't persuade her not to drive herself even though using the brake hurt her right leg. Eleanor was staying on at Carrick Cottage.

'I'll keep an eye on Eliza,' she promised. 'We'll get something sorted out for her. I'm in no hurry to get back.'

London felt entirely different, dirty and ugly. Beth's flat

seemed to her to have been furnished by someone else, someone with a taste for the deliberately uncomfortable. The post was heaped up on the floor and the answering machine had run out of space.

And Beth, all undeserving, was a hero.

It was *The Times* which had first tracked down the origin of the speech and coupled her name to it. The next day one of the tabloids insisted that she had found the inscription while on a mission of mercy to her dying father, had been overwhelmed by its message and had timed its delivery to the Foreign Secretary at the perfect moment to bring all his latent doubts to the surface. 'The Peace Girl' it named her over a long-shot photo she had never seen before.

For an hour or two Beth saw everything she stood for in tatters around her feet but then she began to like this new version of herself, not just in a pragmatic way, not just because it meant she had a future but because somewhere deep in herself, she found she actually felt easier with this new message. It was after all the disproof of the idea that the Kilfillan genes had been pulling her strings. If it might equally have been a proof that the Battock genes were now doing that same job, she chose to ignore that.

That afternoon the phone kept ringing and it didn't stop ringing for over a week. It was mostly journalists asking her for interviews but then, in the second week of her return, when she'd cleared her office and gone through all the bureaucracy of resignation, Robert Baker called and asked her to join him at the Institute he had been invited to lead. She put the phone down after they had talked and stared out of the window at the busy street below and, knowing she should feel happy, was puzzled by the fact that she felt utterly bereft. It was great to be wanted, she told herself. She heard his words again. 'We'll be a real force, you and me. We'll be a force for peace.' She looked down into the street and found she longed to be part of something, part of a community, and this wasn't it.

A few days later, she was on her way to meet Baker for dinner in Bristol when the phone buzzed in her car. She reached out to press the button and heard an American voice on the speaker.

'Beth?'

'Eleanor? Is that you? How *are* you?'

'I'm good. I just wondered what you were doing.'

'I'm in the car, somewhere near Swindon. Heading west.'

'Are you coming down?' Beth heard the sudden happiness in the older woman's voice.

'Sorry, Eleanor. No. I'm going to Bristol to talk about a job.'

'Oh, I see.' Eleanor's voice sounded really flat.

'I could come on down tomorrow. I'll check my diary when I stop.'

'That would be good.' It didn't sound especially good. She still sounded flat.

Beth said goodbye to her and drove on down the motorway, thinking hard, wondering why.

At a petrol station on the outskirts of Bristol, she did check her diary and that was when she realised what date it was and knew exactly why Eleanor had sounded as she had.

Late that night, approaching midnight, Lewis came to meet Eleanor at Carrick Cottage.

'I've told Eliza she doesn't have to come,' he said. 'I had to get a bit firm. She's taken the pills and I've put her to bed. I said we could do it and we'll come back and tell her all about it tomorrow.'

'She's a tough old bird,' said Eleanor. 'I wouldn't put it past her to show up.'

'She says it should be Beth doing it, not us.'

'Well, it's not going to be, I'm afraid.'

'Isn't it?'

Eleanor heard the tone in his voice. 'No, I called her.'

'Where was she?'

'Heading for some job interview.' Eleanor looked at Lewis's expression. 'Are you missing her?'

'So much that it hurts,' he said fiercely.

'Cheer up. She said she might come tomorrow.'

He shrugged. 'She might. She might not. It would be different if she'd come to sing the mass. I'd have a bit of hope then.'

'She may have forgotten all about the mass,' said Eleanor gently. 'That doesn't mean there's no hope for you two. You should talk to her if she comes tomorrow. Tell her how you feel.'

'It's kind of you,' he said, 'but I've been here before.'

'Oh well. Is it time we went?'

'Yes, have we got everything?'

'I think so.' Eleanor followed Lewis as he led them on their circuitous way round to the back of the Chantry tower, groping through the dark. 'Do you know how it goes?' she asked.

'I've played the tape over and over and over again,' said Lewis. 'I hope so.'

'Yes,' she said, 'I've nearly worn mine out too.'

They climbed through the fence and walked cautiously across the garden. 'We're trespassing, aren't we?' she whispered.

'In a good cause. Here we are.'

They stepped in through the arch into the base of the ancient tower. Lewis took a candle out of his pocket, melted its base and stuck it on a fallen stone. In its glow, the tower was timeless.

'Let's sing this for both the Guys,' he said.

Eleanor opened her mouth and let out a pure, high note. Lewis came in with a less-certain bass. Then, as they launched into the first line of the mass, a third voice joined in and Beth stepped out of the shadows.

372

# HISTORICAL NOTE

Sir Guy de Bryan and Sir John Molyns were both real people and I have closely followed the course of what is known of each of their lives, although no source links them together in any direct way. I was thinking about the history of Slapton and its Chantry when I first heard about Sir Guy de Bryan from that great story-teller, Clive Fairweather. The more I learnt about him, the more I wondered why this best of medieval knights had needed to build a Chantry. My son, Ben, an excellent historian, found Molyns for me in the footnotes of books on other men. Molyns was, if anything, worse than he is painted here.

As I researched them both, I realised how well they must have known each other and how the matter of Stoke Trister must have put them at daggers drawn. The main liberty I have taken with Molyns' story is to put him in charge of the cannon at Crécy, which was indeed the first time they were used on a European field of battle. Knowing Molyns, I am sure he would have relished that role.

It was while I was constructing a detailed time line of Sir Guy's life that I first noticed the way in which a younger man, a king's squire, kept cropping up at some of the same places as him – at the siege of Limoges, at Rheims and, most breathtakingly, on a long overland diplomatic mission to Genoa, crossing the Alps in January. The references to the squire's journey and to Sir Guy's appear entirely separately. The dates for the squire are precise, those for Sir Guy a little less so, but the timings broadly coincide and the objective of their journeys was the same.

That squire was Geoffrey Chaucer, who undertook many diplomatic missions for the king. Fifteen years or so after the journey to Genoa, he began to write the *Canterbury Tales*, including of course the *Knight's Tale* where Palamon and Arcite vie for the love of one woman.